Among Wolves

NANCY K. WALLACE

Book One of The Wolves of Llisé

HARPER
Voyager

Harper*Voyager*
an imprint of HarperCollins*Publishers* Ltd
1 London Bridge Street
London SE1 9GF

www.harpervoyagerbooks.co.uk

This Paperback Original 2015

First published in Great Britain in ebook format by Harper*Voyager* 2015

A catalogue record for this book
is available from the British Library

ISBN: 978-0-00-812072-6

Set in Sabon by Born Group using Atomik ePublisher from Easypress

Printed and bound in Great Britain

Among Wolves *is dedicated to my family.*

My husband, Dennie: without his love and support I would never have become a writer. My daughter, Mollie, who provides technical assistance, and my daughter, Elizabeth, the most tireless and dedicated proofreader ever! I cannot thank you enough for believing in me even when I didn't believe in myself

CHAPTER 1

The Beginning

"There's an urgent message for you, *monsieur*," Isaac La Salle said, handing Devin a rolled parchment sealed with the gold signet of the Chancellor Elite. The proctor's whispered message boomed in the compulsory quiet of the examination hall.

Devin nodded silently, aware of the handful of other graduate students still bent feverishly over their exams. He squared the edges on his sheaf of examination papers and retrieved his jacket from the back of the bench. His friend, Gaspard, glanced desperately his way, eyes rolling, his exam barely started. Shooting him a sympathetic grin, Devin walked to the back of the room. La Salle now sat propped against the Académie's stone wall, the seventh volume of Blade's Laws spread across his lap. Devin handed the proctor his completed papers and left without comment.

Devin pocketed the parchment. It was so like his father to think nothing of interrupting final exams with an urgent missive to report home. He knew without reading it what it required of him. He'd already planned a visit to his parents

1

into the flurry of tonight's activity but it would have to be brief. His ship sailed at dawn and he doubted he would even find time to sleep.

He crossed the wide entrance hall, with its two elegantly curving stairways. One led to the Archives, the other to the lecture halls. He mounted neither but walked through the massive double doors into the late spring sunshine. Spray from the central fountain dampened his hair and shirt as he passed through the courtyard. He welcomed the sprinkle of cool water after the stuffiness of the examination hall. Blossoming trees and early bulbs in bloom flanked the perimeter of the cobbled expanse. The fragrance of flowers hung heavy in the air. The sun lying low in the west silhouetted the trees lining the street before him. Horses and buggies hugged the curb, their drivers soliciting fares. He passed by them, content to walk.

Today marked the completion of his first two years of apprenticeship in Llisé's Historic Archives. His Third Year was his own – to explore optional careers – or to rethink his decision to become an archivist. If he returned for the Fourth, and final, Year at the Académie, his choice of profession would be sealed and there could be no changes.

He didn't anticipate any alteration of his plans. He had never been happier than studying Llisé's ancient documents, recopying those whose condition was deteriorating, and compiling meticulous chronological records.

When he reached Independence Square, the clock high on the cathedral arch, chimed seven. He quickened his pace. The windows of the houses bordering the square already glowed softly with candlelight. His family would be waiting and tardiness on his part would only lead to teasing about his possible lack of proficiency in exams.

The Chancellor's mansion dominated the western end of the square, its pillared gates lined by a dozen guards, in blue and silver uniforms. They waved Devin through as he climbed the front steps in the fading light.

Girard, his black suit and white shirt immaculate, opened the door.

"How did it go, *monsieur?*" he asked, with a smile. "Did you pass your exams or should I inquire about a post in the provinces for you?"

"I did well," Devin assured him. "I finished first. The others are still up to their ears in essays."

Girard laughed. "Your father will be pleased." He pointed to the right. "They're in the petite parlor. They've been waiting."

Devin crossed the threshold expecting to have a quiet dinner with his parents. But all five of his older brothers had gathered to see him off. He was not surprised to see that none of their wives had been invited. That was his mother's doing. She actively sought time alone with her sons, where she could claim their complete attention without any distractions.

His father had neatly slotted his first five sons into every branch of the powerful government he controlled. As the youngest, only Devin had been free to pursue his own interests.

His brothers stood clustered in the parlor, waiting for him. Their expressions ranged from anxious to grave, as though they had gathered to stage an intervention.

"It's a celebration not a wake!" Devin exclaimed, clapping his oldest brother on the shoulder. Jean was a district judge; staid and solemn, already tending toward plumpness around the middle. A few gray hairs highlighted his dark temples.

"We're just concerned," Jean replied. "This plan of yours seems ill-conceived."

"Ah," Devin laughed, "and your Third Year was a model of convention? I've heard stories about the places you visited!"

"A few wild oats are understandable . . ." Jean sputtered. "You, on the other hand, seem to have taken this quest to heart."

"Hello, dear," his mother said, extending her hand to pull him closer. "I think it's a shame to waste this opportunity, that's all. The Third Year is intended as a carefree time. You should spend it with friends or traveling before you lock yourself away in the Historic Archives for the rest of your days."

Devin bent to kiss her on both cheeks. "I will be spending my time traveling and with friends, Mother. Gaspard's agreed to go with me, if he can finish his exams in time."

"Oh well, Gaspard," she commented, one hand falling languidly to the side. "Why didn't you choose someone more . . . " Words apparently failed her.

"Intelligent?" André asked with a laugh. He was already Head of the Department of Sciences at the Académie; well-liked and highly respected. "Gaspard will be good fun, Mother. He tempers Devin's bookishness."

"I don't understand your motivation, Devin," Ethan said, stalking to the table to refill his wine glass. "You're a trained historian, why would you want to spend your Third Year gathering Chronicles in the provinces?"

Ethan, a Colonel in Llisé's army, was most like their father, though he lacked Vincent Roché's humor. Devin suspected that he, too, might be Chancellor one day.

Devin extended a glass to his brother to fill. "The current process of preserving the Chronicles seems so fragile," he explained. "Did you hear the Master Bard, who held the Perouse Chronicle, died suddenly last month? He didn't have time to pass on even half of the information to his apprentice. Those stories are lost forever."

"Well, you can't write them down," Jean told him. "Canon Law forbids it."

"I'm well aware of that," Devin answered. "They can't be recorded as historical data."

"You can't record them in any manner," Ethan clarified, his index finger stabbing Devin's chest. "Your degree lends credibility to anything you write. I wouldn't want to see you brought up on charges over this. It could ruin your chances of ever working in the Archives again."

"I know that," Devin assured him. "I only plan to memorize them."

Jacques, an under-secretary in their father's cabinet, hoisted himself from a chair by the fireplace. "Only?" he said with a chuckle. "Devin, no one has ever memorized the Chronicles from all the provinces – no one – in over a thousand years."

Devin, his defenses beginning to crack, took a gulp of wine before answering. "Perhaps, no one has ever tried."

"Give him a chance," his father said from the doorway. "Devin memorized the first volume of Bardic Songs before he was six."

"But the Chronicles are of little importance, darling," his mother protested to her husband. "The work Devin will be doing here, in the capital, is so much more valuable. Surely, the Chronicle of Perouse is only of value to the people who live there."

Devin sighed. He'd fought this battle before and he wasn't about to repeat the arguments over and over again. The Chronicles were not officially sanctioned history but they recounted the important events in each province. They deserved a better means of preservation than to be passed down orally from one generation to the next. He patted his mother's shoulder, knowing she would never understand. "I intend to go, Mother. Tonight's my last night here. Let's not argue."

"Let's not," his father said, "Besides, I've brought you a present."

Money, Devin thought, even though his Third Year stipend would be more than sufficient in the remote areas he intended to travel to. His father would think it necessary that he carry half the treasury along, just in case. "That's not necessary," he protested.

"Ah, but it is," his father continued, "and I must exact your promise that you will take my gift with you."

Devin bowed his head, acquiescing, knowing the futility of attempting to argue with the most powerful man in the empire. "Thank you," Devin murmured. "I'll take it, if you insist."

"I do," his father replied. "Stand just there, if you don't mind, while I make the presentation." Something about the curve of his mouth told Devin he'd been conned.

His father motioned to someone in the hall and then Marcus, his father's bodyguard of some years, loomed into sight. Devin waited expectantly, anticipating some sort of package or little ritual, until the chuckles began behind him.

"You're not serious!" he cried, when the full realization hit him.

"Oh, I'm quite serious," his father replied, putting an affectionate arm around him. "Marcus will accompany you for the full fifteen months that you're gone, or until you're safely home."

Devin ducked out of his embrace, furious. "I won't take him! I'm not going to travel the empire with the Chancellor Elite's bodyguard trailing behind me!"

"Then you won't leave the city," his father said quietly. "I've been sympathetic to your wishes so far, Devin. I even think I understand your motivation but I won't allow my gentle, scholarly son to travel the provinces with no protection but his scatter-wit friend."

"Gaspard's not a scatter-wit!" Devin protested. "And I'm going to be memorizing stories, for God's sake! Who would want to harm me?"

"Your *naiveté* astounds me," Ethan murmured, finishing his wine in one gulp, and reaching for the decanter.

"My empire is certainly not immune to cutthroats and thieves," his father said tightly.

"And if we're traveling students, no one will think we have anything worth stealing! A bodyguard implies wealth and valuables. You might as well put a sign around my neck, proclaiming that I'm your son!"

"Believe me, I considered it," his father replied. "Marcus isn't negotiable, Devin. Should he come back alone, because you've ditched him in some backwater, I'll issue a warrant for your arrest in all fifteen Provinces. I'll have you brought back in irons if necessary."

"Vincent, please!" his mother protested.

Anger had momentarily hardened his father's face. He had not, after all, reached his elevated position by compromise, nor was he about to negotiate on this issue.

"That's my final word on it, Devin."

"Well, you've ruined dinner!" his mother said. "How do you expect Devin to eat after all this? And who knows what kind of meals he'll get for the next year!"

"People eat in the provinces too, Mother," Devin replied.

"Then we'll call it settled," his father said, taking his wife's hand and pulling her to her feet. "Let's sit down to dinner and forget this unpleasantness."

Mathieu, an attaché in the diplomatic service, passed Devin without speaking, but landed one hand sympathetically on his younger brother's shoulder.

Devin jockeyed for a position next to his father as they left the room and walked down the hall toward the dining room.

"Marcus will jeopardize my work, Father," he pleaded. "People are suspicious of the government in the provinces. A man in uniform will make them think I'm conducting some kind of investigation. They won't speak as freely."

"I have no problem with Marcus wearing casual clothing," his father said. "That should solve the problem."

"But he still looks and acts like a soldier," Devin complained. "It's in his nature, he can't help it."

Marcus towered over him, a massive wall of toned muscle. Weapons strained the seams of his uniform.

His father stopped dead, tucking his wife's hand into the crook of his oldest son's arm.

"Jean, take your mother to the table, please. I'll only be a moment." He smiled cordially, as the rest of his family passed them by.

Devin cringed when his father placed both hands on his shoulders and pushed him back against the wall. For a moment, he felt as though he were seven again, facing a spanking for breaking his mother's favorite vase. He stood quietly in his father's grip. He was a man now, and he'd done nothing wrong.

"I want no further discussion on this matter," his father said, his voice held well below the level which might be overheard further down the corridor. "Either you accept my offer of a bodyguard or you do not go at all."

"I'm just asking you to see this from my point of view." Devin begged.

"And I'm asking you to see it from mine," his father retorted. "This quest of yours has ruffled some feathers. Your intentions have been misunderstood. Four council members took me aside last night. They fear you are trying to elevate the Chronicles to the same level as the documents in the Archives. There's some resentment. You are Académie educated, and besides, you are my son. That lends an official tone to your trip whether you intended it or not."

"It has nothing to do with you," Devin protested.

"It has everything to do with me," his father continued. "If Marcus goes with you, it extends my sanction to your undertaking. You can't be censored if I have given you my approval."

"Surely, your approval could come without attaching Marcus to it," Devin grumbled.

"It's a fine line, son, perhaps you can't see it. Marcus's inclusion implies you will be reporting to me."

Devin felt the first shadow of misgiving. "And will I be?"

His father avoided his eyes. "I think it would be best, Dev. This isn't a pleasure trip, and you know it."

"But I'm not going as your representative," he objected. "This trip was my idea from the first."

"And after you gather the Chronicles, what do you intend to do with them? These stories require retelling to keep them fresh in your memory. You cannot set yourself up as a bard, not in your position."

Devin winced at the disapproval in his tone. His prejudice was evident. "I simply want to see them preserved," he answered. "Can't you see that oral records have value just as written ones do?"

His father lowered his voice as a servant passed, a tray of canapés in hand. "The law states that oral records have no validity, Devin. You are in no position to question or change it."

"But you are," Devin pointed out.

His father shook his head. "Oddly enough, at the moment, I am not, and I ask you to leave it at that. It is my job to uphold the law, and yours to obey it. Even in my position, I cannot save you if you choose to disregard it."

Devin sighed. "I know."

His father laid a hand on his arm. "Have you considered that, by learning the Chronicles and not passing them on, you will only preserve them for your lifetime? How will that help the situation?"

Devin's eyes sought the floor. "Gaspard's thinking of becoming a folklorist."

His father's astonishment was obvious. "That's not an Académie-level position! As a folklorist, he'll be barred from the Archives for life. Is he out of his mind?"

Devin sighed. "He can't keep up with his studies. He barely scraped by last term, even with my help. He doesn't expect to pass his exams."

His father shook his head. "What a disappointment for his father. I'm sorry. I had no idea."

"I hope this trip will give him another focus."

His father grunted as the connection became apparent. "I guess I understand this better now. You're planning to pass the songs and ballads on to him and he'll record them. Why didn't you tell me this before?"

"Because none of you credit Gaspard with having a brain in his head," Devin replied.

"Devin, the music is one thing, if that's truly what you have in mind. There are already a few existing pamphlets of provincial songs. But you mustn't ever ask Gaspard to compile any of the Chronicles in written form," his father said. "They've hanged men for less. Be very, very careful what you are doing here. This is dangerous."

Devin clenched his hands. "I would never put Gaspard's life in danger," he protested.

"God," his father murmured, "I'm thinking of your own life, Devin." His face softened. "I know how obsessed you can become with a project. From the time you were a child you have been fascinated by the bards' brown cloaks. Where would you wear one, Dev? They're barred from the Archives!"

"Why would you care what I do with the cloak?" Devin protested. "If I earn an embroidered symbol for all fifteen provinces, I'll be the first man to have a complete set!"

"It's a formidable task, son," his father said quietly. "Don't set yourself up for defeat."

"Can't you understand?" Devin pleaded. "The cloak represents an accomplishment; something no one else has ever done! It would be no different than the trophies you still display from your Académie days!"

His father's face sobered. "Perhaps, you're right. But my trophies didn't put me in any physical danger."

"So, broken bones don't count, then?" Devin asked. His father still walked with a slight limp from a leg that had been broken during a polo match.

"*Touché*," his father replied, stepping back. The distance between them indicated that he'd allowed Devin to score a point, but he considered the argument had already been won. "Look here, I'm sure dinner is getting cold and your mother is fretting. Let's finish this, son, and agree not to discuss it

11

again. Either you abide by my wishes or the trip is canceled. Which will it be?"

"You know which," Devin replied sulkily. He'd planned too long to allow this dream to end on the night of its inception.

"Good," his father said, relief evident in his voice. "You've made the right decision. As of tomorrow morning, you'll be included on the Council's payroll, under my direct authority. I'll expect a full report from each province – I'm not interested in the number of tales you've gathered, of course – but your reflections on them, and observations of the provinces themselves. Marcus will arrange to have them delivered to me. Besides, your mother will want to know where you are and how you are faring. And as always, my resources are available if you need them, Devin, wherever you are. You have only to ask."

"I know that," Devin replied, allowing his father to direct him toward the dining room.

"And, don't be concerned that Marcus will interfere with your plans. I assure you, he will be very discreet. You and Gaspard can feel free to enjoy yourselves. That's what the Third Year has always been about."

Not my Third Year, Devin thought miserably, I'll be tracked, followed, and reported on, make no mistake about it.

His father detained him, a hand still on his arm. "And Devin, I appreciate your being reasonable after receiving my message. I expected you to overreact and yet, when I walked in tonight, I found you calmly stating your case to your brothers. It shows maturity." He smiled. "And courage, too. I'm proud of you and glad we've worked this out."

Devin's hand dropped automatically to the message in his pocket. He'd never even read it. "Thank you," he murmured, inclining his head. He stood for a moment, uncertain what to do. "Could you excuse me, please? I'd like to wash my hands before dinner."

"Of course," his father replied.

He walked quickly down the hall to the gentlemen's lavatory. Wall sconces lighted the huge room designed to handle the needs of the Chancellor's constant entertaining. A bank of porcelain sinks, their brass taps gleaming, covered one wall. He'd come so very close to revealing his entire plan tonight and then he would never have been permitted to leave. Devin retrieved his father's message and broke the seal, spreading it out on the sink in front of him. The note was brief and to the point:

> *Devin,*
> *Under no circumstances are you to leave the city without speaking to me first. There is strong opposition to your trip and I think it would be wise to cancel it. I hate to disappoint you but you'll have to trust my judgment in this. Come to the house after exams, we'll discuss it then.*
> *Affectionately,*
> *Your Father*

He read the message twice. Had his father truly intended to call off his trip? And if so, at what point had he reconsidered? Obviously, the decision had been made before Devin arrived: he'd had Marcus waiting in the hall. He stood a moment wondering whether to admit he hadn't read the message before he came, and decided against it. His hands shaking, he folded the parchment and jammed it back into his pocket. After one quick look in the mirror, he walked back down the hall to the dining room.

13

CHAPTER 2

Leaving Viénne

Devin turned down his father's offer of a carriage to take him back to the dormitory. The cool moonlit walk offered a quiet end to a hectic day. He strolled beneath the budding trees, marking his progress by the luminous pools the gas lights left on the sidewalk. The Académie buildings looked formidable against the dark sky. Only the Archive's windows were still illuminated as first year apprentices labored to shelve the massive quantity of materials which had been used to study for final exams. The examination hall had closed at ten and it was now well past midnight.

The dormitory lobby reeked of pipe tobacco, its table and chairs littered with crumpled study notes, crumbs, and empty glasses. Devin mounted the stairs without seeing another student. An eerie quiet marked the darkened halls. Some students had already departed for the three month summer holiday. Others were celebrating or drowning their sorrows down at Antoine's. Final exams sparked either high spirits or despair. The essays were excruciatingly specific with little room for fabrication. Rarely did a student leave the Examination Hall without knowing for certain he had secured a place in next year's class, or that he would have to return home in disgrace.

Gaspard was not in his room. None of his clothes had been packed and his bed remained rumpled and unmade. Devin packed the contents of his own closet in the large trunk at the foot of his bed, reserving only a few items to put into his knapsack. He intended to take only what he could conveniently carry. He folded his itinerary and placed it flat on the bottom, and then a few shirts and trousers, a warm jacket and blanket, thick socks, and a pocket knife. Only because his father required him to make reports did he include paper and ink. Either item might be misconstrued by the Council members who disapproved of his journey. Whatever else he needed could be purchased along the way. The larger job was to strip the room of his belongings. Next year he would be assigned an apartment in the Archives. He would never return to this dormitory again.

It was after three when he finished marking the boxes of books and the trunk with instructions to be taken to his parents' house. There was still no sign of Gaspard, and their ship sailed at five. He threw his roommate's clothes into another knapsack and started to pack his other belongings.

He was so tired; even the thin, bare, mattress tempted him. The past two weeks he'd had little sleep, spending half the night studying for his own exams and the other half tutoring Gaspard. He gave into temptation, slumping down on the bed and closing his eyes.

A moment later, he heard running feet on the stairs.

"Devin?" Henri Ferrare, a first year student, hung on the doorframe, his breath coming in gasps. "It's Gaspard. Can you come?"

Devin dragged himself up off the bed. "What's the matter? Is he hurt?"

Henri shook his head. "No, just drunk . . . and Antoine needs to close up."

Devin quelled his annoyance. It was typical of Gaspard to go on a binge when he needed to concentrate his energy elsewhere. He clattered down the stairs and out the front door after Henri, feeling a chill as the night closed in around them. The sky was as clear and starry as midwinter, and Devin wished he'd brought his jacket. A spring peeper piped his bell-like solo from the edge of the fountain. Behind them a cabbie shouted anxiously for a fare, but they kept on going.

"Antoine sent for Gaspard's father," Henri confided as they hurried along.

"God," Devin murmured. "I hope we get there before he does!"

At Antoine's, candles burned on every table, though the sign by the front door said "closed." Devin stopped just inside, realizing he'd never seen this room empty before. Its cozy warmth faded without the camaraderie of dozens of students and scholars clustered around the bar and sitting at the tables. The silence seemed jarring, bereft of the sound of laughter and the clink of glasses.

They found Gaspard on the floor under a corner table, a cut oozing blood across his right cheekbone. Antoine knelt beside him, a wet cloth in hand.

"How badly is he hurt?" Devin demanded.

The barman shrugged and stood up. "It's nothing. The cut will heal without a scar."

Devin leaned down to see for himself. Gaspard's breathing was smooth and regular, his parted lips emitting an occasional snore.

"What happened?" he asked.

"I sent for his father," Antoine replied. "I thought you'd gone home."

"I went home for dinner but I had to come back to pack," Devin answered. He had barely a month to spend in each province. He needed every moment of his summer holiday plus his entire Third Year to complete his project. He couldn't have lingered a few days with his parents even if he had wanted to.

"Monsieur Forneaux came himself," Antoine continued, "and Gaspard was not glad to see him."

Gaspard's father was René Forneaux, a high ranking Council member. He must have been very angry or very worried to have come himself to drag his son out of a bar in the middle of the night.

"Monsieur Forneaux tried to take him home," Antoine continued. "Gaspard told him he hadn't finished his exams. He said, when he turned them in, Isaac La Salle told him he need not return to the Académie next fall."

Devin's breath wheezed out in exasperation. The least Gaspard could have done was to finish his exam and not leave it half completed. The implication was that he didn't care if he was ruining his chances at the Académie.

"This is not true?" Antoine asked.

"True enough, unfortunately," Devin murmured. "And then, what happened?"

"Monsieur Forneaux said he would hire tutors for the summer so that Gaspard could be reinstated. Gaspard told him that all the tutors in the world wouldn't help him graduate. He said if his father couldn't accept that, he could go to hell. Then Monsieur Forneaux hit him."

Devin winced, glancing at his friend on the floor. "He knocked him out cold?"

"No, no!" Antoine explained. "Gaspard passed out. He drank a whole bottle of wine after his father left."

Devin rolled his eyes. "Can you help me carry him back to the dormitory, Henri?"

Antoine grabbed his sleeve and pointed. "That won't be necessary. I think your father sent his carriage."

"What?" Devin said in disbelief. He turned to see Marcus's formidable bulk standing in the doorway.

"I'll take care of this," his bodyguard said, bending to pull Gaspard from under the table. "Go back and get your things and his. I'll meet you at the bottom of the dormitory steps."

"How did you hear about this?" Devin asked.

"Your father had me follow you. I called to you from outside the dormitory when you ran down the steps. You must not have heard me."

So the protection his father had assigned him had started immediately, even before he'd left the city of Coreé. Devin found it odd.

Marcus paused, Gaspard slung over his shoulder like a sack of grain. "You're certain Gaspard still wants to go?"

"We haven't spoken since this morning . . . " Devin said, suddenly unsure he was doing the right thing.

Marcus made the decision for him. "We'll take him with us. If he decides to return, your father will pay his passage back. Go now. You'll be late."

"What time is it?" Devin asked.

"Nearly five," Marcus told him.

"The ship . . . "

"Will wait," Marcus replied "You father's seen to that."

Devin smiled. This morning there seemed to be some advantages to being the Chancellor's son.

Even though the sun had yet to rise, the docks in the harbor swarmed with activity. The Marie Lisette sat low in the water, her hold filled with Sorrento wine bound for the Northern Provinces. Marcus carried Gaspard aboard while Devin gathered their belongings from the carriage. He turned to see his father ride up on his dappled gray gelding.

"I decided to see you off," Vincent Roché said, drawing his coat closer around him. "It's a cold morning to be heading north, son. You'll keep an eye on the weather?"

"Of course. But we have to visit the Northern Provinces first; they'll be snowbound again by the first of September," Devin said, even though he'd left his father their proposed itinerary.

"Just be careful and listen to Marcus. He's got a good head on his shoulders."

"I will," Devin replied. "I hadn't expected to see you this morning."

"I have a small gift," his father said, extending a package.

Devin laughed, pleased that he'd come. "I thought you'd already given me Marcus."

"Marcus is going with you to ease my concerns." He held the package out again. "Open it."

Devin tore the brown paper away to reveal a cloak of russet suede.

"A storyteller's cloak?" he gasped in surprise.

"You've always wanted one," his father said, guiding his horse in closer as a wagon pulled by to unload. "You'll need it if you're going to collect all fifteen symbols."

"Thank you," Devin murmured. "I'd planned to purchase one in Arcadia but this will mean so much more."

His father smiled. "It's a peace offering. I didn't want you to think that I agreed with the Council members who

19

would have prevented this trip." He glanced around them. "Where's Gaspard?"

Devin sighed. "In his cabin. Marcus has already proven invaluable." He told him briefly what had happened.

"I'd better let René know, Dev. You can't go, and let him think his son has disappeared. I won't mention that he didn't leave under his own power. That's between the two of you."

They both glanced up at the same time and saw the Captain waiting at the top of the gangplank. "You'd better go, son, we've held your ship up long enough."

Devin nodded, suddenly reluctant to leave. "Give Mother my love."

"I didn't tell her I was coming to see you off. She's feeling quite fragile this morning. She would have begged you to stay."

"It's difficult to say 'no' to her."

"I'm well aware of that!" his father said with a laugh, backing his horse away. "Have a good trip, Devin. Stay safe."

"You too," he called after him. He turned then, not wanting to watch him go, and walked toward the Marie Lisette.

The Captain welcomed Devin aboard himself, first bowing then shaking his hand.

"I'm sorry I've given you a late start," Devin apologized, before he'd stepped off the gangplank.

Captain Torrance smiled, handing Devin the key to his cabin. "Don't worry. Your father made it worth my while. I hope your friend will feel better by this evening. We put him in the cabin next to yours."

Devin couldn't shake the nagging doubt that, perhaps, he'd forced Gaspard to accompany him when he'd decided otherwise. Obviously, Gaspard had made the decision to walk away from any chance of passing his exams and staying on at the Académie. Perhaps, he'd changed his mind about visiting the provinces, too. Devin carried his knapsack down into the hold, passing by the cabin the Captain had assigned to him, and going into Gaspard's instead.

His friend lay sound asleep, snoring loudly. His face had been washed, the cut doctored and bandaged. Someone had even strapped him in his bunk, a basin in easy reach on the table. The Northern channel of the Dantzig was notoriously rough when the snow melt had swelled its course. They weren't in for an easy ride.

The door opened behind him and Devin stepped aside in the tiny space.

"Gaspard's fine," Marcus assured him. "Go up on deck and get some fresh air! When he starts to puke, he won't want you hanging around. Let the man have a little privacy."

Devin nodded, secretly glad to escape sickroom duty. He'd been planning this departure for months. But last night his father's concern and Gaspard's irresponsibility had dampened his enthusiasm. Here with the ship bobbing under his feet he felt the rush of excitement return. He stopped to drop his knapsack on the bunk in his own cabin and went back up on deck.

In the first flush of dawn, the lines were being untied and two tug boats were moving into place to tow them out into the main channel. The wind pulled at the edges of the furled sails and ruffled the water. Whitecaps topped the waves. He stood at the prow, with the wind in his hair, and laughed. This was what he'd waited for, Devin thought. This was the beginning of an adventure!

CHAPTER 3

The Marie Lisette

The first mate tapped his shoulder.

"Move to the forecastle if you want to watch, *monsieur*. When we hoist the sails, these booms will start to swing. You could be knocked overboard before anyone has a chance to warn you."

Devin nodded, embarrassed that he hadn't known better. He'd had no experience with ships and he had sought out the first deck available. He found steps to another level, and stationed himself out of harm's way on the upper deck with a good view of their course.

Devin had the forecastle to himself. The Marie Lisette only carried seven travelers besides himself, Marcus, and Gaspard. The others must have boarded last night, he thought, and were still lingering below deck, sleeping through their departure. Devin enjoyed the solitude, watching as the huge ship made its way out of the harbor. They might have been on the eastern coast of the empire. The Dantzig's waters stretched beyond the horizon in three directions, dividing Llisé nearly in half. Six provinces bordered the eastern side of the Dantzig, separating them from its culture and learning as effectively as an ocean. The Rhine provided almost as great a barrier for the eight provinces to the west. Only Arcadia connected by land to Viénne, the capital province, but the mountain ranges between proved a formidable impediment even in the summer months.

To the south, a scattering of ships negotiated the Dantzig's channels, their sails billowing in the strong east wind. To the north, the river lay cold and deserted. The Marie Lisette's course into the channel carefully avoided ominous white water, where rock and debris threatened to snag ships unfamiliar with the river's shallows.

The wind went right through Devin's jacket, chilling him to the bone, and yet he wouldn't have moved for the world. His father's position had kept them close to Coreé in the past. There had been no seaside holidays for the Chancellor's family even though summers in the capital were uncomfortably steamy and hot. Devin's mother had felt her place lay at her husband's side and she never allowed herself the luxury of a summer cottage on the coast of Tirolien or Cretois. Ironically, Devin had been named for just such a seaside resort where his parents had spent a month celebrating his father's rise to power. Devin had been born nine months later; the sixth and final son of the new Chancellor Elite of Llisé.

Travel, a pleasure denied to Devin in the past, had today become a reality and he was relishing every minute of it. The smell of the harbor, hanging like a stinking cloud over the docks behind them, dissipated as they moved farther from the shore, giving way to the clean scent of wind over open water. Coreé faded to a distant smudge on the horizon once the sails unfurled. The ship leaped forward like a stallion, hurtling through the waves. The stinging force of the wind brought tears to Devin's eyes and he turned his back to wipe them, startled to find someone standing behind him.

A tall middle-aged man held out his hand. "I'm Henri LeBeau, Department of Sciences. I work with your brother."

Devin nodded. The man looked familiar. Perhaps, he'd seen him at the Académie. Although, much to Andre's disappointment, he had no classes in that department.

"Of course," he said, extending his own hand. "I'm sure André has mentioned your name."

"How long have you been out here?" Henri asked, covering Devin's hand with both of his. "You're freezing."

It was an overly familiar gesture and Devin extricated his hand, shoving it into the warmth of his pocket instead. "It's the wind," he murmured, turning back to the view ahead. "But I can't tear myself away long enough to go down to my cabin."

"I understand the fascination," Henri replied. "Unfortunately, I'm too late to see the sun rise over the water."

Devin resisted the urge to point out the sun had risen hours ago. To his right, he saw Marcus lounging casually against the rail. He wondered when he'd come up on deck.

"I'm traveling for a few months," Henri continued. "I have a small summer home in Arcadia but I plan to stay a month in Ombria and another in Tirolien on the way."

That was odd. Devin's plans took him along the same route.

"And where are you headed?" Henri asked.

Devin shrugged, affecting a nonchalance he didn't feel. "Well, after all, this is my Third Year. My friends and I plan to tour all fifteen provinces and still make it back before classes begin next September."

Henri laughed. "An ambitious undertaking! So, you're not alone?"

"No," Devin replied, cocking his head at Marcus. "There are three of us."

Henri's eyes met Marcus's and then slid off. "I see. Well, I'm sure you'll have a good time. Do you plan to stop in Treves?"

Arcadia's Master Bard lived in Treves. Of course, they'd stop there but Devin didn't like where this questioning seemed to be headed. He shook his head. "I haven't thought that far ahead."

"I could show you the sights. The healing springs are world famous."

"I haven't any complaints," Devin murmured. "Perhaps, when I'm your age, I'll pay them a visit." The remark was rude and pointed but his companion refused to be offended.

"The east side of the city is a warren of caves and hot springs. Most are still in their natural state, dripping with ferns and cascading waterfalls. It's worth seeing. Why don't we set a date?"

Devin gave an exaggerated shiver. "You know, I think I will go below decks. I'm really chilled. It's nice to have met you."

But their parting wasn't so easily accomplished. "I'll come with you," Henri offered, tagging along as though they were the best of friends. "Would you like to stop in the galley for coffee or chocolate? Something hot would warm you."

"Not right now," Devin replied, glad to see Marcus following them closely down the steps. "I didn't sleep at all last night. Perhaps I'll nap awhile and go back up on deck later."

"I'll save a chair for you at dinner, then," Henri offered, giving Devin's shoulder a proprietary pat. "Enjoy your rest."

25

Devin ducked inside his cabin, fuming as he saw Henri jotting the cabin number down on a piece of paper from his pocket. The man was almost enough to make him change his itinerary. A moment later, Marcus knocked and Devin let him in, half expecting to see Henri lurking behind him but the passageway was blessedly empty.

Marcus closed the door and leaned against it.

"Henri LeBeau," he said. "Councilman, Alexander LeBeau's oldest son. His father is a constant thorn in your father's side, and he is also one of the Council members who threatened to file a complaint about your trip."

"Shit," Devin muttered.

"And then some," Marcus agreed.

Devin sat down on his bunk. "He wants to be my best friend, apparently."

"I would discourage that."

"I tried! The man wouldn't leave me alone. I was blatantly rude and he just smiled."

Marcus snorted. "Perhaps, I will be rude myself. I've had more practice at it than you have."

Devin laughed, releasing the tension that had threatened to spoil the morning. "Perhaps you could just push him overboard."

Marcus's face was impassive. "I will consider it."

"I was only kidding," Devin said, rummaging through his knapsack.

"I was not," Marcus replied.

Devin turned his bag over and dumped the contents on his bunk, carefully separating his belongings.

"What's the matter?" Marcus asked.

"My itinerary is missing."

"Perhaps you misplaced it," Marcus suggested.

"I haven't taken anything out of my knapsack until now."

Marcus bent over the bunk to help him look. "Are you certain you packed it? You left the dormitory in a hurry."

"It was the first thing I put in my knapsack!" Devin protested.

He'd spent months preparing that itinerary, estimating travel time and allowing for bad weather, always trying to set aside the maximum number of days to memorize each province's Chronicles. He was attempting something that apprentice bards took years to accomplish. There wasn't a spare moment built into that schedule once they set foot in Ombria. The only other copy was in Coreé, on his father's desk. Suddenly, the whole project seemed hopelessly doomed.

Marcus turned to look at the door. "Did you lock your cabin when you went up on deck?"

"Of course," Devin snapped, and then wondered if he had actually locked the door. The Captain had given him a key but he couldn't remember having used it. His hand fumbled in his pocket. With a sinking feeling he pulled out the brass key with the numbered fob. "Maybe not," he amended dully.

Marcus sighed. "I don't suppose you have a second copy?"

Devin shook his head.

"You can ask your father to send you one. Until it comes, can you recreate your plan for the first two provinces?"

Devin laughed. This whole scheme rested on his ability to memorize a great deal of information. If he couldn't even remember the itinerary, they might as well turn around now and save everyone a lot of aggravation.

"Yes, I'm sure I can," he answered. "I'll work on it after dinner. It just makes me angry that someone stole it out of my cabin!"

"The fact that it's the only thing that's missing worries me more," Marcus said. "Why is it important that someone knows exactly where you're going? Do you think Henri LeBeau . . . ?"

"LeBeau said he was spending a month in Ombria and Tirolien before going to Arcadia. That's my plan, too. He could have stolen the itinerary before he talked to me on deck. But if he did, why did he write down my cabin number just now?"

"To divert suspicion?" Marcus suggested.

"Perhaps," Devin answered, refolding his clothing and laying it on the bunk. "But, it seems a funny way of doing it. Who else is on board?"

"I already asked the Captain." Marcus raised his hand and counted off on his fingers. "A merchant and his daughter from Tirolien, a young man who plans to spend his summer in Cretois with his aunt and uncle, another merchant from Coreé who is going to buy Arcadian lace for his shop, a physician returning to Treves with his daughter, and a soldier on a three month leave."

"Counting LeBeau, that's eight people," Devin pointed out. "I thought there were only seven, in addition to us."

Marcus raised his eyebrows. "You're right. That's what I was told. Perhaps LeBeau is the latecomer. I'll go and find out." He turned, with his hand on the door. "And Devin, if you actually plan to sleep, bolt this door when I leave and don't open it for anyone but Gaspard or me."

Devin stood up. "I should go and check on Gaspard."

"I have already done that several times. I was planning to stop again on my way to see the Captain." Marcus gestured at the mess on the bed. "Maybe you should go through your belongings one more time to make sure nothing else is missing. And, lock the door as soon as I leave."

Devin threw the bolt after Marcus went out into the passageway. He found the whole concept of locks distasteful. He'd never lived where he'd had to worry about stealing. Dormitory rooms were never locked. The thought that scholars would steal from each other negated the entire idea of academic freedom and intellectual collaboration.

He spread out his things on the bunk again but nothing else seemed to be missing. It made the theft seem more sinister and pointed. There would be no reason to steal such a thing unless someone intended to follow him. He repacked the knapsack and stowed it underneath the narrow bunk before lying down. The problem of the missing itinerary lingered to worry him only a few minutes. The gentle roll of the ship was hypnotic and before he knew it, he fell asleep.

CHAPTER 4

Allies and Adversaries

When Devin wakened a few hours later, a piece of paper had been shoved under the door. He picked it up, recognizing Marcus's untidy scrawl: I am on deck. M. Devin washed his face and straightened his clothes. The single porthole in his cabin showed the sun already lay low in the sky. He glanced at his watch. It was almost 7 o'clock; nearly time for dinner. He hadn't meant to sleep that long. After he locked his cabin, he knocked softly on Gaspard's door and received a muffled response. The knob turned easily in his hand.

Gaspard sat on the edge of his bunk, his hands clasped between his knees, his dark hair rumpled and standing on end. He glanced up at Devin with bloodshot eyes.

"Ah, my kidnapper shows himself at last."

Devin's stomach clenched. "Had you decided not to come with me?"

Gaspard regarded him icily another moment and then laughed, shaking his head back and forth. "Of course, I meant to come with you, you idiot! Did you think I wanted to stay

30

in Coreé with my father ranting on about my irresponsibility? I hope you didn't tell him I was going with you. It will do the old bastard good to worry about me for a change."

"I'm sure he does worry about you," Devin said. "My father came down to the docks to see me off. He insisted on going to tell your father, personally, that you'd gone."

Gaspard rolled his eyes. "It's more than the old man deserves."

Devin sat down on the bunk beside him. "What did he say to you?"

Gaspard leaned his head against the wall, one arm propping himself upright. "After I gave up on my exams, I went down to Antoine's to get seriously drunk. The next thing I knew my father was in my face, telling me how I had failed him and the entire Forneaux family. He insisted that I spend the summer under a tutor, of his choosing, and attempt to be reinstated at the Académie in the fall."

Devin ran a hand through his hair. "God, I've made things so much worse. I'm sorry."

"Worse?" Gaspard said with a hollow laugh. "How could things be worse than a summer in Coreé with my father breathing down my neck?"

"But he must have forbidden you to go with me."

"Oh, he did. He threatened me, in fact, said if I went on this trip he'd disown me."

"Gaspard!" Devin protested. "My father knew none of this when I talked to him. He'll be furious at me for dragging you along."

Gaspard grunted. "I'm afraid that is your problem, *mon ami*. I have enough of my own at the moment."

"But I've complicated the whole thing! Maybe you should take the first ship back to Coreé when we reach Friseé. I'll write a letter to your father and explain what happened . . . "

Gaspard straightened abruptly. Grabbing Devin's lapels, he shook him.

"You're not listening, Dev! I don't want to go back! I need this time away to decide what I'm going to do with my life. Fifteen months is a long time, my father may relent by then and if he doesn't . . . so what? I can't be responsible for his happiness as well as my own."

Devin shook off Gaspard's hands and stood up, pacing the tiny room. "There must be something I can do to help."

"Pay attention!" Gaspard shouted. "You have done the best thing possible! I can't thank you enough! Now drop it!" He lay back on the bunk, his feet still on the floor and stared at the ceiling. "All the tutors in the world wouldn't have gotten me through those exams. You did what you could for me; spent hours going over all the information."

"What happened?" Devin asked.

"With my exams?" Gaspard replied. He shrugged. "I froze, Dev. I looked at those examination questions and it was as though there wasn't one scrap of information left in my head. I couldn't have told them how old I was let alone who founded the archives!"

"Pierre Gaston," Devin murmured involuntarily.

"I know that!" Gaspard snapped, then his voice softened. "I know it . . . now. But I couldn't have told you then. My mind doesn't work like yours, Dev. I get so on edge about taking an exam that when I sit down with the papers in front of me anything I ever knew just flies out the window."

"I'm sorry."

"Don't be sorry. I can't thank you enough for getting me out of there, honestly. Fifteen months away from school – away from Father – sounds like heaven to me. I don't know that I will ever go back. Maybe you could leave me on some deserted beach in Andalusia. I'll spend the rest of my days in seclusion."

"I've heard seclusion isn't much fun," Devin said.

Gaspard laughed. "That from you! You lock yourself up for days at a time, studying ancient documents."

"I enjoy it."

"Well, thank heavens you have other attributes that are more appealing!"

Devin pulled his watch from his pocket. "Can you eat? It's time for dinner."

Gaspard sat up. "A couple of hours ago, I wouldn't have welcomed that suggestion but I could eat something now. Did you pack me a change of clothes or will I have to spend the next year in these ratty things?"

Devin dragged Gaspard's knapsack up onto the bunk. "I packed very light. We're going to be doing a lot of walking. If there's anything you need that I left out, I'll replace it when we get to port."

Gaspard sat for a moment, his hand on his knapsack. "There's one other issue . . . "

Devin twisted to look at him. "What?"

Gaspard turned out his pockets. "I'm penniless. I spent the last of my money at Antoine's."

Devin shook his head. "That's not a problem. You had no time to pack."

"You did kidnap me," Gaspard pointed out.

"I did," Devin agreed. "To be frank, I couldn't quite face going without you."

Gaspard snickered. "You didn't think Marcus would show you a good time?"

Devin laughed. "Absolutely not! Believe me, when I say that I never expected to have a bodyguard assigned to me."

Gaspard's face sobered. "Marcus may be an asset. My father's a dangerous man, Dev. He is furious with me but now he will be angry at you, too."

"He was already angry at me. My father said he was one of the Council members who objected to this trip. We're on our way. Let's put that behind us. And as far as money is concerned, this is my trip and I'll take care of the expenses."

Devin was also on the Council's payroll now, but something kept him from sharing the information. Now wasn't the time or the place.

Gaspard's smile was pensive. "Thank you," he said. "I'm sorry. I've always thought I should be the responsible one. I'm three years older than you. I should be like your big brother; instead, you are always bailing me out."

Devin laughed. "I have far too many big brothers! I'm much happier to be traveling with a friend. I'll go find Marcus while you change. We'll meet you in the dining room."

Devin passed no one in the passageway. Down the hall he could hear the clink of glasses and silverware and the low murmur of voices. Henri LeBeau laughed louder and longer than necessary and Devin cringed as he went up the staircase.

He braced himself as he crossed the deck. Lowering purple clouds filtered the sun's rays, sending bright shafts of light to illuminate the water. Feathered fringes glowed gold and orange in a glorious display, unencumbered by the clutter of land, trees, or buildings. Their appetites and the rising wind had apparently discouraged any other passengers from admiring the view. Only Marcus stood on the forecastle, his arms resting on the rail. Clutching his jacket around him, Devin stopped beside him.

"It's quite a bit colder but that sunset is spectacular," he commented. "What did Captain Torrance say?"

Marcus turned to face him, the wind blowing his hair into his craggy face. He swiped at it with a massive hand.

"The soldier is the only one who booked passage just before we left. His name is Bertrand St. Clair and he is stationed in Coreé, a member of the Militaire de l'Intérieur."

Devin raised an eyebrow. "Does that qualify him as a thief?"

"Not ordinarily," Marcus replied. "But his haste to come aboard makes him suspect."

"Perhaps René Forneaux sent him."

"Perhaps, but I imagine Monsieur Forneaux didn't know for certain where Gaspard was until your father told him this morning. I think St. Clair's plans were made earlier. He pretends to be on leave but he doesn't act like a man on a holiday."

"I think it's possible that René Forneaux may have had Gaspard followed," Devin said, and then filled him in on what Gaspard had told him.

Marcus sighed. "You've left your father with a pretty mess to sort out."

"I'm sorry about that," Devin said. "But there is nothing I can do about it now. I'll write him a letter tonight and send it back on the first ship. Surely he knows I wouldn't have brought Gaspard if I'd known he was forbidden to go?"

"Oh, he'll realize it once he's calmed down but I doubt he'll be very happy with either of us. I wish I hadn't encouraged you to bring Gaspard along," Marcus admitted. "The best thing would be for him to go back and face his father."

"He won't go," Devin assured him. "If I book him passage on another vessel, he'll simply disappear. There's nothing we can do now but proceed as we had planned." They stood a moment at the rail in silence. "Did you tell the Captain that I'd had something stolen from my cabin?"

Marcus shook his head. "I decided not to. He would have said it was your own fault for leaving it unlocked. Besides, there might be some advantage to letting the thief think you haven't missed it yet."

"I still think he should know," Devin protested. "His other passengers may be at risk too."

Marcus bowed his head, acquiescing. "Then feel free to tell him, *monsieur*. You've heard my advice on the matter." He crossed the deck and disappeared down the stairway.

Devin watched him go. Marcus had made it clear that Devin was in charge but he felt out of his depth. He was facing issues he had never expected to deal with. And now, the missing itinerary seemed less important in light of their other problems. Had he and Gaspard come alone, would he have sacrificed this trip to persuade him to go home? Should he tell the Captain that his itinerary had been stolen or keep the information to himself? He lingered for one more look at the smoldering sunset and followed Marcus below deck.

CHAPTER 5

Rough Seas

The dining room was far more elegant than Devin would have imagined for a ship the size of the Marie Lisette. Paneled in dark wood and trimmed in gleaming brass, the room could have seated forty. But only one table had been lit with burnished oil lamps and set for the inopportune number of thirteen.

"Ah," Devin murmured, coming up behind Marcus and Gaspard, "which of us makes it unlucky thirteen?"

"You, I would think," Gaspard commented mercilessly. "You arrived last and have kept everyone else waiting."

The Captain turned to grace Devin with a smile. "At last, our honored guest has arrived. Ladies and gentlemen, may I present our Chancellor Elite's youngest son, Devin Roché."

Devin saw at once that he had dressed too informally. The rest of the company had donned evening attire for dinner. Only he, Marcus, and Gaspard stood clad in casual traveling clothes. Oh well, it couldn't be helped. He gave a slight bow.

"Good evening. I'm sorry to have kept you waiting. Please sit down." The notoriety annoyed him but he tried not to let it show on his face.

The Captain ushered Devin to the chair on his right and seated Henri LeBeau next to him; Marcus and Gaspard were placed across from each other, further down the table. He quickly introduced the rest of the passengers. The merchant, Gustave Christophe, and his pretty daughter, Sophie, sat toward the end of the table. Across from them, Captain Torrance had put the other merchant, Frederic Putton, and his wife, Margot. Bertrand St. Clair, the soldier they suspected of ulterior motives, had been seated next to Marcus. Devin wondered if perhaps the Captain had done that intentionally. Thomas Reynard, a boy of about fourteen, sat alone at the end of the table. Dr. Lucien Rousseau and his daughter, Josette faced Devin and Henri, completing the company.

St. Clair slid his chair away from Marcus as he sat down. Perhaps, it was only a courtesy – giving Marcus the extra space his huge frame demanded – but Devin saw a momentary look of distaste cross the man's face as well.

The Captain seized his soup spoon to sample the first offering.

"So tell us all the news from Coreé, *monsieur*," he demanded of Devin. "What is troubling hearts in the capital this spring?"

"My friend Gaspard and I are students at the Académie," Devin replied. "We haven't had much time for political intrigue."

"And what are you studying?" the Captain asked, taking a noisy slurp of his fish chowder.

"I'm a certified historian but I am training to work in the Archives," Devin replied.

"Apparently, you don't crave excitement, then," the Captain said with a laugh. His gaze fell on Gaspard. "And you are René Forneaux's son, are you not?"

Gaspard crooked an eyebrow. "Only if you catch him on the rare day that he will admit it."

Sophie giggled and Gaspard rewarded her with a wink.

"You and your father are not on good terms?" Henri LeBeau asked.

Gaspard shook his head and downed a spoonful of chowder. "On the contrary, Monsieur LeBeau, we are on excellent terms, as long as we aren't forced to spend any time together."

St. Clair's spoon hit his plate with a sharp report. "Your pardon," he remarked hastily.

Devin cleared his throat. "Surely, dinner discussion shouldn't center on such private matters. Mr. LeBeau, since you are a professor at the Académie, perhaps you could tell us about some of the courses you teach?"

The Captain laughed, elbowing Devin. "I see your father raised a diplomat, *monsieur*. Perhaps your talents will be wasted in the Archives."

"Surely not," LeBeau said. "Llisé is always in need of scrupulous historians to guard our written records. After all, our history defines us as a people. Wouldn't you agree, Monsieur Roche?"

"I would," Devin said with a nod. "We cannot safeguard our future without venerating the past."

"Well said," Dr. Rousseau chimed in. "I wish more young people shared your sentiments."

"I know you and Monsieur Forneaux plan to visit all fifteen provinces in the next year," LeBeau began. "Of what value will such a trip be to an archivist, *monsieur*?"

Devin chose his words carefully before he spoke. "It is something I have always wanted to do. Coreé has its libraries; the history and literature of a thousand years. The provinces have their Chronicles. Each province, including Viénne, has a unique character, and yet together they form Llisé. How can I understand the whole without understanding the parts that comprise it?"

Dr. Rousseau nodded his head approvingly. "Perhaps our Captain is right. Your skills may be wasted in the Archives. We need more young men like you on the Council. My God, written language is still forbidden in the provinces. A man can only be educated if he is recommended by the village elders, and then he must find a sponsor to provide the financial backing to reach Coreé and attend a school. How many intelligent individuals are languishing in the provinces that might serve us better if they could read and write?"

"You verge on heresy," LeBeau said coldly.

"And yet, we are all human beings, LeBeau," Dr. Rousseau retorted. "Some of us were simply fortunate enough to be born into families where education is taken for granted, not regarded as a privilege for the chosen few."

"My family has personally sponsored a number of bright young men from Tirolien," LeBeau replied. "As I am certain Chancellor Roche's family has done in Sorrento. Every family that holds estates in the provinces recognizes the responsibility to instruct those unique individuals who can tolerate the demands of education."

"A child is a child whether he is born into poverty or privilege," Devin said quietly. "Who are we to determine who can and will be educated?"

"The determination is made by the wisest men of the village. Who is a better judge of a boy's worth than his own people?" LeBeau retorted.

"I am not familiar with the actual process," Devin replied, dipping his spoon into his chowder. "How are potential candidates identified?"

Gustave Christophe raised his hand tentatively. "My own son will receive schooling so he can carry on my business. But a father may also recommend his son to the elders if he shows exceptional promise."

"What if the child is an orphan?" Devin asked.

"The men of the village can speak for him," Gustave replied. "There is such a boy in my own village. His parents died when he was ten years old. He sweeps my shop in exchange for room and board. He shows skill in numbers and counting. I spoke for him to the elders."

"And is he attending school?" Devin asked.

"He has no sponsor, *monsieur*."

"Where do you live in Tirolien?"

"Tarente, *monsieur*."

"I plan to travel through there in July," Devin told him. "I would like to meet this boy, if you will give me directions to your shop. Perhaps my father can sponsor him."

"Thank you very much, *monsieur*," Gustave replied, bowing.

Marcus shifted uncomfortably but Devin ignored him. This was exactly the kind of thing he intended to include in his report to his father. How many other bright young children lacked sponsors to pay for their schooling? It was a problem that needed to be addressed.

LeBeau fixed Devin with a grim stare. "I had heard that there is an ulterior motive for your trip."

"And what is that?" Dr. Rousseau asked.

"It is rumored that Monsieur Roche intends to memorize the Chronicles in as many provinces as he can," LeBeau said. "Is that true?"

41

Devin placed his spoon carefully on his soup plate. Conversation had stopped. All eyes were on him.

"That was my original intention," he admitted.

A slight gasp escaped from the lower end of the table. Devin suspected St. Clair but didn't risk confirming it by a glance.

"And your objective has since been amended?" LeBeau continued.

"Not entirely," Devin replied, aware of Marcus's guarded expression. "I do intend to memorize some of the Chronicles. I cannot and would not record them in any kind of written document. My position as a historian precludes that."

"Then what is the point of your project?" LeBeau demanded.

"It is only for my own information," Devin answered. "I would like to understand our realm better. I am only familiar with our written history. Surely the vast treasury of story and song that makes up the tradition of the provinces is of value, too?"

"Legally, it is of value only to those who live in the provinces," LeBeau pointed out. "Anything of historical importance has been officially recorded in Coreé. The rest is merely hearsay. Why would a man of your education and training waste his time on such a task?"

Devin held a palm up. "Monsieur, I will admit I am at a loss as to why this concerns you."

"You are the son of our Chancellor," LeBeau remarked sternly. "Are the sentiments you have voiced his as well?"

God, Devin thought. He apparently had no diplomatic skills what so ever or he would never have allowed the conversation to have gotten this far.

Gaspard's wine glass smacked down on the table. "Don't be an ass, LeBeau! You have children of your own. Does every one of them share the exact same interests and opinions you do?"

"Of course not," LeBeau stammered. "That's hardly the point!"

Gaspard raised his wine glass and gestured. "I think it is, *monsieur*. My friend Devin is merely a scholar. Unlike his brothers he holds no position of authority in his father's government. His influence on any current policy is as negligible as your own. Why do you care what he thinks or does?"

"His actions reflect badly on his father!" LeBeau protested. "He shows a disregard for authority!"

Dr. Rousseau interrupted. "I disagree! I think that it is time the provinces were recognized for the contributions they make to Llisé. We would starve without their produce and wine. Viénne's business would grind to a halt without provincial horses to pull our carriages and our supply wagons. Their mills provide the paper for every official document that is written in the capital and yet the makers of that paper could be thrown in prison for using it to record their own business!"

"Dr. Rousseau, your opinions could land you in prison, as well. I advise you to keep them to yourself!" LeBeau snapped.

Devin stood up and addressed those at the table. "Excuse me, please. Courtesy requires that meals remain free of political and religious discussion. I, personally, find it difficult to eat with all this shouting. Please continue without me and my companions." He turned to the Captain. "Would it be possible to have our dinners served in my cabin?"

The Captain rose, clutching his napkin, his face the color of the setting sun.

"Of course, *monsieur*, I am so sorry. Please accept my apologies."

Marcus pushed his chair back and crossed the room to wait, glowering, in the doorway.

"Thank you," Devin said with a little bow. "Please enjoy the rest of your meal, if you can."

Gaspard snagged the wine bottle from his end of the table and followed Devin out the door.

They went down the passageway in silence. Devin fumbled with the key and then waited until the others preceded him into the room. When he closed the door, his hands were shaking.

"Well," he said, turning to Marcus. "I suppose you think I handled that badly."

"On the contrary," Marcus replied. "I thought you handled it quite well. You left LeBeau looking very much like the ass Gaspard reported him to be."

"I wasn't expecting him to try to embarrass me publicly."

Gaspard collapsed on Devin's bunk and uncorked the wine. "He embarrassed himself. I doubt that anyone else agreed with him, Dev."

"St. Clair seemed quite pleased with LeBeau's opinions," Devin pointed out. "He was glowering at me through most of the meal."

Marcus folded his arms and leaned against the wall. "St. Clair bears watching and so does LeBeau. LeBeau accomplished what he intended to do tonight. If only one of the other passengers repeats this conversation to someone else, the rumor could spread quite quickly that your father favors education for the masses and elevating the Chronicles to Archival status."

"I never advocated either of those things!" Devin protested.

"No, you didn't but LeBeau made certain that those views entered the conversation. Whether you actually voiced them or not has little to do with it," Marcus said.

"I'll admit I find it difficult to support a system which educates a merchant's son enough to carry on his father's business but denies him the right to become a physician or priest unless he finds a sponsor to encourage his scholarship."

"Apparently, Dr. Rousseau agrees with you."

Gaspard leaned back against the window and grimaced. "Why don't you put your stuff away?" he grumbled, pulling Devin's knapsack out from behind him.

Devin just stared it. "I put it under the bunk when I left."

He and Marcus grabbed for it at the same time, spreading the drawstring at the top to reveal a sheaf of folded papers.

"Your itinerary?" Marcus asked.

"It appears to be," Devin replied. He unfolded it, thinking it seemed thicker than before. Something dropped to the floor from between the pages: two twigs tied with red colored thread that formed a miniature cross. He stooped to pick it up but Marcus grabbed his wrist.

"Don't touch it," he warned.

"Why?" Gaspard asked, bending over to see it better.

"It carries a curse," Marcus replied.

"I've never heard of such a thing," Devin said.

"You would never learn about such things in the Archives," Marcus said, "but cursed crosses are quite common in the rural provinces. Superstition claims that the curse will come true for the first one who touches it."

"What kind of a curse?" Devin asked.

"It depends on the color of the thread," Marcus explained. "A blue center promises misfortune, a yellow one – illness, gray – disappointment, and red symbolizes death."

"So, someone wants me dead?" Devin asked incredulously.

"It would seem so." Marcus stooped to slide the offending object onto a piece of paper but it eluded him, skittering across the polished wooden floor.

"For God's sake!" Gaspard protested, picking the thing up between his thumb and forefinger. "It's only two twigs and some thread. What possible harm could it do?"

Devin watched with a shiver of apprehension as Gaspard unlatched the tiny window and flung it out into the sea. Whoever wished him ill, had entered his locked room and tampered once again with his belongings. The theft and return of the itinerary no longer seemed quite so trivial.

Gaspard turned from the window with a grin. "There, it's gone. Put it out of your head, Dev. You never touched the thing so the curse can't come true!"

"But you touched it," Marcus pointed out darkly.

Gaspard tipped the wine bottle to his lips. "What are friends for?"

CHAPTER 6

Revelations

Gaspard chattered constantly during dinner. The clink of silverware provided a subtle counterpoint to his monologue. Despite his apparent good humor, Devin realized that the incident with the twine-wrapped cross had shaken Gaspard deeply. He simply wasn't about to admit it to anyone.

They had no clue as to who had broken into Devin's room. Gaspard and Marcus had entered the ship's dining room just before Devin, and all the other passengers were present. So, it was impossible to tell who might have been responsible for placing the cross inside the itinerary. Obviously, whoever had done it, either had access to the Captain's master key, or was a trained thief. No one they had met so far seemed a likely suspect, and Devin was tired of speculation. They'd sat for hours over the little folding table littered by fish bones piled on dirty dishes and greasy, discarded napkins. Devin and Gaspard had perched on the bunk, giving Marcus the only chair in the tiny cabin.

Gaspard lifted the wine bottle to refill Devin's glass, but he covered it with his hand.

"I've had enough," he muttered irritably, "and so have you."

"Lighten up," Gaspard demanded, topping off his own glass. "Why don't we just forget about the whole thing? No one's been hurt. It was probably just a childish prank. Someone is simply trying to scare you. If they'd intended to kill you, they could have laced the cross with poison. All you would have had to do was pick it up, and you'd be dead."

"No, you'd be dead," Marcus pointed out. "Devin had sense enough not to touch it when he was told not to."

"So, I'd be dead," Gaspard conceded. "But I'm not, so that proves my point."

Devin grinned. "Maybe it's a slow acting poison and tomorrow when I try to waken you . . . "

"Enough," Marcus said. "This is a serious matter. That symbol represents both a warning and a threat."

"How do you know that?" Devin asked. "I've never even seen one of those before."

"My family has its roots in Sorrento," Marcus answered. "Those curse symbols are common there. I remember my mother showing me one once. A disgruntled customer had left a blue one on someone's stall at the market."

"And people actually fear them?" Gaspard asked.

"Oh, yes," Marcus said. "They are taken quite seriously. My grandmother used to tell the story of a man who was feuding with his neighbor. One morning he left a red cross in the middle of the road so that his neighbor would step on it when he took his vegetables to market. The neighbor packed up his donkey and started to town, never even seeing the cross lying in the road. The donkey stepped on it instead. That evening on the way home, the donkey tripped along the cliff road. It fell into the sea and drowned."

Gaspard grimaced. "Shit, Dev, you owe me."

"Apparently," Devin agreed, his eyes on his bodyguard. "Marcus, were you raised in Sorrento?"

"No, I was born in Coreé."

"And when did you decide to go into my father's service?"

Marcus shrugged. "I don't remember ever being given a choice. My family has served your family for generations both in Coreé and on your father's estate in Bourgogne."

"That's hardly fair to you, is it?" Devin said.

"Your father has been good to me. Not only did he give me a responsible position in his household but he taught me to read and write."

"He taught you himself?" Devin asked in astonishment.

Marcus nodded. "Every evening for several years."

Devin laughed. "That surprises me. I wish I had known before."

Gaspard savored another sip of wine. "Wasn't he breaking the law by teaching you?"

"Gaspard," Devin cautioned.

Marcus extended a placating hand. "It's a legitimate question. Monsieur Roche said that my position as his bodyguard required me to carry correspondence, and it was necessary that I learn to read and write."

"And yet, he didn't sponsor you and send you to school which he could have done legally. He taught you himself," Gaspard pointed out.

Marcus shrugged again. "I was already in his employ. He's a good man. He treats his people with respect, both in Coreé and in Sorrento."

"So, perhaps Henri LeBeau wasn't so wrong in his assessment of Vincent Roché?" Gaspard remarked thoughtfully.

Devin glared at him. "So, you think my father was wrong to educate Marcus?"

Gaspard's hand flew to his chest. "I didn't say that! God, you're touchy tonight! I am actually questioning LeBeau's motives. I was wondering if someone had started a movement to discredit the Chancellor."

Marcus was silent for a moment. "We had the first indications of that several months ago. Unfortunately, we suspect that your father may be one of the instigators."

Gaspard rolled his eyes. "That's hardly a surprise."

"Why didn't Father tell me?" Devin asked. The Chancellor Elite was elected by the Council. The position was normally held for a lifetime, as long as the candidate remained powerful and respected. Only twice in the past thousand years had a Chancellor been deposed by a political coup, and that had been in the early years of the empire.

"There was nothing you could have done," Marcus replied.

"I could have stayed home."

"And what would that have accomplished?" Marcus asked.

"My visit to the provinces wouldn't have sparked controversy which put my father in a difficult position."

"Well, now that your trip is underway, conduct yourself in a manner that won't worsen the problem," Marcus answered curtly.

"Obviously, it is already worse!" Devin said. "LeBeau is intent on starting rumors, and someone is trying hard to deter me from going."

"But the Council's objections and our little folk symbol seem to be at cross purposes," Gaspard pointed out.

"What do you mean?" Devin asked.

Gaspard leaned back against the wall and drained his wine glass before answering. "It seems to me that this trip plays right into my father's hands. Why would he try to discourage you from going, if he intends to use your visit to the provinces to discredit your father?" He fumbled for the bottle on the floor, only to find it empty.

"Maybe your father professes one view publicly and works privately to further the opposite position," Devin said.

"Or perhaps there are two factions working independently," Marcus suggested.

"At least, I see now why your father didn't want you coming with me," Devin said. "Perhaps his plan to hire tutors was just a pretense."

"Well, I'll be happy if I've helped to ruin his plan," Gaspard said, yawning. "He can hardly use you to disgrace your father without admitting I've done the same to him." He stood up unsteadily. "I'm going to bed. Why don't you two figure this out and tell me in the morning."

"Wait here a moment, Gaspard, while I take the dishes to the galley," Marcus said. He turned to look at Devin. "You'd better turn in, too."

Devin snorted. "Who can sleep? There's far too much to think about." He watched the door close behind Marcus, glad to see the last of the debris from dinner.

"The day after tomorrow we'll be off this damn ship," Gaspard reminded him. "And anyone following us will be far more obvious on land."

"A sharp shooter doesn't have to be close to be effective," Devin muttered.

Gaspard shook his head. "It's not like you to be so maudlin."

"I'm just annoyed that a simple trip could be used as a political weapon. I wish my father had been completely honest about why he wanted me to stay home," Devin said.

Gaspard grunted. "And would you have listened to him?"

"Maybe, if I'd known what was at stake and I'd have to watch for assassins at every turn."

"Let me do that," Marcus said, as he slipped back through the door. "That's why your father sent me."

"See you in the morning," Gaspard said, giving him a crooked salute and stumbling out into the passageway.

"Goodnight," Devin said, making no move to get up. He noticed the satchel in Marcus's hand and frowned. "You're not planning to sleep in here, are you?"

"Your father entrusted me with your life," Marcus replied, putting his satchel on the opposite bunk. "Locks are no deterrent to this intruder, so I'm not going to leave you alone."

"But your cabin's just next door," Devin pointed out.

"I've learned only too well that an instant can mean the difference between life and death," Marcus replied. "Gaspard may scoff at that red cross but I take it very seriously."

Devin took off his shirt, pulled off his boots, and lay down. He stared at the ceiling, thinking how little he really knew about the man who was sharing his room. His first memory of Marcus was the day after his seventh birthday. His father was dedicating a new park along the Dantzig. The entire family had accompanied him for the celebration. Clouds had scudded across a brilliant blue sky and sailboats dotted the broad river.

They were standing near the new fountain. His father had just finished addressing the crowd when a man suddenly darted forward, a knife in his hand. Andre, already a graduate assistant at the Académie, had grabbed Devin, shielding him with his own body. But the assassin had only targeted the Chancellor. From the protective folds of Andre's jacket, Devin had heard a startled cry, a scuffle, and the dull thud of a body hitting the cobblestones.

Afraid for his father, Devin had pulled away in time to see Marcus pinning the attacker to the ground. The abandoned knife skittered across the pavement. His father was safe and unhurt, thanks to Marcus's quick action. Oddly enough, after all these years, two things still troubled Devin about the incident. The first was Andre's selfless disregard for his own safety. The other was the haunting image of a single tear running down the cheek of Marcus's prisoner as he lay prostrate on the cobblestones.

Devin turned to look at Marcus sitting on the bunk across from him.

"The day my father was attacked in Verde Park, why did the man cry when you caught him? Was he hurt or simply frustrated that he wasn't successful?"

Marcus stopped unpacking his belongings. On the table between them he had laid out two pistols, three knives, and a lethal looking coil of wire. He looked up at Devin.

"I wouldn't have thought you'd remember that. You were only a baby at the time."

"I was seven," Devin corrected him.

Marcus closed his satchel and shoved it under the bunk. He loosened the buttons on the neck of his shirt and lay down, his hands folded behind his head.

"Your father was attacked by Emile Rousseau, a stone cutter from Sorrento. Emile had made three requests for sponsorship for his son, Phillippe. The boy was bright but not very strong physically. Emile felt he deserved to be educated. He was anxious that his son be removed from working in the stone quarries. Your father had a great many other things to deal with at the time. He had already sponsored a number of boys, and for one reason or another he postponed his decision about Emile's son. About three months later, there was an accident at the quarry; Phillippe was crushed between two slabs when a cable broke. Emile blamed your father. He traveled for nine days on foot to reach the capital and kill him."

Devin found it difficult to breathe. "What happened to him?" he asked.

Marcus extinguished the oil lamp on the table between them. "He was executed," he answered. "Now get some sleep."

CHAPTER 7

Snow in Ombria

After breakfast, Gaspard spent the morning in the lounge dividing his time between Sophie Christophe and Josette Rousseau. For a few minutes, Devin attempted to be equally charming, but Marcus, who took his role of guardian angel very seriously, shadowed his every move, making normal conversation nearly impossible. At last, he sought the relative privacy of the deck, his bodyguard in tow.

The day had dawned clear and cold. It seemed that the Marie Lisette had left spring behind them in Coreé. The trees along the visible shoreline were still bare and leafless. To the north, clouds clustered along the horizon, blue-black and stormy.

"We're in for a blow," Marcus said darkly. "That storm is probably just south of Ombria now."

"Let me guess," Devin teased, "your grandmother was a sailor, too."

Marcus didn't crack a smile. "Sorrento is landlocked," he retorted. "But, it doesn't take a sailor to recognize bad weather. I don't imagine we'll get much sleep tonight."

Devin didn't comment. He wondered if Marcus was aware that he had lain awake most of last night. Every footstep in the passageway had set his heart thumping. He'd always felt safe in Coreé. It wasn't as though he hadn't realized, especially after the incident at Verde Park, that his family would live under constant threat. But that threat had only touched him once, personally. His childhood had remained remarkably charmed and unblemished despite his father's elevated position.

He leaned forward on the rail and watched the churning water as it rushed by the prow.

"Had it occurred to you that Dr. Rousseau might be related to Emile?" he asked, after a moment.

"Dr. Rousseau lives in Treves. His family has resided there for several generations," Marcus responded.

"He told you that?"

"No, the Captain did. I made it clear that, for security purposes, it was imperative I know more than just the obvious things about the others on board. Besides, any good Captain makes a practice of knowing his passengers, especially, when he is entrusted with carrying the son of the Chancellor Elite."

Devin rolled his eyes. He seemed doomed to drag his father's title along with him, like an anchor around his neck. "Do you trust Captain Torrance?"

"Your father booked your passage. He wouldn't have chosen this particular ship had he any qualms about Captain Torrance's loyalty or his skill."

Devin shrugged. He wished he could recapture yesterday's thrill of excitement. Today, he felt jumpy and suspicious. He envied Gaspard's carefree attitude. But now that he knew about both the political turmoil in Coreé and its potential threat to his father, they weighed on him. He thought again about his father's abrupt reversal, the evening before he left, in allowing him to continue with his trip. Had his father wanted Devin out of the city for his own safety? Did he hope that, in fifteen months, the threat of revolution might have been averted or resolved? For the first time Devin truly considered booking his passage back to Coreé when they docked in Pireé.

The wind drove them below deck by afternoon and true to Marcus's prediction the storm hit by nightfall. The choppy water sent half the passengers, including Gaspard, to their cabins. Dr. Rousseau was kept busy tending seasick travelers for most of the evening. Devin had to admit that the heaving floors made him feel a little uneasy himself, but Marcus seemed completely unaffected.

Devin hadn't seen Henri LeBeau all day and was surprised when he came into the lounge after dinner. He crossed the floor and headed immediately to where Josette and Devin were seated talking in the corner of the room. Marcus detached himself from the wall and assumed a protective stance next to Devin. The room fell into expectant silence around them.

LeBeau sketched a small bow. "I wondered if I might have a word with you, Monsieur Roché."

"By all means," Devin said. "What's on your mind?"

"Could I speak with you alone?" LeBeau asked.

"That's not possible," Marcus replied grimly.

Josette rose to her feet and smiled at Devin. "Forgive me, *monsieur*, but I should be going."

Devin stood up, hoping to detain her. "Please stay a little longer. I'm certain this will only take a moment."

She lowered her lashes and shook her head. "I'll try to come back later, *monsieur*, if I can. I need to check with my father and see if there is anything I can do to help him."

Devin watched her go with regret. With Gaspard sick in his cabin, he'd been free of any competition for Josette's attention. Tomorrow, she would continue on with the Marie Lisette and he would begin his journey overland across Ombria. He turned in annoyance to LeBeau.

"What is it that you wanted?"

LeBeau cleared his throat. "I'd like to apologize. I drank too much wine before dinner last night. I'm afraid it tends to make me argumentative. I fear I spoiled everyone's meal. I'm sorry."

Devin raised his eyebrows. "Surely your political views haven't changed overnight?"

"Of course, they haven't," LeBeau assured him. "But the dinner table was not the place to discuss them."

Devin inclined his head. "On that we agree."

"I hope you can forgive me," LeBeau continued. "I have the utmost respect for both your brother and your father. I regret that you may have found my remarks offensive."

It was as though Devin could hear his father's voice in his mind: *Never decline an apology that is proffered publicly. If you do, you allow your opponent to become the injured party.*

"We all speak without thinking sometimes," he remarked lightly. "This trip is almost over. Let's put last night's discussion behind us."

"Thank you," LeBeau said with relief. "My invitation still stands. In spite of everything, I would still like to show you Treves."

"I'm sorry but our plans are not definite," Devin answered diplomatically. "I have no idea when we will arrive in Arcadia, so it is impossible to commit to anything."

LeBeau retrieved an envelope from the inside pocket of his jacket. "I've written down my address for you with directions to my summer home, just south of the city. I'd consider it a favor if you'd take the time to stop for a visit."

When hell freezes over, Devin thought. "Thank you," he replied, making a production of putting the envelope in his own pocket. "If we cannot take time to visit you, at least I am certain I will see you at the Académie next year."

LeBeau laid a hand on his arm. "I hope to see you before that."

Devin resisted the urge to shake off the offending hand, and smiled graciously. "Good night," he murmured.

LeBeau answered only with a bow. He turned and was gone. Bertrand St. Clair followed discreetly on his heels.

Conversation started again as quickly as it had stopped and Marcus glanced at Devin.

"That was well done," he said under his breath.

Devin shrugged. "My father would say it is bad form to call a man a liar in public but I was truly tempted."

The rough night made sleep nearly impossible as the ship tossed uneasily on stormy waters. Both Devin and Marcus were up and dressed before dawn. Up on the forecastle, they discovered a light coating of snow covering the deck. The rigging hung thick with ice. Every movement of the ropes or sails sent glass-like shards smashing onto the deck. Stray flurries still floated down from a leaden sky.

They sailed into a harbor made ghostly with frosted spars and shrouds of mist, docking just as the sun struggled feebly to lighten the skies. They had said their goodbyes to the other passengers last night Devin had received an invitation from Dr. Rousseau to visit his home when he reached Treves. And Gustave Christophe was anxious that he stop in Tarente to meet the boy who swept his shop.

Only Henri LeBeau and Bertrand St. Clair also planned to disembark at Pireé but they had yet to appear on deck when Devin, Gaspard, and Marcus left the ship. Devin's first steps off the gangplank were awkward and halting. His legs had grown used to the roll of the ship, and solid ground felt surprisingly odd in comparison.

The port of Pireé seemed strange and exotic. The first thing Devin noticed were the large signboards hanging in front of every shop. Instead of words, each bore a painted or carved likeness of the merchandise that was sold inside. The bright and unsophisticated images made him feel as though he had landed in some foreign port where he didn't speak the language.

Buildings rose three or four stories along narrow streets, the simple architecture adorned by colorful shutters which bracketed windows and doors. Central gardens showed the first leaves of peas and the bright green spikes of garlic poking through dirt still dusted with last night's snowfall.

"Where are the hotels?" Gaspard asked, looking rumpled and sleepy.

"I would imagine they are toward the central part of the city," Marcus said, pointing at the businesses around them. "These are only small neighborhood shops: the scissors indicate a seamstress, the cake – a bakery – the horseshoe – a blacksmith."

"And where would I find a cup of coffee and a croissant?" Gaspard asked hopefully.

Marcus turned him to face a blue shuttered shop with a steaming cup on its sign. "There I would think."

"Thank God," he murmured. "Do you mind if we stop?"

Devin laughed. "You could have had breakfast on the ship, if you'd gotten up earlier."

"You and Marcus are lucky that the storm didn't make you seasick," Gaspard protested. "If you'd felt the way I did last night, you wouldn't have been anxious to get up early for breakfast either."

"You weren't alone," Devin assured him. "Half the ship was sick."

"Let's not talk about it anymore," Gaspard pleaded, one hand held sympathetically to his stomach.

A bell jangled when they opened the door. Four small tables filled the front of the shop. The smell of fresh brewed coffee and cinnamon wafted from behind the counter. Gaspard sighed and crumpled into a chair by the window.

"I'll have *café au lait* and two of whatever smells so heavenly."

Devin threw his knapsack on a chair. He rolled his eyes and made an exaggerated bow. "Yes, *monsieur*. Right away, *monsieur*."

Two of the other tables were occupied and several men had turned to stare at their entrance. Their eyes took in every detail of their luggage and their clothes.

Devin smiled and said, "Good morning." But only one man echoed his greeting, the rest merely nodded or sat silently watching as he walked to the counter.

He paid for four cinnamon buns and three cups of coffee, ferrying the food back in two trips and setting it on the table. Just before he sat down, he glanced up to see Henri LeBeau talking to Bertrand St. Clair out on the street.

"I see LeBeau has departed the ship," Marcus commented. "And that he and St. Clair have struck up a friendship."

"It doesn't look friendly to me," Devin observed, as LeBeau gestured rudely at St. Clair. LeBeau's face was flushed and angry. St. Clair made some final retort and stalked away.

61

"Apparently, that man can't get along with anyone," Gaspard said through a mouthful of cinnamon bun. "These are wonderful, by the way."

"LeBeau actually apologized to me last night," Devin said, "and invited me to visit him in Treves."

Gaspard made a disgusted sound in his throat. "I hope you told him what he could do with his invitation?"

"Devin was actually very polite," Marcus informed him.

"Then you're a better man than I am," Gaspard said.

Devin looked up and grinned. "That has never been in question has it?"

Gaspard threw a piece of bun which hit Devin squarely in the chest – and bounced off – landing in his coffee cup. Coffee sprayed all over the table and the front of Devin's jacket.

Gaspard leaned back with a satisfied smile. "How clumsy of me! Please accept my apologies."

"Remind me never to buy you a cinnamon bun again," Devin said. He fished in his pocket for a handkerchief and pulled out LeBeau's envelope, as well. He laid it on the table while he mopped at the brown liquid soaking into his jacket.

Marcus tapped the envelope. "Is that LeBeau's address?" he asked.

Devin crumpled his wet handkerchief on the table. "I assume so."

He tore open the envelope and extracted the piece of paper inside. It took only a moment to read it and react. With it still in his hand, he stood up and rushed to the door, hoping that somehow LeBeau might still be in sight. Standing on the doorstep, he could see the street had filled with people going to and from the docks. But there was no sign of either LeBeau or St. Clair in either direction.

Marcus had followed him. "What's the matter?" he asked in alarm, grabbing his shoulder as he came back through the doorway.

"Read it yourself," Devin snapped, throwing the paper down in front of him on the table.

Marcus unfolded the letter and read out loud: "*I know who broke into your cabin. Be careful. Your life is in danger. Please come to see me in Treves.*"

"Shit," Gaspard said, straightening up. "Is there more?'

"Just directions to his house," Devin replied, slumping down into his chair.

"Why couldn't he have told you this last night?" Gaspard asked.

Devin shook his head. "I don't know. He did ask to speak to me alone."

Marcus was watching him closely. "Was there some reason you didn't open this until now?"

Devin sighed. "I intended to throw it away without reading it at all. But I forgot it was in my jacket pocket until I pulled it out just now. I wish I'd found it ten minutes ago."

Had LeBeau been lingering outside to speak to him just now? And what had St. Clair said to him that had made him so angry?

Marcus folded the letter carefully and returned it to the envelope, then shoved it across the table to Devin.

"You won't be in Treves for another two months. That gives you a long time to decide what you want to do. You can either ignore it or take LeBeau up on his invitation. Besides, there's some possibility that you may run in to him along the way and you can ask him what he meant. I wouldn't worry about it now."

While the others finished their breakfast, Devin sat hunched over his coffee cup, toying with his food. He methodically dismantled his cinnamon bun but didn't eat any of it.

Gaspard gestured with his coffee cup. "I would have eaten that if I'd known you were going to destroy it."

"Be my guest," Devon replied, pushing his plate in front of his friend.

Outside the sky had darkened and snow was falling heavily.

CHAPTER 8

The Stones of Ombria

Devin's itinerary called for them to leave the harbor and walk the twenty miles to Briseé to spend the night but Marcus immediately vetoed that because of the weather.

"This isn't Viénne," he told Devin, as they left the cafe. "These spring snowstorms can be deadly. I'm not running the chance of being caught far from shelter and having to spend the night out in the open. We'll stay tonight in Pireé. If the weather has improved by morning, we can go on."

"But if we stay here tonight," Devin protested, "we'll be behind schedule already and we're only three days into our trip!"

"Then I would say the man who planned our itinerary was a fool not to take bad weather into account." Marcus responded harshly. "Use your head, Devin!"

Devin had, in fact, taken bad weather into account. He just hadn't anticipated it being a problem so early in their journey. It was later, as they made their way through the most Northern Provinces, that he had built extra time into their schedule. Apparently, Ombria was having a late spring; he'd had no way of knowing until they'd arrived here this morning. He threw his knapsack over his shoulder and followed Marcus, tight-lipped and furious. Snow blew into his face and melted down the neck of his jacket. A few steps ahead of him, Gaspard's dark hair was already powdered with white, and snowflakes plastered Marcus's hat and shoulders.

"This is nasty," Gaspard said, stopping to let Devin catch up. "You don't want to walk all day in a snowstorm. We'll rent a room at one of the hotels and get a hot bath and a good meal. Besides, it's a shame not to see the capital of Ombria while we're here."

Devin stalked straight ahead without commenting while Gaspard kept pace beside him.

"We could walk around the city this afternoon and then go to the theater tonight. The plays are all unscripted, did you know? Most of the dialogue is improvisation. The director gives the actors a specific plot and they act it out. They claim it's never the same twice."

Receiving no response, Gaspard stopped in front of Devin, placing a hand on each of his shoulders. "You can't control the weather, Dev. You've waited two years for this trip. Lighten up and enjoy it!"

Devin shook off his hold. "It's just that one thing after another has gone wrong. I feel as though the entire project is unraveling and there isn't a blessed thing I can do to stop it!"

"But surely losing one day won't make that much difference," Gaspard insisted.

"It's not the delay," Devin answered. "I'm beginning to have second thoughts about the whole thing."

Marcus turned to face them, sheltering his eyes from the snow with one hand. "Are you two coming or not? I don't intend to stand out here and freeze, while you whine about a change in plans!"

Gaspard grimaced. "God! What's gotten into him?"

"I don't know," Devin answered. "Come on. We can talk later."

They found a large hotel that fronted onto the square. The staff was solicitous and efficient, and except for the strange pictorial signs, they could have been in Coreé. After they took their bags to their room, Devin considered canvassing the other hotels in the area to see if he could find Henri LeBeau. But the heavy snowfall kept them inside the rest of the day. When they went down to dinner, Devin glanced around the large dining room, but he saw no familiar faces.

The theater faced the hotel on the other side of the square. They walked quickly on slush-filled sidewalks, their collars turned up against the huge snowflakes which had begun to mix with rain. Ice coated the street lamps and glittered on the cobblestones and the ironwork that ornamented the front of the theater.

The play was well done and expertly costumed. Devin was fascinated by how the same oral tradition that had produced the Chronicles had also spawned this alternative form of drama. The director proved to be a local storyteller who had turned to theater production. And best of all, the evening's play was based on one of the lesser known tales from Ombria's Chronicle.

"There," Marcus pointed out later as they sipped brandy in the hotel dining room before going up to bed. "You see, the day wasn't a total waste, after all. And I can guarantee that you will sleep better here under an eiderdown quilt than in some snowy hollow along the road to Briseé."

67

Devin allowed his brandy to slip slowly down his throat, enjoying the fiery sensation that drove away the chill of clammy boots and damp clothes.

"I actually wouldn't mind seeing another production some-time," he admitted. "I didn't realize that the theater would be so closely tied to the Chronicle here."

"I heard the man behind us say that some directors are actually bards," Gaspard said. "Apparently, it's important that the plot always remain accurate even though the actors have the flexibility to modify the individual scenes."

The stringed quartet that had played for the evening in the hotel dining room began to pack up their instruments. Across the room, a waiter extinguished candles on the empty tables. Only one other table remained occupied, where a young couple sat talking quietly. Devin stood up.

"We'd better go and let them close for the night."

Marcus pushed in his chair. "Remember, you need to leave the letters to be sent to your father at the Hall of Records in the morning. Is there anyone else you need to write to? I assume your fiancée knows about your trip?"

"I told Bridgette at Christmas," Devin explained.

Gaspard snorted. "Whoa, that's cold, Devin. Haven't you seen her since then?"

Devin avoided their eyes. "No, there hasn't been time. I've been too busy with my studies."

From the time he was seven, Devin had been engaged to Bridgette Delacey, the daughter of a prominent Councilman. They had exchanged tokens, carefully chosen by their mothers, at birthdays and Christmas. For the past few years, they had been paired for dancing at summer soirées and winter galas. There had never been anything remotely romantic between them, at least, not on Devin's part.

Devin turned to leave, hoping to avoid further discussion. Marcus sighed behind him.

"Well, I also need to register our route with the local authorities in the morning."

Devin wheeled to look at him, afraid of another setback. "I want to get an early start tomorrow," he reminded him.

Marcus pointed a finger. "Our departure still depends on the weather, Devin. An ice storm is far worse to deal with than a snowstorm."

"We can't afford any more delays . . . " Devin began.

Gaspard finished off the last of Devin's brandy and laid a hand on his shoulder, the glass still dangling from his finger.

"Don't worry," he predicted, his words slightly slurred, "tomorrow will be beautiful."

Devin wakened to the sound of water dripping off the eaves outside his window. The sky was cloudless and the slushy accumulation of snow had melted overnight. He was surprised to find Marcus already dressed.

"The snow is all but gone and the cold weather seems to have cleared off to the east," Marcus said. "I'll go now and deliver your letters and register our itinerary at the same time. You and Gaspard can have breakfast. Be ready to leave when I get back."

"You're leaving me alone?" Devin asked in surprise.

"I'm leaving you with Gaspard," Marcus clarified. "See that you don't get into trouble while I'm gone." He held out his hand. "Where are your letters?"

Devin rummaged through his knapsack and pulled out two envelopes. One was still unsealed. He'd been reluctant to include everything that had occurred since he left but there was every possibility that Marcus was filing his own report.

Late last night, he'd included the details of LeBeau's note. This morning, he regretted adding it to his father's worries.

He glanced up at Marcus. "Have you written to him as well?"

Marcus raised his eyebrows. "Do I need to?"

Devin shook his head and sealed the envelope. "No, I just hate to worry him."

Marcus slipped on his jacket. "You'll worry him more if you don't report all the information available to you. I'll be back as soon as I can."

Devin and Gaspard had a leisurely breakfast and packed their few belongings, but it was nearly noon before Marcus returned.

"The wheels of our government grind very slowly here," he said, in answer to their questions. "We'll be lucky to reach Briseé by nightfall. Let's get going."

The air had warmed considerably by midday and the sun was welcome on their backs as they left the city. Soon, cobbled streets gave way to unpaved country roads. Wooded areas still sheltered remnants of snow, and deep hollows and valleys harbored pockets of air so cold they could see their breath. Before long, the dirt roads deteriorated into little more than beaten paths threading their way between cow pastures.

They stopped to rest on a high knoll, surveying miles of dry stone walls snaking off into the distance. Clouds raced across the sky casting constantly changing shadows that chased each other across the fields. Grass along the stream beds was already vibrantly green as spring stubbornly advanced, despite yesterday's weather. Coffee-colored cows dotted the landscape.

"Cheese," Gaspard remarked suddenly.

Devin turned to look at him. "Cheese?"

"That's what Ombria is famous for," Gaspard explained. "I was trying to remember last night after I went to bed.

Every province has its own food specialty; I just couldn't remember Ombria's."

"You could have asked," Devin said.

"I'd rather have figured it out for myself," Gaspard replied. "When I admit my stupidity, it only makes you look smug."

"That's not true!" Devin protested.

Gaspard grinned. "I'm not holding it against you. I'm just trying not to give you any more opportunities to prove your superior intellect."

Devin ignored him, sliding from his perch on the top of the stone wall to the pasture on the other side. He walked a few feet forward and bent to unearth a rectangular stone pillar covered by grass and ivy.

"Do you think this could be a monolith, Gaspard?"

Gaspard dropped down beside him. Together they pulled away the vegetation, revealing a cut stone, about eighteen inches square and nearly nine feet in length. Inscribed halfway up on the two visible sides was a solid circle surrounded by four consecutively larger rings.

"What does it mean?" Gaspard asked.

Devin shrugged "I don't think anyone knows for certain. I've read about these. There are supposed to be hundreds of them from Ombria clear to the western coast of Perouse. In the southern part of Arcadia, dozens are still standing, two by two, in perfect alignment, from east to west."

Gaspard traced the circular symbol with his finger. "Surely, there must be some legend or folktale that explains their origins?"

"I hope the Chronicles will shed some light on them," Devin replied. "Viénne's archeologists have traditionally ignored any contribution they might add to their historic data."

Marcus scowled down on them from the wall. "If you two are done excavating, we need to move on. By my calculations, we're only halfway to Briseé."

Devin stood up and dusted his hands off on his trousers. "Give me a minute. I just want to take a rubbing of this design." He scrambled back over the wall and retrieved paper and a piece of charcoal from his knapsack.

Marcus glowered. "Just be quick about it. Do I need to remind you that the symbol of Ombria is a wolf? Unless you relish being eaten tonight, we need to be on our way!"

It was dusk by the time they sighted the first lights of Briseé. The town was built around a community garden with common grazing land around it. Cottages, constructed of the same limestone as the familiar stone walls, stood snug and cozy in the fading light. Some windows were already shuttered against the night but the tavern windows were still bright. Devin didn't miss the furtive look Marcus threw back along the road as he shepherded them inside.

It was there in the public room that Devin saw the first storyteller's cloak. It had been thrown carelessly across the back of a bench and its owner had gathered his audience close by the hearth. He stood with his arms flung wide, his face reddened by the light from the flames. But it was the light in his eyes and the pitch of his voice that attracted Devin. He was inexorably drawn to him, though the story was already in progress. Discarding his knapsack and his jacket on the nearest chair, he fell in with the group gathered in spellbound silence at the storyteller's feet.

CHAPTER 9

Night in Briseé

Devin listened as the mesmerizing voice continued:

"*And so, Gaêtan stood alone in the village square. All around him the windows of the cottages were dark and shuttered. The chimneys stood stark against the forest, not a puff of smoke emerged from their tops. He realized then that the people of Rameau were gone. Not one man, woman, or child remained to welcome him home. He fell to his knees in the overgrown gardens and wept.*"

For a moment no one spoke and then appreciative whispers rippled through the crowd. Devin joined in the enthusiastic clapping that followed. Unfortunately, he had arrived at the end of the recitation. The storyteller smiled and bowed, accepting both congratulations and monetary tributes, and made his way to the bar. Devin ducked in and out of the crowd to reach him. He saw Gaspard and Marcus seated farther down the battered wooden counter finishing their first drink of the evening.

Devin secured a stool next to the storyteller.

"I'm sorry I missed the beginning of that tale. What happened to the people of Rameau?"

The man turned to face him. Dark curly hair framed a face that was young and unlined.

"No one knows," he answered. "An entire village of people disappeared and the only one left to tell the story was Gaêtan."

Devin felt a thrill of excitement shoot through him. "Really?" he asked. "And no one has ever solved the mystery?"

The storyteller inclined his head. "If they have, *monsieur*, it has never been added to the Chronicle of Ombria. Do I know you?"

"I'm sorry," Devin apologized, extending his hand. "I'm Devin Roché."

"Adrian Devereux," he replied. "You're not from around here, are you?"

"We arrived in Pireé yesterday," he explained. "I had expected to spend last night in Briseé but we were delayed by a snowstorm."

Adrian nodded sympathetically. "Spring has been late in coming this year. Our cows were calving in deep snow. We lost a lot of little ones."

"You live close by?" Devin asked.

Adrian smiled. "Does a bard ever really have a place to call home? My parents are from Briseé but I spend most of my time traveling. I'm back in town for a family wedding. It seems I'm always expected to put in a few local performances while I'm here."

Marcus interrupted their conversation, placing a heavy hand on Devin's shoulder.

"There are no rooms available here," he growled. "Perhaps, if you invoke your father's name . . . "

Devin gave a quick shake of his head. The last thing he wished to do was drag his father's position into this situation. Any progress he'd made toward ingratiating himself with the village residents would be lost in a veil of suspicion and contempt.

"I'll take care of it," he murmured, dismissing Marcus with a handful of coins. "Go order something to eat for yourself and Gaspard."

"My sister's being married the day after tomorrow," Adrian explained. "I'm afraid this is the only inn, and it's full of my relatives."

"It's no problem," Devin said. "Perhaps, after we've eaten, we'll just head on to Brisance."

Adrian touched his arm. "I would advise against it. The roads between here and Brisance aren't safe at night."

Devin indicated his knapsack. "I fear we've little to lose."

Adrian raised his eyebrows. "You do not value your life, *monsieur?*"

Devin flushed. "Of course, I just meant that we have little of value to thieves."

Adrian returned to his drink. "I didn't say the roads were unsafe because of thieves, it is the wolves I was referring to."

Devin ordered a glass of wine and a bowl of stew, hoping his companion would continue . . .

"How long have you been a bard?" Devin asked, after a long silence.

"Five years," Adrian replied. "I spent a year studying under Armand Vielle."

"A year?" Devin said in surprise.

"Armand is a perfectionist. His apprentices cannot leave until he's satisfied that they have learned Ombria's stories and legends by heart," Adrian replied.

A year . . . Devin felt his plan dissolving before his eyes. What hope did he have of learning anything in just a month? This Armand Vielle would laugh in his face.

A girl, a piece of striped toweling wrapped around her waist as an apron, brought Devin stew and bread.

"Thank you," Devin said, spooning up the thick broth dotted with mushrooms. "I'd like to hear Monsieur Vielle for myself."

"Well, storytelling is his first love," Adrian replied. "He only takes on one new apprentice at a time so that he is free to tell the Chronicle publicly himself. He's getting on in years. When he can no longer walk the roads of Ombria perhaps he will settle down and spend the rest of his days teaching."

One apprentice at a time, Devin thought, and what if Armand Vielle has already taken someone on this spring? Where would that leave him? Could he skip Ombria and move on to the next province hoping for better luck there?

Adrian was looking at him strangely. "Is something the matter?"

Devin shook his head, restraining the thoughts that had visibly troubled his face. "I'm wondering what we will do for lodging," he said. "If the roads are truly unsafe, we need to find a place to stay the night."

Adrian hesitated, just a moment, before his face broke into a smile. "You know my parents own a little farm. It's not much but there's a barn attached to the house. You'd be welcome to sleep there."

"Thank you," Devin said. "It isn't as though we've any other options at the moment. You're certain your father won't mind?"

Adrian laughed. "He threatened to sleep in the barn himself tonight. My mother and my aunts are driving him mad with the wedding preparations. 'Two more days,' I told him. 'Two more days and you'll have your peace again.' He shook his head and said, 'I'll never last. I'll be in an asylum by morning'."

Devin smiled. "If he's at his wits' end, I don't want to trouble him further."

Adrian shook his head. "His bark is worse than his bite. He'll be happy to help travelers in distress."

Devin knew he had only to mention his father's name or produce the government chit, which he'd been given, to obtain a bed in the best house in the village. But he had no intention of using the influence available to him. He'd done his best to leave his identity behind him in Coreé.

Adrian finished his drink while Devin sopped up the last bit of broth in his bowl with a crust of bread. The stew had been hearty and satisfying at the end of such a long day. He had only just realized how tired he was.

"They'll be expecting me at home. Do you think your friends are ready to leave yet?" Adrian asked.

"I'll go and see," Devin said.

He wove his way down to where Gaspard and Marcus sat and explained the arrangements he'd made.

"A barn?" Gaspard protested. "God, Devin, couldn't you do any better than that?"

"Not tonight," Devin assured him. "There is a big wedding the day after tomorrow. The inn is full and the townspeople are helping to put up the guests. It's the best I could do."

Gaspard stood up, grumbling, but Marcus flicked a coin down angrily on the counter.

"Your itinerary states that we will be staying here at the inn tonight. Should your father need to contact you, it's important that you adhere to the route that you gave him."

"We're not in Coreé, Marcus," Devin said. "I'm sure my father realizes that itineraries are subject to change. There may even be times we have to sleep beside the road.

Be glad we'll have shelter tonight, even if it isn't what I'd planned."

Adrian's parents' farm was located on the outskirts of town, at the edge of the forest. Loud conversation and laughter became audible through the pines even before they could see the lights streaming from the windows. They were welcomed into the midst of a noisy family gathering. The plain wooden table was laden with remnants of a huge meal, and Gaspard, Devin, and Marcus were invited to join them. Small children peered from below the table, their sticky fingers tangled in the fur of a mongrel dog.

"We've just eaten at the inn," Devin explained. "But thank you very much."

"The inn?" Adrian's mother asked in mock horror. "I hope you won't all be ill later. The cook mucks out his stable before he goes to work in the inn's kitchen. I doubt he even washes his hands."

Devin laughed. "We had stew. It was really quite good."

One of Adrian's aunts leaned forward, exposing her ample breasts above a low cut blouse. She winked coyly at Devin. "Where did you find this lovely young man, Adrian? Your friends are not usually so polite."

"Sit," Adrian's mother coaxed, pulling at Devin's sleeve and patting the bench beside her. "Have some wine with us, at least."

Adrian drew them back toward the door.

"They're tired, Mother. They've been walking all day. Let them go and lie down."

"All right," she conceded. "But have breakfast with us before you leave in the morning. Three more mouths to feed is nothing at all."

Devin thanked them and followed Adrian out into the night. The plump aunt giggled and called after them.

"Adrian, did you tell him that you still have two unmarried sisters and a widowed aunt?"

Adrian shook his head and closed the door, laughing.

A full moon had risen, copper and huge, above the eastern horizon. Moonlight silvered the bare tree branches and the peak of the barn roof. Every stone along the top of the wall glowed with reflected light. An owl hooted from the pines around the barn.

Adrian took them up to the loft. He disturbed an old cat, lounging on a pile of grain sacks. He shook the sacks free of dust and spread them over the fragrant hay.

"It's not what you're used to, I'm sure," he apologized. "But you'll sleep safely here till morning. Will you be warm enough? I fear blankets and quilts are in short supply tonight."

"We have blankets," Devin said, unpacking his knapsack. "Thank you again. Your family is very hospitable."

Adrian smiled, pleased at the compliment. "If we weren't housing most of our extended family, you'd have been given a place of honor by the fire for as long as you liked. I think Aunt Genevieve would see that you had the spot right next to her. But then, she'd be demanding you marry her by morning! Believe me you're better off out here!"

Devin laughed. "I'm sure you're right. I'm much too tired for amorous trysts tonight."

Adrian grinned. "Goodnight then. Be certain to go down for breakfast. Mama will expect it."

Adrian made his way down the ladder, and a few minutes afterwards the house door slammed. The barn was quiet and peaceful. The moonlight streaming in through the loft's open window lent a magical quality to the place.

"I think this is very pleasant," Devin said, plopping down on the nearest feed sack.

"You would," Gaspard remarked, sitting down gingerly beside him. "Remind me again, why it is that I ever agreed to accompany you to this god-forsaken place?"

Devin grinned. "To escape your evil father."

Gaspard lay back on the hay with a satisfied grunt. "Ah, that's it! I knew there had to be a good reason."

Marcus said nothing. He retrieved his blanket from his knapsack and lay down facing the wall. His stiff shoulders discouraged engaging him in any further conversation.

It is amazing how quickly and deeply sleep comes to those who are physically exhausted. Devin had spent many nights studying for hours and then not been able to sleep. He assumed it was because his mind was still busy cataloging all the information he'd given it to retain. Tonight, with his feet and back aching from a full day of walking, he fell asleep with Gaspard still chattering next to him.

Devin woke much later. The barn was silent. And yet some small sound outside had roused him. He went to the window. The house was dark and still. He turned to go back and lie down, when a slight movement caught his attention. A man was standing under the trees behind the house, partially obscured by evergreen branches. He stood in shadow and Devin would never have even noticed him if he hadn't turned to scan the area around him. Devin leaned against the window frame to watch.

A moment later, two other men approached, leading horses. The lone man handed over an envelope or paper, which flashed brilliant and white in the moonlight. They stood talking a few minutes before the two with the horses faded into the surrounding woods as silently as they had come.

The remaining man glanced quickly around him and walked directly toward the barn.

Alarmed, Devin whirled around, intent on waking Marcus. But Marcus's blanket lay discarded on the hay. His bodyguard was gone.

CHAPTER 10

Divided Loyalties

Devin snatched a knife from Marcus's stash and resumed his former position, lying on the hay next to Gaspard. Determined to defend his friend to the death if necessary, he listened, as footsteps crossed the barn floor below them and then stealthily mounted the ladder.

He had never been trained to fight. His older brothers were done tussling for supremacy by the time he had been born. Jean was already an attorney with a son of his own, André was in his first year at Coreé University, and both Jacques and Ethan had enlisted in Llisé's army. The only brother left at home was Mathieu and he tended to be almost as bookish as Devin. With fifteen years separating them, a brawl would never have occurred to either of them. And yet, here he was with a knife in his hand waiting for an unknown assailant to attack.

The intruder reached the top of the ladder and Devin sat up, brandishing his weapon.

"My God, Devin," Marcus gasped. "You scared the hell out of me!"

"Well, you scared the hell out of me!" Devin replied, scrambling to his feet. "I woke up and you were gone and then I heard someone coming up the ladder!"

"I had to piss," Marcus replied. "I didn't mean to startle you."

Devin stood facing him, the knife still in his hand. He had two options and neither of them appealed to him. He could call his bodyguard a fraud or accept his explanation and forget what he had just witnessed out the window. Candor won out.

"You're lying," Devin said, breathing hard. "I saw you meeting someone at the edge of the forest. Who was it?"

Gaspard groaned and sat up, turning to stare at them. "What in God's name is going on? It's not morning already is it?"

No one answered him.

"Who did you meet?" Devin demanded, his eyes locked with Marcus's.

His bodyguard's face was white. "I met no one, Devin. God, can't a man take care of personal business without you making a scene?"

Devin gestured at the window. "I watched you. I know what I saw."

"Give me that knife before you hurt someone," Marcus snapped, taking a step forward. He grabbed Devin's wrist, extracting the weapon with a sharp twist of his hand.

Devin winced and stepped back, one hand massaging his wrist. Gaspard stood up, placing himself between them.

"What's going on?" he repeated.

Devin was furious. "I wakened and went to the window. I saw Marcus meeting with two men in the trees before he came back up here."

83

Gaspard sighed and swiveled to look at Marcus. "Is this true?"

"I took a piss," Marcus snarled. "I didn't realize I needed permission from Monsieur 'High and Mighty'. While I was outside, I saw no one. I spoke to no one."

Gaspard turned back again to Devin. "Are you certain you saw Marcus? How clearly could you make out faces from here?"

The explanation was so obvious that it shook Devin. He had never seen the mysterious man's face. There had been nothing in his stance or manner that had made him think of Marcus. It was only when his bodyguard appeared at the top of the ladder that the suspicion had formed in his mind.

"I'm not certain," he stammered, unsure now of what he had actually seen. "I saw a man coming here to the barn and then Marcus climbed up the ladder."

Marcus wheeled and left them, descending the ladder with the skill of a cat. Devin let out a shaky breath as Gaspard went to the window.

"Well, life with you is never boring, I'll say that," Gaspard remarked. "What woke you up anyway?"

Devin shook his head, as he joined him. "I don't know. I was suddenly wide awake. I'm not even sure why I went to the window."

They watched Marcus skirt the yard, moving silently from place to place. Moonlight gleamed on the knife blade in the darkness, and Devin shivered.

Gaspard put a hand on his shoulder. "Are certain you were awake when you saw all of this, Dev?"

Devin knew what Gaspard was thinking. It was an old problem, one that had started in childhood and become nearly unbearable his first year at the Académie. He'd wake from a sound sleep to see some ordinary thing in his bedroom transformed into something terrifying. The illusions faded in seconds but he'd often wakened his parents, and then Gaspard, screaming or confused. Sometimes the episodes had even been accompanied by sleepwalking.

As a student, he'd sought out André's advice and been referred to his friend Pierre Verstegan, a prominent psychologist. Verstegan had listened to his symptoms and diagnosed the malady as "waking dreams," an acute form of "night terrors." He had asked if Devin indulged in laudanum or opium, as a great many of his friends did, citing their penchant for causing hallucinations. When Devin had voiced his loathing for using drugs for entertainment, Verstegan had told him the condition could also be brought on by fatigue or anxiety. He'd prescribed a glass of wine and a mild sedative before bed and Devin had found immediate relief. While he no longer followed Verstegan's recommendation, he'd been free of the disturbing episodes for almost a year. Not even final exams had sparked a recurrence.

"You were exhausted tonight. Do you think it's possible that you imagined what you saw?" Gaspard suggested gently.

Devin had to accept the possibility that Gaspard was right. And yet, he remembered the roughness of the barn boards as he leaned against the window frame and the cool air on his face. But then, that was what had always made his dreams so terrifying. Everything seemed completely believable for the few moments the illusion lasted.

Marcus returned, disgruntled and annoyed.

"There is no one about. I checked the barn and the yard and even the edges of the forest. I don't know what you saw and heard but if there was someone out there earlier, he's gone now."

Gaspard presented his explanation tactfully. "We've discussed the possibility that it may have been a dream," he said. "Devin was very tired when he went to bed."

Understanding softened Marcus's scowl. "Ah," he said. "Your father did warn me about that. He said you've had vivid nightmares since you were a little boy."

Devin flushed. The condition was embarrassing enough but it made his uneasiness about Marcus's activity seem far less plausible. If Marcus was really hiding something, Gaspard had just unwittingly discredited Devin as a witness to it.

And yet, Verstegan had told Devin something else that might have bearing on the situation. He'd claimed that Devin's terrifying visions might play out fears that his waking mind refused to consider. If tonight's incident had, indeed, been a "waking dream" the rational explanation was that Devin no longer trusted Marcus.

CHAPTER 11

Suspicion

Devin couldn't sleep the rest of night. From the occasional snores coming from both Gaspard and Marcus, his companions had no similar problem. He kept going over the incident with Marcus in his mind. He would probably never be certain whether he had actually seen his bodyguard outside or not. The trouble with waking dreams was that, for an instant, a chair could be transformed into a monster or a friend into an assailant. Though the images were short-lived the uneasiness they inspired tended to linger. All that was left after last night's incident was suspicion and animosity on both Marcus's and Devin's part. It promised to make the next few days unpleasant, if nothing else.

Birdsong broke the silence long before the darkness faded into a gray dawn. Devin finally sat up and brushed off a few persistent wisps of hay. Gaspard lay sound asleep but Marcus opened a wary eye. He rolled over without comment when he realized that it was only Devin disturbing his sleep.

Devin went down the ladder and out into the yard determined to ascertain for himself if any evidence lingered to suggest a clandestine meeting last night. The overcast sky promised rain and the dirt in the yard was already damp and muddy. Tracks from cows and wagons marred the ground making it impossible to determine who might have loitered there a few hours before. He had just completed a circuit of the courtyard when the door to the house opened.

"You're up early," Adrian commented, as he thrust his arm into his jacket sleeve.

Devin shrugged. "I had trouble sleeping last night."

"Not enough wine before bed," Adrian diagnosed with a laugh. "My father claims a drunk never misses a good night's sleep, while a sober man lies awake and counts his transgressions."

"He's probably right," Devin agreed good-naturedly.

"I hope our celebrating didn't keep you awake," Adrian replied. "My mother and the aunts were still chattering long after I went to bed."

Devin shook his head. "I didn't hear them. Thank you again for taking us in last night. Would you allow me to make a donation toward the wedding preparations?"

"And incur my mother's wrath?" Adrian asked. "Hospitality is an obligation not a choice. Don't shame her by trying to compensate her for good manners."

Devin smiled. "But surely there is something I can do to thank her?"

"Would you stay for the wedding?" Adrian asked, picking up a bucket and carrying it to the well.

Devin followed. "Thank you, but I'm afraid our plans won't allow time for that. I hope to be in Lac Dupré by tomorrow night."

Adrian hooked the bucket onto the rope and began to lower it. "It's too bad that you will miss Armand."

"Armand Vielle?" Devin asked.

Adrian nodded. "He is coming here for the wedding."

"But I was going to Lac Dupré to hear him!" Devin protested.

Adrian beamed. "Then stay, please. Armand plans to share some of the Chronicle at the wedding reception."

Devin shook his head. "I can't impose like that."

"The entire village is coming and my mother asked me to invite you especially."

"Not Aunt Genevieve?" Devin asked.

"Oh, Aunt Genevieve plans to snag you at breakfast. Your place beside her has already been staked out. Be careful she doesn't drug your coffee and carry you off to her bed."

Devin laughed. "I'll trust you to defend my virtue!"

"What virtue?" Gaspard asked, coming to join them. "You lost whatever virtue you possessed at the Université along with the rest of us." He put an arm around Devin's shoulders and spoke close to his ear. "You should be aware that Marcus is watching you from the loft window. He saw you looking for tracks."

"Let him watch," Devin replied. "I've yet to convince myself that I didn't see horsemen in the yard last night."

The pail of water splashed onto the ground.

"You saw horsemen here?" Adrian asked in alarm.

Gaspard waggled a hand. "Maybe 'yes', maybe 'no.' Devin's not the most reliable witness when he's half asleep."

Adrian left the bucket lying on the ground. He leaned back against the stones of the well, frowning. "Perhaps, you'd better tell me what happened."

Devin told him what he'd seen, omitting his suspicions about Marcus. "My friend," he added, hoping his bodyguard was in earshot, "went down to the yard to investigate but he saw no one."

Adrian grunted. "This is worrisome," he commented, bending to retrieve the bucket. "In Ombria, in case you haven't noticed, only rich men own riding horses. A man on horseback generally means trouble for a small farmer like my father. It could be the *shérif*, a soldier, or the tax collector and none of them are men I want outside my house in the middle of the night." He turned to look at Devin. "You'll do me a favor?"

"Of course," Devin said.

"Let me know right away if you see them again?"

"It's the least I can do," Devin replied.

"Be aware, Adrian," Gaspard said with a playful look at Devin. "That this is an undocumented sighting. Don't concern yourself unless there are further incidents."

"Still," Adrian said, hefting the bucket down from the wall, "Devin saw something in the yard. I think it bears investigation."

Devin smiled. It was nice to be believed without question.

CHAPTER 12

Armand Vielle

Ombria's Master Bard arrived just before supper. The promised rain had fallen by the bucketful all day and Devin had spent most of the afternoon in the tavern playing endless games of cards with Gaspard. By late afternoon, the rain departed, driven before a cold wind. Clouds gave way to brilliant blue sky and sunshine. Mist spiraled up from every stream and valley, shaping spectral figures that drifted and glided through the pine woods as they walked back to Adrian's. And out of the mist, his storyteller's cloak swirling around him, strode Armand Vielle.

Devin stopped dead on the path.

Gaspard ran smack into him. "God, Devin have a care, will you!" he protested.

Marcus drew his knife and looked cautiously around them, in anticipation of some imminent threat.

Devin ignored them both and walked forward, his hand extended. "Armand Vielle?" he asked.

The bard bowed his tall frame dramatically. His gray hair curled around his ears. His beard was close cropped and still streaked with brown.

"The very same," he said with a smile. "And you are?"

"Devin Roché," he said. "We're staying at the Devereaux's." He turned to introduce his companions. "This is Gaspard Forneaux and Marcus Beringer."

"I'm pleased to make your acquaintance," the bard said, shaking hands all around. "And I believe I am nearly late for supper. Is that where you are headed, too?"

"Yes," Gaspard replied. "And Adrian's family has a houseful. If we're late we may go hungry!"

They continued on toward the farm, talking as they walked.

"You are friends of Adrian's, then?" Armand asked.

Devin was not about to misrepresent himself. "Only very recent ones. We were traveling through Briseé last night. The inn was full of wedding guests and Adrian's mother very graciously allowed us to spend the night in their barn."

Armand laughed. "Do you make a habit of sleeping in barns?"

Devin smiled. "No, but it was surprisingly comfortable and we appreciate the Devereaux's hospitality. I'd planned to leave for Lac Dupré this morning to meet you and hear the Chronicle until Adrian mentioned that you were coming to the wedding."

Armand bowed again, his blue eyes crinkling at the corners. "I'm flattered that you would travel so far to hear it from my lips. But Adrian is well versed in Ombria's Chronicle also, why didn't you ask him to enlighten you?"

They had arrived at the crux of the problem and Devin hesitated, trying to ease into his request. "Because I needed to speak with you . . . "

He was saved from any further explanations. They had arrived at the farm and Adrian, who was carrying a load of firewood, saw them coming. He gave a whoop of delight and flung the wood down in the yard. Then he ran, hurling himself into Armand's arms like a small child.

"Armand!" he exclaimed. "How I have missed you!"

Armand pushed him back gently. "How's my favorite student?"

Adrian smiled. "I'm well. How are you?" He frowned, tapping the walking stick that Armand carried. "Is your knee troubling you again?"

"Only when it rains," Armand replied. "It's one of the disadvantages of growing old."

Adrian glanced at Devin. "So you've met my friends?"

"I have," Armand said. "It seems Devin is interested in the Chronicle."

Adrian smiled. "Then we'll have to see that he gets his fill of it." He put an arm around Armand's shoulders. "Come and eat; my mother has been cooking for hours."

At supper, Devin found himself, once again, seated next to Aunt Genevieve, although now Armand seemed to have drawn her attention, as well. The wooden table held far more people and food than it was designed for, and several smaller tables had been set up near the fire. The room was hot and stuffy. People were packed together so closely that it was impossible to move without bumping into someone else. Devin thought his mother would have been horrified at the noisy, chaotic meal where a dozen different conversations were going on at once.

After Devin had eaten, he slipped quietly outside. Marcus followed at a distance. Neither of them had spoken to the other since last night's fiasco, which didn't bode well for the future. They went to opposite corners of the yard.

Devin sat on the stone wall that formed a small courtyard in front of the house and barn. The laughter and conversation from the house was still audible but here he was shielded from the press of bodies and Aunt Genevieve's soft inquisitive hands. He realized that by retreating he might miss the first chance to hear Armand tell a story but there was always tomorrow.

He was surprised, a few moments later, when Armand joined him, his cloak thrown over his shoulders and a mug of wine in his hand. The bard chuckled.

"Is Adrian's family a bit too much for you?" he asked.

"They've been very kind," Devin answered diplomatically. "I just needed a few moments' peace."

Armand sat down beside him. "I was wondering earlier what brought you here. Your lack of an accent suggests that you were raised in Viénne. You're not Vincent Roché's son, are you? There's a remarkable resemblance, you know."

Devin grimaced, irritated that even here in this tiny rural village his identity continued to plague him.

Armand mistook Devin's distress in being identified as his denial. "No, of course not," he amended. "You are far too young to be his son. Are you our Chancellor's grandson, perhaps?"

"No," Devin answered, "You were right the first time: I am Vincent's youngest son. There are six of us. I'm afraid my birth was a shock to both my mother and father, coming so late in life. There are fifteen years between me and my next oldest brother."

Armand laughed. "I met your father once, some years ago, long before he became Chancellor. You weren't even born then, I'm sure. I liked him very much. I thought at the time that he was destined for greatness. It was no surprise when he rose to Chancellor Elite. I'm sure he deserves both the responsibility and the title."

"He's a great man," Devin replied thoughtfully; "a very powerful man, but it's been my experience that he also tries hard to be fair."

Armand smiled. "It's reassuring to hear that from his son." He gave Devin a calculating look. "So, what is the son of the most powerful man in the empire doing searching Ombria for its Master Bard?"

Devin took a deep breath. "I wish to memorize the Chronicles."

"Ombria's Chronicle." Armand corrected him gently, to use the singular.

In the silence that followed, Devin heard nothing but his own heartbeat. Something told him that with this man he could be honest about his ambition.

"No," he said breathlessly. "I want to memorize them all."

Armand's face betrayed nothing, but he studied Devin a long time before he spoke.

"You are obviously an educated man, Monsieur Roché. What is it that you have been trained for?"

Devin shifted uneasily under his stare. "My Université degree certifies me as a historiographer. I am currently training to oversee the Archives at the Académie."

Armand gave a low whistle and shook his head. "I'll admit I am mystified by your interest in me and my Chronicle. Are you certain we aren't breaking canon law simply by speaking to each other?"

"There's no need to worry," Devin assured him. "You would be free of any guilt in the matter. And as long as I don't record your stories I haven't committed a felony, either."

Armand raised his eyebrows and let out his breath in a hiss. "Somehow, I am not reassured."

For a moment they sat in silence, watching the moon rise above the pointed tops of the pines. Finally, Armand spoke.

"What you are suggesting is impossible, my friend. No bard has ever memorized more than four Chronicles, and that has been accomplished only once." He unclasped the neck of his cloak and pulled it over his shoulder to display the emblems of Ombria, Arcadia, Batavie, and Tirolien. "And even after memorizing all four, I am only qualified to teach the Ombrian Chronicles."

"Why is that?" Devin asked.

"Only a native of a province may become its Master Bard, and to protect the authority of the Chronicles only the Master Bard can teach. For example, Adrian may tell you the stories but he cannot teach them to you."

"I am aware of that," Devin said. "That's why it was important to me to track you down."

Armand's hand massaged his bad knee. "Once in a lifetime each Master Bard trains a worthy apprentice to carry on his work. I've often thought that, if he is willing, I will ask Adrian. It's important that I name a successor before my health begins to deteriorate. The Master Bard in Perouse waited too long and now some of those stories are lost to us forever."

"Will you teach me Ombria's Chronicle?" Devin asked.

Armand eyed him a moment. "And how long do you have to devote to this endeavor? Adrian was my best student. I taught him in a year. It wasn't easy for either of us. He was cranky and tired, always short of food and sleep, but he never considered quitting. My worst student was with me for seven years. When I released him, I wondered whether I had made a mistake and done it prematurely. You are an academic, used to late hours and study. Can you match Adrian's precision or do you plan to relinquish the Archives and devote your life to this undertaking?"

Devin cleared his throat. "I have a month," he said quietly. "I can give you no more than that."

CHAPTER 13

Inconsistencies and Allegations

Armand rose angrily.

"You waste my time! Do you think this is some trivial matter; a few fairytales to be put to memory in a month's time? This is the oral history of my province, *monsieur*, a matter of extreme importance!"

"Monsieur Vielle," Devin begged, grabbing his arm. "I do not take this matter lightly. Please let me explain. Can't you see that I value the work you do? I have come a long way, just to meet you!"

"And yet you mock my profession!" Armand protested. "What little respect the men of Coreé must have for the Chronicles that they would send you with only a month's time to memorize them!"

"No one sent me," Devin objected. "I came only because I value very highly what you do. Please, allow me to explain before you assume that I am being disrespectful."

Armand blew out his breath in a great sigh and sat down again. "Mind your words, Monsieur Roché; I am in no mood to be trifled with."

Out of the corner of his eye, Devin saw that Marcus had risen from his perch, disturbed by Vielle's anger. Apparently, he was still taking his job seriously, despite Devin's suspicions.

"I graduated from the Université at seventeen," Devin began, "the youngest man ever to enter, and the first to complete five years of study in only two. I have an excellent memory. Maybe I have mistakenly anticipated the amount of time it will take me to memorize the Chronicle but I only ask that you allow me to try. I will compensate you well for a month of your time."

"You do not pay to learn the Chronicle!" Armand responded in disgust. "Knowledge here is freely given but not to fools or braggarts!"

Devin tried to keep his voice calm. "I did not intend to brag. I only hoped to convince you that, perhaps, I have a better chance than some men to learn your Chronicle quickly."

Armand grunted. "There is a difference between reading a book, where you can go over the material again and again by yourself until you retain the information, and listening intently enough to commit a story to memory. As adept as Adrian was, it was necessary that we work together for many hours to enable him to learn just one story word for word. Accuracy is everything, without it the importance of the Chronicles would have diminished years ago."

"I do understand," Devin replied.

Armand threw a hand in the air. "You have said nothing to convince me that you fully understand the importance of this work."

"Then perhaps, I need to tell you something that I have shared with no one else, not even my father." Devin glanced at Marcus and lowered his voice. "In my last year at the Université a storyteller came to Coreé. Gaspard and I went down to the local tavern to hear him. His name was Gautier Beau Chère."

Armand nodded. "I knew the man. He was Arcadia's Master Bard but he also learned the Batavian Chronicles."

Devin continued. "At the time, I was completing my degree as a historiographer. We had just studied the peasant uprising of 1632."

"Is that what they call it in Coreé?" Armand asked, an edge creeping into his voice. "Do your history books mention that the portion of their livelihood that residents of Ombria paid to Coreé allowed them little or nothing to live on? Combined with the blight that was decimating their crops, people were starving."

"The plight is mentioned. The taxes were considered equitable."

Armand sneered. "Why are you telling me this?"

Devin blundered on. "Because Beau Chère claimed that the government troops murdered the hostages at Beaulieu."

"Do you doubt his word?" Armand snapped, his hands clenched. "They killed nearly three thousand men, women, and children. They were slaughtered like animals and buried in mass graves outside the city."

Devin swallowed hard. "Llisé's official history reports that those hostages died from a particularly virulent type of plague. It concerned me that the Chronicle would differ so completely from our official records."

Armand stood up, but not before Devin saw tears in his eyes. "Did no one ever tell you, Monsieur Roché, history is written by the victors?" He began to walk toward the house and then turned on his heel to face Devin. "I am surprised your father did not prevent you from coming. I think it would be far safer if you abandoned your enterprise now before it is too late. Can't you see that it is no accident that bards are forbidden from entering the Archives? You are treading on very dangerous ground if you seek to reconcile the Chronicles and your history books."

"I am simply asking that you allow me to memorize your Chronicle," Devin said.

"To what end?" Armand asked. "My Chronicle is living history. It is made to be repeated over and over again so that every man, woman, and child in Ombria understands the legacy that precedes them. Where would you tell your stories once you've learned them – in the streets of Coreé – and the houses of your government?"

"I value your oral tradition," Devin replied. "I simply want to be part of it. It takes all of us to make up Llisé, not just the people of Coreé or Ombria or Sorrento."

Armand shook his head. "No! It is impossible to learn the Chronicle in a month's time and I won't cheapen it by allowing you to try! Leave it to Ombrian men who are committed to their heritage and who have the time and ability to do it right."

Devin stood up. "Perhaps Beau Chère will be more accommodating."

Armand shook his head, his eyes glittering with tears. "I see your information is out of date. Gautier Beau Chère drowned returning from his trip to Coreé. His ship foundered in the deep channel off Toulon. All hands were lost. And if you think that was an accident, then you are foolish as well as naive, Monsieur Roché. Thirty-eight innocent people were drowned to silence one man. Should you continue your investigation, I fear our Chancellor will lose his youngest son. And even your friend and your bodyguard will be unable to prevent it."

CHAPTER 14

"Lisette's Lament"

Devin sat for a moment in silence after Armand left him. He had not expected to encounter such resistance to his plan and he was disturbed by the intensity of Armand's position. He could only conclude that Gautier Beau Chère had been Vielle's friend, as well as his colleague, and so his loss was deeply personal. For the moment, he intended to avoid exploring who, in Coreé, might have ordered Beau Chère's murder and the careless extinction of those unfortunate enough to have been traveling with him.

Marcus lumbered across the yard. With the rising moon behind him, he threw a massive, menacing shadow that made Devin scramble hastily to his feet.

"What was that all about?" Marcus demanded.

Devin shrugged, moving out of the malevolent shade that his bodyguard cast. "Armand is angry that I wanted to attempt to memorize the Chronicle in such a short period of time."

Marcus frowned. "But he will still teach you?"

Devin shook his head. "No, he hasn't agreed to anything."

101

"Will we move on to the next province, then?" Marcus asked. "What do you plan to do?"

"I don't know," Devin answered. "But I haven't given up yet. We'll stay here until after the wedding. By tomorrow, maybe I can think of some compelling argument to win him over."

Both of them rejoined the group in the house. Aunt Genevieve had nestled between Armand and Adrian, her hand delicately poised on the bard's left knee. Gaspard was entertaining Adrian's younger sister in the corner with a game of Cat's Cradle. Devin found a seat at the big table next to Adrian's father, Pierre.

"You look like a man who needs a drink," Pierre said, smiling, his cheeks and nose a fiery red. He sloshed wine into a huge earthenware mug and handed it to Devin. "Get some of that down and then tell me what brings you to Ombria."

Devin took a token drink and recounted his stock story of celebrating his Third Year by touring the empire. "I am especially interested in the Chronicles," he added. "I hope to be able to hear them in all fifteen provinces."

"Why not begin now?" Pierre asked. He grinned and pounded the table with a meaty fist. "Armand!" he bellowed, when the room had quieted expectantly. "A story for our guests, please."

Armand's eyes found Devin's and narrowed, assuming that Devin had instigated the request. But the bard stood up and bowed graciously, flourishing his storyteller's cloak with one hand and leaning on his cane with the other. The fire behind him seemed to flare up, at that moment, forming the perfect backdrop. Devin thought afterwards, that he would always remember Armand this way: with the fire at his back, the cloak around his shoulders, and the complete self-assurance that he spoke only the absolute truth.

"Since we have gathered here in anticipation of tomorrow's wedding," Armand announced, "I dedicate my first ballad, 'Lisette's Lament,' to our lovely bride, Colette." He scanned the room for his former student. "May I borrow your harp, Adrian?"

Adrian withdrew a battered harp from a leather satchel stashed under the ladder to the loft. He passed it gingerly, over several people's heads, to Armand. The bard placed his right foot on a stool. Dramatically balancing the instrument on his knee, he paused only a moment to test the pitch of the strings. When he began, the harp notes fell sweet and clear, and Armand's rich baritone provided the perfect counterpoint:

> *In Lamm, a village by the sea,*
> *Antoine first met Lisette,*
> *Along the shore they pledged their love*
> *A wedding date was set.*
>
> *Antoine married sweet Lisette*
> *By the ocean deep and wide.*
> *And yet he held a secret dream*
> *To see the other side.*
>
> *Antoine fished; Lisette kept house,*
> *And yet her heart was sore.*
> *For in his eyes she saw he longed*
> *And wished for something more . . .*

Devin closed his eyes, absorbing every word, listening to the cadence of the language and the repetition of the music. For him there was no other sound in the room but the rhythm of words and notes blending perfectly together, verse after verse, into one harmonious whole.

When the last note sounded Devin looked up to see Armand watching him. There were a few sniffles from around the room. The story had ended sadly and it seemed a peculiar choice for the eve of a wedding but applause drowned out any sounds of dissent. Armand bowed and then threw back his head and sang a fabliau, a bawdy song, which had the men clapping and howling and the women blushing. Devin slipped away to the hayloft in the barn, a plan already forming in his head.

He stayed up most of the night, sitting by the window in the loft. He watched the moon make its way across the sky until it passed from sight behind the barn. At last, when he was satisfied that he had perfected his strategy, he laid his head against the rough barn boards and closed his eyes.

Both Gaspard and Marcus were already in the court-yard setting up tables when Devin wakened. Armand looked askance at his late arrival, but Devin immediately began to help gather supplies for the reception. He worked as hard as any man there, lifting and carrying, and nailing together extra tables from rough-hewn lumber.

The day was beautiful and cloudless, and the sun quickly dried up any mud remaining from the previous day's showers. Garlands of ivy and wild flowers were twined on a hastily constructed arbor that crowned the entrance to the courtyard. Brush and logs were piled near the center for a great bonfire.

At noon, Colette and the other women went inside to dress. Devin and Gaspard washed at the pump and retrieved clean shirts from their luggage. Devin smiled, imagining what his mother's reaction might have been to his attending a wedding in a wrinkled white shirt, rough woolen trousers, and walking boots. And yet, the peaceful simplicity of this country life appealed to him. This afternoon, he felt relaxed and sure of himself. Now, all he had to do was find a few moments alone with Armand before the day was over.

But, Armand was in great demand. He was a celebrity, a special guest, and he had paid Adrian's family an extraordinary honor by attending Colette's wedding. The village folk had come to see and hear him as much as they had come to watch the ceremony. The crowd filled the tiny stone church and spilled out into the small dismal cemetery which surrounded it. Devin found the tilting, weathered tombstones and a recent, freshly mounded grave an eerie contrast to the laughter of the gaily dressed wedding party. Here life and death seemed to coexist hand in hand, each unavoidably a part of the other.

Devin could hardly hear the ceremony over the hilarity of the crowd outside. When the young married couple left the church, both those guests that had been seated inside the church and those who had waited outside, followed them down the road to the farm, singing fabliaux and shouting suggestive comments. Cows gathered along the stone walls, their tails swishing behind them, silently viewing the spectacle that was passing before them.

At the house, Devin helped to bring out the food: huge platters of Ombria's famous cheeses, fragrant breads, crusty cassoulets, sliced hams, beef roasts, dried fruits, and cake. Wine arrived continually by the barrelful and disappeared just as quickly. The huge bonfire both lighted and warmed the courtyard as the sun sunk low in the sky, its light refracted by the giant pines surrounding the house.

Armand gathered an audience near the flames and mesmerized them with his tales of early Ombria. His recitation

105

went on for hours and yet the crowd never seemed to hear enough. Devin could tell the bard was beginning to tire, and yet, always there were shouts of "One more, Armand!" "One more!"

When there was nothing more he could do to help his hosts, Devin found a spot along the wall. He sat down, his legs crossed in front of him, listening to Armand's mellow voice weave its spell over the crowd. It seemed once again that he had miscalculated. He knew Armand planned to leave before dawn the next morning, and as the night wore on, the chance of speaking to him alone seemed more and more remote.

Gaspard came to sit beside him, setting two glasses of wine on the wall between them.

"What do you plan to do?"

"Tomorrow?" Devin asked. Gaspard nodded. "I plan to go to Lac Dupré with Armand."

"Has he asked you, then?" Gaspard inquired cautiously.

"No, but he will," Devin replied confidently. "All I need is a few moments of his time and he will. I'm sure of it."

Gaspard raised his eyebrows. "Have some wine," he recommended, patting him on the shoulder. "You're strung as tight as his harp strings tonight."

Devin shook his head. "I've had enough wine. I need to keep my wits about me."

And then, just like that, his chance came quite by accident. A sudden gust of wind blew the smoke from the bonfire into Armand's face. The bard bent double, coughing and wheezing. Devin grabbed a glass of wine and went to his rescue.

"Here," he offered, drawing Armand away from the fire. "Let Adrian take over for a while."

"Thank you," Armand sputtered, walking with Devin back along the wall. "My voice was going, anyway. You can only do that for so long, you know."

"I'm sure that's true," Devin replied. He was nervous now that the time had come, and his voice faltered. "Could I have just a few minutes of your time? I want to tell you something."

Armand frowned, regarding him darkly under bushy gray eyebrows. "You're not going to spoil the evening by making me angry again, are you?"

"That's not my intention," Devin said. "And I swear to you before I start that the first and only time I've ever heard this song was last night when you sang it." He took a deep breath and stilled his heart before he started, remembering Armand's gentle rhythm and cadence. He began softly:

> *In Lamm, a village by the sea,*
> *Antoine first met Lisette,*
> *Along the shore they pledged their love*
> *A wedding day was set . . .*

He sang each stanza word for word, exactly as Armand had delivered it the night before:

> *He gathered wood and built a boat*
> *Out on the open sand.*
> *One day he sailed to meet the waves*
> *Till he lost sight of land.*

> *He traveled many days until,*
> *One dark and misty morning*
> *He saw the distant shape of land*
> *Draw closer without warning.*

When Antoine stepped upon that shore,
He left his past behind.
For here were fields and forests green,
And birds of many kinds.

He loosed the rope and set adrift
His boat upon the sea.
And back in Lamm his dearest love
Cried, 'Please come back to me.'

But he had found what he had sought
A world all unexplored.
And so he left without a thought
The one that he adored.

Lisette sat out among the dunes
And watched the waves come in.
She never saw his ship return
Nor held her love again.

And yet they say she watches still
And wears his wedding band.
Her ghost awaits him in the dunes,
A lantern in her hand.

Devin stopped, hoping for some small sign of approval from Armand. The bard simply stared at him and then downed the rest of his wine in one gulp.

"You've made your point, Monsieur Roché," Armand said finally. "Your lessons will begin tomorrow on the road to Lac Dupré. If you are late . . . I will not make the offer again."

CHAPTER 15

A Bard's Life

The day dawned sunny and clear. Despite the cool breeze, Devin stuffed his jacket into his knapsack before they'd walked the first mile. It would take two days to reach Lac Dupré, and Armand set a brisk pace, despite his cane. Conversation was sparse this morning. They'd all had little sleep. The celebration had lasted well into the night and they had risen before daybreak. The first rays of the sun had revealed several revelers sound asleep in the trampled garden and an inebriated goat tottering around the empty wine barrels. They'd delayed their departure just long enough to clean up the courtyard and dismantle the temporary tables, after Armand had insisted that Adrian come with them.

Devin had seen Armand draw Adrian aside last night after he had finished his storytelling. Their conversation had been lengthy and intense. Once, Adrian had put a hand on Armand's shoulder but Armand had shaken it off. Devin had turned away, guilty at seeming to eavesdrop. Then this morning, Adrian had explained to his disappointed parents that he wouldn't be staying another week as he had promised but would be traveling back to Lac Dupré with his old tutor, instead. Perhaps, Devin thought, Armand had decided that it would be better to designate his successor too early rather than too late.

As they walked, the melody from "Lisette's Lament" ran through Devin's head incessantly. "Where was Lamm?" he asked Armand, when they stopped in a grove of trees for lunch.

Armand unfastened his cloak and folded it neatly beside him. "Why does it matter?"

Devin shrugged. "Well, Antoine crossed an ocean – he either left Llisé – or he came here. Which was it?"

"I don't know," Armand replied. "Perhaps, it wasn't an ocean at all, maybe it was just the Dantzig. To a primitive man that river would seem like an ocean."

"The Dantzig doesn't have dunes," Devin pointed out. "If he crossed the Dantzig he would have traveled from one province into another one. Then the story would be included in the Chronicles of two provinces."

Adrian looked up from unpacking the food his mother had sent with them. "Perhaps it is," he said.

"Is it?" Devin persisted, bending to pick up a heart-shaped stone.

"Not that I know of," Armand replied.

"Then the ballad can't refer to the Dantzig, can it?" Devin asked.

"What difference does it make?" Armand asked, as he laid out his portion of bread and cheese on his handkerchief.

"But what if he came to Llisé from somewhere else?" Devin said. "Which direction did he travel, do you know that?"

Armand rolled his eyes in exasperation. "It doesn't say, Monsieur Roché. Let it rest, will you? You ask far too many questions! By God, I'm a man of my word but you make me regret having struck a bargain with you."

Admitting defeat, Devin got up and walked to where Gaspard and Marcus were sitting. He pulled his knapsack from his shoulders and slumped down on the ground. Gaspard handed him bread and cheese, and then leaned closer.

"Give Armand a break," he whispered. "It's going to be a long month if you keep this up."

Devin bit into the cheese and shook his head. "It won't be a long month at all, Gaspard. It will be a very short one. I need to learn as much I can, as quickly as possible."

"Well, Armand can't tell you what he doesn't know himself," Gaspard pointed out. "He's a man who's used to being in charge, Dev. Don't push him. Accept what he is willing to give and admit that you may have to leave with some questions unanswered."

Devin worried a root with the toe of his boot. "Surely we can work it out so both of us are satisfied."

"You asked him a favor," Gaspard reminded him. "Accept what he's offering without badgering him."

Perhaps, he was pushing Armand, Devin thought, but it was hard to restrain his excitement. Even though there was so much he wanted to know, he could hardly hound the man all day with questions. He would have to make a conscious effort to contain himself, even though he was interested in where the men originated who first settled in Ombria.

Marcus silently passed him a bottle of wine, but avoided making eye contact. Devin thanked him and took a drink. The restraint between them was beginning to wear on him. First, he had alienated Marcus and now he had annoyed Armand. With any luck he would offend Gaspard and Adrian before the day was over, too.

He ate the rest of his bread and cheese in silence. While the others finished, he amused himself by examining two more monoliths which had been incorporated into the fence that bordered the road. He longed to ask Armand if the Chronicles contained any explanation for their presence but he didn't initiate any other conversation. When Armand signaled that he was ready to move on, Devin walked between Gaspard and Marcus and let Adrian and Armand go ahead of them.

After about an hour, Armand glanced over his shoulder.

"I promised you a lesson today, Monsieur Roché. Walk with me."

Devin joined him obediently.

"Let's assess what you already know," Armand said. "Sing 'Lisette's Lament' for me."

"I've already memorized it," Devin reminded him.

"You knew it well enough last night," Armand responded. "That doesn't mean you remember it this morning. Repeat it now."

At the end of the first stanza, Armand stopped him. "You said wedding day, it's wedding date. Begin again."

Devin started again. He reached the fourth verse before Armand stopped him again. "You said he'd lost sight of land. It's he lost sight of land. Begin again."

Behind him, Gaspard snorted. "Spare us, Armand. Must we listen to Devin sing all the way to Lac Dupré?"

Armand cut him down with a look. "Yes, if necessary. He'll repeat it until it is perfect or he loses his voice, whichever comes first. Tomorrow, we will begin with that ballad again . . . and the next day and the day after that. The Chronicles require precision. Each word must be exact or I will not authorize him to perform them in public."

That was the last mistake that Devin made. He sang the ballad perfectly the next time but Armand made him repeat it ten times more just to be certain his concentration didn't slip with multiple attempts.

The rest of the day went by in a blur. By late afternoon, Devin's feet hurt from walking and his throat was sore from singing. Armand never slackened in his training.

"Who was Ombria's first Master Bard?" he asked.

"Belami Facette," Devin answered.

"Name the eight different types of stories included in the Chronicles."

"Chanson des Gestes, beast tales, fabliaux, romances, legends, historical tales, cautionary tales, and religious tales," Devin replied.

"What are the three types of religious tales?"

"Lyrical, allegorical, and the lives of the saints."

Armand nodded his head. "Good. Now sing 'Lisette's Lament' again."

"He's hoarse," Adrian protested. "Leave off for today, Armand."

Armand's face hardened. "Did I ever grant you any mercy?"

Adrian smiled. "Once or twice after I had demonstrated my dedication."

"When he demonstrates his, I will consider it. Remember, you had a year to learn the Chronicle; Monsieur Roché boasts he can do it in a month. I intend to prove him wrong or break him in the process."

Devin refrained from comment even though Armand had made him angry. He was certain that all of this was a test and he wasn't about to be tricked into failing it.

"Armand," Adrian protested. "Devin will either learn this or he won't. There is no need to turn it into a contest."

"I wasn't the one who issued the challenge," Armand pointed out. He slashed his hand through the air. "Enough, we have work to do!"

He turned to Devin. "Sing!"

Devin's itinerary had them stopping in Nance but Armand called a halt outside of Purview at a small farm.

"There is an inn in Nance," Marcus suggested. "We could reach it by nightfall."

"It is suicide to travel these roads after dusk," Armand replied. "Besides, inns cost money. I am welcome in any home in this province and a good many outside it as well. Any man with me will be treated to the same courtesy. You've slept in a barn before, Marcus, I doubt you will find this one any less comfortable than the last."

Devin was certain Armand and Adrian would rate a spot by the hearth but he kept his opinions to himself. He dropped back to walk with Gaspard.

"I need a bath badly," Gaspard confided. "And I've no clean clothes in my knapsack."

Devin laughed and lowered his voice. "I've noticed Armand has a certain air about him, too. No one seems to care here. Perhaps we'll pass a lake or a river tomorrow where we can take a quick dip."

"And catch our deaths from pneumonia, no thank you!" Gaspard protested. "I'd rather stink than die at twenty-three."

Armand tapped Devin's shoulder. "Sing your ballad again, Monsieur Roché. You're giving your first performance tonight. It's time you earned your room and board."

CHAPTER 16

Mäìte

The gray stone farmhouse had only a small shed attached to it. Ivy covered the roof, dripping down from the eaves in thick garlands. Behind the house, a walled cemetery lay strewn with headstones. It gave the place a forlorn, deserted look and Devin felt as reluctant as Marcus to spend the night.

A tiny old woman answered Armand's knock. She stood a moment, blinking out into the fading light, and then giving a soft sound, wrapped her arms around Armand. Her head barely reached his chest.

"*Grandmère* Mäìte," Armand murmured. "My friends and I are in need of some food and a place to sleep."

She beckoned them in, smiling and bowing. An old man sat at a rickety handmade table, a bowl of stew before him.

"This is my grandfather Emile Vielle," Armand said, with a sweeping bow that was suitable for some great dignitary.

"Who is it, Mäìte?" Emile asked, standing up with difficulty. He was still a bear of a man, despite his age and infirmity, and when he saw Armand, he enveloped him in a hug that might have hurt a smaller man. "You are always welcome here, Armand," he said graciously. "Very welcome. Who's this with you?"

They recognized Adrian and treated him to the same enthusiastic greeting. With Devin, Gaspard, and Marcus they were more reserved but no less friendly. They pulled up two stools and a bench to the table. More bowls were produced and filled with stew and a loaf of bread was sliced.

There was only one bottle of wine for the entire table to share and Devin barely wet the bottom of his glass. He felt guilty accepting their hospitality when he thought of the unlimited budget his father had given him access to. This morning before he had left he'd hidden ten gold francs in the bread basket for Adrian's mother, as well as a substantial gift for the new bride and groom. These country people had so little and yet seemed so willing to share. It made the prosperous residents of Coreé seem selfish, in comparison.

Little Mäite gathered blankets and quilts and spread them on the soft hay in the shed. In truth, the rickety structure was nearly the same size as the tiny house. If tonight, they shared their beds with a half dozen chickens and an old cow, Devin felt it only added another dimension to the experience of touring the provinces. Marcus was not so philosophical. He liked their days to go according to a prearranged plan and the present arrangement did not seem to suit him at all. He left his belongings reluctantly with a wary eye toward the insubstantial roof.

All afternoon, Devin had restrained the impulse to lash out at Armand when he had teased and belittled his ability to learn the Chronicles. But tonight, when Armand insisted that Devin sing, he had unwittingly presented him with the perfect opportunity to show off his talents.

Both Adrian and Armand told tales after dinner. First, Adrian told the story of Emeline and Renèe, two little girls, who wandered into the forest and were eaten by wolves. Laced with warning and regret, Devin recognized it as one of the cautionary tales. It was short and sad, and Devin committed it to memory as quickly as Adrian told it. And yet, he knew it was a tale he would never enjoy telling. When Adrian finished, there was only hushed silence. Their host nodded gravely, and *Grandmère* Mäite turned away, her lips trembling.

"Devin is my new apprentice," Armand announced. "He's only learned one ballad but I'd like him to sing it for you. Forgive his voice; he's been working hard all day to perfect it."

Gaspard pushed his half-finished wine in front of Devin, who took a sip and then stepped to the hearth. He leaned down to whisper to Adrian.

"May I use your harp?"

Adrian gave him a puzzled look but lifted it from where it lay nestled on his lap and handed it over. Devin's mother had insisted he learn to play the pianoforte; but it had been his own idea to cultivate the folk harp. He had become quite accomplished at the Université, and for the last two years had been asked to perform at the Académie's *Gala de Noel*. He tested the pitch, adjusted two strings, and settled down on a stool. He was not about to imitate Armand: Armand was a master and he knew instinctively that any attempt he made to emulate him would be a mistake.

"'Lisette's Lament,'" he announced quietly. He sang the ballad with sensitivity and reserve, intentionally avoiding Armand's flamboyant style. As he told how Antoine left Lisette, his hostess's eyes filled with tears. They trickled randomly through the deep wrinkles of her face. It almost unnerved him, sending a sympathetic yearning through his own chest for that kind of undying love and devotion. He quelled the urge to stop and comfort Armand's little grandmother.

Devin continued, drawing the story out as though it took its life from him alone. He sang the last stanza, imagining Lisette seated alone in the darkness, the waves breaking on the sand, her lantern the only light in her world. He allowed his last few notes to resonate a moment after he had ceased to speak, letting them fade into a silence where he swore he could hear the echo of breaking surf and wind over sand.

Mäite rose from her seat and hobbled to where he sat, wiping away tears on her apron. She bent and brushed her lips against Devin's forehead.

"That was beautiful," she murmured. "Beautiful."

He blushed, embarrassed at her familiarity.

She cupped his chin, tilting his eyes up to meet hers. "I've never heard it sung so well," she whispered. "Not even when Armand has sung it."

Devin glanced away to hide his surprise, hoping his tutor hadn't heard her comment.

Her husband beat on the table with the empty wine bottle. "Enough tragedy! Enough love songs! Send these *enfants* to bed, Armand," he demanded, indicating, Devin and Gaspard, "and sing me some fabliaux!"

Armand laughed. "Bring out another bottle of wine, you frugal old fool, and I will!"

Devin rose and returned the harp to Adrian. All of sudden he felt shaky, as though he hadn't eaten anything all day. For a moment, he was afraid he was going to be sick and he stumbled unsteadily outside. He was surprised when Armand followed him.

The bard put a hand on his shoulder. "Sit down. Take some deep breaths. It will pass."

Devin put his back against the house and slid down till he sat on the huge stone doorstep.

Armand eased himself down awkwardly beside him and forced a glass of wine into his hand. "Drink that," he advised. "It'll settle your stomach."

"I don't like to take it," Devin protested. "They have so little."

Armand waved a hand airily. "They have a whole wine cellar underneath the house. *Grandpère* is as tight as they come."

Devin took a sip and put the glass on the ground. His hands were shaking. He leaned back against the stones of the house. "I don't know what made me sick at my stomach . . . "

"It's called nerves," Armand told him. "It hits most of us right before we begin a presentation. A few like you breeze right through the performance and then fall apart afterwards. You'll get used to it in time."

"Used to it?" Devin asked in surprise. "Won't it go away?"

Armand laughed. "No, it never goes away completely. You just have to accept it and go on from there."

"I hadn't expected to have to perform so soon," Devin confessed.

"It's part of the job," Armand said. "Being a bard requires performing every night, usually. And it takes a special talent to keep the stories fresh and new each and every time."

They sat for a moment, listening to the muffled sound of voices and laughter inside the house. Armand shifted uneasily.

"Perhaps, it's none of my business, but I've noticed that you and Marcus seem at odds. It's not wise to alienate your bodyguard."

Devin hesitated, unsure whether to tell him what had caused the rift between them. "It's a long story," he said.

"I'm a good listener," Armand replied. He tapped the wine glass at Devin's side. "Drink that and tell me about it."

Devin swirled the crimson liquid a moment before drinking it. He told Armand about his itinerary disappearing, and the cursed cross which had been included when it was returned, and Le Beau's strange note. He described the horsemen that he'd seen in the middle of the night from the hayloft at Adrian's. Reluctantly he added his own penchant for waking dreams, and his uncertainty, afterwards, about what he had actually seen.

"And Marcus denies meeting anyone?" Armand asked.

Devin nodded. "He was very angry. And at this point, I don't honestly know what I saw."

Armand shook his head. "You're in a dangerous position if you don't trust your bodyguard."

"I know," Devin answered. "And yet, if he's telling the truth, I've obviously hurt him with my suspicions."

"I know it would take some time but could you request that your father send you another bodyguard?"

"Marcus was my father's own personal bodyguard. He handpicked him to go with me," Devin said. "I don't think replacing him is an option."

Armand stretched his legs out in front of him. "And you have no reason to suspect that your father might benefit in any way from your death?"

Shocked, Devin turned to stare at him. "God, no! Never! I . . . what would make you even suggest such a thing?"

Armand shrugged. "Even our Heavenly Father sacrificed his Son to make a point. The world hasn't been quite the same since. It never hurts to consider all the possibilities."

"That," Devin replied, shaking his head, "is not a possibility."

"All right then," Armand continued. "In that case, you'll have to have faith that your father has sent a trustworthy bodyguard with you and let go of your suspicions. There's an apothecary in Lac Dupré. I can get you a sedative if you need it to sleep."

"I'd prefer to get along without it," Devin said, imagining himself too drugged to evade an assailant.

"Suit yourself," Armand replied. "But keep in mind, your training will be more grueling because of this self-imposed time limit. Sleep will be a luxury, in very short supply. I have no idea how disturbing these waking dreams can be."

Devin took another sip of wine. "It varies. The frightening part is that they transform some normal object or person into something or someone else. It is not just a hallucination; parts of it are real and parts of it are imaginary. One night at the Université I had just fallen asleep, when Gaspard came in from a party. He walked past my bed. For an instant, I could have sworn he was one of my professors and I even called him by name. Gaspard thought it was funny. He assumed I was drunk, until it was obvious that I had been sleeping."

Armand raised his eyebrows. "So you are saying that, even if Marcus wasn't in the courtyard that night, someone else was?"

"Yes," Devin said.

"So this is not a simple thing?" Armand asked.

"Not at all," Devin replied. "And if Marcus didn't meet someone in the courtyard, who did?"

Armand patted Devin's knee. "I think I might not have been so quick to take you on as a student, Monsieur Roché, if I had realized all the baggage you were carrying."

"Well, at least, if the incident at Adrian's farm was a waking dream, it is the first I have had in over a year,"

Devin said, knowing that even putting it into words would probably doom him to another episode, soon.

Armand struggled to his feet. "Let me know if I can help. Don't think about it anymore tonight. Sit and relax for a few minutes and then go to bed. Tomorrow will be a long day."

His hand was on the doorknob when he turned back to look at Devin. "And by the way, if, in a month's time, your final performance is as good as tonight's, Monsieur Roché, I'll embroider Ombria's wolf emblem on your cloak myself."

He was gone before Devin could thank him. He sat quietly for a moment and finished his wine, savoring Armand's praise. It was unexpected so early in their relationship. Tonight, he had to admit, he'd tailored his performance to impress Armand, and yet Mäìte's words had touched him more.

Something almost magical had happened when he had sung tonight. This afternoon, when he'd recited that song over and over again, he had simply repeated the correct words in the proper order. Tonight, he'd become a part of the story, and on some level Mäìte had entered into it, too. He'd actually felt like a bard, creating the kind of atmosphere that provoked a strong emotional response from his audience. It had been exhilarating, and for just a few minutes, Marcus, LeBeau, and the mysterious horsemen had all been banished from his mind. He leaned his head back against the stones and smiled.

CHAPTER 17

Night Terrors

Devin dragged himself up out of a deep sleep. Thunder and the sound of rain on the roof had wakened him. Something brushed his arm, and he opened his eyes to see his father bending over him, a distressed expression on his face. For a moment, Devin struggled to remember where he was. Surely they weren't back in Coreé already?

"Forgive me," his father said. A knife blade glinted for an instant in the darkness as it descended toward Devin's heart.

Devin rolled to avoid it, his scream echoing through the night. A chicken shrieked and flapped off its roost. Several others joined it in raising the alarm, as the cow struggled to its feet.

Hands grabbed Devin, yanking him upright and holding him. Marcus materialized out of the darkness in front of him.

"What is it?" he demanded, shaking him slightly. "Are you hurt? Was someone here?"

Devin shook off his hands and pushed him away, his heart pounding.

"No," he answered, dry mouthed and shaking. "No, there was no one here."

He was drenched in sweat, and sick in his stomach, embarrassed that this had happened again so soon. Damn you, Armand, he thought, for making me doubt my own father.

The house door slammed shut and Ombria's Master Bard arrived as though he'd been summoned. His bare chest was speckled with rain and his unfastened trousers hung precariously from one hand. Adrian trailed behind him, his cloak thrown haphazardly over his shoulders. The light from the lantern in his hand splashed around the shed, reflecting in the cow's wildly rolling eyes, and elongating the chickens' shadows into weird mercurial shapes.

"What happened?" Armand asked. "Is everyone all right?"

"We're fine," Gaspard explained, laying a hand on Devin's shoulder. "Dev sometimes has nightmares . . . "

Armand waved away his explanation. "He warned me earlier. Although, honestly, Monsieur Roché, you hardly did them justice! I didn't realize they were quite so spectacular!"

Devin hated him for being cheerful enough to joke after having been startled awake in the middle of the night.

"I'm sorry I woke everyone up," he apologized.

He sat down in the hay and bent his head against his knees for a moment, trying to dispel the nausea that was washing over him.

"Would a glass of wine help?" Armand asked, suddenly serious.

"No." Devin said, glancing up. "Thank you. But please, go back to sleep if you can. You have my word that I won't disturb you again tonight."

Armand didn't linger. "*Merci!*" he said, giving him a little bow. "I wish you sweet dreams, *messieurs.*"

He waded back through the puddles toward the house, holding one hand above his head to ward off the raindrops.

124

"Thank God, my grandparents are half deaf," he confided to Adrian, just loud enough so that the residents of the shed could hear him. "They would have thought the *Militaire* were attacking."

"Well then," Marcus mused, leaning back against the side of the shed. "That was exciting. My heart's still pounding."

"I'm sorry," Devin apologized again. "It's not something I can control."

Gaspard ran a hand through his hair and blew out a long breath. "I think we should look for an apothecary, Dev, at the earliest opportunity."

"I think you're right," Devin agreed. "Armand told me that there is one in Lac Dupré."

"Then tomorrow, if we arrive in time, we'll pay him a visit," Gaspard said. "I'll look forward to it." He lay back down on the hay and then grimaced, as he shifted to the right. "Sweet Jesus, this roof leaks like a sieve."

Marcus settled down on the hay, too. His movements were slow and studied as though he had yet to decide whether the crisis was over and he could truly relax.

"If you intend to stay a month in Lac Dupré, may I suggest that we find an inn with real beds and a lavatory?" he asked.

"I'll see what I can do," Devin promised. He realized with a jolt that this was the first time that Marcus had spoken to him directly in the last few days.

His surprise turned to panic. As Marcus took his hand from behind his back, Devin saw a familiar metallic glint. A moment later, Marcus sheathed a knife and slid it underneath his pillow. Devin remained propped in the corner, his heart beating erratically. Despite Armand's advice to the contrary, he could not bring himself to trust Marcus. Nor had he any intention of sleeping again tonight.

125

CHAPTER 18

"Emeline"

Armand slapped Devin on the back.

"Sing for me, *monsieur*," he requested, as soon as they were on the road in the morning.

Devin was in no mood to sing. A cold rain pounded the countryside around them, pooling in the rutted road and dripping from the branches that formed a canopy above their heads. If Armand had noticed the dark circles under Devin's eyes or his avoidance of Marcus, he hadn't commented. The bard was as cheerful this morning as when he had been faced with Devin's nightmares in the middle of the night.

Devin cleared his throat and sang "Lisette's Lament."

"Adequate," Armand pronounced when he finished. "Considering."

"Considering what?" Devin growled.

Armand gave him an engaging smile. "Your mood and your lack of sleep. Although, it wasn't half as good as your performance last night. Perhaps you'll do better tonight."

"I can't sing the same song night after night," Devin protested. "Teach me something else."

Armand chuckled. "That's what we do, *monsieur*, we tell the same stories over and over again but we try to make them original for every new audience." He adjusted the hood of his cloak. "Some men have a way with melody but are hopeless with prose. Let's see how you do with a narrative. What about 'Emeline'?"

"I already know it," Devin replied.

"I thought you might say that," Armand replied. "And how did you learn it?"

Devin frowned, wondering what he was getting at. "I memorized it last night when Adrian told it."

"Ah, *monsieur*," Armand said, shaking his head. "Then you broke the first rule as my apprentice."

Devon stopped dead in the road. "And what was that?"

"You learn the Chronicle only from me," Armand said, shaking his finger. "Not from Adrian and not from any other bard we should happen to meet in Ombria. If you are my apprentice than no other storyteller's work matters to you but mine. I am the original, your Bible, so to speak. The rest are simply imitations of a great work."

"Forgive me," Devin said sarcastically.

Armand's face hardened. "You'll get no points from me with that attitude. Remember I can dissolve this agreement at any time."

Devin bowed his head. "Forgive me," he repeated. "I'm not myself this morning. Will you teach me 'Emeline'?"

Armand nodded, completely amiable once again. "Of course. Please listen carefully.

"*Once upon a time there were two sisters. Their names were Emeline and Renée. Emeline's hair was dark and curly, and Renée's was golden like the summer sun. They lived with their Mama and Papa at the edge of a deep forest. Every day before they went to play, their Mama would say, 'Girls do not go under the branches of the trees, stay in the sun and play.' And each day their Papa would say, 'Girls do not go into the shadow of the trees, stay by the house and play.'*

"One fall day, the girls played by the house. They had a little ball their mother had made out of bits of rags. It was all different colors: red, blue, yellow and green. That day they threw the ball, back and forth, back and forth. Until Renée, who was the smallest, threw the ball under one of the oak trees.

"Now behind that oak tree, a wolf was waiting. The wolf would not come near the house. He would not come into the sun but he waited in the shadows. He waited because he knew one day that Emeline or Renée would forget what their Mama had told them. He knew one day that they would forget what their Papa had said and they would come under the shadow of the oak tree and he would eat them up.

"And that day, when the ball went under the tree, Renée looked at Emeline and Emeline looked at Renée. The little rag ball was their only toy and they didn't know what to do. 'I will get it,' said Emeline. 'I am the oldest. I will grab the little rag ball and run back here quickly.'

"Renée started to cry. She said, 'No, Emeline, I threw the little ball under the tree. I will go and get it.' So they decided to go together, one little girl with dark hair and one little girl with hair like the sun. So they held hands and they crossed the yard, step by step, until they reached the shadow of the oak tree. They walked, step by step, until they could see the little rag ball.

"And when Emeline bent down to pick up the ball, the wolf jumped. He was so quick that their parents never heard them scream. He was so quick that no one saw him drag

128

their dead bodies into the woods. All that was left of Emeline and Renée was the little rag ball in the shade of the oak tree and the red, red blood on the grass."

Gaspard turned away. "That is such a revolting story! Why in God's name would anyone ever tell it to a child?"

"Perhaps you'd like to explain that to him, Monsieur Roché," Armand said.

Devin shook his head. "I'm sorry but I agree with Gaspard. I see no good reason to tell that story to anyone. Is it even true?"

Armand ignored his question. "It is included in the Chronicle for a reason. What kind of tale is it?" he asked.

"A cautionary tale," Devin answered.

"And as such, what is it designed to do?"

Gaspard laughed uneasily. "Appall and disgust the audience?"

Armand glowered. "Have you considered how many lives that tale may have saved? How many little girls or boys, for that matter, may have stayed out of the woods after hearing it?"

Devin hadn't considered that. Wolves had never been a problem in Coreé. They were not something he had ever had to worry about as a child. And at the moment, his immediate troubles seemed to center around bodyguards with big, shiny knives.

"Are wolves really a danger in Ombria?" Gaspard asked.

"Oh yes, *mon ami*," Armand replied. "The wolves of Ombria are legendary for being particularly vicious. In the past forty years they have become even more dangerous. Why do you think the roads are unsafe after dark?"

Devin felt a chill run down his back that had nothing to do with the rain. Everyone had warned them about wolves and traveling after dark. It explained a great deal if Ombria's wolves were famous for their savagery.

"I guess I can understand why you might tell that story to children, then," he said. "But why did Adrian tell it at your grandparents' house last night? They are old and their children have long since grown up."

Armand fixed his gaze on the road ahead. "My grandparents lost a son to the wolves when he was only seven. He was my father's youngest brother. He had gone out to the yard to play, just like Emeline and Renée. By the time they heard him scream, it was too late. I think sometimes that, hearing "Emeline" comforts them, because it is clear that the mother and father have warned the little girls over and over about the dangers of the forest. It is the children who make the decision to disregard their parents' good advice, and they forfeit their lives because of it." He wiped either rain or tears from his eyes and continued. "Now, Monsieur Roché, let me hear you tell the story. If you learn it quickly enough, I'll see you are given the opportunity to tell it tonight in Lac Dupré."

CHAPTER 19

The Forêt d'Halatte

The clouds above them deepened and the wind rose. Devin had never seen such heavy rain. Or to be truthful, he'd simply never been outside in rain like this before. The deluge was never-ending. Their clothes clung to their skin, sodden and heavy. Even their knapsacks were soaked through. They were wet, miserable, and chilled to the bone, and yet they hadn't passed a cottage or farm for hours.

They'd entered the Forêt d'Halatte around noon. The heavy cloud cover had left the woodland as dim as twilight. With "Emeline" running through his head, Devin had felt more than a little reluctant to walk under its canopy of branches. Armand had long since abandoned trying to teach him as they traveled. The bard was limping badly but refused to call a halt while they were still within the confines of the forest. Mid-afternoon came and went and still they walked on, sometimes in water that rose to their ankles. The mist hung in diaphanous curtains, making the deep woods around them seem mysterious and forbidding. Evergreens provided the only variety in a sea of bare and sodden tree trunks.

The road descended into a deep ravine where the river had overflowed its banks. Broken branches swirled in the muddy current. When they reached the bridge which allowed the road to continue to the other side, the raging water was lapping at the floorboards. They stopped, viewing the only way across with apprehension.

"This isn't safe," Armand pronounced. "I know another way around, up through the hills. It's treacherous, even in good weather, but it is preferable to having this bridge give way while we are on it, or being caught in the forest after nightfall."

He directed them back the way they'd come only a few minutes before, to where a narrow path left the main road. It curved steadily upward under rocky outcroppings which hung precariously over the trail. Hemlocks clung to the huge boulders, their roots gnarled and exposed. Giant ferns lined the path. Some of their tightly curled fronds had opened to reveal surprisingly delicate, lacy foliage. The moss growing on the stone was a garish, brilliant green giving the place an eerie, unnatural look.

They had lost valuable time in backtracking and evening was drawing dangerously near. Armand had to stop time after time to rest his knee. He became increasingly pale and short tempered, lines of pain marking his face. Not only did climbing the steep trail which skirted the cliff aggravate his knee, but the footing was uncertain, as well. Rivulets of water and mud cascaded down the hillside, forming gullies which had eroded the path. Below them, the river rushed through the forest, its waters devouring its banks and gobbling debris as it went. A splintering crash announced the destruction of the bridge they'd almost crossed.

Devin glanced apprehensively at Gaspard. Nothing in his life or training had prepared him for this. He sidestepped to avoid another rush of mud and water tumbling down the slope toward them. Without warning, the earth gave way beneath him.

He fell, skidding over the edge of the cliff in a rush of water, earth, and stones. A hand clamped onto his left wrist, halting his descent and nearly jerking his shoulder from its socket. In one heart-stopping instant, he hung suspended above the ravine, swinging from Marcus's hand. Seventy-five feet below him, the rock-strewn riverbed promised a swift and painful death.

Marcus knelt above him, his face beet red with exertion.

"Someone grab his other hand!" he shouted to his companions.

Devin spit dirt and water. Twisting frantically, he searched for another anchor, terrified that Marcus's grip wouldn't hold. He snatched at a root with his right hand but it snapped off, pitching him forward. His face smacked into rock on the side of the cliff, splitting his lip and bruising his cheek. He blinked to clear his eyes, his shoulder burning with pain. He groped for a handhold, anything to keep him from that final plunge into the ravine below him, but the hillside crumbled away at his touch.

"Devin, hold your right arm up!" Marcus shouted.

Devin tried to obey him, swinging against Marcus's grip to bring his hand above his head. Strong fingers latched onto his right wrist, biting into the bone, but taking some of the pressure off his left shoulder. Slowly, they hoisted him upward.

Another cascade of earth and stones battered his head and shoulders, eroding the cliff face still further. For an instant, he feared his rescuers might die, too, in the act of trying to save him. But more hands grabbed and held him. Gaspard and Marcus hauled him up until his head and arms were back above the edge of the cliff. Adrian grasped the waist of Devin's trousers and hoisted him over the edge, pulling him backwards to safety.

His rescuers collapsed on the ground around him. Devin lay face down on the muddy path for a moment, his breath ragged. He still half expected the entire hillside to give way beneath him. When the ground remained solid and steady, he could have sobbed with relief. A hand touched his back and he turned over cautiously. Armand was crouched beside him.

"Are you hurt?" the bard asked, his voice anxious.

Devin shook his head. "Not seriously, anyway."

He sat up unsteadily with Armand's assistance. He looked for Marcus first, in the figures gathered around him. His bodyguard was seated a few feet away, grimacing as he massaged his arm. Devin extended his hand.

"Thank you for saving my life," he murmured.

Marcus looked him in the eye and drew a shaky breath. "That's my job, *monsieur*, in case you've forgotten," he said curtly. "And while you're being grateful, I doubt that I could ever have pulled you up from there alone."

"I realize that," Devin said, looking at Adrian and Gaspard. "Thank you, *mes amis*, I owe you my life."

Gaspard gave a nervous laugh. "Thank God you don't take after your brother Jean," he teased. "We'd all have landed in the ravine with you."

It was a grim joke, Devin thought, because for a few moments he'd been afraid they all might die here. In his desire to learn the Chronicles, he had personally put them all at risk. If Gaspard or Marcus lost his life accompanying him on this trip, he would never forgive himself.

A low thin howl broke the silence followed by several sharp yips.

Armand flinched. "Wolves," he groaned. He stood up awkwardly, leaning heavily on his cane. "We have to find shelter. Or believe me, Monsieur Roché, you might rather have died quickly on those rocks down there."

CHAPTER 20

Among Wolves

Devin thought the scene might as well have been conjured from one of the Gothic novels his mother loved to read: twilight on a treacherous cliff trail, rain, thunder, and flickering lightning, thickening mist swirling up from the river below, and the howl of wolves echoing across the foothills. He needed no urging to set off toward shelter and firelight.

Armand suddenly seemed less concerned about his knee. He walked briskly, wielding his cane before him like a weapon. Marcus drew his pistol and Adrian unsheathed a hunting knife. Every cluster of bushes or fallen tree might hide a potential predator, and they were taking no chances.

When a frightened rabbit rushed out from beside the path, right under Devin's feet, he startled, jumping out of its way. Marcus gripped his arm, steering him to the opposite side of the trail.

"For Christ's sake, stay to the inside of the path!" he bellowed. "If you slip again, I'll have to let you fall. I haven't the strength to save you a second time!"

The rain tapered off before they reached the top of the cliff. The thunder became more distant, rumbling off to the east. Ragged clouds scattered before the wind, revealing the waning moon rising above the treetops. Tonight, the moon looked eerie and misshapen, like a yellow apple beginning to go bad. It only added to the nightmarish aspect of the dimly lit scene before them. A main road cut through the clearing in front of them. Across it raced a herd of deer, pursued by a pack of wolves.

Marcus threw out his arm, keeping them within the deeper shadow of the forest. They watched in horrified silence as a doe near the back of the herd faltered; one wolf locked on her throat, another latched onto her side. She crumbled under their attack, thrashing feebly for a moment in the tall grass. She raised her head, mutely, only once before she lay still in the moonlight. The remaining deer bounded into the forest, the sounds of their terrified flight fading away as they descended the steep slope down toward the river. The rest of the wolf pack turned, smelling fresh blood, and loped back to the kill. Their lips curled, exposing savage teeth.

Armand moved his hand slightly, indicating that the route they must take lay diagonally across the near edge of the meadow where a bridge crossed the river chasm. The town of Lac Dupré lay several miles further along the road on the other side.

Gaspard let out a shuddering breath that sounded like a smothered sob. Devin reached out a tentative hand and rested it on his friend's shoulder. Gaspard's face was pale and ghostly and Devin could feel him shaking. There seemed to be no way to reach their destination without attracting the wolf pack's attention. For the second time that day, he questioned the wisdom of this venture. What had possessed him to think that two scholars from the Académie could make their way through fifteen primitive provinces and return home in one piece? No wonder his father had argued against his making the trip from the very beginning.

Marcus gestured slightly with his pistol but Armand shook his head. Armand held up six fingers indicating six wolves and then nodded toward the upper meadow where a furtive movement caught Devin's eye. Another wolf pack was moving cautiously toward the first.

The wolves devouring the deer saw the rival pack approaching and began to growl and snarl, dragging the deer carcass back toward the tree line. The second pack followed; their noses to the ground, their hackles raised.

Armand touched Devin's arm and indicated that they should move toward the bridge quietly, while remaining under the shadow of the trees.

They walked sideways, turned toward the wolves but proceeding toward the bridge on the right. The plan appeared to be working until Gaspard stepped on a brittle stick that snapped like a gunshot. The wolves froze, then turned as one body and focused on the five men gathered under the trees.

Devin's mouth went dry as both packs wheeled and headed directly for them. Marcus's pistol cracked and the lead wolf went down; a second shot reduced the pack by two. But they didn't falter in their attack, and they were coming much too fast to pick them off one at a time.

"Run!" Armand shouted. "They won't cross the bridge!"

The men crashed through the woods, racing toward the bridge but the distance seemed to lengthen in front of them. Even as they leaped over fallen branches and debris, it was obvious that it was impossible to reach safety before the first wolves were upon them.

A huge wolf hurled itself at Devin. The jarring impact of fur and muscle swept him off his feet. He rolled, throwing his arm up as savage jaws snapped at his throat. The wolf clamped down on his wrist instead, snarling and wrestling his arm back and forth as though it were a small animal.

Marcus's pistol cracked. Devin felt the impact as the wolf jerked once and fell dead across his chest. Then more gunshots joined Marcus's, filling the night with one concussion after another, the pounding of horse hooves, and the reek of gunpowder.

Devin clawed his way out from under the furry, blood-covered body.

Marcus dragged him to his feet. "How badly are you hurt?" he demanded, his eyes going to Devin's arm.

"It's just a bite," Devin said, but his sleeve was already soaked in blood.

Marcus took his knife and split the fabric on Devin's sleeve but it was nearly too dark to see. He mopped at the blood with his own handkerchief and then bound the wound with Gaspard's.

Armed horsemen surrounded them. The ground around them was littered with the bodies of wolves, but miraculously everyone else was still standing and appeared unhurt.

The leader of the mounted men inclined his head to Armand. "It is late to be out walking, Master Bard," he said. "You shouldn't subject yourself or your friends to such danger."

"It is late to be out hunting, Monsieur Chastel," Armand responded coolly.

"It depends entirely on what prey you are seeking," Chastel retorted.

"Tonight, my men were preparing to reduce the size of the Forêt d'Halatte's wolf pack. Thank you for gathering so many here in one spot. You made our job a simple one."

"Most men hunt wolves with rifles," Armand said, suspiciously. "Why would you carry nets, as well?"

Chastel shrugged. "Don't question the techniques of those who just saved your life, Armand," he answered. "I may not be inclined to intervene in the future."

Puzzled by Armand's animosity, Devin pushed past Marcus to thank their rescuer.

"Thank you for your assistance, Monsieur Chastel," he said. "Another moment and I fear we might not have survived."

Chastel bowed. "And who do I have the pleasure of addressing?"

Devin lifted the leather pouch that held his official papers from around his neck and passed them up.

"Devin Roché," he said. "This is my bodyguard, Marcus Beringer."

Chastel returned the pouch without opening it.

"I'm Jean Chastel," he said. "I had heard rumors that you might be coming through my province. I would have thought Armand would know better than to bring you through my forest at dusk. I would prefer it not fall to me to have to notify your father that his youngest son was killed by wolves on my estate." He extended a hand to Gaspard. "And you must be Gaspard Forneaux."

Gaspard shook his hand. "I am, *monsieur*."

Chastel's hand fluttered. "Enough formalities, you are obviously wet and chilled. Let me offer you the hospitality of my home, tonight."

"An escort into town will be sufficient," Armand growled.

"Nonsense," Chastel replied. "My house is closer. Besides, our Chancellor's son seems a bit worse for wear. Surely you won't deny him a hot meal and medical attention? Tomorrow

you can take him to your house, Armand. Tonight, allow me
to entertain all of you."

Chastel made five of his men dismount and give Armand's
party their horses. Devin felt instantly safer, traveling well
above the level of snapping jaws, but he questioned, after
what he had seen tonight, whether a horse could truly outrun
a wolf. In spite of the size of their group and the large number
of armed men, Chastel didn't linger in the forest. He led
them across the meadow, past the massacred deer carcass,
and through several miles of pasture beyond.

Chastel's mansion faced the famous Lac Dupré. The water lay
peaceful and still, its glass-like surface luminous with moonlight and stars, mirroring the night sky above it. Tendrils of
mist played across the water, resembling sylphlike dancers,
twirling in the moonlight. The serene atmosphere dimmed
as the howls of wolves echoed again in the distance. Devin
imagined their teeth tearing into the still-warm flesh of the
fallen doe, and shuddered.

They were treated like royalty from the time they crossed
the threshold into Chastel's beautiful château. Greeting them
in an elegant entrance hall, Chastel's servants directed them
immediately to spacious guest rooms, arranging for baths
and clean clothing.

Surrounded by the familiar comforts of servants and airy,
lighted-filled rooms Devin was truly tempted to abandon
his quest and return to his father's house in Coreé. Tonight,
the glaring inconsistencies between the information in the
Archives and the Chronicles seemed like too great a problem
for him to tackle.

He was taken upstairs to one of Chastel's guest rooms,
where Marcus unwound Gaspard's blood soaked handkerchief

141

and examined his wrist. The bite was still bleeding, the tooth marks deep and painful. A ragged flap of skin lay open, revealing the tendons and muscle beneath. His wrist was already bruised and discolored.

"This is bad," Marcus pronounced. "I've already sent for Chastel's physician. This could easily become infected."

Devin nodded, acquiescing. He wasn't about to question the judgment of a man who saved his life twice in the same day.

"Thank you again, Marcus. I'm sorry that . . . "

Marcus cut him off. "I'll go and see about that physician."

Devin smiled; Marcus seemed to be back to normal, and he had pushed away the nagging doubts that had been haunting him about his bodyguard. It felt good to be free of them.

CHAPTER 21

The Beast of Gévaudan

Devin arrived late for dinner, his wrist swathed in bandages. Dr. Mareschal had let him go with a stern warning to report back to him if there were any signs of fever or infection. Marcus had hovered like an anxious mother during the doctor's examination and then followed Devin silently downstairs afterwards.

They found the others in the dining room, gathered around the lower half of a massive table. Five candelabras lit the long expanse of white linen, while sconces illuminated the walls with golden pools of light. The heads of deer, wolves, and mountain lions, stuffed and mounted, stared down on the gathering with sightless, glass eyes.

Chastel rose from his seat at the end of the table when Devin entered.

"I trust everything is well?" he asked, his eye on the bandages.

Devin, who was blessedly insulated from pain after a glass of red wine laced with a strong pain killer, affected nonchalance. "There's no permanent harm done," he answered.

"Except that you might have lost a hand," Marcus observed ominously, "or bled to death."

A servant pulled out a chair, seating Devin at his host's right. Chastel settled back down beside him, pressing a glass of wine into his hand.

"Perhaps a taste of home will ease some of your discomfort. This wine comes all the way from Sorrento, from your father's own vineyards."

Devin accepted it with thanks, obediently sipping the proffered glass before considering any of the food spread out before him. Dr. Mareschal's treatment had been painfully thorough, including a meticulous swabbing of the wound with strong antiseptic and at least a dozen stitches. Though he was trying hard not to show it, he felt shaky, and sick in his stomach, and would much rather have stayed upstairs in the guest room Chastel had assigned him.

Marcus helped himself to bread and several thick slices of roast venison.

"Your wolves seem especially aggressive, Monsieur Chastel," he said offering the platter to Devin.

Devin shook his head after one look at the meat. The sight of deer flesh, prepared for human consumption, was revolting tonight. If anyone pressed him to eat it, he would be forced to leave the table.

"They are not my wolves," Chastel corrected Marcus. "The wolves of Ombria have always had a reputation for ferocity. Our Chancellor has wisely instituted a bounty on wolf pelts to reduce the population. Our governor encourages our residents to capitalize on it."

"Most people have neither the weapons nor the training for such a dangerous undertaking," Armand protested.

"I agree," Chastel answered. "That is why I consider it

144

my duty to protect the people of Lac Dupré by conducting a quarterly wolf hunt. Thank God, my men and I arrived when we did tonight."

Marcus speared a large piece of the dark red meat. "This is excellent venison, *monsieur*."

Devin took another swallow of wine and looked away. He noticed that, although Gaspard was toying with his meat, he had yet to put a piece of it in his mouth.

"I have never known wolves to attack a party of armed men before," Marcus said, wielding his knife with the precision of a surgeon's scalpel.

Chastel shrugged. "The wolves do not fear the local men who cross my forest because they do not carry guns."

"The law forbids peasants to own firearms," Armand pointed out coldly.

Chastel continued as though he hadn't spoken. "I'm sure you noticed the yips interspersed with the howling tonight. That is the young pups calling to the pack. Early May is whelping season, by June the bitches are hunting to feed their young. That's why more people are killed and injured by wolves in early summer than any other time of year."

"Surely, there are some safeguards that could be put in place?" Gaspard said.

"Wise men avoid this forest at dusk," Chastel said, looking at Armand. "You were raised here, Armand. Surely, I do not have to remind you of how dangerous this area can be. Why did you risk the lives of your friends tonight?"

Armand's fork clattered onto his plate; his face flushed with anger. Before he could respond, Adrian sprang to his defense.

"We intended to reach Lac Dupré by late afternoon, Monsieur Chastel, but the weather delayed us. The bridge

145

at Beaulieu washed out. We had no alternative but to take the long way around."

Chastel grunted and then gestured with his knife in Armand's direction. "My apologies, I did not know about the bridge. I'll send some men in the morning to assess the damage. I'll see it is repaired and back in service as quickly as possible."

Adrian inclined his head. "Thank you, *monsieur*, and thank you for rescuing us earlier." He hesitated a moment before adding. "Your hospitality tonight is very welcome."

Chastel smiled. "Ombria's Master Bard is guaranteed food and lodging in any home in this province. Surely, you never thought that mine would be excluded."

"I could have slept with both eyes shut in my own house," Armand muttered.

Devin winced at the insult but Chastel merely seemed amused by his guest's continued resentment.

Their host waved a hand airily. "Fortunately, you must bear with my poor accommodations for only one night. Tomorrow, my men will see you all back to town safely." Chastel held up a finger. "I must admit I intend to require the normal compensation for the lodging of a bard. Tonight, Armand, you must favor us with several tales from the Chronicle when dinner is over."

Devin downed another glass of wine in the hostile silence that followed Chastel's request.

After dinner, Chastel directed them to gather by the fire in the sitting room. Devin would have given anything just to go to bed but he rose to follow the others. When he stood, the floor swayed disconcertingly beneath him. He put one hand on the table to steady himself.

Gaspard took his elbow. "God, Dev, are you drunk?" he hissed.

"Maybe," Devin responded. He'd had multiple glasses of wine and nothing to eat.

Gaspard grunted. "Well, I can hardly blame you," he confided, as they walked. "After today, I've even considered going home."

Devin stopped unsteadily to look at him. "Have you?"

"Haven't you?" Gaspard retorted. "God, you almost died twice today. I didn't sign on for this and neither did you. Are you certain this business with the Chronicles is worth it?"

Devin resumed his progress down the long paneled hall. "I don't know," he murmured.

When they reached the sitting room, Devin slumped into an armchair by the fire, not certain whether he would be able to get up again without help. Everything around him had assumed a pleasant haziness, which just made him want to close his eyes. He passed a hand over his face and tried to focus on Armand.

He'd half expected Adrian to take Armand's place tonight as storyteller. Armand's face had been gray with fatigue at dinner. Now, as he stood before the fire, his stance was rigid. Whatever quarrel he had with Chastel, it was obvious tonight's rescue had not improved Armand's opinion of the man.

Armand waited for them all to settle around him and then bowed dramatically. It seemed that he refused to allow exhaustion to alter his performance.

"*The Beast of Gévaudan,*" he said, introducing his story.

"*Many years ago, in the Mageríde Mountains just north of Lac Dupré, there were many wolves. In the spring, they decimated the flocks and stalked the shepherds' children. Each season it seemed the wolves grew more aggressive and*

147

the peasants were less able to protect their flocks and their families. Even though they build great bonfires at night to protect their sheep, every morning at least two or three more were missing. At night, the wolves crept in silently, always attacking the sheep at the back of the neck, breaking their spines or tearing out their throats."

Devin's hand involuntarily cradled his right wrist against his chest, imagining what might have happened to him, had he not imposed his arm between his throat and those snapping jaws.

". . . the peasants appealed to the powerful nobleman who owned all the land around to kill the wolves. But the nobleman seemed more interested in studying the wolf packs instead. He watched them from the safety of his château, and took notes about them in a little book he always carried with him. He even followed them into the mountains, to observe their behavior. Rumor claimed he had acquired a wolf cub as a pet. He fed it on the scraps from his table and trained it to obey his commands. As time passed the cub grew much bigger and stronger. Soon people saw a huge wolf running with the pack. It was twice the size of a normal wolf and its fur had a reddish tinge. The shepherds began to call it the Beast of Gévaudan.

"Now, at the foot of the mountain, lived a shepherd named Jacques and his ten-year-old son Emile. Emile's mother had died the winter before and there were only the two of them raising their sheep together. Little Emile watched his father's flock during the day but at night his father insisted that he stay safely inside the house. Each night, Emile's father told him to bolt the door and not to open it until light dawned on the mountain above their cottage.

"One night, just before Emile went to bed, he heard the howling of the wolves. It started in the forest below the

house and came closer and closer. Emile thought of his father alone on the slope, watching the sheep, and he took the poker from the fireplace, weighing it in his hand. He stood inside the door of the cottage, his heart beating like a drum, and waited. Soon the sheep began to bleat and Emile could hear his father's voice trying to calm them but the howling came closer and closer. Then the terrified cries of dying sheep filled the night, and above that sound was the anguished cry of a wounded man. Emile knew it was his father. Without hesitation, he unbolted the door. Carrying the poker in his hand, he ran out to save him.

"Now, that night the moon was full and Emile could see the wolves silhouetted against the light of the bonfires. The sheep were scattered, they lay dead or dying, but what chilled him to the bone was the sight of the Beast of Gévaudan poised above his father's still body. Emile took no thought for himself but ran toward his father, brandishing the poker in his hand.

"The Beast raised its head, its muzzle smeared with blood, and growled at Emile. And in that instant, Emile noticed its reddish fur and its strange haunting eyes; round and blue like a man's. And then Emile swung the poker, striking the wolf across the face. The wolf cried out and backed away, and Emile struck it again across the shoulders. The wolf threw up its head, howling in pain. It backed away, slinking into a clump of bushes on the hillside.

"Emile bent down quickly and began to drag his father toward the house. But suddenly he heard rustling in the bushes, and he stopped, raising the poker again. In the moonlight, Emile saw a naked man stumble from the bushes. Blood dripped from his forehead and his back. As he ran off into the forest, the other wolves followed him in a pack.

"*Now, Emile saved his father's life that night, but all their sheep were dead. They had no way to make a living there at the foot of the mountain. So, when Jacques was able to travel, they packed up their few belongings and moved to the town of Lac Dupré, away from the mountains, and the forest, and the wolves.*"

Devin realized he had been holding his breath. He exhaled, releasing his clenched fist. Armand's stories rarely ended happily and he was relieved to find that this one had.

But then, Armand held up his hand. He hadn't finished.

"*On the day that Emile and Jacques left for Lac Dupré,*" the bard continued, "*they passed the nobleman and his son out riding. Now the son had always been a big, handsome young man with red hair and blue eyes, but now Emile saw that he bore a terrible l-shaped scar across his forehead. It was exactly the same shape as the poker Emile had used to fight off the Beast.*"

"Enough, Armand!" Chastel protested, rising. "You disappoint me. You insist on the authenticity of your Chronicle, and yet you spout off fairytales to frighten the children."

Armand's gaze was cool and steady. "As Master Bard, I assure you that my information comes from a reliable source."

Chastel shook his head. "A frightened ten-year-old boy is hardly a dependable witness."

"In your opinion," Armand said.

"In my opinion," Chastel agreed. He took a deep breath. "Perhaps we should call the evening to a close." He glanced at Devin. "Young Monsieur Roché would be better off in bed, and so would the rest of you. I pray tomorrow will be a better day for you all."

When Devin made no attempt to drag himself up from the depths of the armchair, Marcus offered him a hand. It was as though he had just watched a stage production where Armand and Jean Chastel were both actors. He felt peculiarly distanced from the action and yet apprehensive at the same time, as though this conflict might somehow expand to involve him, if he wasn't careful to avoid it.

"Goodnight," Devin said to Chastel. "Thank you again for your help."

"I was glad to be of assistance," their host answered. "Please, sleep as long as you like in the morning. And don't hesitate to call for Mareschal in the night should you need him."

When they walked upstairs, Devin pulled Armand aside in the hallway.

"I don't understand what went on here tonight," he said. "Chastel has been nothing but courteous to us, and yet you continue to antagonize him."

"You have no idea what he is capable of," Armand replied. "I have known him and his family for a long time."

"Whatever he may have done in the past, he saved our lives tonight," Devin reminded him. "I have no illusions; I would have died, if he and his men hadn't arrived in time to drive off those wolves."

"I have been trying very hard to like you," Armand said, his face set into hard lines, "even though we come from very different backgrounds. At first, I thought you were merely young and naïve, but now I fear you are short-sighted as well. Things here are not what they seem and you would do well to look beyond the obvious."

Devin ran a hand over his face, trying to reorder his thoughts. Tonight, he was poorly equipped to fight verbal battles.

"All I know is that I owe Chastel my life," he replied. "I would much rather be here than back in that forest among wolves."

151

Armand's smile was strangely feral. "You are still among wolves, Monsieur Roché, and you aren't even wise enough to realize it." He tapped Devin's chest with one finger. "Go back to Coreé while you still can. You don't belong here."

CHAPTER 22

Unavoidable Delays

By the time Devin crawled between the crisp linen sheets, in one of Chastel's guest rooms, he was almost too tired to appreciate them. The drug and alcohol induced stupor that had allowed him to remain upright all evening was beginning to fade. His head ached dully, his wrist throbbed, and the shoulder he'd wrenched in the fall on the cliff trail hurt every time he moved it. He slept fitfully, dreaming of savage packs of wolves and vicious snapping teeth.

Wakening once in the middle of the night, he was certain that he heard the click of claws on the floor outside his room. The sound repeated, growing louder and then softer, and then louder again, as though an animal crossed in front of his closed door time and time in the darkness.

Softly, the door opened. Candlelight flickered in the hall. Claws tapped across the threshold then muffled as they hit the thick carpet by the bed. The plume of a tail fluttered once above the footboard as a shaggy head appeared beside the bed, tongue lolling, blue eyes glowing softly in the darkness.

Devin jerked upright. "Marcus!" he yelled. The wolf vanished; the door closed soundlessly an instant later.

Marcus emerged from the covers on his cot in the corner. "What's the matter?" he asked.

"There was a wolf . . . ," Devin began. "I heard it in the hallway!" He stopped before putting his thoughts into words. His waking dreams made everything he experienced during the night suspect, and he was reluctant to share his fears with Marcus.

"It's only Chastel's wolf hounds," Marcus said quietly. "I heard them earlier in the night and got up to look. They seem to pace endlessly up and down the hall. It gave me a start, too, after Armand's story."

Devin's laugh was shaky. If only he could believe Marcus's explanation. "I was dreaming of wolves. I thought I'd imagined them here, too."

"How's your wrist?" Marcus asked him.

Devin didn't answer. The bandage felt tight and even his fingers throbbed. He suspected that, despite Mareschal's thoroughness, the wound might be infected.

Marcus lighted the oil lamp by his cot. "Let me see," he said, rising to examine Devin's puffy fingers and bandaged wrist. "Your hand and arm are warm. Do you think you're feverish?"

"I have no idea," Devin answered. It had been years since he'd suffered from any childhood illnesses and their symptoms were long forgotten.

"Let me send for Mareschal," Marcus said. "If nothing else, he can give you something to help you sleep."

Mareschal arrived promptly, a cloak thrown over his evening clothes. It was obvious that he had yet to retire for the night but he seemed unwearied and affable.

"This isn't unexpected, Monsieur," he said, folding his cloak over the back of a chair. "Those puncture wounds were deep and there was significant tearing. I would have been surprised if you escaped without infection. Let me examine your wrist again, and then I'll give you more laudanum for the pain."

Laudanum? So, that's what he'd been given earlier. Devin should have suspected as much. He'd felt oddly detached all evening but he hadn't made the connection.

"That's hardly necessary," he protested.

When Mareschal unwrapped the bandage, Devin's wrist looked red and swollen. Several tooth marks still oozed blood. Mareschal took Devin's pulse and put a hand against his forehead.

"You are running a fever but it's not particularly high. I insist that you stay here a day or two until I'm certain there's no further cause for concern. I'll speak to Chastel."

"Surely, we've bothered him enough," Devin protested.

Mareschal waved away his objection. "It won't be a problem."

He swabbed Devin's wrist with antiseptic again, and wrapped it in clean linen.

"Elevate your wrist when you're lying down," he instructed. "That will help with the swelling and the pain."

He left a glass of red wine spiked with a few drops of laudanum on the night table. Now that he realized what he'd been given, Devin was reluctant to take it.

"Drink it and get some sleep while you can," Marcus urged him after Mareschal had left them. "Who knows what kind of accommodations we will find at Vielle's house."

Devin grudgingly swallowed some of the red liquid.

"When did you write to your father last?" Marcus asked.

"Not since Pireé. We've been nowhere that we could send letters, anyway."

"And yet a great deal has happened," Marcus pointed out. "Your father promised the Council that you would be sending reports back from each province. Don't make him a liar."

Devin gestured at his wrist. "At this point, I'm not sure I can write."

"Then dictate your letters to Gaspard," Marcus suggested. "We've veered from your original itinerary. It's important that your father knows where you are and what you're doing."

"Hearing that we were attacked by wolves won't reassure him."

Marcus sat down on his cot. "If he asked you to come home, would you do it?"

Devin considered it for a moment before answering. "I guess I would have to, if he insisted. I feel I have barely scratched the surface here. Armand has shared nothing with me except love ballads and cautionary tales. He continues to withhold the portions of the Chronicle I am most interested in."

"Armand doesn't trust you," Marcus replied. "I'm not certain he trusts anyone but Adrian. It won't improve the situation if you have to spend additional time here with Chastel."

"Chastel saved my life," Devin objected. "I will always be grateful for that, no matter what Armand thinks of him." A pleasant lassitude was creeping over him and he lay back on the pillows. "Can we talk about this in the morning?"

"Of course," Marcus said. But his lamp was still burning when Devin closed his eyes.

Devin wakened much later, when Gaspard sat down on his bed. The rays of the sun streaming in the window indicated it must be nearly noon. He pushed his tousled hair out of his eyes.

"I didn't mean to sleep so long," he apologized.

"I only got up a little while ago myself," Gaspard replied. "I think all of us were exhausted. How do you feel?"

"Better, I think," Devin answered. He flexed his fingers, and wished he hadn't.

"Mareschal says you still have a fever. I'm supposed to call him when you waken." Gaspard toyed a moment with the maroon fringed comforter, avoiding Devin's eyes.

"What is it?" Devin asked, sitting up awkwardly.

"Armand's gone," Gaspard replied. "He and Adrian left this morning."

"Gone?" Devin asked, his heart thumping. "Gone where?"

Gaspard pointed. "Just into town. His home is in Lac Dupré. Have you forgotten?"

"No," Devin answered. "He's just so unpredictable."

"He was angry because Marcus told him that Mareschal wanted you to stay here for a few days more," Gaspard continued. "He suggested that Armand could stay too, and teach you the Chronicle while you're recovering."

"I imagine that went badly," Devin murmured. "What did Armand say?"

Gaspard gave him a sideways glance, a smirk spreading across his face. "Do you want a direct quote?" he asked.

Devin grinned. "Of course."

"He said, 'If Monsieur Roché is foolish enough not to take my advice and return to Coreé, tell him to come and find me when he's done kowtowing to Jean Chastel.'"

Devin smiled; it was no worse than he would have expected.

"Armand advised me to go home last night," he explained.

"Perhaps you should consider that," Gaspard said, his dark eyes unreadable.

Devin shook his head. "I don't intend to, but I think you should."

"Go home without you?" Gaspard asked, raising his eyebrows. "I don't think so."

"Listen," Devin said, "up until last night, it never occurred to me that one of us might actually die on this trip. I don't want that person to be you. I can call on the resources my father gave me. We can purchase horses and guards to escort you back to Pireé. You can board a ship home and leave this all behind. It would relieve my mind if you'd go. If something happens to you, Gaspard, I will feel responsible."

Gaspard laughed and shrugged. "I won't go back to Coreé without you. We were attacked by wolves last night, and all of us survived. How much worse could it get, for God's sake? Besides, so far, nothing's happened to anyone but you," he pointed out. His face turned sober. "Did Marcus tell you, I found another one of those creepy, little red crosses outside your door this morning?"

Devin felt a chill slither up his spine. "I haven't even talked to Marcus this morning."

Gaspard grimaced. "I probably wasn't meant to tell you. It's gone now. Marcus took it out onto the gravel drive a few minutes ago and burned it."

Devin dropped his head back on the pillow. "Someone must be following us. I can't think of any other explanation."

"There are several other possibilities," Gaspard hinted darkly. "But none that I would like to put into words at the moment. Maybe you should reconsider going home, Dev. I would go back to Coreé, if you'd come, too."

Devin shook his head. "I can't. Armand keeps hinting at all these dark secrets that the Chronicle contains and yet, so far, he has only taught me fairytales to prevent children from wandering off alone. He's keeping the historical part of Ombria's Chronicle to himself. I have to stay long enough to find out why he's holding back. If I am supposed to be reporting to my father about the state of things in Ombria, then I need to be able to give him actual facts. And if I discover huge discrepancies between the Chronicles and the Archives, then I need to tell him that, too. He'll expect the truth from me, if nothing else."

Gaspard turned to look at him, his face deadly serious. "Your father's the Chancellor Elite of Llisé, Dev; don't you think he already knows the truth?"

CHAPTER 23

Family Secrets

When Mareschal returned to check on Devin, he left another glass of red wine mixed with laudanum. Devin didn't drink it. He already felt lightheaded and disoriented, and he didn't intend to spend the afternoon sleeping. When Marcus reappeared, Devin insisted on going downstairs to thank his host for agreeing to let them stay a few days more.

A servant directed them to the study, where he found Chastel seated at a huge desk. Three walls were lined by book shelves; the fourth was covered in framed portraits. Above the shelves, more hunting trophies encircled the room. It reminded Devin of a wing in the Natural Science Department at the Académie.

Chastel rose to greet Devin. "How are you this morning?" he asked kindly.

"Much better than I would have been without Mareschal's ministrations, I'm sure," Devin replied. "I simply want to make certain we are not causing you any added inconvenience by extending our stay. We can easily continue into Lac Dupré. I'm sure there is a physician there, as well."

Chastel grunted. "There is only a midwife and an apothecary. So believe me, you are better off here. I am more than happy to be of assistance. Your father would expect nothing less of me."

"Still," Devin said. "Unexpected house guests are a bother."

Chastel shook his head. "Not in my home. This is primarily a hunting lodge. My friends often spend a month at a time here. There is no lack of game and, despite the disadvantages of a healthy wolf pack, they provide exciting prey for my guests."

The memory of snarling wolves hurtling across the meadow toward the defenseless deer rose unbidden in Devin's mind. He put a hand on the back of a chair and took a deep breath.

"Please, sit down," Chastel invited.

"Thank you," Devin said, settling into the huge leather armchair in front of his desk. Marcus wandered off to examine the mounted heads along the wall.

"Can I get you some coffee or wine?" Chastel asked.

Devin shook his head. "I just ate. Your servants are very efficient. I had breakfast delivered to my room."

"At my request," Chastel said, dropping back into his own chair. "I thought you might want to spend the day in bed."

"I may go back upstairs again shortly," he admitted.

"Please, treat my home as your own. Whatever you need or want, you have only to ask."

Devin smiled. "Thank you. I appreciate your kindness."

"Tell me about your trip," Chastel requested, "René Forneaux and I went to the Université together. We correspond on a regular basis. He mentioned your intention to tour the provinces with his son when he wrote to me at Christmas. I had hoped to be able to meet you both if you came through this area. I'll admit, I was puzzled to find you on foot, though. Surely, you would be safer traveling on horseback?"

"I'm sure we would be," Devin admitted. "But I didn't want to call attention to myself."

"Ombria's roads can be dangerous," Chastel warned. "It was prudent of your father to send a bodyguard with you. There is no love for the residents of Coreé in the provinces."

"That is why I chose not to advertise my identity by arriving on horseback," Devin replied.

"Well, you travel in strange company; I never expected to find you with Armand," Chastel said, "but then, René did mention your interest in the Chronicles. He found it an odd obsession for an archivist."

Devin shrugged. "I view the Chronicles as just another manifestation of history."

"An imprecise one," Chastel retorted. "Surely, Armand's performance last night demonstrated that?"

"I can't judge the merit of his story because I am not familiar with its historic context, but I feel as though I should apologize for Armand's behavior," Devin replied.

Chastel smiled. "Why? It is a quarrel of long-standing, and not anything you contributed to. Just because Armand and I must live in the same village, doesn't mean we have to like each other." He leaned back easily in his chair and laced the fingers of his hands. "All of the unpleasantness started a long time ago, before my lifetime, and despite his adamancy, long before Armand's. And that is the crux of the problem. Little Emile in the story was Armand's grandfather, and the nobleman was mine."

Devin frowned. "So, the nobleman's son was your father?"

Chastel shook his head. "He was my uncle, Charles Chastel. He died when he was sixteen."

Chastel rose and walked partway around the room, pausing before a portrait. He beckoned to Devin to join him.

"The artist was very kind. The scar Armand mentioned was extensive."

Devin studied the face of the boy in the portrait. His strange blue eyes were lighter than normal and fiercely feral. An l-shaped scar marred his forehead, rakishly ending above his left eye.

"I'm not certain what you are implying," Devin said, afraid to draw his own conclusions. "Where did the scar come from?"

"He fell from his horse onto a stone wall. He almost bled to death. I think, it might have been better if he had," Chastel said softly. He looked toward the window, his eyes unfocused. "My uncle was deeply disturbed. He was odd from the time he was born, fascinated by animals but unable to cope with people. He was large and awkward, and he never talked. The village children teased and chased him. They called him a monster. He was happiest out in the woods alone. People frightened him, even the servants here in my grandfather's house. I have no doubt that he roamed the mountainsides half naked when he could evade his father's bodyguards. He was fascinated by wolves, and my grandfather's preoccupation with them only stemmed from trying to keep track of his son." He pulled a leather-bound journal from a nearby bookcase. "Here," he said, handing it to Devin. "I believe this is what an archivist calls a primary source."

Devin flipped through the pages. Each dated entry contained intimate details about Charles's life:

Thursday June 10 – Charles released all the rabbits from the game keeper's cages. He is still smiling, going around the

163

house humming those strange little wordless songs he invents when he is happiest.

Sunday Oct. 20 – Charles brought home a wolf pup. God help us, I believe he intends to keep it in the house. It follows him like a shadow and he murmurs strange sounds to it, as though they are actually communicating. I feel as though I have been given a changeling. I don't know what to do with him.

Devin closed the journal and gave it back to Chastel.

"This is too personal. I don't feel right reading it."

Chastel's face was flushed. "I want you to know that Charles was never some strange hybrid who could change from man to wolf at will, as Armand implied," he said in disgust. "And yet, that was the rumor that developed about him, thanks to Emile Vielle."

"So, there never was a Beast of Gévaudan?" Devin asked.

"No, there was; that part of the story is true and well documented," Chastel admitted. "The Beast was just a huge, oddly colored wolf. My grandfather killed it." He swiveled to view the wall behind him. "It's mounted right there."

Devin glanced up to see the snarling lips and vicious teeth of a giant reddish wolf. The glass eyes had been tinted blue as though in imitation of Armand's legend. A sudden chill swept over him; a long violent shiver that shook him from head to toe. He rested a hand on the bookcase for support.

"You should be in bed, resting," Chastel said in concern, "and here I am, keeping you from it, by droning on about my sordid family history."

"No, tell me the end of the story," Devin protested, folding his arms over his chest. "If your grandfather killed that huge wolf while Charles was still alive, then why did people come to associate your uncle with the Beast of Gévaudan?"

Chastel turned away from him, his face lost in shadow.

"My grandfather returned home from the forest, the morning after the Beast was killed, to discover Charles was missing. He rode to town with some of his men, where he saw my uncle fondling the lambs in the marketplace. He had released them all once before, and Jacques Vielle began to throw stones at him, shouting for him to go away. He hit Charles several times and knocked him down. Before my grandfather could reach him, Charles threw himself on Emile's father, biting him on the throat." Chastel's voice trailed off and Devin leaned closer to hear him. "My grandfather shot him."

Devin slid back down in the leather armchair, his heart beating erratically. For a moment he thought he was going to be sick.

"Your grandfather killed his own son?" he asked, unable to focus on anything else.

Chastel's voice was devoid of emotion. "My grandfather had no choice. He was trying to protect him from the townspeople. You see, Charles killed Jacques Vielle. Dozens of people saw it happen. Can you imagine what that crowd would have done to him?"

"But your grandfather had a gun!" Devin protested. "He had his men with him. They should have protected your uncle! Surely, your grandfather could have used his influence to save him!"

"Save him for what?" Chastel asked angrily. "Weeks in a jail cell and then a hanging? A bullet was kinder."

Marcus loomed up behind the armchair. "How did Charles kill Vielle?" he asked.

Devin had almost forgotten he was there. It was a relief to know he hadn't been told this story alone . . . that there would be someone else he could talk to about it later.

"He crushed his windpipe, just like a wolf would do," Chastel answered tightly. "And, of course, that just fed the legend further."

Devin was speechless. Suddenly, Armand's animosity made much more sense but then so did Chastel's anger last night when Armand had told his version of the "Beast of Gévaudan". It had been incredibly rude to tell that story here, to flaunt it in Chastel's face. It was inevitable that such a dramatic tale would find its way into the Chronicle, but it was extraordinarily cruel of a Master Bard to subject a host to that kind of humiliation in his own home.

"Monsieur Chastel," he stammered. "I am so sorry."

Chastel exhaled audibly. "Armand would have told you the rest of the story eventually. I thought it best that you hear the Chastels' side of it, too."

Devin ran a shaky hand over his face. "Forgive me, but I still don't understand the connection to the Beast. If dozens of people saw the attack on Vielle, they knew it was simply an angry boy defending himself."

Chastel sighed. "But don't you see? My grandfather killed the Beast the same day. People assumed that because they never saw it again after Charles died . . . that Charles and the Beast were one and the same."

"But that's insane!" Devin protested.

"To you or to me, yes, but these people were ignorant and superstitious. Emile told his story over and over again about seeing a man rise up from the bushes where the wolf had fallen. Maybe he actually saw Charles that night; we'll never know that now. But I can tell you one thing for certain: Charles was not some kind of half-wolf, half-man."

"What a tragedy," Devin said.

Chastel grunted. "They refer to it locally as the 'Curse of the Chastels'. And believe me, the curse still lives on. My mother gave birth to a stillborn baby the year before I was born. But the good people of Lac Dupré decided that it must be another wolf/child. They even claimed that my father killed it at birth rather than have to deal with another scandal." He gave a hollow laugh. "And do you wonder that I have yet to find a woman who will marry me . . . their fathers all enjoy the hunting on my estate, but they don't want Chastel blood in their grandchildren's veins."

Devin shifted uncomfortably. "I don't know what to say."

Chastel shrugged. "It's not necessary that you say anything. It's done me good to get this off my chest. I apologize for airing the family's dirty linen at your expense."

"Don't apologize," Devin said. "I'm only sorry that I can't do something to correct the injustice that has been done."

"Perhaps you could appeal to Armand," Chastel suggested. "Though I doubt it will do any good."

"I intend to," Devin replied. "Armand and I have disagreed before. But if this story has truly been added to Ombria's Chronicle, I would think he would want to make certain that it is accurate."

"Oh, he was very careful," Chastel answered, bitterly. "Didn't you notice? He never claimed Charles was the wolf, he just made it seem that way. He isn't about to be brought up on charges of slander. Who would teach his precious Chronicle, if he's in jail?"

Adrian would, Devin thought. But surely, Armand wasn't foolish enough to risk his position, just to get back at a long dead boy who had killed his great-grandfather? It was the current Jean Chastel that Armand hated, and he would bet that there was some more recent hurt that had put these two men at odds.

Chastel touched Devin's shoulder. "You need to go rest," he said. "Mareschal will have my head if you aren't any better. Perhaps, you'll join me later for dinner if you're up to it?"

"I'll look forward to it," Devin replied. But he knew that, secretly, he would be relieved to leave this place behind as soon as possible, and move on.

CHAPTER 24

The Quest for Truth

Devin went back up to his room, still reeling from the information Chastel had told him. He'd been shown another side of Armand today – a cold and ruthless side – and he was shocked and confused by it. Armand claimed to be adamantly committed to the truth, and yet the story of the Beast of Gévaudan, which had involved members of his own family, was hopelessly skewed. It threw into question everything that Devin believed to be true about Ombria's Chronicle.

"Why don't you lie down and rest?" Marcus suggested, when Devin began to pace.

"Where's Gaspard?" he asked.

"He just went down to the stables," Marcus replied. "I believe Chastel asked him to go riding. They've also scheduled a card game for later this evening."

Devin sat down on the bed, his mind racing. This fever was an inconvenience he could do without. He felt shaky and ill, and without the laudanum, the pain gnawed away at his wrist. The glass of wine Mareschal had left on the table was still there. Devin downed half of it in a single swallow. At the moment, oblivion seemed more attractive than the present reality. He wanted to be free of this château with its vicious wolf packs and morbid history. More than anything, he wanted to go on to Lac Dupré and confront Armand.

Marcus frowned. "Do you feel worse?"

"My wrist hurts," Devin admitted. He grabbed a silk throw off the bed and drew it around his shoulders with shaky hands. "What did you think of Chastel's story?"

Marcus shrugged. "Life is often cruel."

"It goes beyond cruelty when a man murders his own son," Devin replied. "That is the worst kind of betrayal, when death comes unexpectedly at the hands of someone you trust."

Marcus turned away and walked to the window. "It happened a long time ago, Devin, there's no sense getting upset about it now."

"But don't you see? Now I am beginning to doubt some of what Armand has told me," Devin continued. "If he's been inaccurate with the Beast story, what else has he lied about?"

Marcus sat down on the window sill, and propped his ankle on his knee. "Perhaps, he's not lying," he said calmly.

"Well, one of them is," Devin protested.

"Not necessarily," Marcus replied. "Perhaps it is just a matter of perception. Armand told the story from one point of view, Chastel told it from another. Both of them were told the original story by a family member, someone they trusted implicitly. Ultimately, the truth probably lies somewhere between the two. Remember, you haven't heard the whole story from Armand yet."

"Nor, do I want to," Devin retorted, pulling the throw more closely around him.

"And yet, you are intent on learning the entire Chronicle," Marcus reminded him. "Surely, you can't imagine that this story will be the only one that makes you uncomfortable."

Devin pointed a finger at Marcus. "That story should have been kept private. A family tragedy shouldn't be open to public scrutiny."

"And yet, the story had a very public ending," Marcus said. "I doubt it could ever have been kept quiet."

Devin didn't answer. Chastel's story had horrified him. His mind continued to imagine the final scene with brutal clarity, and he wished he could erase it from his memory forever. He was deeply disappointed in Armand, and frustrated beyond words with the delay his injury was causing. Nothing seemed to be going along with the naïve itinerary he'd conceived in the safety of his dormitory room. He'd spent months planning, and yet he hadn't allowed any time for sickness, injury or – who would have guessed it – duplicity on the part of the Master Bard of Ombria.

Marcus shifted on his perch. "What would you do, if you found two documents in the Archives that seemed to contradict each other?"

The answer required no thought. "I would hunt for more information," Devin answered, "something that would corroborate one side or the other."

"Can you not use the same technique here?" Marcus asked.

Devin glanced up. "What if there isn't any additional information? Anyone associated with the Chastels will support them. The villagers are apt to back Armand's version of the story; most of them will have only heard the account preserved in the Chronicle, anyway."

"And yet, there might be a few older citizens," Marcus insisted, "who actually remember the event."

Devin nodded slowly. "Perhaps," he said. His mind skittered back to his conversation with Gaspard earlier. "Marcus, do you think someone is following us?"

His bodyguard's face was expressionless. "It's possible."

Devin could feel the laudanum dulling his senses, gently seducing him into a peaceful, pain-free cocoon. He gave in and lay back against the pillows, letting his head sink into the lavish softness.

"How do you think he got into the château to leave that second red cross?" he asked.

Marcus stood up abruptly. "What second cross?"

Devin had to fight to keep his eyes open. "Gaspard said you found one outside my door this morning," he murmured.

"You must have misunderstood him, "Marcus said with a frown. "I didn't find another cross."

"You burned it on the driveway," Devin insisted doggedly, his eyes closing.

"Get some sleep," Marcus growled.

Devin wakened to a dark, silent house. Dinner had long since come and gone. Marcus lay asleep on his cot. He remembered their earlier conversation. Somehow, in his distress over Chastel's revelations, he had forgotten there was information right here that corroborated Chastel's story; Chastel had handed it to Devin in the study, himself. He got up and crossed the room, careful not to waken Marcus.

When he opened the door, he muffled a startled exclamation. He'd forgotten the wolfhounds. Three of the huge dogs surrounded him, nosing his hands and sniffing at his bare feet. He moved carefully through them, offering harmless open palms to their questing muzzles. In spite of their size, they were surprisingly calm and gentle. They followed him down the stairs, apparently delighted to have found companionship.

Devin lighted an oil lamp on Chastel's desk. The journal lay on the shelf of the bookcase where Chastel had laid it. He took it and sat down in the leather chair where he'd sat earlier in the day. He'd read enough previously to know that Charles had been far from normal and a constant worry to his father. What he needed was an entry that would substantiate that the injury to the boy's face had come from a fall not a poker wielded by a small boy. He'd didn't have to look far.

June 15 – I took Charles riding down near Beaulieu Bridge. He seemed to enjoy the time we spent together. It made me feel guilty. I don't do it often enough. His gratitude is so apparent.

On the way back, I jumped Viveur over the stone wall in front of the house, the way I always do. Charles always goes through the gates but for some reason today he followed me. His horse balked, refusing the jump, and unseating Charles. He landed directly on the wall. I dismounted and ran back, fearing the worst . . . my father died of a broken neck in that very spot after a fall from a horse.

Charles was unconscious. He'd cut his head. I don't believe I've ever seen so much blood. René saw it happen from the house and came running. Together we got him back to his room but it was an hour or more before he came to. René says he'll have a terrible scar – not that it will matter – I guess. Marriage is out of the question and those of us who care for him love him one way or the other. I wonder if he'll be able to understand what happened . . . associate the scar with the injury. He has had so much hurt in his short life, and so much of it is totally incomprehensible to him.

Reluctantly, Devin flipped ahead. There were only a few more passages. His hand trembled as he found the final entry.

July 1 – I buried my oldest son today. How can I ever justify his death to anyone? I can never forgive myself, as long as I live. I took Charles's life with my own hand in view of half the village. Because yesterday, Charles killed a man – Jacques Vielle – that shepherd who moved here from the mountains only a few weeks ago. Vielle was throwing stones at Charles, trying to keep him away from the spring lambs in the marketplace. Vielle thought Charles was going to let them loose again, and no doubt that was his intention; he can't bear to see anything locked up. Vielle hurt Charles, knocked him clear down, and God help him, Charles fought back. He bit Vielle on the neck and crushed his throat. He killed him right there in the marketplace with dozens of people watching. And these peasants, who fear wolves above all things, went after Charles with a viciousness that rivaled any wolf pack. They would have killed him with their bare hands except that I killed him first. Before the first hand was laid upon him, I shot him through the heart. I don't think he ever realized what hit him or that I was the one firing the shot. Dear God, I hope he didn't. What greater burden could a father endure, than to have killed his own son?

Devin laid the journal in his lap and wiped his eyes. The end was every bit as wrenching as he had imagined. He was glad that Marcus wasn't present to witness his current emotional reaction to it. His bodyguard's voice echoed in his head. *"It happened a long time ago, Devin, there's no sense in getting upset over it now."* Hadn't Marcus realized he was speaking to a historian? What was the point in identifying personal or corporate mistakes if a man or an empire couldn't try to avoid them in the future? Chastel viewed his uncle's murder

174

as a mercy, and so, apparently, had his grandfather. And yet, which death showed more compassion: a swift death by someone you loved or a painful, lingering, one at the hands of an angry mob? He shook his head, avoiding that train of thought. Armand would turn it into a religious commentary.

All of a sudden, the dogs jumped up from the rug beside him and went to the door, their scraggly tails wagging. Chastel stood on the threshold.

"Can't you sleep?" he asked, parting the trio with a gentle hand.

Devin stood up, acutely aware of his trespass into Chastel's inner sanctum. "Forgive me . . . " he began.

Chastel waved a hand in dismissal. "Sit down," he said, taking the chair behind the desk. "Please," he added, when Devin remained standing in front of him.

"I apologize for invading your study," Devin persisted, sinking subsiding into the leather chair. "My father would be appalled."

Chastel smiled. Devin saw no hint of repressed anger, and yet he still felt uncomfortable. There was something about Chastel's eyes, in this light, that reminded Devin of someone else.

"Don't worry," Chastel said. "Your father will never hear it from me. I told you to make yourself at home and I meant it. I have nothing to hide from Coreé." He gestured at the journal on Devin's lap. "I see you decided to read that after all."

Devin tapped the cover of the journal. "It suddenly occurred to me that you were right – this is a primary source – and it offers proof of how Charles's injury actually happened."

"What good will it do?" Chastel asked.

"I could read the entry to Armand," Devin offered, "if you would allow me to borrow it."

Chastel laughed. "And do you actually think he would take my great grandfather's word over Emile Vielle's?"

"I don't know," Devin replied. "But I thought, from what I have learned about him, that he cherishes the truth above anything else."

Chastel's face darkened. "Then you don't know him very well."

There was a rush of footsteps on the stairs and the dogs barked, dashing into the hall as though they were some bizarre single entity with twelve legs and three heads. Marcus and Mareschal appeared in the doorway, both of them out of breath.

"I didn't realize you'd planned a party," Chastel said, glancing at Devin in amusement. "Shall I have cook prepare some fresh canapés?"

Marcus crossed the room in a few long strides to loom over Devin.

"Why didn't you waken me?" he demanded.

Devin avoided his eyes. "I assumed you'd rather sleep. You suggested that I search for further information. I wanted to read more of this journal."

Mareschal appeared to be every bit as concerned as Marcus.

"I came in to your room to check on you, *monsieur*, and found you were gone. We were afraid . . . " The Doctor hesitated, and suddenly Devin knew exactly what they had feared.

"I haven't sleepwalked in years," he said coolly, wondering if it had been Marcus or Gaspard who had warned him.

Mareschal inclined his head. "Waking dreams are often accompanied by sleepwalking, *monsieur*, I meant no offense.

176

The last few days have been stressful. It would not be unexpected if you suffered an episode here when you are ill and so far from home."

Devin barely restrained his annoyance. Next, one of them would be suggesting he sleep with a toy to comfort him.

"I assure you, I was completely awake when I came downstairs. I read for only a few moments before Monsieur Chastel joined me. I think he will verify that I have been quite coherent as we talked."

Chastel grinned, apparently enjoying the repartee. "Indeed, you have been. Can I order some coffee or wine for you gentlemen? It may be the middle of the night, but everyone seems wide awake now. We may as well make ourselves comfortable."

Mareschal cupped Devin's forehead with a cool hand and then grasped his wrist.

"You're still feverish, *monsieur*, and your pulse is very rapid. You belong in bed."

"I'm sorry to hear that," Devin remarked. Apparently, his extended nap hadn't done him much good. "I wanted to move into Lac Dupré tomorrow."

"Well, that is out of the question," Mareschal replied. "A wolf bite is quite serious. This infection could have grave repercussions."

"Take care with your choice of words," Devin remarked lightly.

Mareschal continued to hover. "Monsieur Forneaux mentioned that you wanted to acquire medication to help you sleep. How long have you been having nightmares?"

Devin cleared his throat. "I am in need of a supply of sedative," he said carefully, "not a diagnosis. I have already consulted with the leading expert in sleep disorders in Coreé."

Mareschal shifted uneasily. "Still, I prefer not to prescribe drugs without taking a medical background first, *monsieur*. Laudanum has too often been used indiscriminately among Université men."

Devin stood up. "Yesterday evening was the first time I have ever used laudanum, and it was at your insistence, Doctor. I don't intend to use it again unless there is an urgent reason for it. What I need is valerian."

"But laudanum is used extensively for sleep disorders," Mareschal protested. "Valerian is only a mild herbal preparation."

"I am well acquainted with valerian's properties and its use," Devin replied. "It is entirely adequate for my needs."

Chastel stood up, dislodging a few papers from his desk. "For God's sake, Mareschal, give the man what he asked for! He has only to visit the apothecary in town if you refuse, anyway."

"Very well," Mareschal replied. "I will see that you have a supply of valerian before you leave, *monsieur*." He bent to retrieve Chastel's papers and handed them to him without making eye contact.

The camaraderie they had shared earlier had dissolved. Marcus looked haggard, Mareschal ill-at-ease; Chastel probably only hoped that they would all go back upstairs and leave him in peace.

"Perhaps," Devin said, patting the head of the largest wolfhound, "I'll just go back to bed."

"An excellent idea," Mareschal agreed. "Rest is very important. I'll come up and see that you are settled comfortably. In a few days, we'll discuss when you can safely move into Lac Dupré."

The faintest of smiles tugged at Chastel's lips. He touched Devin's shoulder as he passed. "Sweet dreams," he said.

CHAPTER 25

Armand

It was actually four days before Mareschal allowed them to leave. Devin was nearly wild with the delay. While his fever continued to fluctuate, Mareschal regaled him with horror stories of deaths and amputations resulting from infected wolf bites. When they finally boarded Chastel's carriage, Mareschal presented Devin with a list of instructions and promised to visit in a week's time to remove Devin's stitches. Chastel merely chuckled and winked at Devin. Devin was sorry to say goodbye to Chastel, but he was infinitely relieved to escape Mareschal's ministrations.

Devin was thrilled to be outside. The spring rains had brought out new foliage on every tree and bush. The grass was brilliant green and multicolored crocuses peeked from below the hedges. The air was warm and fragrant.

Gaspard was unusually quiet as they headed down the road. Devin wondered if he would have been happier staying at the château where he could spend the day riding, flirting with the serving girls, playing cards, and sampling Chastel's extensive wine cellar. He realized he had given little thought

179

to what Gaspard would do while he studied with Armand. The prospect left him vaguely uneasy.

"You know I can't guarantee your safety, Gaspard," Devin said, reluctantly turning away from the lush countryside displayed outside the coach window. "But I'm very glad you decided to continue."

Gaspard grinned. "Don't worry! I think my safety at home may be in question, too, with my father on the rampage. What are a few wolves in comparison to René Forneaux?"

Devin laughed, feeling light-hearted for the first time in days.

"The provinces hold worse dangers than wolves," Marcus cautioned grimly. "This isn't a journey to have undertaken lightly. I hope we can all return home in one piece but I wouldn't bet on it."

"Ahh," Gaspard chuckled. "Then you're not a gambling man. I'll bet you a hundred francs that all three of us return to Coreé. Dev, you can hold the money and put my bet in; don't forget, I'm penniless."

Ombria's Master Bard was quartered in a large stone house that faced the village square. The building rose two stories, with seven windows across the top and six below. The shutters had faded to a dusty blue; the heavy wooden door was painted red. It opened just as Devin raised his hand to knock.

"Devin!" Adrian greeted him warmly. He ushered them into a spartan hallway, adorned with only a small wooden chest and a row of coat hooks on the wall. "How is your wrist? We've been worried."

"It's well enough," Devin answered. "Is there an inn here in town? Can you tell us where to go so we can leave our things?"

Adrian's smile dimmed. "So you have decided to continue, then? Armand wasn't certain what you intended to do."

"Of course, I want to continue," Devin said. "I've already lost valuable time. Is Armand here?"

"He was a few minutes ago," Adrian answered. "Come back to the kitchen."

Devin dropped his knapsack on the floor. Chastel had replaced his ripped and bloodstained woolen jacket with a beautiful suede one. As he hung the elegant chestnut garment on a hook in the hall, he thought it would probably provide Armand with another opportunity to make derogatory comments about the aristocracy. He followed Adrian and Gaspard to the kitchen, with a feeling of dread.

Gaspard had stopped in the doorway, one arm draped languidly against the doorframe, his head tilted to one side.

"Good morning, *mademoiselle*," he said, his voice soft and silky. "No one told me that Armand had such a beautiful cook."

Devin ducked passed him to see Armand seated in a rocking chair by the fire, a striped cat curled on his lap. To his left, a pretty young woman with dark, curly hair stood barefoot, stirring an immense soup pot.

Armand uncoiled from the rocker with amazing speed, sending the cat shooting into the corner, and swung his cane up as though he meant to strike Gaspard. He stopped it inches from Gaspard's face and then lowered it to rest in the center of his chest.

"The young lady's name is Jeanette Vielle," he said coldly. "She is my only daughter, and off-limits to any young men from Coreé."

Gaspard was surprisingly unruffled by Armand's performance. He deflected the cane with one hand and strode into

181

the room with the arrogance and assurance of a prominent Councilman's son.

"I'll try to keep that in mind," he replied curtly.

Armand grabbed his sleeve. "I meant what I said, Forneaux!"

Devin swallowed. Everything was already off to an explosive start and he hadn't even greeted Armand yet. He stepped forward, hoping to placate him.

"He meant no harm, Armand," he said.

Armand swung around to face Devin. "I don't want any misunderstandings, Roché!" Armand shouted. "Having just come from Chastel's château where serving girls are trained to cater to your every need, I don't want you anticipating the same amenities here."

Devin was offended by his insinuation. "There was no catering . . . " he stammered, glancing at Gaspard for affirmation, "at least, not to my knowledge."

"Forneaux knows what I am talking about," Armand replied, his eyes locked with Gaspard's. "You've been ill, Roché. Perhaps, Chastel felt you weren't up to it."

"Excuse me?" Devin said, angrily. "Should we go out and come back in again? Somehow, we've gotten off on the wrong foot this morning. I will apologize for my friend's lack of courtesy but I fail to see how I have offended you. If you'll direct us to an inn, we won't bother you for the rest of the day."

"You can stay here," Armand growled. "The province maintains rooms for my students. Adrian can take you upstairs. I expect the most circumspect behavior from the three of you. If there are any problems with any one of you, you will all be asked to leave."

"Understood," Devin said, inclining his head. He was completely baffled by Armand's behavior.

He bowed to Jeanette. "Good morning. I'm Devin Roché, I apologize for any misunderstanding. Thank you for allowing us to stay in your home."

To his surprise, she smiled and extended her hand.

"I'm pleased to meet you, *monsieur*. Welcome to Ombria's Bardic Hall. My father gives performances every Friday and Saturday night, and the rest of the week he teaches. Most of his students are with us for a long time. I'm sure I'll get to know you better."

Armand stepped between them, breaking Devin's tenacious hold on Jeanette's fingers.

"This is a special situation, my dear. Monsieur Roché will only be staying a few weeks. He will be spending every available moment studying with me. There will be little time for anything else."

Jeanette lowered her eyes and stepped back. "Yes, Papa."

"Go and take your things upstairs," Armand directed Devin. "Have Adrian bring you down to the Hall when you are done. We'll start immediately."

Generally, Devin had a high tolerance for Gaspard's impertinence, but this morning he was annoyed.

"Why did you do that?" he hissed on the way up the stairs.

Gaspard shrugged. "She's a very pretty girl. How was I to know she was Armand's daughter?"

"Common courtesy demands that you determine her position in the household first, before you make any assumptions . . . "

"For God's sake, don't you go all prim and proper on me!" Gaspard protested, throwing up his hand. "I've already had my fingers smacked. I'll stay out of the cookie jar! I don't need to hear it from you, too!"

Ignoring the exchange, Adrian opened a door halfway down the hall.

"Gaspard, you can use this room and I'll put Devin and Marcus in the room next to you. Lunch will be . . . "

"Thank you," Gaspard interrupted. "But I intend to be out the rest of the day." He didn't even enter the room. He stood in the doorway and threw his knapsack onto the bed, making the shutters rattle.

"Where are you going?" Devin demanded.

"Why the hell do you care?" Gaspard replied, stalking down the hall. "Go learn your damn Chronicle, Dev, and leave me out of it!"

Devin took a step after him but Marcus grabbed his arm.

"Let him go. He'll have his little tantrum and be back later."

"He doesn't even have any money," Devin protested.

Marcus grunted. "Perhaps, that's for the best."

CHAPTER 26

Secrets

Adrian took Devin downstairs; Marcus followed. Devin was certain that Armand would object to Marcus sitting in on his sessions but he decided to let his bodyguard and Armand fight it out.

"You need to choose your battles," Marcus advised Devin on the way down the stairs.

Devin smiled. It was as though Marcus had read his mind. "What do you mean?" he asked.

"I mean," Marcus replied, "that if Gaspard acts like an ass, it shouldn't fall to you to apologize for it."

Devin sighed. "Well, Gaspard wasn't about to."

"Then, it only makes him appear more churlish. If you apologize, it gives the impression that you are assuming responsibility. That could be a dangerous position to be in."

Devin laughed. "I wasn't in the direct line of fire. The cane wasn't aimed at my chest."

Marcus frowned, apparently annoyed by his nonchalance. "There's a lesson to be learned from it, nonetheless. Someday, the weapon might not be a cane wielded by a cranky old man."

Devin bowed. "Point taken," he murmured.

Marcus grunted. "I wonder. Will you remember if the time ever comes?"

Adrian turned to face them. "I'm sorry to say that Armand is always harsh when a new student comes. He claims that if he explains the house rules at the very beginning then it saves misunderstandings later."

"So, the only house rule is to stay away from his daughter?" Devin asked.

Adrian shook his head. "Oh no, there are more. I'm sure he'll tell you the rest today. He overreacted because Gaspard made him angry. He is just very protective of his daughter."

"That's understandable," Marcus replied, as they reached the bottom of the stairs. "Most fathers are."

Adrian opened the door on the right and guided them into a large performance hall. Benches lined the walls and formed two rows in the center. A huge fireplace dominated the opposite end but Devin doubted that it would do much to dispel the chill of four stone walls. Armand sat alone on a stool, adjusting the logs over a newly kindled blaze. Adrian left them silently, closing the door behind him.

Armand waved a hand at another stool.

"Sit here. I'm trying to warm the room up a bit." He turned to study Devin. "You're looking very pale, Monsieur Roché. Are you certain you are up to this?"

"I've been looking forward to it," Devin replied. He sat down opposite him as Marcus drifted into the far corner. Armand followed Marcus with his eyes but he didn't comment on his obvious intention to stay.

Devin cleared his throat and decided to plunge in head first. If Ombria's Chronicle was riddled with bigotry and

186

personal opinion, then it wasn't worth his time. He had to find out before he went any further.

"When we were at Monsieur Chastel's you told the 'Beast of Gévaudan', but you never finished the story because Chastel stopped you. Could you start with that?"

Armand looked up from the fire a moment, his eyes cold. "Are you in the habit of telling your instructors where to begin your course of study?"

"No," Devin said. "But I would like to hear the end of your story." He realized his inappropriate choice of wording as soon as it was out of his mouth but it was too late to correct it.

"My story?" Armand asked in surprise. "Who else's have you heard?"

Devin didn't meet his eyes. "Chastel gave me his grandfather's diary to read."

Armand massaged his knee with one hand. "Did he? And what revelations did you find there?"

"The injury to Charles's head was caused by a fall from a horse," Devin said. "You implied something entirely different."

Armand sat back and looked at him. "Why are you here, Monsieur Roché?"

"I've already told you," Devin replied. "I am interested in your oral tradition. I came to learn Ombria's Chronicle."

"And . . . ?" Armand prompted him.

Devin sighed, acutely aware of Marcus lounging on a bench in the back of the room. "I have discovered that, in some cases, the historical records in the Archives and the Chronicles appear to present very different accounts of the same events. I want to know the truth."

"And yet, you have already decided that written accounts are more accurate."

"I never said that!" Devin objected.

Armand held up a hand. "But that is what you believe. You have just read Jean Chastel's journal, and already you are questioning me . . . and my integrity."

Devin threw diplomacy to the wind. "Yes, I guess I am," he said. Marcus's breath hissed out in disproval but Devin blundered on. "If the Chronicle is to remain true and accurate, it must be free of personal prejudice."

Armand pursed his lips. For a moment, the room was incredibly quiet.

"I agree," Armand said finally, "But did you know that any Master Bard may add stories of lasting historic value to the Chronicle?"

Devin shook his head. "No, I didn't."

"There is a great deal you don't know, *monsieur*. You would be wise to keep your opinions to yourself until you know enough to ask relevant questions. And by the way, I haven't bastardized the Chronicle. The story I told at Chastel's was only slightly different than the official account."

"Why?" Devin asked. "What has Chastel done that you would intentionally humiliate him in his own house like that?"

Armand's eyes closed briefly, like a cat feinting disinterest in a mouse. "How much do you know?" he asked.

"I know that Jacques Vielle was your grandfather, and that the first Jean Chastel was the present Jean Chastel's grandfather. I know his Uncle Charles was flawed in some way, unable to deal with people but drawn to animals. Apparently, he was fascinated by wolves." Armand listened without comment. "And I know that the day he died, your great grandfather, Jacques, tormented Charles. He threw stones at him and knocked him down." Devin's voice lowered to a whisper. "And then Charles killed Jacques."

"Charles tore his throat out . . . like some vicious animal . . . like . . . a savage wolf," Armand interjected angrily. "Did Chastel happen to mention that?"

Devin nodded. "And then Jean Chastel wrote about shooting Charles." He almost choked on the words. "He shot his own son, Armand, to keep him from being killed by an angry mob."

Armand's head jerked back, his nostrils flaring. "Both Chastel and I lost family members in that particular catastrophe, and yet I feel your censure is directed against me personally. What part do you think I have played in all this?"

Devin's voice was shaking. "Your story implied that Charles was some kind of wolf-man."

Armand corrected him. "The word is werewolf, Monsieur Roché."

"It's absolutely absurd!" Devin answered with more vehemence than he intended.

"I would have thought one night in the forest with that pack of wolves might have made you a believer," Armand responded.

"In werewolves?" Devin asked incredulously. "Give me credit for a little intelligence."

Armand's expression didn't change. "Did Chastel tell you that the Beast was never seen again after Charles was killed?"

"Yes, and he said that it was because his grandfather killed the Beast early the same morning that Charles died."

"And was that corroborated by Jean Chastel's journal?"

For the first time Devin faltered. "It wasn't in the part I read. I was more interested in proving that Charles's injury wasn't caused by Emile's poker."

Armand inclined his head. "Well, I don't think you will find any mention, at all, of the Beast's death in that journal.

189

But by all means, ask Chastel the next time you see him," Armand replied.

"Its head is mounted in Chastel's study," Devin snapped. "I'm sure he would be happy to show it to you."

"The head is probably from a very large wolf. Unfortunately, Ombria is famous for them. I imagine that Jean Chastel even gave this one blue glass eyes when he had it stuffed. But I have no desire to see it," Armand replied, rising to throw a log on the fire. He turned to Devin. "What is it you want from me, Monsieur Roché? We are wasting a good deal of your precious time. By my count, you have only twenty-three days left. Do you want to spend it arguing or do you want to learn the Chronicle?"

"I want to hear the 'The Beast of Gévaudan'," Devin insisted, "the way it is included in the Chronicle."

Armand held up a hand. "There is a specific progression to these stories, Monsieur Roché, and you will learn it eventually, if you stay long enough. But I don't intend to teach it to you today. Besides, you've already heard it at Chastel's château. It ends when Emile and Jacque decide to move to Lac Dupré."

Devin looked up in surprise. "The part where Charles killed Jacques is not included?"

Armand shook his head. "That is an entirely different story. A very sad one, I'm afraid."

"Then why did you add the part about the injury to Charles's face?" Devin asked.

Armand's face was cold and impassive. "Because I hate Jean Chastel. Is that enough of an answer for you, Monsieur Roché, or must you pry out all the gory details?"

Devin sighed in frustration. "I have the greatest respect for who you are and what you do, Armand, but I don't understand you."

"What makes you feel that is necessary?" Armand asked.

"I guess it isn't," Devin remarked, feeling curiously close to tears. "I expected more from you, somehow."

Armand laughed, a low, hollow sound that gave Devin chills. "So, I've disillusioned you, have I? A man your age should have lost his illusions a few years back. Your father must have truly sheltered you."

Devin clenched his hand but didn't respond. "You're right," he said, sitting back down on the stool. "We are wasting time. Where did you intend to begin today?"

Armand turned toward the fire. "With the lives of the saints, Monsieur Roché," he said. "Perhaps, those holy men will live up to your expectations."

Devin grimaced. The lives of the saints always ended badly. They'd all been sainted for a reason. Most had died nasty deaths, been tortured, stoned, or maimed for their faith. Many had their heads or other body parts hacked off. But there was obviously no way to sway Armand into revealing any more about the Beast story than he already had. If Devin wanted to know why Armand hated Chastel, he would have to wait for another day.

CHAPTER 27

News from Home

The morning hours passed quickly. Armand didn't pause for lunch but worked straight through the long afternoon, reciting one saint's life after another. He insisted Devin repeat them continually, going back to the first tale each time before adding on a new one.

Devin's stomach growled but he didn't complain. He assumed, by missing lunch, that he was being penalized for questioning Armand's integrity and judgment earlier. He had some small satisfaction that Armand was punishing himself, as well. This was, after all, what he had waited for. At last, he was sitting in a bardic hall memorizing the Chronicle, as he had fantasized about doing. But today, learning the Chronicle seemed dull and pointless. He obediently delivered each new story carefully and precisely, although, he was certain they lacked the energy and animation of Armand's versions.

There seemed to be an established formula to the lives of the saints – a boy or girl identified in childhood as having special powers or as being unusually kind or benevolent – some event that solidified his or her heavenly calling – a miracle here and there and – last of all, a horrific death, usually at the hands of a brutal, angry mob or some cruel and arrogant individual. After so many hours, their identities began to blur in Devin's mind, becoming one analogous conglomeration rather than six separate people.

Only Genevieve stood out: the saintly virgin who, at sixteen, had traded her own life to a sentient wolf, to save a small child. She'd died horribly, viciously torn apart by his savage teeth. She had been eaten alive and had never even allowed a scream to escape her lips. Genevieve had only whispered a hushed "Our Father" before the final darkness of death descended.

Armand pounded his cane on the floor. "Monsieur Roché," he said impatiently. "Am I boring you?"

Yes, Devin thought, the answer was definitely, yes, but he gave Armand a polite smile and lied. "Not at all," he said. "I'm sorry. Saint Genevieve brought back some unpleasant memories of our recent experience in the forest. My mind wandered for a moment."

"Well, see that it doesn't," Armand said, standing up awkwardly. "Begin again from the first, with Philippe." He began to pace slowly around the room, his hand kneading at the muscles in his hip and his back. "And mind that you speak loudly enough for me to hear you clear back here."

Devin would have given almost anything for a small glass of wine or a cup of cold water. His throat was dry and scratchy; his wrist ached. He was beginning to wish he'd worn the sling that Mareschal had advised him to use. For a moment, he sat very still, trying to organize his thoughts. By the look of the fading light outside it was early evening. He suspected it was Friday but he didn't know for certain. Perhaps Armand had a performance tonight and they could finish soon.

Armand stopped pacing, his cane hit the floor. "Monsieur Roché! Please begin!"

Devin cleared his throat.

"*Saint Philippe was born in the southern part of the province in the little town of Bien Terre. He was small for his age and he spent most of his time in his father's garden . . .*"

"That was Saint Michel," Armand growled. "Begin again."

Devin looked at him in confusion. "Which was wrong?" he asked. "The garden or the town?"

"Both," Armand replied. "Begin again."

For a moment, Devin's mind went blank. He scrambled in vain for details. It wasn't like him to make a mistake. Philippe's story was the first one he had learned today. He had repeated it more often than any of the others. He'd recited all of them perfectly, only minutes before. Michel must have been the herbalist then, or was it Clement? Was it Philippe who had brought a frog back to life when he was six? It was all a horrible jumble in his head. He simply couldn't remember the first part of Saint Philippe's story. He expected that Armand would be furious. Desperate, Devin turned, his open hand extended.

"Forgive me, Armand, I can't remember the beginning."

Marcus had stepped out over an hour ago. Shadows had gathered in the corners of the room. Only the fire lightened the gloomy interior with its flickering light. They were alone, and for just a moment, Devin felt uneasy facing Armand's tirade by himself. It must have shown on his face.

All of a sudden, Armand's shoulders slumped. Gone was the irritation and arrogance of a moment before.

"You're tired and so am I," he said affably. "We've been at this too long, Monsieur Roché. Leave it for today." He beckoned to Devin. "Come on, I'm sure it is almost time for dinner. The stew smelled delicious when Jeanette began it early this morning, by now it will be perfection." He extended an arm as Devin reached him, and draped it amiably over Devin's shoulders. "The Chronicle was never meant to be learned in such haste. Perhaps, you could extend your stay by just a few more days? It would be much easier on us both."

Marcus had made the same suggestion at Chastel's just that morning, although now it felt like days ago. He'd said it would be better if Devin learned one Chronicle completely than several only partially.

"I'll think about it," Devin agreed, allowing Armand to escort him from the room.

The hall was redolent with the smell of freshly baked bread and savory stew.

"Before we go into the kitchen, though, tell me the beginning of Saint Philippe's story again," Devin requested. "Otherwise, I'll never remember it correctly."

Armand withdrew his arm from Devin's shoulders and grabbed a lighted candle from the chest. He held it out in front of him.

"*Our Saint Philippe was a chandler's son. From an early age, he grew up knowing the awesome power of light in a dark and frightening world . . .* "

Devin nodded then, remembering. There was no frog in this story. He took up the recitation:

"*One night, when Philippe was barely four, he sat on his mother's knee playing with a misshapen candle that his father intended to remold. The child took the candle in his chubby little hands and held out before him. 'Light' he said and the candle burst into flame.*"

Surprisingly, Armand halted Devin when they reached the kitchen door.

"Enough," he said. "The beginning is the key, once you have that down pat, then the end follows it logically."

But Devin continued to summarize, to fix it again in his own mind. "Later in life, Philippe was sentenced to be burned at the stake for witchcraft, but he put out the bonfire again and again to the astonishment of his executioners, and he was beheaded instead. Flame answered his commands but apparently steel did not." He tried to push the image from his head of the gentle saint falling from the cruel blow of an axe, but it refused to leave him. He rubbed at his forehead wearily. "Why do men do such things to each other?"

Armand was surprisingly cheerful. "You need a drink," he advised, pushing him forward into the warmth of the kitchen.

They found Adrian and Gaspard sharing a bottle of red wine at the kitchen table. Armand sobered a bit as they walked in but he greeted Gaspard pleasantly enough, as though nothing had happened earlier.

Gaspard snagged his sleeve and pulled Devin down beside him. "Sit, Dev, you look exhausted."

"I kept him too long at his studies," Armand replied, evicting the cat from its perch on the rocker. "I'm sure Mareschal wouldn't approve."

Gaspard poured two more glasses of wine. He set one in front of Devin and passed the other to Armand. Devin sipped it gratefully, allowing the conversation to flow around him. It was a relief not to have to talk for a while. He could easily have put his head down on the table and slept while the others chattered companionably.

The kitchen was light and warm and cozy. The scents of food cooking filled the room. Jeanette hummed contentedly as she sliced bread and stacked bowls near the soup kettle. Used to the young ladies of Coreé who viewed everything through a studied mask of boredom, Devin found great pleasure in watching her graceful movements, the joy she derived from the simple tasks she was performing. How had Armand produced such a beautiful, happy daughter?

Devin heard footsteps on the stairs and Marcus came in with a handful of envelopes. Gaspard sloshed wine in another glass and gave it to Marcus, before topping off his own.

"We had mail waiting at the Town Hall," Marcus said, waving the letters in his hand. "Do you see why it is important that we keep to your itinerary, Devin, or at least, keep your father informed when we are delayed?"

Devin nodded, silently taking the five letters Marcus handed him. One was addressed in Gaspard father's cramped and precise script. He passed it onto Gaspard and laid the others on the table. Two had the Chancellor's seal and were stamped "Official Business," one was from his mother, and surprisingly, one was from André.

He opened his mother's first. It was filled with endearments and familiar admonitions: "stay warm, don't eat strange foods, get enough rest," and ended with a sweet request for Devin to plan his trip so that he could come home for Christmas. He smiled and slipped it back into the envelope to reread later.

He opened the one from André next because it was unexpected. He quickly scanned the contents and then read them a second time to be certain he hadn't misunderstood. The news came as a shock.

"LeBeau's dead," he said, in surprise.

"The Councilman?" Gaspard asked, looking up in alarm from his own letter.

Devin shook his head. "No, Henri. They found his body in his hotel room in Pireé, the morning we left for Briseé.

197

He had been stabbed to death, and his room had been searched."

For a moment, no one moved or spoke. Then at the same time, both Devin and Gaspard turned to look at Marcus, who stood with his back to the fire, his face in shadow.

Marcus raised his glass and took a long drink before commenting.

"If I recall correctly, I last saw LeBeau when you did, outside that little shop in Pireé. He was an annoying little man. I can't imagine that he will be missed."

CHAPTER 28

The Edge of Sleep

Armand seemed oblivious to the undercurrents of tension in the room.

"So this, LeBeau, he was a friend of yours, Monsieur Roché?" he asked, dipping up a spoonful of the rich brown stew.

Devin chewed and swallowed before answering. "Not a friend, no, but I knew him. We all did. He taught with my brother André at the Académie. They are . . . ," he faltered, "they were both in the Science Department together."

Armand pointed his spoon at Marcus. "And you did not like him?"

"He sailed on the Marie Lisette from Coreé with us," Marcus replied, helping himself to more bread. "I found him ingratiating. He followed Devin all over the ship like a puppy."

"Why do you think he did that?" Armand asked Devin.

Devin finished his wine and wiped his mouth with his napkin. When Gaspard moved to refill his glass, he made no move to stop him. Maybe after a third glass, his hands would stop shaking.

"I have no idea," he answered Armand. "But, the night before we disembarked, LeBeau asked me to visit his home in Arcadia this summer. He was quite insistent." For days, he had carried LeBeau's directions in his jacket pocket. The note had probably been destroyed when his jacket was discarded at Chastel's.

"You seem disturbed by his death," Armand commented.

Devin downed half his wine and avoided looking at Marcus. "I am. He was an annoying little man, as Marcus said, but I believe he was harmless. I'm sorry he was killed like that. He must have been terrified."

"Perhaps, it was a robbery," Gaspard suggested.

"Perhaps," Devin replied, laying his spoon down. He'd been so hungry, moments before, now Jeanette's carefully prepared stew seemed to stick in his throat. His mind was spinning. Marcus had been gone for so long that morning they'd left Pireé. He'd claimed that he was delayed at the Hall of Records. But several hours would have been enough time to canvass the hotels in the area and locate LeBeau. They'd all been disturbed by Henri's message claiming to know who intended to kill Devin. But surely, that wasn't a reason for Marcus to have murdered him . . .

"Do you know, Monsieur Roché?" Armand asked.

"Do I know what?" Devin responded, unsure what they had been discussing.

"Do you know if Henri LeBeau had any enemies?" Armand repeated. He leaned forward, his wine glass cradled in his hand, appraising Devin. "Perhaps, you should retire after dinner, *monsieur*, it is obvious that you are tired but you seem distracted, as well."

Devin put his hand on the table and stood up.

"You're right, I am. Please excuse me; I think I will go up to bed now. I'm not feeling very well."

200

Marcus pushed back his chair with a screech and started around the table toward him but Devin held out his hand.

"No, please, finish your meal. I just want to lie down." The last thing he wanted was for Marcus to follow him upstairs. He needed time alone . . . time to think. "Please," he added, realizing he'd disrupted their dinner, "continue."

He turned to find Jeanette's eyes on him and was filled with an irrational desire not to disappoint her. "The stew was delicious, Jeanette, I'm sorry not to have finished it."

Afterward, he didn't even remember climbing the stairs, just the soft pressure of the mattress as he sat down on it. His room was dark except for the dim light filtering in from the hall. He sat there shivering, wondering if, perhaps, he was feverish again. Or maybe, it was just shock. Marcus had killed before in the Chancellor's service. He knew that. But why would he kill a man who had information that might save his charge's life? What did LeBeau know that was damaging to either Marcus or to Devin? And why would Marcus kill him to prevent him passing that information on?

Devin shook his head. He was dealing in conjecture. He was assuming that Marcus had killed a man simply because he was late returning from an errand. And yet, Gaspard had thought the same thing. Devin had seen it in his face when he'd told him about LeBeau's death. What would make them both jump to the same conclusion about a man they had known for years?

Devin raked his hair back from his forehead and lay down. He propped his wrist on a pillow and dragged the quilt up from the bottom of the bed. He wrapped it around his shoulders, but the soft worn material did nothing to dispel the terrible chill that had settled into the very center of his being. He wished he hadn't eaten. His stomach churned

201

ominously: too much wine and not enough food. He knew better than that. At the moment, he would have welcomed Dr. Mareschal's suffocating attention. He longed to feel comforted and safe.

After about a half hour, he heard Adrian open the door in the hall downstairs. People were entering from the street. Their voices drifted up the stairs even though individual words weren't discernible at this distance. Devin had been right: Armand did have a performance tonight. He still wasn't certain whether it was Friday or Saturday. He'd lost track of time completely, even though Armand seemed to know exactly how many days Devin still had left of the thirty he had allotted him.

Before long, Marcus came upstairs, apparently forgoing Armand's presentation. Devin pretended to be asleep. Marcus stood for a long time next to his bed. Devin breathed slowly and steadily, wondering if Marcus could hear his heart beating frantically. Finally, Marcus lighted a candle and went to sit in the chair by the window.

Devin wakened much later. The door was shut and only a faint glow emanated from the window. Marcus still sat in the chair but now a knife lay across his lap. Was he guarding Devin, or did he intend to harm him? Devin considered yelling for help but who in this house would try to save him? Gaspard's instinct for self-preservation was too strong. Armand might be all too glad to be rid of him. Adrian and Jeanette owed him nothing. He sat up slowly, his eyes on Marcus. There were some things he needed to have resolved.

Devin chose his words carefully. "Under what circumstances would you have killed Henri LeBeau?" he asked softly.

Marcus hesitated a moment before answering. "Only if he represented a threat to you or to your father, or to me."

"And did he?" Devin asked, his voice shaking.

Marcus apparently chose not to understand his meaning. "Did he what?" he replied.

Devin cleared his throat. "Did he represent a threat?"

"Yes," Marcus whispered.

Devin waited, but his bodyguard didn't move. Gradually the lines of Marcus's body shifted and softened. They flowed and resolved into the lines of clothes thrown casually across the back of the chair: Marcus's coat and trousers, a woolen shirt. The glint of the knife was only a belt buckle.

Devin swallowed, his hands shaking. He'd forgotten to take the valerian Mareschal had given him. Thank God, this whole episode had been nothing but a waking dream. He slid back onto the pillow, soaked in sweat, and stared at the ceiling, willing his heart to stop racing.

Then Marcus's voice rose out of the darkness. "Get some sleep. Tomorrow will likely be another long day."

CHAPTER 29

Acquainted With Death

By morning, Devin was able to convince himself that the entire conversation with Marcus had been a waking dream. He was, after all, a historian; he dealt in facts not speculation and innuendo. There was absolutely no hard evidence that pointed to Marcus as LeBeau's assassin, and he didn't intend to hunt for any. Some things were better left alone. Obviously, his father had sent Marcus with very specific instructions. Whatever they were, they were intended to protect and preserve Devin's life. He needed to believe that and cease questioning both men's motives.

He walked downstairs and found the house deserted. The fragrance of last night's bread still lingered in the spotless kitchen. The table had been scrubbed and laid with silverware and napkins but Jeanette was nowhere to be seen. He lingered a moment in front of the cooking fire, savoring its warmth. The striped cat gazed up at him from the rocker and then went back to meticulously licking its paws. He walked out the back door onto the terrace bordered by herb beds. The air was cool but pleasant, the sky cloudless and blue. He found Marcus gazing into the distance, a pipe in his hand. Not far away a church bell tolled.

"God," he gasped, "it's Sunday!" Everyone had gone to church and left him to sleep.

Marcus seemed undisturbed. "Do you want to go?"

"Yes," Devin answered irritably.

He went back inside, grabbing his coat from the hook in the hall and went out the front door. The spire was visible from the street and the voice of the bells drew them through the ancient graveyard to the church.

The service had started before they entered. Devin dipped his fingers in the font of holy water and made the sign of the cross. The symbol he'd made so often mechanically seemed special this morning and intensely sacred. Jean Chastel sat by himself in the very front of the sanctuary. A few rows behind him, Gaspard, Adrian, Jeanette and Armand filled half a pew but Devin didn't join them. When Marcus knelt and slid into a pew, Devin chose the one behind him, preferring to sit alone and enjoy the solitude. He found peace in the familiarity of the service and the Latin words. If he closed his eyes to block out the simple sanctuary, he could have been in the cathedral in Coreé on any given Sunday.

It wasn't until Devin went forward to receive the host that Gaspard spotted him. When his friend joined him, Devin returned to his pew but the pleasant anonymity and peace he had felt at first were shattered. He found himself staring at Marcus's broad shoulders which strained the fabric of his jacket; his large head and muscular neck gave the impression of formidable strength and power. Did such men ever become priests or professors, he wondered? Or were they predestined by their physical attributes to turn toward more militant professions: soldiers, gendarmes, and assassins?

He rose when the mass ended, and waited obediently for the others to come to him. Gaspard circled his shoulders roughly with an arm and shook him.

"You're back in the land of the living, I see."

Armand studied him critically a moment. "Since today is Sunday, Monsieur Roché, we'll forgo further study. Take some time to rest this afternoon."

Devin shook his head in frustration. "That's not necessary. Please, Armand, my time here is so limited. I need to spend every possible moment memorizing your stories."

"I insist," Armand replied, brushing past him. The hard edge to his voice told Devin there was no sense in pursuing the issue any further.

Armand's mercurial moods required constant adjustment on Devin's part. He swallowed his anger, and intentionally fell behind as they exited the church. He walked down the steps alone, aware of Marcus trailing at a distance.

The graveyard lay spread before him. The morning sunshine did nothing to soften the hard angles of the stones that marked the final resting places of the village dead. Devin lingered a moment, reading the names: *Marie, beloved wife of Henri Bassett, died in childbirth*; *Henri Bassett, infant son of Marie and Henri, stillborn*. Five other Bassett infants had never reached their first birthday. Henri, the father, had married three wives, all of them died before the age of twenty-four.

Tragedy wasn't limited to the Bassetts. The pattern was the same in family after family: one husband, several wives, and multiple children, either stillborn or struck down in the early years of life. Perhaps one child, or at the most two in a family, survived to adulthood.

Devin stood, his hands jammed in his pockets, gazing down at the stones. They offered cold comfort and mute testimony to lives marred by constant heartbreak and sorrow.

"Dev?" Gaspard came up behind him and tapped his shoulder.

Devin didn't look up, his eyes still on the inscriptions. "Did any of your brothers or sisters die as infants?"

Gaspard circled, to stand in front of him. "What?" he asked.

Devin pointed to a row of tombstones. "Look at this. Eleven children – every one stillborn – what do you think happened?"

Gaspard shrugged. "How should I know?"

"My mother never lost a child," Devin mused, "or, at least, if she did she never mentioned it."

"What's your point?"

Devin rubbed distractedly at his forehead. "There's so much death here."

"Everybody dies, Dev, whether it's here in Ombria or at home in Coreé. One way or the other death comes to all of us."

"But this is different," Devin protested. "These babies never had a chance, neither, apparently, did their mothers." He walked a little further on, weaving between the headstones. Gaspard followed.

"Could I have some money?" Gaspard asked, after a moment.

Devin looked up. "Of course, I should have given you some before now. How much do you need?"

Gaspard hesitated, looking back at the door of the church. "Chastel asked me to play cards tomorrow night with some of his friends . . . "

"Gaspard . . . ," Devin protested. His friend had never been prudent where gambling was concerned. Devin had bailed him out several times in the last year when his losses had reached critical proportions. He had not brought enough money with him to cover any major debts.

Gaspard was suitably contrite. "I know . . . I know . . . I'll be careful. I promise. Look, I'll let you set the limit. I can't lose any more money than you give me!"

"Yes, you could," Devin reminded him. "You have lost more than you had in the past, because you never know when to quit!"

Gaspard shrugged. "There's nothing to do here, Dev. Before we left yesterday, Chastel invited me to come back to the château for a few days, to do some hunting and meet some of his friends . . . "

"You don't hunt," Devin pointed out.

"I could learn," Gaspard replied. "I can't sit for hours in the corner and listen to you tell stories, the way Marcus does."

"Well, once we leave Ombria, you'll have to begin recording all of these songs," Devin told him. "It's going to take you a great deal of time. I'll be learning a new Chronicle while I'm retelling the songs and ballads to you."

Stringent laws forbade folklorists from obtaining material directly from the Chronicle through a Master Bard. The information had to have been passed on to a second source, first. He was certain the original intent was to prohibit any part of the Chronicle from being preserved as a written, rather than oral record. The Council, apparently, had no idea of the complete accuracy men like Armand exacted from their students.

"Maybe I'm not cut out to be a folklorist," Gaspard replied glibly. "I only said I'd try it to please you."

"You decided to try it because you were afraid that you wouldn't pass exams. Don't blame that on me!" Devin retorted.

Gaspard grinned. "Well, if I will be busy next month . . .

that's even more reason for me to enjoy my free time while I can!"

Devin rolled his eyes and withdrew his wallet. "How long will you be gone?" he asked as he pulled out a handful of bills.

Gaspard brightened. "I'll be back by Friday night. Armand will have you performing by then, and I'll be there to cheer you on."

Devin felt strangely bereft; marooned with a bodyguard he didn't trust and a Master Bard who appeared to hate him most of the time. "All right," he agreed. "But don't get in over your head, Gaspard. I don't have access to my bank account here and I cannot use a government chit to cover your gambling debts."

"Noted, monsieur." Gaspard tipped his hat merrily. "I'm eternally grateful."

Devin turned to see Chastel descending the church steps and realized he must have been waiting for Gaspard. They'd had it all planned. Chastel's carriage was drawn up on the street, ready to take Gaspard back to the château. Devin tried to erase the annoyance from his face. But Chastel didn't look pleased either as he strode across the cemetery toward them, a grave expression on his face.

"What's the matter?" Gaspard asked.

Chastel stopped in front of them. "I need to talk to you both."

Gaspard waited expectantly but Chastel directed them toward the street. "I need to speak with Marcus, too. Let's go back to Armand's."

Devin laughed uneasily. "Armand doesn't like you, Chastel; surely you know that! I doubt he will want you visiting his house."

"I'll deal with Armand," Chastel murmured.

They walked the few blocks quickly, catching up with Armand and Adrian at the front door.

"We need a place to speak privately," Chastel announced when Armand would have slammed the door in his face.

"Then you best be quick about it," Armand replied. "You aren't welcome in this house."

"I have urgent business with Monsieur Roché," Chastel said. "I won't darken your doorstep a moment longer than necessary."

Armand flung the door open and stood to one side. "Take them to the kitchen, Adrian."

Jeanette had arrived before them and was already placing wine-filled mugs on the table.

"Monsieur Chastel," she murmured, curtseying.

"Jeanette," he murmured. "How are you today?"

She smiled. "I am well, thank you."

"You said your business was urgent," Armand growled. "Get on with it."

Marcus moved to stand in front of the fire, his eyes on Armand. Chastel sat down without being asked, and Devin and Gaspard settled on the bench across from him. Chastel gestured at the suede coat Devin was wearing.

"Oddly enough, it involves your coat, Monsieur Roché. The woolen one you wore was badly damaged during the wolf attack. I had sent it down to our seamstress but she said it would have to be patched extensively – not something a gentleman would want to wear in public – "

"For God's sake!" Armand interrupted. "Surely wardrobe issues don't require clandestine meetings!"

"Let me finish!" Chastel demanded, his eyes flashing. "I didn't know until last night but she gave the jacket to Robert Foulard, one of the young men who worked in the kitchen. He is barely twenty, slight, with light brown hair and blue eyes."

Devin nodded, wondering what possible crisis could have arisen because of his old jacket.

"Robert wore it when he left to return home Thursday night. He and George Matisse walked back to Lac Dupré together after dark. Neither of them ever reached home, and their families made inquiries at the château on Friday. No one had seen either man; they seemed to have simply disappeared. Last night my gamekeeper found their bodies."

Jeanette stifled a gasp. Armand went to her, folding his arms around her and pulling her close.

"Were they killed by wolves?" Devin asked, a chill creeping up his back.

"No, both men had been shot in the head," Chastel explained. "They had been killed several days ago. Their bodies were buried in a shallow grave at the edge of the forest. The remains had been dug up by wild animals but there was still enough flesh to make an identification, that, and your jacket."

Jeanette was crying against her father's shoulder. Armand rubbed her back distractedly, trying to soothe her, but his attention was on Chastel.

"Have you notified the authorities?" Devin asked.

"I intend to do that as soon as I leave here," Chastel assured him. "But I thought you should know first."

Puzzled, Devin shook his head. "I'm terribly sorry that you have lost two men, Chastel, but why tell me first? The loss of life is a tragedy but that old jacket was worth nothing to me."

Marcus intervened. He put both hands on the table and

leaned over to look Devin in the eye. "Robert Foulard was wearing your jacket, Devin," he said, his voice surprisingly gentle. "He was killed because someone mistook him for you."

CHAPTER 30

Investigation

"Come inside," Marcus urged for the second time. "Jeanette has lunch ready."

Devin stood on the terrace, facing away from the house, his heart still beating unsteadily. Two decent men had died because of him, he thought. Something as trivial as eating seemed disrespectful under the circumstances.

"Tell them to go ahead without me," he murmured.

Marcus stood in silence a moment. "There is no way you could have prevented this," he said gruffly. "You had no idea that your jacket would draw an assassin."

"Did you?" Devin asked accusingly.

Marcus drew a ragged breath. "No, Devin, I didn't. I would have taken greater care if I'd had any idea something like this would happen."

Robert Foulard had been a childhood friend of Jeanette's . . . a neighbor of long standing. Even in its damaged state, Devin's discarded jacket had been finer than anything he'd ever owned. He'd been glad to have it. He'd had no idea that its warm woolen folds would lead to his death, and his companion's, as well.

"Who's trying to kill me, Marcus?" Devin demanded. "I'm certain you know more than you've told me."

"I don't know," Marcus replied. "I wish I did. I told you that there's been a movement to discredit your father. His concern was that you might be targeted because of him. But your trip seemed to play right into the opposition's hands: offering the Council another reason to question his motives. This threat to you personally is puzzling."

"Henri LeBeau knew who was behind it."

"I suspect that Henri, himself, may have been a danger to you," Marcus answered. "His message may have been a ploy to get you alone in some remote location."

Devin swung around to face him. "Did you kill him, Marcus?"

Marcus's face was carefully neutral. "No, but I did go looking for LeBeau that morning. I would have been remiss if I had not followed up on his message. I can't protect you if I don't know where the threat is coming from. He was already dead when I arrived; his belongings were strewn about but there hadn't been a struggle. He was killed with one precise thrust of a knife blade at close quarters. The assailant must have been someone he knew and trusted. I suspect that St. Clair was responsible."

Devin looked away.

"Chastel went to speak with the shérif quite a while ago," Marcus continued. "He said he would be back if there were any additional developments."

"Did Gaspard leave with him?" Devin asked tightly.

"No," Marcus replied. "Gaspard thought you might need him here."

Devin blinked, surprised and touched by his friend's sensitivity.

Marcus reached for Devin's elbow. "Come in. We'll sort this thing out. There's nothing to be gained by standing out here alone."

Devin evaded his grip. "Can't you see I feel responsible?" he snapped.

"Armand and Jeanette don't blame you for what happened," Marcus assured him. "Don't blame yourself."

"Am I putting them in danger by staying here?" Devin asked.

Marcus shook his head. "I can't answer that. I would hope not, but there's no way to know for certain."

"Then, perhaps, we should make alternate plans," Devin replied.

Armand opened the door, his eyes going from Marcus to Devin and back to Marcus again. "The shérif is here with Chastel, will you come in?"

Devin gave in to the inevitable. Entering the warm room, he realized how chilled he'd become on the terrace. He avoided Jeanette's eyes and concentrated instead on the rotund little man standing behind the table, his hand held out in greeting.

"Monsieur Roché? I'm Jacques Picoté."

Devin merely nodded, his good manners strained to the limit with the current situation.

"As you already know, two men were murdered on the road to Lac Dupré. Would you mind answering a few questions, *monsieur*?" Picoté asked, taking out a small notebook. Devin made a mental note that, apparently, shérifs were taught to read and write, while so many others were not.

"I'm not sure how much help I can be," Devin answered, sitting down beside Gaspard. "I'll tell you what I know."

Picoté inclined his head and sat across from him. "I can ask no more than that." He rummaged in his pocket and withdrew a piece of paper. "This was found in Robert Foulard's pocket, *monsieur*, do you recognize it?"

Devin took it from his hand, unfolding it on the table in front of him. "This is a note that was given to me by Henri LeBeau."

Picoté's stare was unwavering. "It indicates that your life is in danger. Can you tell me why you chose to ignore it?"

"I didn't ignore it," Devin objected. "I was simply unable to find out who wished me ill."

Picoté gestured with his hand. "You have not tried to contact this Monsieur LeBeau?"

"Henri LeBeau was murdered shortly after he gave me that note," Devin replied. "It would be impossible to obtain further information from him now."

Picoté's eyebrows shot toward his hairline. "Has the murderer been apprehended?"

"I don't believe so," Devin said.

"Is it fair to assume the same man might have killed Robert Foulard and George Matisse?" Picoté asked.

Marcus intervened. "I think it would be foolish to make any assumptions, at this point."

Picoté picked up his pen. "And you are?"

"Marcus Beringer: Monsieur Roché's bodyguard."

"And you have information about the man who murdered this Henri LeBeau?"

"I have no information about either murder," Marcus clarified. "I simply think that making suppositions at this stage is pointless."

Picoté's eyes narrowed. "It is useful, *monsieur*, to have a place to start. The last murder in Lac Dupré occurred seventeen years ago, when a drunken butcher accidentally killed his wife during an argument. To have two young men from our village struck down together is unprecedented."

"I'm extremely sorry," Devin said, rubbing his forehead with his left hand. "What can I do to help?"

216

"Both men were shot. That eliminates almost all of the men in the village as suspects, since they are not allowed by law to own a gun." Picoté gestured at the note in Devin's hand. "That note is the only lead we have. I understand Foulard was wearing your coat, *monsieur*. Perhaps, someone mistook him for you and your companion, Monsieur Forneaux, in the dark?"

"That seems possible, under the circumstances," Devin replied.

"Monsieur Roché did not give that coat to Robert," Chastel pointed out. "It was to be discarded because it was badly damaged after Monsieur Roché was attacked by wolves. My seamstress gave it to Robert, instead."

Picoté jotted down a few words. "You didn't know Foulard personally, *monsieur*?" he asked Devin.

"To my knowledge, I have never met him," Devin said.

"To your knowledge?" Picoté asked.

Devin restrained his irritation. "I may have seen him during my stay at Monsieur Chastel's château. I was not introduced to him; there wouldn't have been any reason for me to be."

Picoté's face hardened. He leaned forward, his hands braced on the table. "I see, Robert was just a simple servant and unworthy of your notice. And yet, he took a bullet in the head for you, Monsieur Roché. I would think you might be grateful for that, at the very least."

Devin shot to his feet. "I find your attitude insulting, Picoté! I am as shocked as you are that Foulard was killed. If I could bring him back to life, even at the cost of my own life, I would do it. But I am at a loss as to how to remedy the situation, now. I do feel responsible for his death and I will have to live with that guilt for a very long time. If there is nothing more, I believe we are finished here. Please see yourself out!"

Picoté stood up slowly. "This is not your house, Monsieur Roché, nor even your province. You have no authority over me."

Suddenly, Armand stepped forward, his hands resting lightly on Devin's shoulders in a proprietary manner.

"Say good afternoon, Picoté," he said calmly. "Monsieur Roché will cooperate fully with your investigation, as will we all. There's nothing further that you need to know today."

Picoté took a deep breath and retrieved his hat from the table. "Why don't you make plans to go home and leave us in peace, before we are forced to bury more of our young men in your stead, Monsieur Roché?" He roughly extracted the note from Devin's hand, and picked up his notebook and pen. "This investigation isn't finished. Inform me, *monsieur*, before you intend to leave Lac Dupré."

He gave a slight bow to Jeanette and stomped down the hall. A moment later, the front door closed with a bang.

CHAPTER 31

Aftershocks

Armand's hands flexed once on Devin's shoulders and then withdrew.

"Robert Foulard was Jacques Picoté's nephew; his sister's only son. He is understandably upset."

"I didn't know," Devin murmured. "That makes the situation worse. I'm sorry."

"You've done nothing wrong," Armand replied. "The circumstances are unfortunate. Robert was a good man. He was well liked. Picoté's looking for someone to blame."

"I wish I'd had Marcus burn the damn coat," Devin growled.

Armand shook his head. "If you think these things lie in our hands, you are mistaken, Monsieur Roché. It was apparently Robert's time to leave us. What we want or wish for has little to do with it."

"I don't believe that," Devin muttered.

Armand smiled. "You are very young. Perhaps, a few more years will convince you otherwise."

"I need to be going, too," Chastel said. He spared a glance

for Gaspard. "I'll be in touch. Perhaps, we can arrange a visit later in the month."

Devin cleared his throat. "Please Gaspard, don't cancel your stay on my account."

Chastel shook his head. "Now isn't the time, Monsieur Roché. I think you need your friend here. We'll schedule something again."

He bowed to Jeanette and Armand. "Thank you for allowing me into your home. I'm sorry the circumstances couldn't have been more pleasant."

"You'll let us know if they discover anything else?" Devin asked.

"Of course," Chastel replied.

"Please tell me when the funerals will be held. I'd like to attend," Devin added.

"I would advise against it," Armand interjected. "Local feelings tend to be volatile. You're better off staying out of sight the next few days. If the murderer is caught, blame will shift to him. Right now, many people may feel as Picoté does, and hold you responsible."

"He's right, you know," Chastel agreed. "Spend your time learning Ombria's Chronicle. Hopefully, this will be resolved before you need to move on."

He smiled at Jeanette before turning to go.

"I'll see myself out."

Armand captured Devin's shoulders again lightly. "Sit down and eat. Life goes on. We must enjoy the days allotted to each of us or we dishonor God's plan."

Devin folded beneath the pressure of Armand's hands, sinking back onto the bench beside Gaspard. Jeanette had placed platters of cold sliced meat, and pungent aged cheese, bread and butter, and last fall's wrinkled apples on the table.

Overall, the scent of wine predominated in the kitchen, along with the pervasive fragrance of sweet wood smoke. This kitchen offered warmth and comfort, and yet it was likely that, in a similar kitchen in this same village, a mother wept for her only son.

"George Matisse," Devin said, breaking the uneasy silence around him. "Who was he?"

Armand sat down heavily at the head of the table. "George was married just a little over a year ago. His wife is expecting a baby in the next few weeks."

He bowed his head and said grace.

Devin swallowed, hardly registering the words Armand offered in prayer. What had he expected to hear? What had he hoped for? That the man had been a drunkard or a thief? That the village would be a better place without him? He thought of all those tombstones in the cemetery. He had mourned their dead as an outsider, saddened by the frequency and inevitability of death in their small village. Now, he'd added two more graves to their total. It would have been better had he not come here.

Gaspard passed the platter of meat. "Last night, when you went upstairs, Dev, you left your father's letters here on the table. I put them on the chest in your room."

Devin hadn't opened them. The news of Henri LeBeau's death had driven everything else from his mind.

"Thank you," he said. He passed the meat on to Marcus without taking any. "You had a letter from your father, too. How are things in Coreé?"

Gaspard's eyebrows rose slightly. "I have no idea. The letter was quite personal. He spoke entirely about how his eldest son had dishonored him by his failure at exams and subsequent expulsion from the Académie. He intends to name my younger brother as his heir."

"Gaspard . . . " Devin floundered, uncertain whether his friend was joking or serious. Then, for just an instant, he witnessed a chink in Gaspard's armor, as his eyes darkened with hurt.

Gaspard blinked hard and turned away. "He was quite serious, Dev. He's given me until the end of the summer to come home, or face the consequences."

"Then you must do it," Devin told him, painfully aware of their audience. "Go back, before it's too late, Gaspard. It's not worth risking your future. I should never have brought you with me. All of this is my fault."

Gaspard shook his head. "You think I would have stayed there if you'd left without me? What kind of life would that be – gratifying my father's every whim – to make up for my woeful lack of academic achievement? I'm glad that you have given me this chance to get away. Who knows, I may find a place that is just right for me, and stay in one of the provinces. My life in Coreé is finished."

"You have to consider the rest of your family," Devin protested, taking a sip of his wine.

Gaspard turned to face him. "Why? My mother only cares for parties and fashion. If I stayed away from Coreé for twenty years, I doubt she'd notice I was missing. My brother, Louis, will be only too happy to take over the reins as Father's heir! If he and I were standing on Girard's Tower at the Académie tomorrow, he'd gladly push me off to assure his inheritance!"

Devin laughed uneasily. "You exaggerate. Louis has always idolized you!"

"That's a thing of the past," Gaspard said. "He has heard too often from Father that I am a dismal failure, and he's clever enough to take advantage of it. You have no idea what it means to be the eldest son; the responsibilities and expectations that are heaped upon you. Everyone isn't blessed with a family like yours, Dev. Your father and your brothers cater to you; let you dabble in whatever new thing catches your interest. They trot you out on state occasions: the brilliant young protégé who captivates everyone with his intellect and charm. Then they shoo you off to go play with your expensive toys while they go about the serious business of running the empire."

Devin relinquished his mug with a thump that splashed wine on the table.

"That's not true!" he protested. "Have a care what you're saying, Gaspard."

Gaspard scowled. "You have no idea how often I have wished I could change places with you! You have everything, Dev, and you don't even know it!" He rose from the table, throwing his napkin on the bench. "Excuse me, please. Lunch was excellent, Jeanette."

Marcus loomed up behind him, one hand snagging his right arm. "Don't forget, you may be in danger here too, Gaspard. It was not only Robert Foulard who was killed but his companion, as well. Don't leave the house without an escort."

"Then I'll be in my room," Gaspard replied. "It's been a bad day all around. I'd prefer not to end it by having my head blown off!"

Devin watched him go, with a knot in his stomach. He turned to Armand and Jeanette.

"I'm sorry to have disturbed your meal with personal matters."

"I think you apologize overmuch," Armand replied. "It is Gaspard who owes you an apology. We were only the unwilling audience."

Devin flushed. "The dinner table is never the place for such intimate conversation."

Armand laughed. "Then manners are very different in Coreé. Here in Ombria the most private details of our lives are dissected around the kitchen table. Don't assume your friend's burden, Monsieur Roché. If Gaspard has a problem with his family, it is not your doing. Jealousy serves no purpose except to inspire bitterness."

Devin shook his head. "And yet, I feel as though I have brought nothing but turmoil to your household. This venture seems ill-conceived."

"And yet, you have embarked upon it, and there is nothing to be done but to see it through," Armand replied lightly. He glanced at Marcus, and forked a large slice of pork. Leaning forward, he deposited it on Devin's plate, along with two pieces of bread.

"Eat, Monsieur Roché," he advised. "If you're interested, I'm planning to spend some time in the hall this afternoon, brushing up on some historical ballads. If you can sing at least one perfectly by tomorrow, I'll schedule you to perform it this Friday night."

"Thank you," Devin replied. He was surprised and grateful for the diversion. Perhaps the familiarity of studying would take his mind off the troubles that were currently hounding him. And if he was lucky, maybe later on, Gaspard would have regained his good humor.

Devin gathered the platters from the table when they had finished, as a means of having a word alone with Jeanette. She dried her hands on her apron and turned to face him, her eyes still red from crying.

"Can I help you, Monsieur Roché?"

"I'm so sorry about your friend," he began.

"Robert," she added gently. "He was a very good friend."

"I know," he assured her, fumbling for the right words. "I'm not sure what else to say. I can't believe that this happened."

"It was not your fault," Jeanette replied.

He sighed. "I feel that it was. I wish I could undo it and make things right."

"No one can reverse time, Monsieur Roché, not even your scientists at the Académie in Coreé can do that."

"If I could," he said, "I would. Perhaps it would have been better if I had stayed in Coreé."

She touched his hand, her dark eyes still brimming with unshed tears. "I am glad you did not stay in Coreé because then I would never have met you."

"Monsieur Roché?" Armand bellowed from the doorway into the hall. "I'm waiting."

CHAPTER 32

The Storyteller's Sack

The weather turned cold and miserable, as though it joined the village in mourning the two young lives so recently lost. With wind and rain beating constantly against the windows, Devin didn't object to remaining indoors. The days fell into an easy pattern, as Armand constantly presented new material and Devin memorized it, parroting it back flawlessly. With the successful memorization of each additional story, Devin's confidence grew. For the first time in the last few weeks, he felt confident that he could actually master Ombria's Chronicle in the time he had allotted to it.

On the day of the funerals, both Jeanette and Armand left after breakfast to attend the services. Gaspard and Adrian started a card game in the kitchen. Marcus carted the laundry downstairs, after warning Devin not to go out without telling him. Free to pursue his own interests, Devin closeted himself with a paper and pen and began a long overdue letter.

Dear Father,
Thank you for your letters. I apologize for being

such a poor correspondent. I fear my trip has not gone according to plan. We stayed nearly a week at the château of Jean Chastel after having been attacked by wolves in the Forêt d'Halatte . I was the only one who was injured but the wound is nearly healed. I would consider it a personal favor if you wouldn't tell Mother. I don't want to do anything to increase her worry. Please do not be concerned, the wound is slight and easily mended.

We are now staying at the Bardic Hall in Lac Dupré. I expect to be here at least three more weeks. We are housebound at the moment. Two local men were shot to death last week on the road into the village. One of them was wearing a jacket which I had discarded after the wolf attack. The current theory is that the assassin mistook the two of them for Gaspard and me in the dark.

I have taken to heart your recommendation that I go nowhere without Marcus. But I am concerned about the threats you have received personally, which you mentioned in your letter. Perhaps, Marcus belongs with you. I feel guilty having taken your most loyal defender with me. Please be careful and take no chances, just as you have counseled me.

You asked for my observations on each province. Ombria is more wild and rugged than I had ever imagined. Transportation is difficult – some roads are little more than paths. In the interior of the province, wolves are a constant threat. Sanitation and health care are minimal. Even a village of importance, like Lac Dupré, does not have a physician. It was fortunate that Chastel came upon us in the forest when he did, slaughtering the wolf pack that was intent on killing us, as well as later providing his personal physician to tend my wound. The infant mortality rate here is extremely high, as is the death rate for young women undergoing childbirth. I find the system for providing schooling to local residents discriminatory and biased. There are so many areas which require reform. It would be difficult to suggest to you a good place to begin.

Ombria's Master Bard is Armand Vielle. He is an unpredictable man – reasonable one minute – and irrational the next but I like him. On good days, he is like a favorite professor – on bad days – he becomes a tyrant. At first, I feared he would not take me on as his student but I think I have proven my worth to him. I expect to perform for the first time in public this Friday night. I had no idea of the precision required in learning the Chronicles. It is an exacting assignment and one I do not take lightly. I realize now that I have undertaken an impossible task. I may have to settle for learning the Chronicles in only one or two provinces instead of all fifteen. Please don't tell Jacques. He makes enough jokes at my expense as it is!

I was puzzled to hear in your last letter that René Forneaux has begun to support our trip publicly. Gaspard received a letter from him this week claiming that if he didn't return by summer's end, he would confer his inheritance on Louis, instead. Gaspard is understandably upset but not moved to bow to his father's wishes. At present, he vows he will never return to Coreé and I doubt that even I *can change his mind.*

In answer to your last question, I am not in need of money. I have spent very little so far and am more than adequately supplied for the next few months, at least. Bards are amply provided for by each province and so are their students. I want for nothing.

Give Mother my love. Tell her I am well and happy and extend my best regards to my brothers. I will write again when I have time.
Affectionately,
Devin

He laid the pen aside and dusted the ink lightly to keep it from smearing. There was a satisfaction in having finished this tally of the current crises. He hoped he had presented them in such a way that his father wouldn't be overly alarmed. He remembered briefly the romantic image he had cherished of this trip, envisioning himself ensconced at the foot of a Master Bard before a roaring fire with a cup of mulled wine at his elbow. There had been times in the last two days peculiarly like his daydreams; moments when he could forget, that two men had died here for him and that, somewhere close by, an assassin might still be planning his murder.

Adrian knocked on his open door. "Do you have a few minutes, Devin? If you could come downstairs, I'd like to show you something."

"Of course," Devin answered, folding the letter and placing it in an envelope. He laid the missive aside to give to Marcus.

Adrian went down to the kitchen and beckoned Devin toward the table where Gaspard was engrossed in a game of solitaire. Marcus had settled by the fire, cradling the tiger cat.

Devin laid a hand on his friend's shoulder. "Who's winning?" he asked.

Gaspard gestured at the cards. "No one, at the moment. Care to join me? Adrian's luck has run out and he refuses to play anymore."

"Perhaps, later," Devin replied. He wanted to borrow Adrian's harp and practice this afternoon while Armand was out.

"Later, Armand will come back and you will shift into study mode," Gaspard replied petulantly. "Can't you spare me a few minutes of your time?"

Devin sensed veiled animosity beneath his invitation. "Of course," he answered. "Give me a moment with Adrian."

Adrian removed a small brown velvet sack from his pocket.

"I wanted to give this to you while Armand isn't here," he said. "I asked Jeanette to make it for you. She made one for me when I was learning the Chronicle and I still carry it."

He loosened the ties and spilled out the contents: dozens of brightly colored beads, which rolled and darted on the tabletop. He gathered them into a pile with his hands.

"Some bards string the beads and wear them on their belts; others fill the bag with pebbles of different colors instead of beads. I suppose you could even use coins, although I wouldn't want to tie up my money for this." He sorted them quickly into piles. "You see there are eight kinds: one each for the different types of stories in the Chronicle. You can use whichever color you like, but I usually designate the red ones for the Chansons de Gestes, brown for the beast tales, yellow for the fabliaux, white for the romances, black for the cautionary tales, blue for the religious ones, and green for the historical accounts, and these speckled ones for the legends. I've given you one bead for each story. It is simply an easy way to remember the titles. Name them as you count out the beads. I don't know about you, but if I can remember the title, then that's half the battle won."

Devin gathered the twenty-three green ones in his hand and raised his eyebrows.

"I hadn't realized there were so many. Armand only began to teach me the first historical accounts this week. I believe we've only finished six. We spent a great deal of time on cautionary tales and romances. I was afraid he would never reveal the rest of these to me, and they are the ones that interested me most."

Adrian laughed. "Armand likes to be in charge. If you try to tell him what to do, he is stubborn as a goat. The only way around it is to make him think something is his idea. But don't let him fool you, Devin. He has been very impressed with your abilities at memorization. He simply doesn't want you to know it."

Devin sat down beside Gaspard. "I seem to make him angry."

"He's angry at what you represent," Adrian replied. "He feels that Coreé treats the residents of the provinces unfairly."

"I would agree with him there," Devin said. "I said as much today in the letter I wrote to my father."

"Perhaps, you could tell Armand that, as well," Adrian said. "I worry that his outspokenness will get him killed. He wouldn't be the first bard to be silenced for defying Coreé."

Devin took the deck of cards and shuffled them idly.

"I have difficulty believing that the Council fears the Chronicles so much that they would kill to keep certain information quiet," he said. "A Master Bard is only the vehicle to pass on that information, but there are other bards who will still repeat the stories that they have learned."

Adrian hesitated. "The teaching of the Chronicle is strictly regulated. Did you know that every bard must be registered in his province?" he asked.

Devin shook his head.

"Armand took a chance teaching you," Adrian continued. "For all he knew, you were an agent of the imperial government sent to ferret out any heresy he had been teaching. Ombria's Master Bard was executed for treason at the turn of the last century because he dared to report events that were at odds with the official government accounts at the time."

Devin felt oddly responsible. "I'm sorry. I had no idea. That isn't a fact that's widely known."

"And you are a historian," Adrian pointed out.

In the distance the church bells tolled: one stroke for every year of two men's lives. Devin shifted uneasily at the sound.

"Deal!" Gaspard demanded. "Armand will be back soon."

Adrian gathered up the beads, funneling them through his fingers and into the little bag.

"It's called a storyteller's sack," he said. "I thought you might want to know that. Perhaps you'll want to make a more ornate one someday, but this will get you started."

Devin dealt the cards into three hands, aware of Gaspard's impatience.

"Thank you very much, and please thank Jeanette," he said to Adrian. "I rarely have a chance to speak to her alone." He picked up his cards and winced. He'd dealt himself a miserable hand but Gaspard was grinning.

"What are we playing for?" Devin asked.

"Our souls," Gaspard replied. "I'm out of money."

CHAPTER 33

High Stakes

Gaspard's comment indicated that he must have already been in debt when he had asked Devin for money on Sunday. If he'd still needed to pay off Chastel then it would explain his lack of funds today. It made Devin angry that Gaspard had lied to him, pretending he needed money for an impending card game. He knew for certain that Gaspard hadn't lost his money to Adrian. Armand didn't allow gambling in his house: when they played around the big kitchen table, the stakes were beans or matchsticks.

Devin was preoccupied the rest of the day, wondering how to handle it. They were on their way up to bed before he had a chance to speak to Gaspard alone. He waited until Marcus had entered the bedroom they shared, and then walked into Gaspard's room and casually kicked the door closed behind him.

"So, why didn't you tell me that you already owed Chastel money?" he demanded.

Gaspard shrugged, looking young and vulnerable in the light of the single candle on the bedside table. "I hoped you'd give me enough to pay Chastel off and I'd still have a little leftover to begin to win some of it back."

Devin sighed. "So you've cleared it up, then?"

Gaspard avoided his eyes.

"How much do you still owe him?" Devin asked.

Gaspard's response was barely audible. "A thousand francs."

"A thousand francs!" Devin gasped. "That's more than three times what I gave you on Sunday!"

Gaspard simply nodded.

Devin shook his head in disbelief. "But Gaspard, when did you lose it all? We didn't even stay at Chastel's that long."

"You weren't feeling well," Gaspard explained, slumping down on the bed. "And there wasn't a lot for me to do. When Chastel asked me if I would like to play cards with him and Dr. Mareschal, of course, I said 'yes'." He laughed self-consciously. "They are both experts, Dev. Don't ever gamble with either of them!"

"I don't intend to," Devin replied.

Gambling was a hobby for the idle rich and Devin didn't see himself as belonging to that category. For the last two years, he had done manuscript restoration at the Académie to avoid making unnecessary demands on his father's resources. Once he took his place in the Archives, he would be self-sufficient and no longer dependent on his father's income.

"They played for much higher stakes than I am used to," Gaspard continued. "My losses got out of hand very quickly. Chastel seemed amused. He and Mareschal exchanged glances a few times, as though they both knew something I didn't. At first, I thought maybe he was cheating, but then I began to wonder if he wasn't getting back at my father for some past loss he had suffered. Chastel even offered, several times, to request the funds from my father if I didn't have enough ready cash. Surely, you can understand why I couldn't let him do that? So, I told him you were holding my money for the trip, and as soon as you were feeling better, I would settle up. I thought you would give me what I needed, if I asked."

Devin turned away, his hands jammed into his pockets. "And yet you never told me how much you needed, or why you needed it. Was I just supposed to guess?"

"I didn't want you to know how much I owed," Gaspard confessed.

Devin swung around to face him. "Listen Gaspard, I will gladly buy you food, clothes, or anything else you need on this trip, but I can't continue to assume your gambling debts. I simply can't afford to. I will pay this off, but it will leave us short of cash. It will be another three weeks before we can reach a government center where I can make a withdrawal from the account my father set up. I've spent less than fifty francs in two weeks to support three of us. You dropped thirteen-hundred in four days! I don't know how to make it any clearer. You simply can't gamble any more unless you can raise the funds yourself. I can't risk losing the money we need to get back home on a card game."

"I can win it back," Gaspard protested. "Give me an extra ten francs now, and I can replace your money by the end of the week."

"No," Devin replied, shaking his head. "Absolutely not." He grabbed the doorknob and wrenched the door open. "And as far as the thousand francs go, I will pay Chastel myself. It's time he understood where the money's coming from."

Gaspard followed him, grabbing his arm as he crossed the threshold.

"Dev, please. Don't embarrass me in front of Chastel!"

Devin shook off his hand. "Embarrass you? God, doesn't it embarrass you not to be able to pay your debts? I'd be mortified."

Devin was too angry to go to bed. He started downstairs but Marcus appeared, half dressed, on the top step before he was halfway down.

"Where are you going?" he demanded.

"Downstairs," Devin told him. "I can't sleep right now. Don't worry, I'm not going out."

"See that you don't," Marcus answered before stalking back down the hall to their room.

Devin heard voices coming from the performance hall. The door was only partially closed and he pushed it open to find Adrian and Armand seated before the fire. Armand shifted, shielding whatever they were looking at from Devin's view.

"I'm sorry," Devin said. "I should have knocked."

"It is not a problem," Armand answered smoothly, sliding something into Adrian's harp case. "I thought you'd gone to bed."

"I did," Devin explained.

"You sound upset," Armand said, turning around. "Is something the matter?"

Adrian stood up, looping the handle of the harp case over his shoulder.

"I'll see you in the morning, Armand. Goodnight, Devin," he said.

"I didn't mean to interrupt," Devin protested.

"It's truly not a problem. I was on my way up anyway," Adrian answered graciously.

"Good night, then," Devin said.

"Come. Sit, Monsieur Roché," Armand said, patting the stool beside him. "Tell me what is bothering you."

Devin slumped down beside him, watching as Adrian walked out and closed the door behind him.

"I had an argument with Gaspard," he confided. "Apparently, he spent most of our four day stay at Chastel's playing cards. He just told me he owes Chastel a thousand francs, and that's in addition to the three hundred that I gave him on Sunday."

Armand grunted. "Gambling is an addiction, Monsieur Roché. Any gambler who denies that is only fooling himself."

Devin rubbed at his forehead. His head was thumping. "I will have to pay this off for him because he has no resources of his own at the moment, but I told him tonight that I can't do it again."

"I doubt it will stop him," Armand replied, lighting a long pipe with a splinter from the kindling bucket. "He will just go further into debt, or worse yet, steal, to support his habit."

"I don't know what to do," Devin said in frustration.

"There is nothing you can do," Armand answered. "It is not your problem, it is Gaspard's. As long as you bail him out, you are giving him permission to continue gambling. By saying 'no' and meaning it, you are removing yourself from the equation. Believe me, he will find another means to get the money. I only hope it will be a legal one. I think your friend needs to swallow his pride, and go back to Coreé. He will never survive in the provinces."

"We have been friends a very long time," Devin said, dreading the prospect of fourteen months without Gaspard. "I can't imagine this trip without him."

"I am sorry for you, then." Armand blew smoke out of his nose, his eyes on the fire. "And Chastel," he said after a moment, "do you feel any differently about him? It would have been more courteous not to continue offering credit to a man who was already overextended."

Devin didn't answer immediately. "I have always judged a man by the way he treats me personally," he said at last. "Chastel has given me no reason to distrust him." However, Gaspard's hunch that Chastel had fleeced him to get even for a past grudge, continued to nag at him.

"And yet," Armand observed, as though sensing his doubts, "you do not really know the man or his family."

"So, tell me about him," Devin said.

Armand was so quiet that Devin assumed he didn't intend to answer. Then suddenly the bard turned to face him, his face haggard.

"Jean Chastel is my brother," he said.

Devin's mouth dropped open. "Your brother?" he gasped, and yet the statement was not that unbelievable. All through their stay at the château, Chastel had reminded Devin of someone. He realized now that it was the affable side of Armand that he had recognized and responded to in Chastel. If Armand's darker side also coexisted within Chastel's genial façade, it was a little too disturbing to think about at the moment.

Armand continued, "I only know all of this because Mäite told me the night of my eighteenth birthday. She felt it was important that I know my heritage. My grandfather has never spoken of it to me and I doubt that he ever will.

"Apparently, when my mother was fifteen, my grandfather was nearly crushed by a falling tree. It broke both his legs and no one ever expected him to walk again. My mother took the only job available to help support her parents. She went to work in the château kitchen. She and my grandmother kept it a secret from my grandfather. Emile hated the Chastels because Charles had killed his father. They told him she worked for the baker in Mirrelle, and slept in a room above the shop. Emile had no reason to doubt them. Richard Chastel, Jean's father, was a bachelor at the time, and it seemed that the Chastel curse was likely to keep him one. None of the high born families wanted to marry their daughters into a family of werewolves."

Devin made a disgusted noise in his throat. "Surely, they didn't believe . . . "

Armand clamped a hand on Devin's knee. "Don't interrupt," he said. He sat silently a moment, as though to reorder his thoughts, and began again. "Richard Chastel may have been cursed but he was also lonely, and my mother was very beautiful. After a few months, my mother told Maïte that she was expecting a child and that Richard Chastel was the father." He tapped his hand on Devin's knee. "My mother assured her that Richard had never forced himself on her. My mother claimed they fell in love. Richard even offered to marry her when she discovered she was pregnant. He wanted his child raised at the château.

"At that point, there was no way they could hide the situation from Grandfather. He was furious, of course. I think, had he been physically able, that he would have killed Richard Chastel with his bare hands. My grandfather insisted that Mother quit working at the château.

"A few days later, Chastel came to the house. He tried everything he could to convince my grandfather to allow Mother to marry him but my grandfather wouldn't agree to the marriage. Mother was afraid not to abide by her father's wishes and so she agreed never to see Richard Chastel again. And so, I was born, Armand Vielle. The village people suspected that Richard was the father but no one dared voice it within my grandparents hearing. And after a while, I think most people forgot that I was a bastard.

"Richard asked to sponsor me when I was seven. He offered me a room at the château while I was being tutored. My grandparents realized the value of an education, but insisted that I live in the village. And so I was taught to read and write at Richard's expense.

"Eventually, Richard Chastel did marry, but his first son was stillborn and his wife seemed too fragile to survive another birth. Again, he approached my family about allowing me come to live with him at the château but Grandfather refused. When the present Jean Chastel was born, Richard finally ceased his campaign to have me legitimized. At last, he had a son and heir to carry on the family name."

Devin shook his head. "But none of this was the present Jean Chastel's fault. From what you've said, your mother and Richard were in love. It was your grandfather who prevented the marriage. Just think, Armand, it could have been you living at the château right now, not Jean."

Armand raised a hand in annoyance. "Hush or I won't finish the story!" he threatened.

Devin apologized. "I'm sorry. I thought you were finished."

"Well, I'm not," Armand growled. "And I'm not even sure why I am telling you this. It's none of your business anyway."

"You're right; it's not," Devin agreed, "but you can hardly stop now."

Armand glowered, but continued. "Some years later, on the day of my wife's funeral, Richard Chastel came here, to this house. I'd lost my wife in childbirth along with our infant son, and I was devastated. I was already a Master Bard and had been married ten years. Jeanette was just three. Richard's wife had died the year before. He gave me a letter, stating that he was my father, and that I was his first born son, even though I was illegitimate. With it was a copy of his will,

240

leaving half his estate to me and my descendants, the other half went to Jean. He said he had always loved my mother, and that he wanted to see that her children and grandchildren were adequately cared for. He died a few months later.

"Several weeks after that, Jean came to visit me. He was probably about your age, and completely overwhelmed with the responsibility of his father's estate. He was aware of both the letter and the will his father had given me. He asked me to take over the management of the Chastel estate. He wanted me to run it. We would have split the profits. And I did actually consider it. Not for me, but for Jeanette. Death often comes unexpectedly: I wanted to be certain that Jeanette would be cared for if something happened to me."

"And yet, you didn't accept his offer," Devin said. "Why?"

Armand leaned back in his chair. "Because it would have broken my grandfather's heart. As long as he lives, he deserves my loyalty. He and Mäìte raised me, Monsieur Roché. My mother died when I was born."

"And so you hate Jean Chastel because your grandfather hates him?"

Armand nodded.

Devin shook his head. "When Chastel told me that your grandfather was Emile Vielle, he omitted the fact that the first Jean Chastel was your grandfather, too."

Armand shrugged. "It isn't a fact that I am proud of, and I give Jean credit for keeping it to himself."

"But how long will the animosity go on?" Devin asked. "You continue to taunt Jean with that werewolf nonsense, even though the same blood runs in your veins, and Jeanette's."

Armand's hand grasped the front of Devin's shirt and yanked him closer.

"If you ever repeat that," he snarled. "I will call you a liar to your face! All of this may seem like foolishness to you, but a man's family is very important here!"

Devin met his eyes without flinching. "It's important in Coreé too, Armand. Ombria doesn't have the corner on family ties!" He pried himself free of Armand's grip and stood up, putting some distance between them. "Does Jeanette know?"

Armand shook his head, his anger visibly dissipating. "No, if I feel she needs to know, I will tell her myself. But I think that, perhaps, it would be best if the knowledge dies with me. Every family has secrets that are best kept hidden, Monsieur Roché."

Devin took a deep breath. "I pray there are no such volatile ones in mine."

Armand grunted. "If you think your family is exempt from secrets, then you simply haven't discovered them yet."

CHAPTER 34

Undercurrents

Picoté arrived before breakfast the next morning, asking for Devin and Marcus. Adrian knocked gently on Devin's door to tell them of his arrival. Marcus was already dressed but Devin was still in bed. He'd spent a restless night agonizing over his argument with Gaspard and wishing he had handled it differently. Sleep had finally come near daybreak and hadn't lasted nearly long enough. He slid wearily into yesterday's wrinkled shirt, buttoning it as he followed Marcus downstairs, barefoot.

Armand was pouring coffee but Picoté stood facing the fire, his hands clasped behind him. He turned as Marcus and Devin entered. Picoté took one look at Devin's rumpled hair and hastily donned clothes, and raised his eyebrows.

"I'm sorry to have disturbed your sleep, Monsieur Roché," he remarked sarcastically. "Country people rise early. It didn't occur to me that you wouldn't be up yet."

"Monsieur Roché and I worked very late last night," Armand explained, a mug of coffee in his hand. "I told him we could delay our lessons this morning."

"And yet, I find you presentable and ready to start the day," Picoté pointed out.

Armand simply extended the mug. "Would you like some coffee?" he asked.

Picoté shook his head, his eyes still on Devin. "No, thank you, I've already eaten. I just have a few questions for Monsieur Roché."

"Have you learned anything more about the murders?" Devin asked, sitting down at the table.

"Unfortunately, no," Picoté said, parting the tails of his coat before seating himself across from Devin. "No one remembers seeing any strangers in the village last week. The killer or killers appear to have vanished into thin air."

"If they were professional assassins," Marcus observed darkly, "they would be careful not to be seen and they wouldn't have left any evidence behind."

Picoté nodded. "I'm sure you are right. I'm afraid I have little hope of catching them now."

Devin wondered, apprehensively, whether the killers had vanished that night, confident that they had achieved their purpose in assassinating the Chancellor's son and his companion. Or, had they lingered long enough to realize their mistake? Perhaps, even now, they were planning another more successful attempt.

"The people of Lac Dupré have no knowledge of professional assassins," Picoté continued. "They would not know how to contact such persons, let alone commission them to carry out such a crime. The only conclusion I can reach is that you, Monsieur Roché, have drawn these men to our small corner of the province and placed all of us here in jeopardy."

Marcus stepped forward, towering over Picoté. "No one is currently in jeopardy except Monsieur Roché and his companion."

Picoté's eyes were cold. "I believe Robert Foulard and George Matisse would disagree with you if they were able." He shifted to glance behind him. "By the way, where is Monsieur Forneaux?"

"I think he is still asleep," Devin answered.

"Ah," Picoté commented, his eyebrows arching a moment before resuming their normal position. "Was he also up very late last night?"

Devin barely restrained his annoyance. "You said you had some questions for me? I trust they are more important than my friend's sleeping habits."

"My sources have informed me, Monsieur Roché," Picoté continued, his gaze fixed on Devin, "that there was an unsuccessful attempt made on the Chancellor's life last week. Do you think it had any connection to the murders here?"

Devin didn't even remember rising to his feet. "What did you say?" he asked, his heart beating unsteadily.

Picoté's smiled smugly. "Ah, you didn't know then, Monsieur Roché? When did you last hear from your father?"

"Two days ago," Devin stammered. "Is he all right? Was he hurt?"

"Not seriously," Picoté replied, obviously relishing his knowledge of the event. "An assassin hid on the seventh balcony of Council Chambers. Fortunately, light glinted off the barrel of his rifle when he aimed. The man was shot in the head before he could fire. The Chancellor was thrown to the floor by his bodyguards. I believe he only suffered bruises and a minor head injury."

Devin wheeled to look at Marcus.

"Did you know this?" he demanded.

Marcus nodded, his eyes locked with Picoté's.

Picoté's mouth twisted into the semblance of a smile. "And so I ask again, Monsieur Roché, do you think the two events are connected in some way?"

"How could I possibly know that?" Devin retorted. "There has been conflict among Council members for some time. My father indicated in his latest letter that he had received a personal threat. I did not interpret it to mean someone had actually made an attempt on his life! But obviously, I did not receive the same information you obtained."

"Do you know which Council members might pose a threat to your father?" Picoté asked, flourishing his notebook.

He could compile quite a list, Devin thought grimly, but he was unwilling to lay random suspicions before Jacques Picoté. He shook his head, and sank back onto the bench.

"I can provide you with names," Marcus replied. "Although, how that will help your small investigation here
. . ."

"My small investigation?" Picoté interrupted angrily. "Two good men are dead, *monsieur*. Perhaps that doesn't matter in the overall scheme of things, but it matters very much to me!"

Armand intervened. "He meant no offense, Jacques. It is just that if this crime has repercussions as far away as Coreé, surely, it is out of your hands to solve?"

"It occurs to me," Picoté replied furtively, "that Monsieur Roché may bear some culpability in the matter."

"In what way?" Armand demanded, frowning. "He came here as my student."

"And yet, he was aware of a threat to his life. He should have informed me as soon as he arrived in Lac Dupré. Two murders might have been averted!"

"I have my own security," Devin replied, his mind still reeling, imagining the assassination attempt in Council Chambers. He wished Picoté would leave so that he could question Marcus further about exactly what had happened. "I trust Marcus to see to my protection not the local authorities!"

"And yet, I am entrusted with the lives of the people in this village, Monsieur Roché," Picoté replied. "Your bodyguard has no authority here."

"In that you are wrong," Marcus said, pulling his packet of official papers from the neck of his shirt. He slapped them down on the table. "I believe the Chancellor's dispensation supersedes your authority."

Picoté's face paled. He reviewed the papers silently, the corner of his mouth twitching.

"You are quite right," he murmured, handing them back to Marcus. "Your authority exceeds mine in this matter."

"Since you have eliminated any local suspects or motives for these murders, I hereby advise you to cease your investigation," Marcus said. "Coreé has been informed and is taking action as we speak. You will be informed when and if the perpetrators are apprehended."

"And will they be returned to my district for trial and sentencing?" Picoté asked.

"I doubt that's possible," Marcus muttered. "The attempted murder of any member of the Chancellor's family is a treasonable offense. It carries the death sentence just as any murder charge would. Be assured, the assassins will be executed, whether they are tried here or in Coreé."

Picoté stood up and bowed stiffly. "I will make an official note of our conversation, Monsieur Beringer. Should the magistrate have any questions about the investigation I will refer him to you."

He hesitated uncertainly for a moment. "I actually came here this morning regarding another matter. I feel it is my duty to inform you that Monsieur Roché is not well liked in this community. Many people hold him personally responsible for Robert's and George's deaths. There are those who intend him physical harm. You should be aware of that and take appropriate precautions."

"I already have," Marcus replied. "But allow me to remind you that, anyone implicated in a threat against the Chancellor's son, will be dealt with very harshly. Be certain that your people understand that. I will show no mercy to anyone involved, should Monsieur Roché be hurt."

Picoté's eyes narrowed. "Don't forget, you are a long way from Coreé, Monsieur Beringer."

He retrieved his hat from the table, and was gone.

Devin only waited until he heard the front door slam before he turned on his bodyguard.

"Damn you, Marcus!" he said angrily. "Did you think it was a mercy for me to hear about this attack on my father from a pretentious small-town shérif instead of from you?"

Marcus took a deep breath. He glanced down at Devin and lowered his voice. "Your father never intended for you to hear about it, at all. He asked me not to tell you unless absolutely necessary."

"And what else are you keeping from me?" Devin snapped. "If I can't trust you, Marcus, who can I trust?"

Marcus leaned over, his mouth only inches from Devin's ear. "This isn't the time or the place," he hissed. "These are private matters between you and me."

"But surely, there is no need for so much secrecy!" Devin said breathlessly. "My God, my father could have been killed! Would you have told me then?"

Marcus's hands latched onto Devin's shoulders. "Come upstairs," he ordered. "I'll tell you what I can."

Devin yanked away. "What you can? Do you plan to dole out just enough information to keep me satisfied until the next crisis? Sometimes, I suspect I am in more danger from you than these villagers!"

"Then you would be wrong," Marcus muttered, shoving him toward the door.

Devin was halfway down the hall, when someone turned the knob on the front door. He stopped angrily, assuming it must be Picoté returning. But Gaspard stumbled through the doorway, his forehead covered in blood. He wavered unsteadily for an instant before he fell forward into Devin arms.

CHAPTER 35

Sticks and Stones

Devin staggered, trying to support Gaspard with his left arm and slam the door with his right.

"What happened?" he gasped. "Are you all right?"

Gaspard righted himself, one hand pressed to his forehead.

"Someone hit me with a rock."

Marcus took Gaspard's arm. "Sit," he directed, pushing him down on the hall bench.

Devin knelt beside him. "Did you see who threw it, Gaspard?"

He shook his head and then winced. "I didn't see anyone."

"For Christ's sake, Devin!" Marcus growled, pushing him aside. "Get out of the way!"

Suddenly, Armand was there, too, both of them bent over Gaspard. Devin shifted up against the door, feeling useless, and yet wanting to help. He folded his arms over his chest, his breathing erratic.

"Shall I go for Dr. Mareschal?" he asked, after a moment.

Marcus spared him a look. "You are not to go anywhere! How many times do I have to tell you that?"

Armand glanced at Devin. "There's no need for a doctor," he said, quietly. "It's just a gash. He'll be all right. Jeanette's on the terrace. Would you ask her to come in?"

Devin slid past them and ran down the hall. Jeanette was just coming into the kitchen, a basket on her arm.

"What's wrong?" she asked in alarm.

"Gaspard's hurt," Devin blurted out. "Your father asked for you to come. They're in the hall."

She put her basket on the table and rushed to help. Devin followed her at a discreet distance, afraid of incurring Marcus's anger again but compelled to see for himself that Gaspard wasn't seriously injured.

He stood in the doorway with Adrian. Gaspard's face was deadly white except for trickles of blood which stood out vividly against his pale skin. Jeanette was dispatched for a needle and thread, and Devin grimaced. Gaspard always claimed that it was his good looks that consistently brought him luck with the ladies. Devin hoped the scar would be a small one.

He watched Jeanette's small hands, so efficient, and yet gentle and comforting at the same time. He almost envied Gaspard his injury.

A few minutes later, Gaspard walked to the kitchen with Marcus's help. Armand installed him in the rocker with a mug of red wine, and sent Adrian for Picoté.

Devin paced in front of the fireplace, his stomach churning.

"Why would someone attack you?" he demanded, after a moment. "I'm the one they're angry with."

"Most of these people don't even know what you look like!" Marcus pointed out irritably. "They only know there are two young men from Coreé staying with Armand. All they want is someone to blame. One of you is as good as

251

the other, I imagine. I've told you both before that neither of you is to leave the house without me. What was so important that you had to go out alone this morning, Gaspard?"

Gaspard took a drink before answering. He slipped his hand into his pocket and pulled out his watch. It dropped and spun on the end of the chain, the sunlight glittering off the links.

"I tried to sell my watch," he murmured.

Devin's stomach clenched. "Please tell me this has nothing to do with Chastel," he protested guiltily. "I told you last night that I'd pay off the thousand francs you owe him."

Gaspard let his head fall back against the chair, his eyes narrowed against the pain.

"You were so angry; I decided to take care of the debt myself."

"With your watch?" Devin asked incredulously. "Gaspard, it's not worth a tenth of that!"

"It was a start, Dev," Gaspard replied. "Give me credit for trying."

"It's not worth getting killed for!" Devin replied.

"And, I'm not dead, in case you hadn't noticed." Gaspard took a sip of wine, eyeing Devin over the rim of his mug. "It seems to me you are overreacting."

Devin took a shaky breath. Perhaps he was overreacting, but only because of Picoté's revelation earlier.

"Someone tried to assassinate my father, Gaspard," he said.

Gaspard sat up. "God, Dev, I'm sorry. Is he all right?"

Devin nodded. "A man tried to shoot him in Council Chambers. According to Picoté, he wasn't badly hurt. His bodyguards knocked him down in time."

Gaspard drained his mug. "What does Picoté have to do with it?"

Devin glanced at Marcus. "Picoté's the one who told me. Apparently, Marcus chose not to share the information."

"Enough!" Marcus's hand slammed down on the table. He stood up, his face suffused with anger. "Devin, I'll see you upstairs."

Acutely aware of Jeanette looking on in horrified silence, Devin reluctantly complied. He patted Gaspard on the shoulder.

"I'll be back shortly," he murmured.

Gaspard raised his mug. "God, I hope so," he quipped. "Yell, if you need assistance. I'll send someone up."

Devin turned and walked down the hall, Marcus stalking behind him like an executioner. When he reached their bedroom, he turned his back and walked to the window.

"Sit down!" Marcus roared, slamming the door behind him.

Devin swung around to face him. "Don't give me orders! Do you have any idea how angry I am?"

"That's two of us, then," Marcus replied. "Because it never occurred to me that you would question both your father's judgment and mine."

Devin ran a hand across his forehead. "How could you keep that assassination attempt from me? God, Marcus, he's my father! You had no right to keep it to yourself."

Marcus sighed. "I was simply following you father's orders, Devin. If I can't do that, I am worth nothing to him."

"And you have no obligation to me?" Devin retorted.

"My obligation to you is dictated solely by his instruction," Marcus replied. "I am sworn to protect you, Devin, not to do your bidding."

Devin stared at him in frustration. "So what specific instructions have you been given concerning me?"

Marcus's eyes slid away from his and rested on the chair under the window.

"I am not at liberty to share that with you right now. You'll have to trust me that both your father and I have your best interests at heart."

Devin's hands clenched. "This isn't a game of semantics, Marcus. How do you expect me to make intelligent decisions without accurate information?"

A flicker of amusement crossed Marcus's face. "What monumental decisions are you wrestling with at the moment?"

"Perhaps I need to go home," Devin said.

Marcus laughed. "Because some idiot tried to take a shot at your father?"

Devin nodded.

"What could you possibly have done to prevent it? You're his son, not his bodyguard," Marcus replied. "What you are doing here is much more valuable to him."

Devin snatched at this new crumb of information. "How?"

Marcus sat down on his cot. "I said I would tell you what I could. Your father was dead set against your touring the provinces to gather the Chronicles. We discussed it at length. He felt it was too controversial considering the present political climate. That's why he sent you a message during your exams, asking you not to go."

"But he changed his mind . . . " Devin reminded him.

"He changed his mind because he decided that you and I together could be his eyes and ears in the provinces. He needs to know how far this opposition goes – whether Council members have poisoned their districts against him – or if the dissension is only in Coreé. He would handle political opposition differently than a full-blown rebellion."

"Has it come to that?" Devin asked, his lungs grappling for breath.

"Nothing is certain yet," Marcus replied. "But we're standing on the brink of something monumental, Devin. The empire is changing radically. In the next few years – either the provinces will begin receiving equal access to education and medical care under your father's leadership – or the old order will be rigidly maintained, at the cost of your father's life and the Council members who agree with him. Either way, your existence and mine will never be the same again."

Devin swallowed. "Do you think the opposition has a chance of winning?"

"No one knows that. But I'll tell you this; even if Forneaux and his allies win, it will be a short-lived victory. You've seen the resentment here. Men like Armand won't be suppressed for long; the masses will rise up the way they did in 1632. And it will happen soon, Devin, if you and I can't take the pulse of this empire so that your father can find a remedy."

"But, why me?" Devin asked. "Surely Ethan or Jacques would have been better suited . . . "

"Don't you see?" Marcus interrupted. "You were the perfect choice for the job. No one could ever accuse you of being political. You are known only as a scholar – an archivist – and therefore a neutral party."

"And yet, there were still objections to my trip," Devin reminded him.

"Only among those who fear the contents of the Chronicles. Your father became aware of disturbing inconsistencies once he became Chancellor. Written files that crossed his desk differed from the initial oral reports. At first, he attributed it to occasional inaccuracy, until a subtle pattern began to emerge, which always presented the official government position in a favorable light and provincial affairs in an unfavorable one." Marcus lowered his voice. "In Coreé, provincials are always made to appear primitive – illiterate and backward – like a race apart. It is ironic that you noticed similar disparities between the Archives and the Chronicles."

"Has Father confronted anyone on the Council about this?" Devin asked.

"Not yet. He needs concrete proof. And should he inadvertently approach the wrong person, someone who appears trustworthy, but isn't, he won't live very long."

Devin's breath hissed out. "But if he can't get to the bottom of it, who can? He is the most powerful man in our government, Marcus, and yet what you're telling me makes it appear that someone else is control."

The silence that followed made a chill run up Devin's back. He didn't want to be away from home for fifteen months when everything he loved might be in jeopardy. He remembered his departure from the dock in Coreé, and his father's attempt to smooth over their disagreement the night before. Had his father suspected then that they might never see each other again?

"What has he done that angered the opposition so?" he asked, trying to accept the idea that a conspiracy threatened his father's life.

"He has begun to institute some changes in Sorrento. He was deeply affected by the death of young Phillippe Rousseau, the stone cutter's son I told you about. He founded the first provincial school so that children could be educated in their own region, instead of removing them to Coreé. Students don't have to be sponsored; any boy who shows an interest is given the opportunity to attend, at no cost."

"Why would that make anyone angry?" Devin asked.

Marcus raised an eyebrow. "Think, Devin. An educated man is a threat. He wants to be paid for his labor. He isn't satisfied with simply receiving food and housing and living as a vassal of his aristocratic landlord. He is bound to compare and resent the inequality between the provinces and Coreé. Men like Forneaux don't want to have to share their wealth, and they are determined to keep the reins of power in the hands of a very few individuals. Educating the provincials is dangerous in their eyes."

Devin sank down on the bed. "I don't understand why Father didn't just tell me all of this."

"He thought you would be more objective in your reports if you didn't know the whole story. I have no doubt that excerpts from your letters will be read at Council meetings and reviewed by committee. If your observations simply support your father's sympathies they will lose their validity and impact. You should include as much factual information as possible."

"No wonder you kept urging me to write to him."

"I've done nothing on this trip, Devin, except protect you so that you can gather the information your father so desperately needs," Marcus said.

Devin ran a hand over his face. "God, I've suspected you of far worse."

"What now?" Marcus asked.

"Oh murder . . . treachery . . . corruption," Devin remarked "Nothing out of the ordinary."

Marcus grunted, his chin rising. "I do have a confession to make."

"By all means . . . " Devin said.

"That night we slept in Adrian's father's barn, I did meet someone in the yard."

257

"I knew it!" Devin cried. "And you let me think . . . "

"Let me finish," Marcus said, interrupting him. "Your father made arrangements for a military escort in each province, to be used at my discretion. That's one of the reasons following your itinerary was so important. The men met with me secretly that night, and I ordered them to trail us at a discreet distance. They're camped just south of Chastel's château. I think now their presence here might be a deterrent to any more violence."

"Or cause a riot, Marcus," Devin replied. "The villagers won't welcome an armed regiment."

"I'm not interested in making friends at this point. We have two more weeks here before you expect to move on. I want to make certain I can get you out of town in one piece."

"You're sure my father's all right?" Devin asked, his mind still on the assassination attempt.

"I have only his word for that," Marcus replied. "But this is what he told me: apparently, a gunman came through the roof and hid all night on the seventh balcony. He made his move when your father gave his opening remarks to the full assembly last Monday morning. The gunman neglected to take into account the way the sunlight streams through that huge glass dome during a morning session. Pierre Vacher saw the light reflecting off the rifle barrel and dived for your father. Both André Sommer and Charles Marchand shot the gunman before he could pull the trigger.

"Your father hit his head on the podium when he fell. When they got him upright, his head was bleeding, and some Council members assumed he'd been shot too. It caused a great deal of panic until he was able to assure them that he was all right. They recessed long enough for a physician to treat him but he refused to go home and rest. He went back out to the podium and addressed the full assembly, continuing his remarks as though nothing had ever happened."

Devin shook his head, laughing shakily. "That sounds like something he would do. And my mother, do you have any idea how she's taking all this?"

"I would imagine your mother was only given an abridged version of what went on. Your father has always been very careful to shield her from the more disturbing aspects of his chancellorship."

"I can understand his wanting to protect her, but why didn't he tell me?" Devin asked.

Marcus raised his eyebrows. "Did you give him an accurate account of your fall from the cliff road and your injury during the wolf attack?"

Devin shook his head.

"Well, I guess we tend to protect those we love, even if means lying to spare them worry," Marcus said. "Don't be too hard on him."

A tentative knock startled them both.

"I'm sorry to interrupt," Adrian called out. "But Dr. Mareschal is here to check your wrist, Devin. Can you come downstairs or should I send him up?"

"I'll come down," Devin said, glancing at Marcus. "I think we're finished here."

He sent Marcus down alone before he withdrew a thousand francs from his wallet and slipped them into his pocket. He would give the money to Gaspard today, before his friend put himself at risk again to pay his gambling debts.

CHAPTER 36

Solutions

Mareschal turned from reattaching the bandage that bound Gaspard's head, to smile at Devin as he walked into the kitchen.

"Ah, here's the patient I came to see. Come sit down at the table where I can have a look at your arm." He gave Jeanette a patronizing smile. "Excellent stitches, young lady. If you were a boy, I'd ask Chastel to sponsor you for medical training. Could I have a clean towel, my dear?"

Devin almost pointed out that he saw no reason why a woman couldn't become a physician if she had the aptitude, but he was reluctant to have any more radical ideas attributed to his father's influence. He sat down obediently and unbuttoned his cuff, laying his arm on the towel that Jeanette placed on the table.

"So," Mareschal asked, as he rolled back Devin's sleeve, "what have you two boys been doing to make people throw rocks at you?"

"There continue to be hard feelings about the murders," Armand murmured, hovering close by. "I suspect that Picoté has been fueling the fire."

"He always was an arrogant little bastard," Mareschal replied, sliding a knife blade skillfully under the bandage on Devin's wrist. "Chastel can have him replaced. Stirring up insurrections hardly falls under the responsibilities of a shérif."

"Don't," Devin protested softly.

Mareschal looked up, quickly retracting the knife. "Did I cut you, *monsieur?*"

Devin shook his head. "No, I meant, don't have Picoté removed. It won't help anything and it will probably make the situation worse. We're treading a very narrow path here. I don't want any resentment directed toward my father."

"If Picoté isn't doing his job," Mareschal said, wielding his blade again, "he needs to be replaced."

Devin cleared his throat. "He's lost someone he cares about. It's understandable that he's angry."

Mareschal glanced at Devin. "It seems to me that you have a right to be angry, too, *monsieur*. You did nothing to contribute to Robert's death, and now your friend has been hurt because of something neither of you had any control over."

Devin nodded. "Of course, I'm angry that Gaspard was hurt. But I don't know who attacked him. I have no idea who killed those two young men either. There is a great deal going on that I have no control over."

"Well, Chastel holds the reins of power here," Mareschal replied. "Picoté only serves as shérif at Jean's behest. One word from you, *monsieur* . . . "

"I'll keep it mind," Devin replied, watching the discarded bandages fall away onto the table top.

Here was another blatant abuse of power, he thought. Apparently, even provincial authorities owed their livelihoods to the aristocrats who ruled their districts. An angry complaint from the Chancellor's son and Chastel would bring Picoté's world crashing down around his shoulders.

Mareschal smiled when he saw Devin's arm.

"Oh, to be young again! I tell you, Armand, you and I couldn't have an arm nearly torn off by a wolf and have it heal like this in a week! This looks far better than I had hoped."

Across fading green and yellow bruises, jagged furrows twisted from the middle of Devin's forearm to the base of his hand. Fortunately, the greater part would always remain hidden beneath his shirt sleeve. But he felt certain the scars would be with him till he died, a prominent reminder – should he ever be inclined to forget it – that, currently, civilization ended on the borders of Viénne.

"Any loss of feeling or impaired motor function?" Mareschal asked, as he gently probed the area around the stitches. "No lingering fever or chills?"

"No," Devin answered. "Nothing."

Mareschal shook his head. "You're a very lucky man, *monsieur*. I'll get those stitches out now." He took out a pair of small, narrow scissors and a pair of tweezers. He slid the scissors under the first stitch and snipped.

"Monsieur Roché," Armand said, setting a mug of wine beside Devin's left hand. "I have seen you wear only casual clothing on this trip. Did you bring anything more formal with you?"

Devin glanced at his wrinkled shirt, now spotted with Gaspard's blood.

"I dressed in a hurry this morning . . . " He sucked in a breath as Mareschal yanked the first stitch out and laid it on the towel.

"No, no," Armand replied. "I mean something you might wear at home in Coreé, not traveling clothes."

The second stitch snaked out, puckering the skin and leaving a glistening drop of blood. Devin raised the mug and gulped before answering.

"I have tried to blend in with the provincial people. I didn't think it was wise to emphasize the differences between us."

The third stitch snagged and Devin winced as Mareschal worked the scissors under it a moment.

Armand rested a hand on Devin's shoulder. "Well, I think that on Friday when you perform, you should dress like the Chancellor's son, for a change. Perhaps, a gentle reminder that your father rules this empire might not be amiss."

He turned to Mareschal. "Since Monsieur Roché's brought nothing suitable with him, do you think you could lend him something, Dr. Mareschal?"

Mareschal shook the third stitch off the tweezers onto the towel. He paused to size Devin up.

"He's smaller than either Jean or me. I doubt I have anything that would fit, but I imagine Chastel has something left from his younger days that might do. What are you up to, Armand?"

Armand leaned nonchalantly against the table, a slight smile on his lips.

"I just think that we might be able to soothe some angry neighbors if Monsieur Roché were to tell the right story Friday night. I need him to look the part."

Marcus joined them. "I don't think this is wise, Armand. With feelings running as they are, I don't think Devin should perform at all tomorrow."

Drops of blood stood out like tiny red currants across his forearm. Devin wished Armand would stop talking. He

263

couldn't concentrate. His mind was full of the pull and tug of Mareschal's tweezers. He took another swallow of wine and looked away.

"No one would dare attack a storyteller in a Bard's Hall; even an unpopular storyteller," Armand assured Marcus. "You have my guarantee on that."

"Well, a room full of people is too much for me to handle alone," Marcus protested. "I can't swear to Devin's safety without additional men."

"Chastel can provide extra guards, if you need them," Mareschal offered. "You have only to ask."

Devin eyed Mareschal warily. Most of the stitches weren't coming out cleanly. They needed to be pried loose where the skin had begun to heal around them. He winced as the next one scored a fresh furrow across a row of ragged tooth marks.

"You'll have to let Monsieur Roché come out to the château, then," Mareschal was saying, "I can't guess what clothes will fit him. He'll have to try them on." He paused to glance at Marcus. "Our coachman carries a pistol if that relieves your mind any."

"I wouldn't let Devin go without me," Marcus replied, "and I don't like to leave Gaspard alone."

Gaspard stirred and yawned. "So, take me with you. I'm feeling much better and I'd be happy to get out for the day. Chastel and I have a bit of unfinished business anyway."

"Well, that's settled, then," Armand said, tapping Devin's shoulder. "By the way, I have a new story that I want you to perform tomorrow night, Monsieur Roché. If you go with Mareschal you must be back by dark or else you will be up all night learning it."

"I'll do my best," Devin replied, through gritted teeth.

"I will insist on it," Armand said. "This will be the most important story I have taught you so far. It is imperative that you repeat it flawlessly."

Devin nodded. "I promise, I will." He flinched, as another stitch tore his skin. "God, will you hurry up, Mareschal?" he begged.

CHAPTER 37

"Remi Reynard"

Armand patted Devin's shoulder.

"You'll do fine," he assured him for the second time. "Remember what I told you, begin with "Lisette's Lament," do "The Dead of the Dantzig" next, and then finish with "The Story of Remi Reynard;" I guarantee you a standing ovation."

"I'd bet you on that," Devin replied, "but I've spent all my money."

Armand grunted. "It will be worth it, Monsieur Roché, mark my words."

They stood by the banister at the end of the upstairs hall overlooking the front door. The performance hall would be crowded tonight, Devin thought, judging from the steady influx of guests surging through the entrance. Had they come to hear the Chronicle, or did they just want to see the man responsible for bringing assassins to their little village?

"Most of them have probably only come to catch a glimpse of you and Gaspard," Armand said, echoing Devin's thoughts.

"But we'll give them more than they bargained for tonight."
He glanced approvingly at Devin's black velvet jacket and
open collared white shirt. "Chastel came through, I must
say. It was thoughtful of him to have his seamstress tailor
that jacket for you. You look different, *monsieur*, far more
like the aristocratic archivist that you are. The clothes were
an excellent choice."

Devin didn't feel any different. Although they'd spent most
of last night rehearsing "The Story of Remi Reynard," he
still felt uneasy. Chastel's hastily arranged costume hadn't
inspired any confidence in him. The jacket was twenty years
out of fashion and the shirt was more suited to a young art
student. But he guessed the overall effect implied wealth and
authority, which was exactly what Armand had in mind.

"I hope you know what you're doing, Armand," Marcus
growled, from his stance behind Devin. "If anything goes
wrong, I'm holding you personally responsible."

Devin glanced at his bodyguard. Tonight, at Armand's
insistence, Marcus had donned the blue and silver livery of
the Chancellor's Personal Guard. Together, he and Devin
presented the very image Devin had tried so hard to avoid.

"Nothing will go wrong," Armand assured him. "These
are good people."

"Who throw stones at innocent strangers," Marcus
reminded him.

"Picoté is certain that it was only children who targeted
Gaspard," Armand told him.

"Until I threatened to conduct my own investigation,"
Marcus replied. "He took the incident more seriously then."

"Well, there will be no stones thrown tonight," Armand
said. "Come on, Monsieur Roché, the crowd at the door is
thinning. Let's make a grand entrance."

By the time they descended the stairs, only Adrian stood by the door. He gave them a grin.

"A very good night," he said, shaking a basket loaded with coins. "There is standing room only."

Marcus made an exasperated noise. "That will complicate security."

"Chastel has four guards on every wall, plus more outside," Armand pointed out. "Anyone would have to be crazy to move against Monsieur Roché tonight."

"It's been my experience," Marcus muttered, "that every town has at least one or two crazy people in it. I doubt that Lac Dupré is any exception."

Armand ignored him.

Jeanette appeared suddenly from the kitchen, her cheeks flushed and her dark hair curling around her face. Devin thought she'd never looked more beautiful.

"I just wanted to wish you luck, *monsieur*," she said brightly. "I'm sure your performance tonight will be wonderful."

"Thank you," Devin murmured, touched that she took the time to wish him well. He wished fervently that he could spend a quiet evening in the kitchen with Jeanette, rather than have to face a crowd that might well have come to see him murdered.

"Come on, Monsieur Roché," Armand urged, dropping his arm over Devin's shoulders in a show of support. "Let's not keep them waiting."

The room was packed. Every bench was lined, shoulder to shoulder, and people had gathered toward the back and along the sides, standing in small groups. At the feet of those in the front row, children sat giggling and tussling on the floor. Chastel's men, their faces grave, stood at attention, rifles pointing at the ceiling. Conversation stopped when Armand

and Devin entered the room. Inquisitive faces turned to watch them walk down the center aisle; furious whispering began as they passed, and continued as they reached the front of the room.

Devin turned to face them, glad of Marcus's imposing figure beside him. The roaring fire at his back did nothing to dispel his inner chill He stood slightly behind Armand and viewed the sea of angry faces, wishing the evening was over and done with.

Armand raised his hands and the audience quieted.

"My friends," he said, beaming confidently at the assembled group. "Welcome to tonight's performance. I am pleased to introduce Devin Roché, our Chancellor Elite's youngest son. He has come to Lac Dupré as my student. Tonight is his first public performance of Ombria's Chronicle."

He took Devin by the elbow and drew him forward. Devin bowed graciously, as though the audience had received him warmly. He retrieved Adrian's harp from the stool beside him and sat down.

"Good evening," he announced. "My first selection will be 'Lisette's Lament.'"

Looking up, he froze. Two late arrivals stood framed in the doorway. He exhaled as he recognized them. Gaspard and Jean Chastel had come in together. They walked behind the last row of benches, and settled against the wall next to one of Chastel's guards. Devin gave them a shaky smile over the heads of the villagers. He was glad that he had apologized to Gaspard for his outburst over his gambling debt, and given him the money to settle up with Chastel himself. Now, at least, the restraint between them had eased.

As he scanned the crowd he realized that Jeanette was conspicuously absent. A chill touched his heart. Had Armand excluded her because he thought there might be trouble? Jacques Picoté sat in the first row. Devin wondered if he'd come to represent authority or cast the first stone.

He bent his head and ran his fingers over the harp strings. At the first notes, the room quieted. He tried to visualize little Mäite before him, instead of a room full of bitter villagers who'd lost two of their cherished young men. They sat stony faced and unresponsive, totally unreachable, even though the harp begged their attention. Devin realized that it was only out of deference to Armand that they were listening to him at all. To begin with, he looked just over the heads of his audience, but as he neared the end of the song, he began to selectively make eye contact with a few of his listeners. He hoped it was not his imagination that he saw several faces soften as he finished.

There was no applause, and he faltered, wondering whether to go on. Had they orchestrated this ahead of time, he wondered? Or was the feeling against him so intense that not one of them would recognize publicly that he had done an adequate job of storytelling? Instinct told him that this crowd could go from anger to riot with little provocation, and he longed to walk out now before the unthinkable happened.

Armand touched his shoulder. "Continue," he whispered.

Marcus's anxiety was palpable. His eyes flicked constantly over the crowd, his hand poised over the pistol in his belt. At the total lack of positive response from the crowd, Chastel's men had stiffened, their weapons ready to be lowered at an instant's notice. At the back of the room, Gaspard and Chastel were poised for flight, if things went from bad to worse.

Please God, let them escape if there is trouble, Devin prayed, don't allow anyone else to die because of me.

"'The Dead of the Dantzig,'" he announced, willing his voice not to tremble or break. He stroked the familiar strings

of the harp and began, concentrating exclusively on the music
and the words.

The Dantzig winds from Northern Seas
To the southern Orleans shore.
In frozen parts, its waters start
Its chilling currents pour.

Its flow across the continent,
Divides Llisé in two.
And no good land, escapes the brand,
Of that water running through.

And north to south the people speak
Of the depths beneath those waves.
And some maintain, those killed for gain,
By its waters will be saved.

For the Dantzig's waters deep and cold,
Preserve their dead with care.
And legend tells, that those who fell,
May one day, soon, be spared.

For where those frigid currents run,
The depths have not been probed,
And bards will long recite in song
The prophecy foretold.

So mourning friends and family
Still bear their ravaged dead,
With tears and prayers, they leave them there
In the river's watery bed.

So all of Ombria's patriots,
Her brave and valiant men –
All those who've dared – lie silenced there
And wait to rise again.

For those who fight for Ombria
Who for her rights have bled,
Will all join ranks, along her banks,
To greet the Dantzig's dead.

For when the fate of Ombria,
Lies poised upon the scale,
All men will fight to set things right
And we will never fail!

Devin allowed the last notes to linger and then stilled the harp strings with his open palm. The room fell deadly silent. He waited mutely for any response. Surprise had registered on several faces, confusion on others. Everyone in the room knew that Robert's family had just returned from the three-day trip to bury his body in the Dantzig at Museé. The choice of interment had been a political statement, defining Robert as a hero, and Coreé and the Rochés as the enemy. The lines had already been drawn, but with Armand's help, Devin intended to make a political statement of his own before the evening was over.

A smattering of applause began and grew more enthusiastic. Devin realized their accolade was in honor of Ombria, not his meager performance, but it gave him hope, nonetheless. These people's pride and allegiance was to their province not Llisé. But at least their response showed that things were going according to Armand's well-orchestrated plan. It called for Devin to speak of love and patriotism first, and then at last, to remind them of Remi Reynard.

The applause died away as quickly as it came. Devin wasn't certain if what he heard next was the last few tentative claps or raindrops on the roof. Distant thunder confirmed the latter, and with it the tension in the room increased. All eyes were on Devin.

He stood up, leaning the harp carefully against his stool.

"For my last selection," he announced, "I will tell 'The Story of Remi Reynard.'" He ignored the gasps that followed. Armand had thought they might have forgotten. It was Chastel who had first put the thought in Armand's head, when he'd mentioned at the funeral that Robert had aspirations to join the Chancellor's service in Coreé.

Devin cleared his throat and began:

"*Remi Reynard was born on a farm just outside of Pireé, the only son of a carriage maker. When he was only a little boy, he loved to hear stories of Coreé, where his father's carriages graced the streets, and ten thousand oil lamps lighted the city at night. He told his father that one day he would join the Chancellor's service. He longed to become one of the Chancellor's Personal Guards, to defend him and protect him, and wear the blue and silver livery of that high office.*

"*When Sébastien Rouse was elected Chancellor Elite of Llisé in 1787, the opposition grumbled. Rouse had won by only a few votes and they demanded a second tally. But Council allowed the election to stand after the first count, citing Rouse's small but significant margin. Rouse began to prepare for his Grand Tour of the provinces while the opposition plotted his assassination.*

"*Remi had just turned eleven. He looked forward to the Grand Tour with great anticipation. Only once in a Chancellor's* reign does he visit every provincial capital in Llisé and Remi was fortunate enough to live within walking distance of Pireé. The months seemed to pass slowly but at last, news reached Pireé that the Chancellor's party should arrive by ship within the week. Unknown to the Chancellor, André Follett, a professional assassin, had already made the trip by land and waited quietly in the best hotel in Pireé for the opportunity to kill him.

"People crowded the docks at Pireé for days, hoping to catch a glimpse of Chancellor Rouse when he arrived, some even prayed to venture close enough to touch his robes. Remi imagined that somehow he might attract Rouse's attention and be allowed to join his entourage. His father tried to reason with him, explaining that there was no way that one small boy could be singled out for special notice among the thousands of people gathered in Pireé but Remi believed that somehow it would happen.

"At last, on June 23rd, the Chancellor's ship arrived. Remi climbed a high post so that he could see Rouse come ashore. Not far away, André Follett lay in wait, perched in the branches of huge maple tree. He ignored the gangly boy dangling excitedly from the post and aimed just under the child's feet at the gangplank below.

"Rouse came down the walkway preceded by a dozen guards and followed by a dozen others. Above him, Follett took aim. Remi had eyes only for the Chancellor, one hand waving frantically to catch his attention, the other anchoring him to the post. And just as Follett pulled the trigger, Remi slipped and fell. Follett's bullet hit him in the center of his chest. Remi's father caught him in his arms, but his son was dead before he hit the ground."

Devin heard a stifled sob from somewhere in the audience. He took a breath and continued:

"*The sound of the shot and the boy falling alerted the guards. Rouse was hustled back to the ship, unharmed. Follett was grabbed by the angry crowd as he tried to descend from the tree. He was beaten to death before Rouse's bodyguards could obtain the names of the men who had hired him. Poor Remi lay dead, at the age of eleven, from a bullet through the heart. And yet, unknowingly, Remi had fulfilled his dream: he had saved the Chancellor's life.*

"*Rouse was grateful and humbled that a child had given his life for him. Remi was buried in the blue and silver uniform of the Chancellor's Personal Guard. In honor of Remi's sacrifice, Chancellor Rouse erected a statue which stands in the square at Pireé to this day. He hoped that it might offer some comfort to his family since Remi had given his life for the Chancellor he had yearned to serve.*"

Devin took a deep breath and looked out over the audience. He even saw tears on some of the faces of the men. Picoté refused to meet his eyes, and several rows behind the shériff, a pregnant woman sobbed openly into her apron. Devin had come to the hard part, now. Memorization was one thing but this next speech had to come from the heart. He cleared his throat.

"Robert Foulard and George Matisse died for me. I don't believe that they knew it at the time . . . or that it would have made their deaths any less horrifying if they had. I assure you that I would have spared them, if I could. But I had no way of knowing that a simple thing like my discarded jacket would lead to their deaths."

Devin swallowed hard and continued.

"In my father's name, I have authorized a statue in honor of Robert and George to be placed in your town square. This morning, I spoke to Claude Deville, the stone mason, and

275

he will begin work immediately. I thought it was important that we employ someone local, who knew both Robert and George," he gestured to include them all, "and who knew all of you. The Chancellor has also authorized a payment to each of the families of one hundred francs a year," he said.

There was a gasp from the crowd and he felt guilty that such a small amount would seem like a fortune to them. The money had actually come from Devin's own pocket, but under the circumstances it was the least he could do. The monument and the gifts to the families had exhausted his reserve but he'd vowed not to think about that for the moment. He waited until the uproar died down before he spoke again.

"In addition, you have my personal assurance that any male child from either family will be guaranteed schooling from this time forward." Devin nodded toward the back of the room. "Monsieur Chastel has offered to oversee the educational arrangements."

The pregnant woman crossed herself. Clutching at her belly, she began to weep again. Devin exhaled before finishing.

"As for myself, I cannot tell you how much I regret that my presence in your village has caused such tragedy." He bowed his head. "I am profoundly sorry."

He held his breath, waiting in silence to receive their forgiveness or condemnation. For an instant, nothing happened at all, and then there was a roar of sound around him. People had risen to their feet. Some were clapping, some were crying. Others were hugging each other.

Armand joined him, slipping an arm around his shoulders. "Breathe," the bard instructed. "It's over."

People began to line up at the stage to shake Devin's hand. They greeted them together, Armand carefully introducing each person, so Devin could call them by name.

Picoté wormed his way to the front.

"Why didn't you tell me about this earlier?" he demanded. "It might have saved a great deal of unpleasantness."

"You didn't ask," Devin replied.

"Money won't replace two men's lives!" Picoté blustered.

Devin took a breath and looked him in the eye. "You're right, it won't," he agreed. "But it will make life easier for those they left behind."

He turned to greet the pregnant woman, who Picoté had pushed aside. "Mrs. Matisse?" he asked, taking both her hands in his. "I am so sorry about your husband's death."

Picoté spat in disgust and walked away. Marcus watched his every move until he left the performance hall and walked out into the night.

CHAPTER 38

Celebration

It was nearly an hour before the performance hall cleared completely. After the last person left, Adrian closed and locked the front door, slumping against it dramatically.

"I'm glad that's over!" he admitted. "You could have cut the tension in that room with a knife tonight. I was afraid there would be a riot before the evening was over." He sketched a playful bow at Devin. "Until your final presentation, that is. My compliments, Devin! You outdid yourself!"

Devin was running on nerves. He wasn't certain how much longer he could have continued to calmly shake hands and smile. The evening had been nerve-wracking and he heartily agreed with Adrian. He was glad it was over!

Armand, still wildly exuberant, rumpled Devin's hair and caught him with a hand around his neck, dragging him backwards toward the kitchen.

"Come, let us celebrate!" The bard turned to Adrian. "Have I ever had such a protégé, Adrian? The Chancellor's youngest son was born with a silver tongue and I, Armand Vielle, have polished it to perfection!"

Adrian rolled his eyes at Devin. "I wondered how long it would be before he took credit for your performance!"

Devin laughed. "He deserves it. He orchestrated the entire thing."

Armand turned to beam at him. "Ah but, save some of the praise for yourself, Monsieur Roché! I did not script that final speech, that came entirely from you."

"But you told me what to say!" Devin protested.

"I simply made suggestions," Armand maintained. "I should have known better than to try to coach the son of a consummate politician!"

Devin shook his head. "Believe me; my father has never instructed me in rhetoric."

"Then it must be natural talent," Armand replied. He threw one hand dramatically in the air. "God, that is frightening! You may have us all wrapped around your finger by the end of the month."

"He already does," Gaspard said with a laugh.

Chastel had dismissed all but a few of his men. The last four had retreated outside to stand guard at both doors. Devin had been surprised to find Dr. Mareschal hovering in the hallway when they emerged from the performance hall. Apparently, Chastel had posted him in the kitchen in case there were casualties tonight. Thank God, a physician was never needed.

Chastel and Mareschal still lingered uneasily in the hallway. Chastel's gaze was carefully directed away from Armand. He raised his hand in farewell.

"We'll be going," he said. "I can't tell you how relieved I am that everything went smoothly tonight, Monsieur Roché. You did well!"

For just a moment, Armand hesitated. "Please," he said finally, drawing his brother into the kitchen. "Come and join us. After all, it was you who set this all in motion, Jean, with your comment about Robert's desire to move to Coreé and train for the Chancellor's Personal Guard. You also provided the guards and Monsieur Roché's wardrobe. You deserve a place at this celebration!"

Jeanette had sliced bread and cheese on large platters. Delicate little pastries were artistically arranged on trays, and several bottles of wine were standing on the table. The room was warm and bright with candles. Devin felt as though he were coming home.

Armand popped a cork and poured wine for everyone. Grinning from ear to ear, he held his mug aloft.

"I propose a toast," he declared, "to Monsieur Roché and the power of the spoken word!"

Devin watched in amazement as Jean Chastel tapped his mug against Armand's and received a smile in return.

Jeanette touched Devin's elbow. Her dark hair curled around her flushed cheeks. "I sat on the stairs in the hallway during your performance, Monsieur Roché. You were wonderful tonight!"

He was irrationally pleased at her comment and felt his own cheeks redden.

"Thank you," he murmured with a slight bow. "That is high praise from you, considering your father is the finest bard in Ombria."

She lowered her lashes. "And yet every bard brings his own touch to his storytelling. I don't believe I have ever heard my father sing 'Lisette's Lament' with such tenderness or emotion."

Devin inclined his head. "Thank you. And thank you for all of this." He gestured at the table laden with food and wine.

"I hoped there might be cause for celebration." She hesitated a moment, as though searching for words. "I hoped that, tonight, people might find that those who live in Lac Dupré and those who live in Coreé have more in common than they might have thought."

Devin shook his head. "And yet there are such horrible inequities, Jeanette. Why should people in the provinces have to go without proper medical care or education while those in Coreé have so much?"

Marcus caught Devin's eye and shook his head in warning. Devin looked away, concentrating instead on Jeanette's lovely face.

"Surely, everyone in Coreé isn't wealthy," Jeanette said. "Isn't it more that the imbalance lies between rich and poor there, as it does here?"

Devin visualized the streets of Coreé. To assert that there was no poverty or hunger in that great city would be foolish. The poor were everywhere; begging alms at the dormitories at the Académie, and lining the steps after Council meetings. But the inequality he had found in Ombria was something else entirely.

"It is complicated, Jeanette," he explained. "Yes, there is poverty in Coreé. There is terrible poverty in the midst of great affluence. And in Coreé, it is very definitely a disparity between rich and poor, or perhaps, more accurately, between the fortunate and the unfortunate. But here in the provinces the inequality is legislated. The influential in Coreé pass laws which enable them to retain and increase their own wealth and yet limit what provincial people are able to attain."

"How?" Jeanette asked.

Devin gestured with his hands. "When education and transportation are strictly controlled, initiative and enterprise are stunted. Basically, only exceptional people succeed."

"Isn't that true even in Coreé?" asked a voice behind him.

Devin turned to see Chastel standing with a mug of wine in his hand.

"Perhaps," he agreed. "But opportunities to succeed are also more prevalent in Coreé."

"For whom?" Chastel asked.

"For. . . " Devin faltered.

"I think you will find that, as a rule, only exceptional people succeed in Coreé too, Monsieur Roché," Chastel said quietly. "It is called survival of the fittest. And it is as true for the wolves of Ombria as it is for the people of Llisé. Even education won't change that."

"Perhaps not," Devin replied. "But education levels the playing field, allowing more people a chance at success. An educational system in the provinces would ultimately strengthen Llisé."

Chastel took a sip of his wine and nodded. "I agree."

Devin nearly dropped his mug. "You do?"

Chastel raised his eyebrows. "Well, I realize it is an unpopular sentiment but I found the argument compelling years ago."

"Then why haven't you supported it?" Devin asked, earning a frown from Marcus.

"I'm not a Council member, Monsieur Roché," Chastel replied.

"And yet you are friends with several of them," Devin pointed out.

Chastel retained his composure, the corners of his lips curling a little in amusement. "And I intend to stay friends with them, Monsieur Roché. I do what I can here in my little corner of the empire, and keep my mouth shut whenever controversial issues arise."

"Have you considered becoming a Council member?" Devin asked.

"I would have to be appointed, as you well know," Chastel replied, refilling his own mug and then topping off Devin's.

"And yet there are vacant seats each term," Devin continued, taking a drink. "I could indicate to Father that you are interested . . . "

"Please," Chastel said, laying a placating hand on Devin's arm. "Don't bother, Monsieur Roché. I am quite happy as things stand. I wouldn't want to spend more than half the year in Coreé." He threw a mischievous glance at Armand. "I would miss running with my wolves."

"You could be a real force for change," Devin urged.

"Or a source of contention," Chastel replied. "Leave it, *monsieur*. I am content as things are."

Gaspard joined them, his face unusually pale under the swath of bandages around his head.

"Have a care what you are saying, Dev. What you're preaching is blasphemy to the old-line Council members. If Chastel were appointed to a Council seat with his views, you'd be sending him into a lion's den. My father would literally have me beaten for spouting the opinions you've just voiced. And he'd see that you received even worse treatment, if you had intentionally convinced me to your way of thinking. When and if things change, it won't be a swift or an easy process. If you push too hard, you will never live to see the results of your efforts."

Devin began to protest but Gaspard held up a hand. "Listen, you may tell stories like a Master Bard but I think you need to learn a little subtlety, Dev, before you begin airing your political opinions publicly."

"Subtlety isn't one of Devin's virtues, Gaspard," Marcus replied wryly. "Thank you for reminding him that it's worth cultivating."

"But change has to start somewhere!" Devin protested. "Someone has to be willing to be the first to speak up!"

"Don't ask me to volunteer!" Chastel responded, holding up a hand. "I prefer to keep my head off the chopping block."

"And yet, you truly understand the issues here in the provinces. You have seen the problems first-hand that the present system causes," Devin insisted. "You are the perfect . . . "

"Enough!" Armand shouted. "Monsieur Roché, this is a celebration not a political forum! We have just extracted you from a great deal of trouble, don't be foolish enough to blunder right into it again." He pushed him gently toward the table. "Sit! Eat! Drink lots of wine! Tomorrow, I intend to be merciless. I will teach you at least five new stories, if it takes all day and all night. So enjoy yourself while you can!"

Devin yielded, with a small sound of protest. He dropped onto a bench, his back to the fire. To his delight, Jeanette sat down beside him. Her eyes sparkled as she reached for a wine bottle. After filling her own mug, she replaced the bottle on the table and extended her mug to Devin. He laughed and drank half of it in a single swallow. Handing it back to her, he smiled as she finished the rest herself.

"Monsieur Roché," Armand called out, tapping him on the shoulder with his cane. "Perhaps, you'd better go up and get me that cloak your father bought you. It's time I started embroidering one of Ombria's wolves on it."

Devin turned to look at him in amazement. "But I haven't finished learning the Chronicle yet!"

Armand shrugged. "You will. I'm certain of that now. Besides, I am an old man, and my needle work has never been very good. It will take me a while to finish it."

Jeanette stood up and linked affectionate arms around her father's waist.

"I will embroider it, Papa, just as I always do. Why would you suggest such a thing! Monsieur Roché doesn't want his cloak to look like it was embroidered by a child!"

Armand splayed his hand across the center of his chest.

"Ah, but I made a vow that I would embroider it myself if he performed well at his final presentation. I didn't believe him that he could learn the Chronicle in a month. Now, I find I must eat my words. And . . . ," he said, gesturing grandly, " . . . embroider his cloak."

Devin laughed. "Then, I release you from your vow, Armand. Please, allow Jeanette to do it for me." He took a sip of wine. "Besides, I still have more than a week as your student. Surely tonight wasn't my final presentation?"

Armand waggled his hand and shrugged. "Perhaps it might be better to end on a high note, Monsieur Roché. The people of Lac Dupré tend to be a volatile lot. Tonight, they loved you; next week, maybe, not so much. Why don't we quit while we are ahead?"

Devin ducked his head playfully. "Then, I bow to your expertise, Armand."

Armand grinned and motioned with his mug. "See, Adrian, I have Monsieur Roché dancing to my tune at last. I told you he would come around!"

Adrian shook his head. "I believe it is only a momentary aberration. The acclaim and the wine have gone to his head. By daybreak, he will likely be questioning your judgment again. I wouldn't count on his cooperation tomorrow."

"I will enjoy his acquiescence while I can then," Armand replied amiably.

Devin laughed and leaned back against the table. It was good to see Armand so jovial and happy. For the moment, the bard was even at ease with his brother. Tonight, maybe Devin had made a tiny step toward promoting understanding between the people of Ombria and the government of Coreé. Tomorrow was another day.

CHAPTER 39

Admonitions

"What were you thinking?" Marcus demanded when they reached their room.

The merrymaking had gone on for hours, and Chastel and Mareschal had just staggered out into the dark for the ride back to the château. Devin had offered to stay and help Jeanette tidy up the kitchen but Armand had waved him off to bed.

Devin stumbled over the threshold and sank down wearily on the bed.

"What are talking about, Marcus?" he asked.

Marcus closed the door quietly behind him. "You were discussing education in the provinces with Jean Chastel in the kitchen. He's René Forneaux's friend for God's sake! Tonight, Gaspard showed more sense than you did, although I never thought I'd say that!"

"Chastel's in favor of educating the masses, too," Devin replied. "He told me so, himself."

Marcus shook his head. "Did it ever occur to you that he might have lied?"

Devin ran a hand over his face. "Why on earth would he lie to me?"

"So that you would declare yourself," Marcus replied. "Did your father never tell you that you don't lay all your cards on the table in front of a professional gambler, Devin?" He turned away, unbuckling his belt and laying his pistol on the chest beside the bed. "One moment you conduct yourself like an experienced diplomat and the next you act like a schoolboy!"

"I don't think I am such a bad judge of character," Devin protested. "And I truly believe that Chastel is an ally."

"I sincerely hope you are right," Marcus said, shedding the jacket from his uniform and arranging it neatly over the back of the chair. "But I would warn you not to trust anyone."

Devin raised his eyebrows. "Not even you, Marcus?"

"Oh, sleep it off!" Marcus retorted. "Maybe, you'll be more sensible in the morning."

Devin chuckled and lay back on the bed. He closed his eyes, his feet still planted on the floor.

"And take off that jacket and shirt!" Marcus demanded. "If Chastel had the good grace to have it tailored for you, the least you could do is hang it up!"

Devin pushed himself into a sitting position.

"Since when are you in charge?" he grumbled.

Marcus grunted. "I have always been in charge. You have simply been too preoccupied to notice."

Too tired to argue, Devin unbuttoned the jacket and folded it, laying it over the trunk at the foot of the bed. The shirt followed it, before he dropped his trousers and crept between the covers.

Marcus was still sitting on the edge of his cot. "One other word of warning," he said gruffly. "It seems you have forgotten Armand's admonition about Jeanette."

Devin settled into bed wearily, drawing the blanket up around his shoulders.

"I believe that was directed mostly at Gaspard."

"At the time, maybe, but you know he meant it to apply to you as well, Devin. Armand's done a great deal for you. Don't let this become an issue that drives the two of you apart. In a few days, we'll be moving on. Considering your position and the short time we still have to spend here, it's hardly fair of you to encourage Jeanette, anyway."

Devin called to mind a cloud of dark curly hair and eyes that seemed to touch and warm his soul. In all fairness, he hadn't been the one to encourage Jeanette tonight. It had been the other way around, and he would have had to be made of stone not to respond to her. He closed his eyes.

Marcus's cot creaked.

"And don't think for a moment that Armand didn't notice what was going on right under his nose tonight," he said in the dark. "That man's never too weary or too drunk to keep an eye on his only daughter, and you'd better not forget it!"

Devin sighed and snuggled more deeply into his blankets.

"Good night, Marcus," he said sleepily.

Devin wakened mid-morning. Sunlight streamed in through the window, flooding the somber little room with a golden glow. Marcus had already gone, leaving his cot precisely made. Devin dressed quickly and went downstairs. Following the delicate sound of a harp, he found both Armand and Adrian in the Performance Hall.

"You slept late," Armand commented, without interrupting the fragile melody he was picking out on the instrument.

"I'm sorry," Devin replied, folding up gracefully to sit at his feet.

Armand stilled the strings and handed the harp to Devin.

"Can you duplicate that, Monsieur Roché?"

Devin blinked. The tune had barely registered as he entered the room. Thank God, he had always had a good memory for melody.

"I think so," he replied. He picked out the notes carefully the first time. When there were no corrections from Armand, he played it more confidently a second time.

Armand grinned holding out a hand to Adrian. When Adrian placed a coin on Armand's palm, the bard began to laugh.

"I bet Adrian that you could play a tune after hearing it only once."

Devin inclined his head, passing the harp back to Armand.

"Well, you were very lucky, then. Because I wasn't even certain I had heard the entire thing."

Armand laughed. "That makes it even better. Are you ready to work?"

Devin nodded, refraining from mentioning that he had yet to visit the kitchen for breakfast.

"Good," Armand said approvingly. "We still have a great deal to cover. And since Jeanette is already hard at work on your cloak, I think we need to finish your training."

"I'll leave you then," Adrian said, rising.

Armand sat in silence for a moment after the door closed, and then shifted the harp to a spot on the floor. He folded his hands between his knees and looked at Devin.

"Before we start, I thought it wise to mention that I intend for Jeanette to marry Adrian."

Devin straightened, a sudden and unexpected pain stabbing through his chest. He struggled to catch a breath, aware of Armand's blue eyes watching him closely.

"You make it sound as though this is something you have arranged yourself," Devin said, carefully. "Does Jeanette have any say in the matter?"

"Adrian and I have arranged it," Armand replied. "But it is for Jeanette's welfare. Let me assure you, Monsieur Roché, it is for the best. Should something happen to me, it will allow her to continue to live here, in a capacity that she enjoys."

Devin scrambled to his feet. "But Jeanette doesn't love Adrian!"

He had watched Jeanette's polite refusals of Adrian's advances. Oh, she smiled at him but there was no sparkle in her eyes when she spoke to Adrian. And her face did not light up when Adrian entered the room. It was very obvious she was not interested in pursuing a relationship with him. Besides, surely she would never have behaved the way she had last night, if she was in love with Adrian. Devin was certain of that!

Armand swallowed. "I am sorry if this is distressing to you. The situation is unfortunate. I think my daughter has fallen in love with you, Monsieur Roché. And that is a situation that you and I, both, must try to remedy. I'll be asking you to spend as little time with her as possible until you leave Lac Dupré. Last night's little tête-à-tête should never have taken place. I want your word that it won't happen again."

"Armand . . . " Devin protested.

Armand's face was drawn. "You cannot pretend that your intentions are honorable, *monsieur*, not a man in your position. Here in Ombria, a man only courts a woman with one purpose in mind. Unless you intend to ask my daughter to marry you, I must insist that you leave her alone."

Devin was momentarily speechless. "Armand," he sputtered. "I would never deliberately hurt her."

291

The lines around Armand's eyes deepened. "Your very presence here hurts her, *monsieur*. Although, I must say, in all fairness, that I don't think you have actively pursued her. You have been too preoccupied with your work. And I believe it is your intensity and your earnestness that attracted her in the first place, not your aristocratic heritage. For a girl like Jeanette, falling in love with you must have been rather easy, I would think. The problem is there is no future in it; just the certainty of a broken heart when you move on in another week. Surely, you can't believe that you would be able to offer her anything more than that?"

Devin imagined writing to his father to say that he had fallen in love with the daughter of Ombria's Master Bard. He would be advised to enjoy himself, provide for any bastard child that might arise from the union, and be home in time for Christmas to please his mother. He stood mute and embarrassed before Armand.

"I thought not," Armand replied. "And since we are both men of the world, perhaps we will just leave it at that. I would imagine your father has made arrangements long ago for your own marriage. Even with five older sons, a man in his position would never leave something like that to chance."

Words jammed in Devin's throat. How could he have found eloquence so easily last night? At this moment, he couldn't formulate a single sentence in his own defense. Armand was right. And yet, Devin had never carried on an intelligent conversation with his fiancée, Bridgette Delacey, in the entire time he had known her. She lay as far from his heart as some classmate he had met only once and whose name he had forgotten. Last night, Jeanette had touched him with her intelligence and her passion in a way no other woman ever had. He had not pursued her before, for the very reasons Armand mentioned, but how could he ignore her now?

"Armand . . . ," he pleaded, searching for some means to justify himself.

The bard turned away from him.

"I would prefer not to speak any more about it. I've been feeling rather pleased with you of late, Monsieur Roché. Please, don't say anything that might change my mind."

Armand retrieved the harp and slung it into his lap, a little roughly.

"Shall we start your lesson? There's a great deal I want to cover today. While you learn these stories incredibly quickly, I find I cannot put in the long hours at this that I once did." Armand patted the stool beside him. "Sit down, will you? It hurts my neck to have to look up at you all the time."

Devin slumped down, wishing he could be anywhere else at the moment. He hated himself for enjoying and encouraging Jeanette's attentions. What had he been thinking? Marcus had tried to warn him, but he had preferred the gentle fantasy that, someday, Jeanette might be in his arms, her skin soft and cool against his. He didn't deserve Armand's dispassionate judgment. His cheeks were scarlet as attempted to shift his focus to what Armand was attempting to teach him. But he found it impossible to concentrate on his lesson.

"And Adrian," he asked after a few tense minutes, "does he love Jeanette?"

Armand hesitated a moment too long. He avoided Devin's eyes when he answered. "He will be a good husband, Monsieur Roché. In time, I think they will grow to love each other."

That's not enough, Devin thought fiercely. For a woman like Jeanette, it would never be enough.

CHAPTER 40

Bishops and Blacksmiths

The next few days passed quickly, sliding toward their inevitable conclusion: Devin must leave Ombria, Armand, and Jeanette behind. His mission, both apparent and implicit, required him to move on, but it was going to be harder than he had ever imagined. He had consciously avoided Jeanette's company, turning his gaze away from the hurt in her eyes when he failed to accept her invitation to have coffee on the terrace or to sit by the fire in the evening. Perhaps she assumed that his work with her father kept him constantly occupied, or perhaps she too sensed that circumstances were set against them. Devin ached to reassure her, and yet, he knew it would be a lie.

"I've lost you again, Monsieur Roché," Armand commented with a sigh. "You cannot daydream and learn Ombria's Chronicle at the same time. If you plan to keep to your itinerary, you need to concentrate."

Devin raised his eyes to look at him, "I was thinking about Jeanette."

Armand cut him off. "I know exactly what you were

thinking about and I consider the subject closed. Please, don't make me angry with you."

Devin gestured hopelessly. "I'm sorry. But, I can't help but be concerned about her future."

"Let me worry about Jeanette," Armand retorted. "Tell me the story of Edmond Leferre."

Devin took a moment to compose his thoughts.

"*Edmond Leferre was a blacksmith from Genevois. He lived on the estate of Monseigneur Leveque, a Bishop of the church. One day, Leveque was to be honored at a special mass in the Cathedral in Pireé. But one thing after another conspired to delay him. By the time he left, he was in a terrible hurry. But just as he drove out of the courtyard, his carriage horse threw a shoe.*

"*He went to find Edmond Leferre himself. Edmond's wife greeted the Bishop at the door with many bows and curtseys. Leveque explained what he needed but she told him that Edmond was sick in bed. 'Let me see him, please,' Leveque begged. Now, the bishop saw at once that Edmond was truly very ill, tossing and turning with a high fever and a cough. 'Shoe my horse,' Leveque requested, 'and I will give you anything you ask.' 'Anything?' Edmond asked. 'Anything,' the Bishop agreed. And knowing that Leveque was a man of his word, Edmond got up and put on his warmest cloak and went out to the forge to shoe his horse.*

"*It was mid-winter and the snow was sifting under the edges of the smithy and the wind howled around the corners. Edmond shoed Leveque's horse and then went back to his bed, shivering and coughing.*

"*Now Edmond's wife had heard the Bishop's promise and was thinking about what Edmond could request as payment for his services. Wealth could assure the future of their children or a comfortable old age.*

"*Leveque was gone for two days and when he returned he went immediately to Leferre's home. A neighbor opened the door and ushered him in. Edmond's wife was sobbing into her hands, her children gathered around her. Edmond was laid out on the kitchen table all still and cold. The neighbor explained that Edmond had passed away during the night. The Bishop was shocked. He was immediately filled with guilt that he had persuaded Edmond to go out into the cold when he was so ill. He knelt in front of Edmond's widow. 'I made a promise to your husband and now, I say the same to you. I will give you whatever you ask: a large house or riches for your children. What do you desire?' And Edmond's widow simply looked at the Bishop with tears in her eyes and said, 'I want my husband back.'*"

Devin paused before he continued, loving the way the story built to its unbelievable climax.

"*And then the Bishop said, 'As you wish. There is nothing that the power of Almighty God can't accomplish.' And he asked everyone in the house to leave him alone with the body. Huddled in the other room, the mourners could hear nothing but the steady rise and fall of the Bishop's voice praying. But after about an hour the praying ceased abruptly and the room fell quiet. Edmond's widow went to the door and pushed it open. She found the Bishop lying dead on the floor, his Bible in his hand. And Edmond was sitting up on the table, his burial shroud still wrapped around him. He held out his arms to his wife and she ran to embrace him.*"

Devin finished and grinned at Armand. "Have you considered that maybe Edmond wasn't really dead, and when he sat up the Bishop died of shock?"

Armand shook his head. "A bard's job is to recite these stories word for word not to speculate about their authenticity, Monsieur Roché. Some other bard, centuries ago, was convinced of this story's credibility and added it to the Chronicle. You must accept it with the same conviction you would devote to any other story."

"Still," Devin replied. "It makes me wonder just the same."

"You can wonder all you like," Armand said, "just don't ever introduce doubt into your performance. Your personal opinions have no place in this work. You must always keep them to yourself." Armand lighted his pipe, drawing the sweet smoke through the long stem and releasing it in perfect white circles. "I did like how you paused before revealing the ending. It heightened the suspense. That was nicely done, despite your reservations."

"Thank you," Devin said, inclining his head. "I've been wondering, Armand. When will you tell me about those monoliths we saw along the road? Surely they appear somewhere in the Chronicle. I can't leave Ombria until I've satisfied my curiosity about them."

"All in good time, Monsieur Roché," Armand replied. "I have told you before that there is a sequence to these stories but I promise you will know before you leave my province."

Adrian opened the door to the performance hall. Dr. Mareschal stood behind him.

"Armand," Mareschal said with a little bow, "Chastel would like to invite you all to dinner tomorrow night, if you can release Monsieur Roché from his studies for a few hours. I know you are pushing to meet a deadline."

"Monsieur Roché's deadline is self-imposed," Armand replied. "I have all the time in the world for dinner parties. It is my student you must convince."

"Of course, we will come," Devin said graciously. "I owe Chastel a great deal. I would be honored to spend the evening in his company."

Mareschal bowed again. "I will tell him. We'll send a carriage at six o'clock."

"Thank you," Devin said. "We'll look forward to it."

"One last thing," Mareschal said, "bring a harp. Chastel requested that you sing for him after dinner."

"Can I borrow yours or Adrian's?" Devin asked Armand.

"Of course," Armand replied. "But you need your own. You are so concerned with having a bard's cloak, and yet you lack the harp. Surely you want to look the part?"

"I have a harp at home," Devin replied. "I didn't bring it because it seemed just one more thing to cart along."

"A necessary thing, nonetheless," Armand said. "My predecessor presented me with this one when he asked me to be his apprentice. I believe my old one is still here in the attic somewhere. I'll make you a present of it, Monsieur Roché."

"That's not necessary," Devin protested, embarrassed by his kindness. "I can buy one."

Armand waved a hand. "Nonsense, I have no need for two. It's a fine harp, though it is a little battered. Take it with my blessing. I hope you will use it for many years."

CHAPTER 41

Death and Secrets

My Dear Devin,
I hope you are well and quite recovered from your encounter with Ombria's wolves. I dare not dwell on what might have happened had Chastel not arrived in time to help you. Guard your life, son. I want you back home safe and sound at the end of this adventure.

Unfortunately, René Forneaux announced news in Council of both the wolf attack and the murders of the two young men from Armand's village. He chose to use them as an example of the barbarism still present in the provinces. I barely headed off a motion to have you and Gaspard recalled to Viénne with an extensive military escort. Could you have a word with Gaspard in private? While I cannot tell him what to write, caution him that what he shares with his father in his letters is being broadcast to all of Council.

Of course, it didn't take long before your mother heard the news. She was completely distraught. She

*has taken to her bed, refusing to speak with me for
the past three days – but not before reminding me
that she tried to dissuade you from this undertaking.
I share her concern, Devin. As you have found out,
the provinces can be uncivilized, dangerous places. I
cannot caution you enough to be constantly on your
guard and place your full confidence in Marcus.*

*There is worrying news from Arcadia. Lucien
Reynard, Arcadia's Master Bard, was found shot to
death in his own performance hall. The man was
apparently well liked and venerated by his people.
The killer has not been found. Fortunately, his
apprentice was safely away at the time of the murder.
Your friend, Armand, may already know of Reynard's
death but if he doesn't . . . break it to him gently. I
believe all of those men are good friends, especially
those who reside in neighboring provinces.*

*If you veer from your intended itinerary, please let
me know as soon as possible. As always my
resources are at your disposal. Do not hesitate to
allow Marcus to select additional bodyguards if he
feels it is necessary. Your safety is of the utmost
importance.*
Affectionately,
Your Father

Devin folded the letter and placed it back in its envelope. He
slid it into his inside jacket pocket, where it rested uneasily
against his heart. His mother's reaction was not unexpected
but he still felt responsible. He felt guilty for not having
shared more information with her. It had been cruel and
unkind that she had heard about the murders here in the

village, and the wolf attack through such a public venue. Tonight, before their dinner at Chastel's, he would write to her and try to explain his reticence.

He was certain that Armand did not know of Lucien Reynard's murder. This was catastrophic news following on the heels of the death of Perouse's Master Bard only a few months before. It made his original mission even more imperative. The oral history of the provinces must be preserved.

Devin went downstairs unwillingly, reluctant to be the bearer of bad news. He found Armand polishing a beautifully carved harp at the kitchen table.

Armand looked up and smiled when he came in.

"There, what did I tell you, Monsieur Roché? I knew I had this old harp around here someplace. It has a few nicks and dents, but it plays more beautifully than the one I use now." He drew an experimental finger over the strings, filling the room with mellow, resonating notes.

Armand's smile faded when he saw Devin's expression. "What is it?" he asked. "What is the matter?"

Devin avoided his eyes. "I just read my father's letter. Armand, I am sorry to tell you that Lucien Reynard is dead."

"No!" Armand protested, one hand to his chest. "How? When did it happen? I saw him not two weeks before the wedding. He was the picture of health."

Devin's chest contracted painfully. "He was murdered, Armand, shot to death in his own performance hall. They have no idea who is responsible."

"God!" Armand slumped down at the table but with enough presence of mind to ease the harp down gently. "God," he whispered again. "What does this mean?"

301

Devin sat down across from him. "You once told me that you believed that Gautier Beau Chère had been murdered. Is it possible . . . .."

Armand raised his head, his eyes red. "Careful what you say," he warned. "You may incriminate what you hold most dear."

"My father wouldn't order such a thing," Devin protested.

"Are you certain?" Armand asked.

"Yes," he answered, "I am very certain."

"Then who would?" Armand demanded.

"Certain Council members, perhaps," Devin suggested. He was afraid to say too much. "I have begun to suspect that my father's power isn't absolute."

Armand stared at him. "What are you saying?"

"I cannot elaborate," Devin replied. "But there are very strong factions within the government that threaten to undermine the Chancellor."

"So the attempt on your life . . . "

"Goes far beyond this village, as Marcus implied," Devin said. "And apparently, you may be in danger, as well, but from other sources."

"I have been in danger for a long time," Armand retorted. "A bard walks a fine line, Monsieur Roché. There is an old saying: if you misjudge your audience, you must watch your back. The wrong story told within hearing of a government official can be fatal."

Devin's stomach clenched. "So there have been others?"

"In addition to Beau Chère and Reynard?" Armand asked. "There have been two Master Bards who have died under suspicious circumstances in the last two years. I'm surprised you haven't heard."

"Perouse's Master Bard died of natural causes," Devin protested.

"Do you call murder natural?" Armand retorted. "Phillippe Duvoison was poisoned."

Devin gasped. "I hadn't heard that."

"I have it on the authority of his housekeeper, who watched him sicken and die before her eyes."

Devin shook his head. "Was she certain? Sometimes a weakness of the heart can cause a sudden death, Armand."

"The woman was a trained herbalist, Monsieur Roché; she knew enough to recognize the signs but was unable to save him."

"Then his murderer must have been someone close to him," Devin speculated.

"One might assume so," Armand replied. "A young man came to him asking to learn Perouse's Chronicle. He stayed two weeks and disappeared the same night his master died in agony. Do you wonder that your own request was met with skepticism?"

"Oh God, Armand, I'm sorry," Devin whispered. "I had no idea."

"At present, Perouse has a half-trained apprentice serving as its Master Bard," Armand continued. "And now, with Reynard gone, Arcadia has lost two Master Bards in five years. Even you cannot believe that is coincidence."

Devin sat silently a moment. "And the other bard?" he asked finally. "Who else died recently?"

"Remi Maigny, Master Bard of Ferrare," Armand replied. "He died of a broken neck on the road to Tarente last October – a fall from his horse – the official report concluded. Remi didn't even own a horse, Monsieur Roché. He walked the roads of Ferrare just as I walk the roads of Ombria."

"Is there anyone to carry on for him?" Devin asked. "Please tell me he had an apprentice."

"He did," Armand said quietly. "But the man has been afraid to declare himself. Ferrare's Bardic Hall lies empty while he hides in secret. There is no doubt among us that, one by one, the Master Bards of Llisé are being silenced."

Devin took a shaky breath. "Armand, these Chronicles will be lost if something isn't done."

Armand stood up. "If you truly wish to become a bard, then perhaps it is fitting that you share some of the burden as well. Come with me, Monsieur Roché."

They passed Marcus in the hallway. He raised a questioning eyebrow at Devin.

"We'll be in the performance hall," Armand told him. "I'd prefer we remain undisturbed until we leave for Chastel's."

Marcus merely nodded. He had grown used to their lengthy sessions and simply amused himself elsewhere in the house while they were working.

Adrian and Jeanette had gone to the market, and Gaspard had spent last night at Chastel's. They had the house to themselves. Armand opened the door to the performance hall, allowing Devin to precede him into the room, and then locked the door behind them.

"Sit down," he directed as he took the stool by the fireside. He took a great deal of time lighting his pipe, and then turned to Devin.

"When you become a bard, you join a brotherhood. You become part of a tradition that predates your beloved Archives. It transcends written record. It and only it contains the very roots of the people of Llisé. These stories, Llisé's history, are a sacred trust, passed down from one generation to the next virtually intact. It is only in the last few weeks that I have finally become convinced that you share my belief that the loss of the Chronicles would be incalculable.

"When you first came to me, I was never sure of your intent. You claimed to want to learn and yet you might have been an assassin sent to kill me. I have tried to hold you at arm's length, Monsieur Roché, but you have earned my trust. It is only because of that trust that I am about to share something with you that no one but a Master Bard knows.

"What I am about to tell you must never leave this room. Should you repeat it to anyone, even your father, it would jeopardize the existence of the Chronicles forever. I would hunt you down myself. Is that understood?"

Devin swallowed, trying to quell the sinking feeling in his stomach.

"Perfectly," he said.

CHAPTER 42

The Last Supper

"You're unusually quiet," Marcus observed. And yet, the creak of the coach and the clatter of the horses' hooves left little room for conversation. "What was so damned important that Armand needed to lock the door to the performance hall this afternoon?"

Devin glanced at Jeanette sitting beside him. The ribbons on her bonnet were fluttering in the breeze from the open window. She turned her head away from them, as though pretending not to hear their discussion. The evening shadows heightened the curve of her cheek and the gentle slope of her neck.

"I didn't realize you had noticed the door was locked," Devin replied. "Armand asked that no one disturb us. He was simply making sure of it."

"Well, I'll tell him myself if you won't," Marcus said, his jaw set. "No one locks you in a room without my permission. See that Armand understands that."

Devin inclined his head. "He meant no harm by it. He taught me the final story in the Chronicle today. It was important to him that I get it right." Even to his ears the explanation sounded hollow. And here he was, offering it to Marcus who was trained to detect deception. Jeanette stole a questioning glance his way.

"You've never had a problem 'getting it right' before," Marcus muttered. "Memorization comes to you as easily as spreading butter on warm bread."

Devin's eyes narrowed. After what Armand had told him this afternoon, he was in no mood to deal with Marcus's disapproval.

"Is that how it appears to you?" he asked irritably.

Marcus shrugged. "It's not like you have to work to learn any of it. I've seen your brothers bent over their books all night before an exam. You always sailed right through."

Devin settled his head back against the coach seat, his eyes on Jeanette, and ignored the passing countryside.

"Oh, I have to work for it, too, Marcus. You just don't see the effort that goes into it."

An uneasy silence descended.

"You're like your father," Marcus said after a minute. "That man's mind amazes me. At least, one of his sons inherited it."

The compliment was meant to smooth over the disagreement, but Devin refused to be soothed. He turned instead to Jeanette.

"I'm sorry Armand was too upset to come tonight."

"He knew Lucien well," she answered. "To him, it seemed disrespectful to celebrate when one of his comrades died so violently. I offered to stay behind but it was kind of Adrian to spend the evening with him."

Devin was glad that Adrian had stayed behind, too, but it would have been rude to say so. Armand had seemed very depressed when they had left. Perhaps it would have been kinder if they had all stayed to cheer him up.

His eyes strayed again to Jeanette. It was so rare that she wore anything but a simple smock and apron. The sleeves of her rose-colored dress accentuated her slender arms and wrists. The soft fabric matched the natural blush across her cheekbones exactly.

Devin had seen nothing in the past few days that indicated Jeanette's attitude toward Adrian had softened. Just this afternoon, she had snubbed her suitor's gentle offer of help carrying the laundry downstairs. Devin had no way of knowing what passed between Jeanette and her father when they were alone but he suspected she would not go willingly into this marriage of convenience.

He closed his eyes, his head swimming with the information Armand had told him this afternoon. He had known that, because of Richard Chastel, Armand had been taught to read and write. But he hadn't guessed what had occupied Armand and Adrian in their private sessions. Devin had failed to register the significance of those hastily hidden pages, secreted into the harp case, when he had accidentally walked in on them. Armand had been teaching Adrian to read and write, too.

The greater revelation was that every Master Bard taught his apprentice the same skills. The Master Bards of Llisé had been outwitting the government in Viénne for centuries. The Chronicles already existed in written form. What Devin had committed his Third Year to accomplish was a reality. And yet, he could tell no one, not his father or Marcus or even Gaspard who had pledged to help him fulfill his mission. Whoever was carrying out the extinction of Llisé's Master Bards had no knowledge of the arcane library that guarded their ancient legacy. And Devin was barred both by his position at the Académie and his pledge to Armand to ever reveal its secrets. If Llisé's Chronicles were ever to be evaluated against the Académie's Archives it would only be through Devin's awkwardly conceived plan to memorize them. He was the only one in the unique position to do so. The deaths of Llisé's Master Bards made it even more imperative that he succeed.

The jolt of the coach halting broke his revelry. He allowed Marcus to descend and then helped Jeanette from the coach. Her hand lingered in his longer than necessary. It was he who finally broke the contact as he allowed her to precede him into the house.

As always, Chastel's Château enveloped Devin in its opulence. Here, he could so easily fall back into the patterns that had been so deeply ingrained in Coreé; never questioning the effort that brought such luxury to the wealthy few and left the majority to struggle for a meager existence. Around him, servants moved on silent feet, attending to their master's every need. Devin wondered if he might have glimpsed Robert Foulard when he stayed here before. And yet, he had never even taken notice of the man's face or bothered to learn his name.

"Monsieur Roché!" Chastel greeted him warmly, taking Devin's right hand in both of his. "You seem much too pensive for a celebratory occasion! Come have some wine to lighten your mood!" His sweeping glance took in his other guests, as well. "Jeanette, Marcus, welcome to my home. Come this way."

Chastel began to lead them toward the dining room, and then turned.

"Where is our Master Bard? I'd hoped he and Adrian would attend. Surely Armand isn't boycotting my dinner party."

"My father sends his regrets," Jeanette responded. "A friend of his, Lucien Reynard, Arcadia's Master Bard, died very suddenly. My father thought his grief might spoil the evening."

Chastel bowed. "I am very sorry to hear that. Arcadia's Master Bards seem not to be a hearty lot. I believe something similar happened about five years ago."

"Lucien was murdered," Devin said brusquely.

Marcus seized Devin's shoulder. "Speaking of ruining the evening," he hissed. "Are you certain of that?"

"Quite certain," Devin replied. "My father told me in the letter you gave me today. Reynard was shot in his own performance hall."

Chastel blanched. "And the killer?" he asked.

"Apparently unknown and still at large," Devin answered.

"So there is good reason for your sober appearance," Chastel replied. "Forgive me. I assumed you had simply been working too hard."

The double doors of the dining room stood open. Gaspard was at the sideboard refilling his empty glass.

"Dev!" he called, his words already slurred. He gestured with the bottle, dribbling wine on Chastel's fine Andalusian carpet. "Come, have some of your father's excellent wine."

Devin stepped forward and carefully righted the bottle. Taking it from his friend's hand, he replaced it on the sideboard. "Perhaps you need to show some restraint," he suggested quietly. "The evening's just begun."

Gaspard threw a companionable arm around Devin's shoulders. "Loosen up, Dev. This is your last party in Ombria."

"Our last party," Devin corrected him.

Gaspard drew him closer, swaying unsteadily. "Perhaps not, *mon ami*. Chastel has invited me to stay."

Devin recoiled, as though he'd been stung. "Gaspard!" he protested. "I need your help! You have to record the musical part of the Chronicles after I memorize them."

Gaspard shrugged. "This trip has turned dangerous, Dev. I agreed to tour the provinces with you, but I don't want to die doing it." He patted Devin's shoulder in an effort to placate him. "You've got Marcus for company. I think his skills may prove more useful than my feeble wit, anyway."

Devin pushed his friend's hand away, his face flushed. He felt betrayed – not only by Gaspard – but by Chastel, as well. His eyes sought Marcus's in mute appeal, but his bodyguard only shrugged.

Chastel snagged Devin's arm with the desperate air of a host whose party has gone awry.

"Here now, nothing definite has been decided yet. I merely made the offer because Gaspard's situation with his father is so strained. At my château, he is only a week away from home should the situation change."

"What makes you think the situation will change?" Devin demanded. "Gaspard doesn't want to go home!"

Chastel looked faintly embarrassed. "I have intervened on his behalf."

"What?" Devin asked in disbelief. He turned to look at Gaspard swaying unsteadily on the carpet. "Did you ask him to do that? Is that what you want?"

His friend shrugged. "I have no income of my own. Unlike you, my father hasn't left his empire at my disposal. I have no skills. How do you expect me to survive in the provinces?"

"You would have been with me!" Devin protested. "I have taken care of all your expenses so far."

"And the first time I asked for extra money, you bit my head off," Gaspard reminded him bluntly. "I need to go home, Dev. I'll make my peace with my father, and go back to school. I can defy him all I want but I will never win."

311

Devin was still trying to process the information. "But we were to leave Ombria in two days' time. When were you planning to tell me?"

"After dinner," Chastel said, intervening, "and not so abruptly. I apologize, Monsieur Roché, I never meant for you to find out like this." He took a deep breath and poured a glass of wine, proffering it to Devin. "Please, don't let this spoil the evening."

Devin refused to be placated. Propriety demanded that he accept the wine but he felt like throwing it in Gaspard's face like an angry child! Instead he fell into sullen silence, his well-thought out plans in disarray.

"I had no idea that Gaspard was essential to your mission or I would never have suggested this," Chastel said quietly.

"And apparently, Gaspard didn't volunteer the information," Devin retorted.

"He seemed at loose ends while you studied," Chastel continued. "I was only offering an alternative."

"So you've made up your mind?" Devin demanded of Gaspard. "Is there nothing I can say to change it?"

Gaspard downed another glass of wine before answering. He avoided meeting Devin's eyes. "I don't think I have an alternative. I'm sorry if it ruins your plans, but I have to think of my own future for a change."

Devin swallowed. He was going to ruin the evening, personally, if he didn't put some distance between himself and Gaspard. He took a gulp of wine. The rich flavors of his father's province did nothing to ease the tension in his chest.

"Would you excuse me, please?" he said, turning away.

Jeanette radiated concern. Her fingers grazed his as he passed her, but he continued down the hall. A servant bowed, sweeping the front door open in front of him.

The shame of his retreat only added to the anger boiling inside him. He stopped at the portico, fixing his eyes on the smooth gray waters of the lake, willing that same calm to ease his own troubled thoughts.

The door closed quietly behind him. For an instant, he hoped desperately that Gaspard had changed his mind and had come to tell him so. But when he turned it was Marcus who stood leaning against the door.

"That was smooth," his bodyguard commented, his tone faintly amused.

"I'm not interested in a critique of my behavior," Devin replied.

"I didn't expect that you would be," Marcus said. "But, you are my responsibility. I can't have you wandering off on your own."

Devin drew both hands through his hair, leaving it tousled and on end.

"Gaspard blindsided me," he explained tartly. "He should have told me when we were alone, not in a room full of people."

Marcus shrugged. "And yet, you have encouraged him to go home at least twice. Why are you so upset that he chose to do the sensible thing, now?"

"Is it the sensible thing?" Devin asked, his gaze searching Marcus's face. "Have you ever known René Forneaux to be a forgiving man?"

Marcus's face remained impassive. "Forneaux told Gaspard that he had until the end of the summer to come home. It would be best if he didn't push that deadline."

Devin turned his back to Marcus. Perhaps Marcus was right, but he felt an uneasiness that had nothing to do with his personal disappointment.

"René Forneaux is a ruthless man," he pointed out.

Marcus corrected him. "He is a powerful man. Powerful men are ruthless."

"Not always," Devin retorted.

Marcus interrupted. "Your father is the Chancellor Elite of Llisé. He didn't reach that position without compromising some of his ideals. Don't insist I disillusion you by making comparisons to Forneaux."

Devin swung around to face him. "Don't you think that I know who and what my father is?"

Marcus stood taut and still. "I doubt you know the half of it, Devin."

Devin clenched his hand. Just once he would have liked to throw propriety to the wind but now was not the time. He dropped his fist to his side.

"A wise choice," Marcus remarked, as though he had read his mind.

"Don't push your luck," Devin muttered, his mood reckless.

Marcus's face looked ominous. "Don't push yours," he warned. "Stop behaving like an angry child. You need to go back in. You've made a shambles of Chastel's dinner party."

Devin's stomach was tied in knots. "I can't eat," he said.

"Then you'd better pretend to," Marcus retorted. "If you truly believe Chastel is an ally then I would recommend that you treat him carefully. We're a long way from home and we may need his assistance before we're through."

Marcus opened the door, ushering Devin into the quiet coolness of the hall. Dr. Mareschal stood waiting for them, his brow furrowed.

"May I be of service?" he asked.

314

"I don't believe so," Devin replied brightly. "It's a lovely evening. I just thought I'd enjoy the sunset over the lake before dinner."

"God," Marcus murmured under his breath. "Have a care, Devin. Playing the clown doesn't suit you."

CHAPTER 43

Changes

Dinner was uncomfortable. Gaspard, heavily influenced by alcohol and remorse, was either completely silent or chattered incessantly. Chastel, Mareschal, and Jeanette determinedly held the conversation to neutral topics but any chance of a normal evening had been effectively shattered. Devin retreated into sulky silence, endlessly rearranging the food on his plate.

When the dessert dishes had finally been cleared away, Chastel turned to Devin.

"I am glad that you brought your harp, Monsieur Roché," he said cheerfully. "Can I trouble you for a song?"

Devin nodded, anticipating the request. "Of course," he said. When he was officially a bard, similar requests would become a frequent part of his travels. The realization eased some of his earlier distress over Gaspard's decision. Fourteen months with no one but Marcus for company seemed interminable, but he would have his performances. And somehow, he would have to memorize as many of the Chronicles as he could before going home.

Devin had selected and then discarded several ballads during dinner as his mood skittered erratically from anger into despair. Nothing adequately suited his current frame of mind. He pulled the harp case onto his lap wondering what he could offer that might defuse the situation. He and Gaspard had been friends since they were children. In a year's time they would be back at the Académie together. He didn't want his disappointment in Gaspard's current decision to influence the course of their friendship from here on.

Chastel stood up. "Let's retire to the parlor," he suggested. "I have some fine brandy to complement your performance."

Devin found himself next to Gaspard as they walked down the hallway. He moved a few steps ahead, anxious to avoid another confrontation, his harp tucked under his arm.

Gaspard matched his pace, placing a tentative hand on his shoulder. "I'm sorry, Dev," he murmured. "I really have to go home. After all my anger and rebellion, he's still my father. I love him and yet I am terrified of him at the same time. I have little choice but to do as he wishes."

Devin stopped. He doubted that he had the strength to defy his own father either. If he were officially recalled to Viénne, he would have to go. If he even considered resisting, Marcus would have no qualms about dragging him back kicking and screaming.

"I'm disappointed that you won't be coming with me," he said, leaning back against the wall behind him. "But I do understand, Gaspard. You just surprised me earlier with the news."

"That was badly done," Gaspard admitted. "I apologize. You know me, I rarely get anything right."

"That's not true," Devin protested.

"It's true enough," Gaspard replied. "But I realized in the last few weeks that I really want to graduate from the

317

Académie. I don't want to be the first Forneaux in centuries who couldn't measure up. I just wish that you would be there to help me get through my exams." He shifted apprehensively and leaned closer. "Would you consider going back with me, Dev? This trip you've planned isn't safe. I don't want to hear you've been eaten by wolves or beaten to death by angry provincials."

Devin smiled in spite of himself. "I doubt that either of those things will happen. This is very important to me, Gaspard. Although, with you gone, I will now have to memorize all fifteen Chronicles, including every song and ballad. I'm fairly certain that I can't do that."

"Your brothers will mock you if you don't!" Gaspard reminded him.

Devin laughed. "As unpleasant as that might be, it is of less importance than being able to compare the Chronicles with the Archives. Unfortunately, it seems that memorizing them is the only way I will be able to do it."

"Have a care," Gaspard cautioned. "By himself, my father is a formidable adversary. But he has many other colleagues who agree with him. Most are adamantly opposed to any credence being given to the Chronicles. If they realize what you intend to do they will kill you."

Devin shrugged, trying to look nonchalant. "I believe they have already tried."

"Come back with me," Gaspard begged.

Devin glanced down the hall. "The others are waiting for us. Don't worry. I'll be fine," he assured him, feeling a weight had already lifted from his heart. "Come on, I owe Chastel a song for my supper. I think you'll like what I have chosen."

He settled by the hearth on the stool Chastel provided. It was traditional to grant a seat at the fire to a visiting bard, and Devin took a certain pleasure in accepting it. He plucked his harp strings, found them still perfectly in tune, and turned to his audience.

"When I came to Ombria," he began, looking at Chastel, "I found your great monoliths fascinating. I knew that their origins must appear somewhere in Ombria's Chronicle. Today, Armand taught me the ballad of "The Standing Stones," as my last story. I think perhaps that it should have been my first."

They've stood for centuries in silence,
Some have fallen at their task,
But the Standing Stones of Ombria,
Were carved and placed to last.

They wind across our province,
Through woods and fields for miles,
And they trace our true beginning
To Terre Sainté's sacred isle.

Sacred Center of Creation.
Holy birthplace of mankind,
Lost for centuries in mystery,
Shrouded in the mists of time.

Hallowed garden full of wonder,
Home of man before his Fall,
Sacrificed in thirst for knowledge,
Lost forever to us all.

Man turned away from comfort,
Toward a cruel and rocky coast,

Forfeit safety for adventure,
And left the place he loved the most.

They built their boats of timber,
Sailing with the evening tide,
They ran short of food and water
And many of them died.

When at last they found Llisé,
They steered onto her shores.
Found both hardship and adventure,
In their quest for something more.

Llisé's fields were tilled with suffering,
A living wrestled from its earth.
Many times they must have yearned for
The island of their birth.

A few set sail with longing,
In hope of being saved,
But the current ran against them
And they drowned beneath the waves.

In Ombria they gathered,
To mark the way that they had come
So it would never be forgotten
If they ever could go home.

So they cut the Standing Stones,
Aligning each with care
And carved each sacred symbol
So that all would be aware,

They'd left a paradise behind them
That could never be regained
They left the Standing Stones as tribute
To the sacred island's name.

Oh Blessed Terre Sainté
Oh, why did we depart?
May your sacred memory lie at peace,
Forever in our hearts.

Devin stilled the strings with his open palm and looked up. Chastel gave an enthusiastic sound of appreciation and began to clap, as did Jeanette and Gaspard. Marcus followed suit.

"Ah," Chastel murmured, "The Legend of Terre Sainté." I haven't heard that in years. Why did Armand teach it to you last, I wonder?"

Devin laughed, knowing he could never disclose the real reason. "I think Armand waited because I have asked him time and time again to tell me about the Standing Stones. Nothing gave him greater pleasure than to withhold information that I wanted so badly."

Jeanette laughed too. "It is very like him to do that," she said, standing up. "But perhaps you will forgive him because he did send this with me." She unfolded a length of russet suede from her bag. Devin's heart skipped a beat. "I finished the embroidery several days ago, but Father wouldn't let me give it to you until tonight," she continued, shaking out the folds.

In the center of his cloak, she had embroidered the symbol of Ombria: a wolf's head against the full moon. She leaned forward and draped the cloak over his shoulders, bending to kiss him on one cheek and then on the other.

321

"He told me that an apprentice must have a final performance before he becomes a full-fledged bard. He left it to
me to judge whether you had measured up." She smiled, her
eyes shining. "You have my unqualified approval."

Devin flushed. "So, you planned this dinner together?" he
asked, looking at Chastel.

Chastel nodded. "Armand felt that it was too dangerous to
risk a second performance in Lac Dupré. He asked me to surprise
you with a farewell dinner party. That way you could fulfill
your final requirement by performing among friends. Now you
understand why I was so puzzled when Armand didn't come."

"Did you know about this, too, Marcus?" Devin asked.

His bodyguard smiled. "I did. And between Gaspard's
announcement and your reaction, I was afraid you had
wrecked all our plans!"

"I'm sorry," Devin apologized. "Forgive me, please."

"It was actually my fault," Gaspard said gaily. "I saw no
reason for Devin to have all the attention tonight!"

Devin laughed, glad that they had made peace even though
he would be traveling on alone.

"I think I owe you a few more songs for your trouble,"
he said to Chastel.

Chastel bowed graciously. "You owe me nothing. I've
been only too glad to help you along your way. It's been an
honor to get to know our Chancellor's son. It is I, who am
in your debt."

"Never," Devin replied, hiding his embarrassment by rearranging his harp. "Would you like another ballad?"

"Nothing sad," Jeanette begged. "Would you sing
'Reymond and Eleanor'?"

Devin beamed. "Of course," he said, striking the beginning
notes of the familiar love song.

As he played song after song, he realized that performing was heady stuff. Of course, there were the initial jitters – the fear of failure – but once he'd tasted success, and his audience's enthusiastic response, he found he enjoyed the applause. Tonight had held the elements of disaster, and yet somehow he knew that his disagreement with Gaspard was not what he would carry with him. Instead, he would remember the warmth of Chastel's friendship, the look on Jeanette's face when he sang, and the uneasiness that his life would never be quite this simple again.

CHAPTER 44

Unexpected Visitors

Somehow, Devin managed to catch Jeanette alone in the hallway, while Marcus said goodbye to Chastel and Gaspard. He draped her light cape over her shoulders, his hand lingering first on her arm and then sliding down over the silky fabric to catch her cool, small hand in his. He was acutely aware of Armand's admonition, even without his physical presence, and yet this was his last night. There would be no more chances to say what he needed to say.

He drew her gently back into the parlor and turned her toward him. Then, the right words failed him.

"Thank you for embroidering my cloak for me. I will always treasure it," he offered inadequately.

Jeanette's face lit up as she squeezed his hand gently. "I enjoyed doing it, Monsieur Roché. A bard's first symbol is always placed in the center of his cloak. Most bards have only one, but I hope that you will amaze us and collect them all."

He shook his head, flattered by her optimism. "For the first time, I truly doubt that will be possible. Your father was right. There is too much information. If I held fifteen

Chronicles in my head, I would be incapable of speech for fear the wrong words would come tumbling out."

Her laugh was sweet and musical, and he finally had the courage to tell her what was truly on his heart.

"I am afraid, even now, that the wrong words will tumble out," he admitted. "I wish that, somehow, things could be different between us."

Her finger touched his lips. "I know," she whispered. "You don't have to say it."

"I want to say it!" Devin protested fiercely.

"Hush!" she admonished. "It can never be. You are the Chancellor's son and I am the daughter of the Master Bard of Ombria."

"It shouldn't matter!" he objected.

"But it does," she whispered. "Perhaps in a hundred years things will change, but for now, I must marry Adrian, and you must marry the woman your father has chosen for you."

"Bridgette," he choked. "Her name is Bridgette."

Her eyes were sympathetic. "Do you love her?"

"No," he said miserably. "Do you love, Adrian?"

She shook her head. "No, but he is a good man . . . a kind man. He will take care of me. He will take care of my father, too, when he is no longer able to walk the roads of Ombria."

Devin covered his face with his hands. "It's not fair."

She gently took his hands in hers and brought them to her lips. "No, it's not but it is the way of the world and we must adhere to it. I will always remember you."

"And I will always remember you."

He drew her forward and felt her melt against him. He cradled her head in one hand, pressing it against his shoulder, memorizing the shape and feel of her body. Bending his head, he kissed her forehead, her eyes, and at last her mouth, regretting a hundred lost opportunities.

"Jeanette, I love you," he whispered, his hands buried in her dark hair.

Footsteps echoed in the hall and they spun apart. Marcus cleared his throat.

"We were just saying goodbye," Devin stammered as Jeanette brushed the hair back from her face.

"I can see that," Marcus replied. "The coach is waiting. I'm sure Armand is anxious to have his daughter home safely."

The ride home was quiet. Jeanette fell asleep, one hand under her cheek against the side of the coach. The evening air had turned cool. Devin spread his cloak over her and watched as she settled sleepily into its soft warmth. Gaspard had agreed to return tomorrow to Armand's to gather his things and see them off. So, they hadn't said goodbye. Devin was glad they would have another chance to say anything that needed to be said between them.

He tried to imagine the next year without Gaspard's levity and good spirits. He felt guilty that he had spent so little time with him in Ombria since they had been staying with Armand. His commitment to the Chronicles had been necessary but now he wished he had devoted less time to his work and more to his friend.

His heart ached every time he looked at Jeanette. There had been no promises between them, nothing, but the grim realization that they must both fulfill their destinies without the other's love and support. On this celebratory night of his first achievement, he felt miserable. Life seemed full of missed chances.

He was nearly asleep himself when the coach pulled up before the Bardic Hall. He touched Jeanette's shoulder lightly, heard her father's voice, and blinked in the sudden glow of lantern light as the coach door swung open.

"Did they catch you?" Armand asked, his brow furrowed.

"Who?" Marcus demanded.

"The men from Viénne," Armand explained, helping his daughter down to the street. "They arrived here in the last hour, saying they had urgent news from Coreé. You didn't pass them on the road?"

Marcus shook his head. "We passed no one."

"I sent them directly to Chastel's," Armand replied. "I don't understand."

"Who were they?" Marcus demanded.

Armand shook his head. "They gave no names. They were dressed in uniform. They asked first for Gaspard, and then for you, Monsieur Roché. I can't think how you could have missed them."

"They asked for Gaspard first?" Devin repeated.

"Yes," Armand replied. "I thought it was odd at the time."

Devin looked at Marcus. "Messengers from his father, perhaps?"

Marcus shrugged. "We need to go back," Devin said. "Perhaps, something is wrong."

His head was suddenly filled with catastrophes. Perhaps Gaspard's father was angry, or something had happened to Devin's father or mother, or maybe a revolution had started and they had been summoned home.

"I'll go with you," Armand said, handing Jeanette into Adrian's keeping.

Marcus leaned out the door after Armand had clambered aboard.

"We have to go back," he instructed Chastel's coachman. "Do you carry a weapon?"

The answer came down out of the dark. "Always, *monsieur*!"

They made the turn at the end of the street and started back toward Chastel's. A whip cracked and the horses leaped forward, rushing toward home much faster than they had left it.

"Who do you think they were?" Devin asked Marcus.

"I have no way of knowing," Marcus replied, his own pistol in his hand. "Have you ever fired one of these?"

Devin nodded. He'd had a few lessons in firearms but nothing beyond the basics.

Marcus handed him the pistol, butt first.

Devin, surprised at the weight of the gun, held it gingerly between his knees and pointed it toward the floor.

"Don't pull the trigger until you've aimed it," Marcus commented dryly. "You'll shoot yourself in the foot."

Devin was surprised to see Marcus hand a similar weapon to Armand while still retaining a third pistol in his hand.

"How many guns do you have?" he asked.

"Enough to get the job done," Marcus replied obscurely.

"You expect trouble?" Devin asked.

"I always expect trouble," Marcus replied.

They questioned Armand over and over. What kind of uniforms had the men been wearing? Armand wasn't certain – not the blue and silver of the Chancellor's personal guard – but military uniforms of some kind. He wasn't positive of the color, something dark with lighter trim. It had been hard to see in the dark as they stood at the door. The trip back seemed interminable, Devin's mind was racing. He kept going over the incident in his head – why would someone in Coreé send soldiers as messengers? Or were they an escort? None of it made any sense.

When the coach finally stopped at Chastel's, Devin leaped over Armand and reached for the door. Marcus stopped him.

"I go first!" he ordered. "You stay behind me, at all times!"

There were no horses standing in the yard, no sign that anyone but the household staff were about. Marcus knocked and the door was opened by Chastel himself.

"What's going on?" Chastel asked. "What's happened?" He had removed his jacket. He stood with his vest unbuttoned, his shirt loosened at the throat. Dr. Mareschal stood at his elbow.

"Did some men come here from Coreé?" Marcus demanded.

Chastel nodded. "They're with Gaspard in the study, right now."

"Who are they?" Devin asked.

"I don't know," Chastel replied. "Gaspard seemed to know them. He called one of them by name."

"Who sent them?" Devin asked.

Chastel shook his head. "I have no idea. Is there a problem?"

A sudden feeling of dread overwhelmed Devin. He turned and ran, ignoring Marcus's shouts to stop. He yanked open the study door and then crashed headfirst onto the floor as Marcus flattened him from behind.

Armand and Chastel halted behind them.

"There's no one here," Chastel said in surprise.

Marcus rolled off Devin and staggered to his feet.

"God, will you never listen to me, Devin?" Marcus growled angrily. "If there had been a man with a pistol in this room, you might be dead right now!"

Devin dragged himself to his knees. The room was empty! Chastel circled the walls in disbelief.

"You saw no one leave?" Marcus demanded of Chastel.

Chastel shook his head. "Mareschal and I were in the hall the entire time. I assumed Gaspard would tell me what was going on when he had finished talking with them."

Devin pulled himself upright, an awful realization suddenly shaping itself in his mind.

"You assumed they were his father's men, didn't you, Chastel?" he asked, his voice shaking.

"God, yes," Chastel replied. "I thought they had come in response to my letter."

"There wasn't time for that," Marcus pointed out.

"Of course not," Chastel stammered. "I realize that now." He stood with his hands clenched. "I think I may have left Gaspard alone with assassins in my study."

"Had they simply been assassins," Marcus said grimly, "we would have found his body by now. Something else is at work here."

Devin turned to Marcus. "Gaspard called one of them by name," he said, repeating what Chastel had told them. "He knew them, Marcus. He trusted them!"

Marcus turned to look at Chastel. "Do you remember the name of the man Gaspard knew?"

Chastel frowned. "I think it was St. Clair."

"Dear God," Devin murmured.

Marcus whirled, slamming the doors to the study, shutting them safely inside.

"Is there another way out of this room?"

For only an instant Chastel hesitated. "Yes," he admitted. "It leads to the back door by the orchard."

"Where?" Marcus demanded.

Chastel went to the fireplace mantel and released something with his hand. The bookcase on the left swung out from the wall, revealing a dark passageway. Marcus took a candle from the mantel to illuminate the entrance. Recent boot prints marked the dust along with huge paw prints, double the size of either a wolf or a hound.

Armand swore.

Chastel cleared his throat. "Sometimes, I let the dogs run through here . . . " he began.

Armand shook his head. "We've only begun to trust each other, Chastel. Don't lie to me. I'd actually prefer not to know."

"Chastel, send your men after them," Marcus directed. "Perhaps we still have a chance of catching them."

"I'll go with them myself," Chastel offered, taking a rifle off the wall rack. He paused in the doorway and glanced at Mareschal. "I'll get my men together. You'll see that our guests have anything they need . . . anything at all."

Mareschal nodded. "Of course."

"I'm going, too," Devin insisted as Chastel left the room.

"Absolutely not!" Marcus snapped, "Sit down and be quiet! I need to think."

Devin paced instead, crossing the floor time after time.

Mareschal forced a glass of brandy into Devin's hand. "You'd probably be more comfortable across the hall. There's still a fire in the parlor."

"I'd rather stay here," Devin replied.

"Chastel will come and find you as soon as he gets back," Mareschal pointed out. "If they locate Gaspard, you will be the first to know."

Devin glanced at Marcus. "And what are the chances of that?" he asked.

Marcus's face was forbidding. "Very little, I think. You need to accept the fact that he may already be dead."

CHAPTER 45

Lac Dupré

Chastel and his men returned just before dawn, their clothes smudged and muddied. Chastel's face was grim.

"Nothing," he said, before Devin could question him. "It's as though they disappeared from the face of the earth."

One small fear eased inside Devin. "Then Gaspard's not dead," he murmured.

Chastel glanced at Marcus over Devin's head. "I wish I could assure you of that, *monsieur*. If they were foolish enough to head into the forest, they may all be dead. My wolves show no mercy."

"They had horses," Devin reminded him.

Something like compassion crossed Chastel's face. "A wolf can take down a running horse, *monsieur*, have no doubt of that."

Devin slumped down in an armchair.

"Will you continue the search this morning?" Marcus asked.

Chastel nodded. "I've already sent out a second party of men. At least they will have daylight on their side."

"Perhaps, if we contact the local authorities . . . " Devin suggested.

"Believe me," Chastel said, "you do not want Picoté and his band of fools involved. Besides, I have a great many more men at my disposal than he does."

"I agree," Marcus said. "The fewer men who know about this, the better."

"But surely we could use help from the men in the village," Devin protested.

Marcus loomed before him. "Devin, this has nothing to do with the villagers. This business goes straight to Coreé, surely you realize that!" He turned to Chastel. "Who else knew about your secret passageway?" he asked.

Chastel rubbed a hand over his face. "Only one other man," he said, after a moment. "René Forneaux."

"God," Devin murmured. It confirmed what he had feared most. Gaspard's father had kidnapped his own son!

"René visited here once over the Christmas holidays when we were at the Université," Chastel continued. "We'd both had too much to drink one evening and René persuade me to reveal some of the family secrets. I've never shown that passageway to anyone else until last night."

"Your secret's safe with me," Marcus muttered. "I can't vouch for anyone else." His steely glance fell on Armand.

Armand averted his eyes. "Many of these old châteaus have hidden passages," he replied, his voice amiable. "It's no cause for alarm."

"Why would René Forneaux have Gaspard kidnapped?" Devin asked.

Chastel sighed. "Perhaps he was just tired of asking him to come home," he speculated quietly.

Armand cleared his throat. "Let's be honest. Gaspard had

become a liability. Perhaps, René Forneaux believed he could salvage something from the situation. His son's untimely death at the hands of provincial barbarians would further his agenda."

"He could hardly publicize that when we know the truth!" Devin protested.

"Then I suggest you watch your back, Monsieur Roché," Armand said grimly. "I would imagine you are next in line for assassination and your bodyguard with you. If Forneaux is behind this, he can't risk letting you return to Coreé alive."

Devin closed his eyes, a chill running down his back.

Marcus took a deep breath. "We need to leave Ombria as soon as possible."

"What about Gaspard?" Devin asked, jumping up. "Isn't it possible . . . ?"

Marcus flushed beet red. "Devin," he demanded angrily, "use your head. In what scenario do you imagine that Gaspard is still alive?"

"I don't know," Devin replied. "Maybe he went willingly. Have you considered that?"

"Would he leave without taking any of his things, or thanking his host?" Armand asked. "The only way that Gaspard could still be alive is if he is an active participant in this conspiracy. Have you considered that, Monsieur Roché?"

"I will never believe that! Gaspard is my friend!" Devin snapped, hoping his nagging doubts didn't show on his face. He remembered how hard Gaspard had tried to convince him to go back to Coreé. And the odd conversation they'd had about a second red cross at the château that Marcus couldn't substantiate. He ran a hand across his forehead. "Gaspard never even made the decision to come with me voluntarily," he added. "Marcus and I brought him on board the Marie Lisette while he was dead drunk."

Chastel made a placating gesture. "We may never know for certain what happened, Devin. But I agree with Marcus. You need to leave Ombria as quickly as possible. You can stay here tonight and leave early tomorrow morning. Marcus, I can offer you a dozen men to go with you."

"They'll only slow us down," Marcus retorted. "Or call attention to us."

"Where will you go?" Armand asked. "It surely isn't safe to return to Coreé right now."

Devin glanced at Marcus. "We'll finish what I started. I left Coreé to gather as many of the Chronicles as I could. That task seems more imperative now."

"And more dangerous," Chastel pointed out.

"There seems to be no prospect open to me that's not dangerous," Devin replied. "I should have followed my father's advice and stayed at home."

"The correct decision is always easy after the fact," Armand told him.

"What about you?" Devin asked Chastel. "Surely you aren't safe either."

Chastel smiled. "I think René Forneaux still believes me sympathetic to his cause. I am in no danger at the moment." He rubbed a weary hand over his eyes. "I suggest we all get some rest."

Devin objected. "I can't sleep," he said. "Can we borrow your coach to go into Lac Dupré? I need to collect my things."

"Of course," Chastel said. "Let me send some men with you."

No one spoke on the journey back to Armand's. Devin had already faced the loss of Gaspard's companionship on the journey ahead; he refused to face the possibility that his friend was dead. He held his emotions at bay by mentally reciting Ombria's Chronicle, retelling the stories that Armand had taught him so painstakingly.

They finally drew up in front of the Bardic Hall. Armand disembarked first, calling Jeanette's name before he'd even opened the door to the house. Marcus followed him, glancing quickly at the street, before motioning Devin forward.

Armand came clattering down the stairs as Devin entered the hall.

"They're not here," he said, his voice rough with anxiety.

"Where would they be?" Devin asked, walking quickly into the kitchen. The fireplace was cold. Nothing hung cooking over the hearth. The house felt strangely empty. Even the cat was missing. "Is there a market this morning?"

"No!" Armand snapped. He opened the front door and stood a moment with his hand on the doorknob.

Except for Chastel's men, the street was devoid of villagers and curiously quiet. Armand stalked to his nearest neighbor's house and pounded on the door. When there was no response he flung the door open and entered. He was gone only a moment.

"There's no one here either," he reported, before rushing to the next house.

Marcus dispatched four of Chastel's men to the other side of the street. Every house and shop was empty.

"Could they be at the church?" Devin asked.

They all set off running. The church door stood open. A few stray leaves had blown across the threshold but both the sanctuary and the rectory were vacant and silent.

After an hour of fruitless searching, they returned to the Bardic Hall and gathered in the kitchen. Armand slumped into the rocker by the fireplace, his face gray with fatigue. Devin stood by helplessly, his fists clenched, his heart pounding.

Gaspard's disappearance was bad enough; the thought that Jeanette and Adrian might be dead made him physically ill.

"What can we do?" Devin asked. "Someone must know something."

"Who would you suggest that we ask?" Armand snapped.

"It's like Gaêtan returning to Rameau and finding it deserted," Devin murmured his chest tight. "How many people lived in this village?"

"Nearly eight hundred men, women, and children," Armand answered. "And now they have vanished!"

"They can't have vanished," Marcus protested.

"Then what is your explanation?" Armand demanded sharply. "I've lost both my daughter and my apprentice; I'd be interested in your assessment of the situation, Marcus Beringer!"

"If they are dead," Marcus replied quietly. "There would be a mass grave. If they are alive they are being held somewhere close. You can't physically move that many people quickly."

"We need help," Devin said. "We need to get back to Chastel's."

Armand turned to look at him. "And are you certain that you can trust him, Devin?" he asked, his voice lowered. "After all, Gaspard disappeared from his château. The people of Lac Dupré vanished while we were occupied with Gaspard's disappearance. What if Chastel is part of this, too?"

"If he were," Marcus replied. "He could have killed Devin any number of times. We have no one else we can trust, Armand. We need Chastel if we are going to make it out of here alive!"

"I'm not leaving this place until I find out what happened to my daughter," Armand replied stubbornly.

"We are all leaving," Marcus replied. "If you don't walk to the coach on your own, I will have you bound and carried. Devin, get your things."

Devin ascended the stairs two at a time. He opened his bedroom door and stopped.

"There is nothing here," he called down. His clothes and knapsack were gone, along with his letters. Nothing remained but the furniture.

Marcus pushed past him. His breath hissed through his teeth. "They were very thorough," he said, grabbing Devin's arm. "Come on. We need to get out of here now."

Epilogue

They left the château at twilight. A full moon lay huge and orange just above the horizon. Armand limped along beside Devin. He seemed to have aged ten years in the last day. Chastel's men had found no sign of the people of Lac Dupré, just as so many years before, Rameau had been left totally devoid of life. It was Chastel who had finally persuaded Armand to accompany them. There were no answers to their questions here, and death seemed to lie in wait for all of them in Ombria.

Each of them carried a pistol. Travel during the day was suicide with unknown assassins looking for them. Travel at night seemed just as dangerous. Yet, Chastel had suggested it and assured them of their safety, mapping the route to a neighboring province himself.

They followed the road in the gathering darkness, alert to the slightest sound that might indicate pursuit. The howl of a single wolf echoed across the valley. A chill ran down Devin's back. Were they destined to die so quickly? A chorus of howls joined the first. Devin's eyes followed the sound. On the hillside above them, a pack of wolves had gathered, watching their progress. Marcus yanked his gun from his pocket and cocked it.

Armand forced the gun barrel down with his hand. "Don't," he said hoarsely, "Don't you see? That's how he assured our safety."

"What?" Marcus asked.

"Chastel's provided an escort," Armand replied.

Devin's eyes were on the huge wolf at the front of the pack. "My God," he murmured, "he's leading them himself!"